THE *Christmas* HEIRLOOM

Four
HOLIDAY NOVELLAS
of LOVE THROUGH THE GENERATIONS

KAREN WITEMEYER

KRISTI ANN HUNTER

SARAH LOUDIN THOMAS

BECKY WADE

BETHANYHOUSE
a division of Baker Publishing Group
Minneapolis, Minnesota

Legacy of Love © 2018 by Kristi Ann Hunter
Gift of the Heart © 2018 by Karen Witemeyer
A Shot at Love © 2018 by Sarah Loudin Thomas
Because of You © 2018 by Rebecca C. Wade

Published by Bethany House Publishers
11400 Hampshire Avenue South
Bloomington, Minnesota 55438
www.bethanyhouse.com

Bethany House Publishers is a division of
Baker Publishing Group, Grand Rapids, Michigan

Printed in the United States of America

Library of Congress Cataloging-in-Publication Data
Names: Witemeyer, Karen. Gift of the heart. | Hunter, Kristi Ann. Legacy of love. |
    Thomas, Sarah Loudin. A shot at love. | Wade, Becky. Because of you.
Title: The Christmas heirloom : four holiday novellas of love through the
    generations / Karen Witemeyer, Kristi Ann Hunter, Sarah Loudin Thomas, Becky
    Wade.
Description: Minneapolis, Minnesota : Bethany House, [2018]
Identifiers: LCCN 2018019427| ISBN 9780764230783 (trade paper) | ISBN
    9780764232800 (cloth) | ISBN 9781493417094 (e-book)
Subjects: LCSH: Christmas stories, American. | Romance fiction, American.
Classification: LCC PS648.C45 C4464 2018 | DDC 813/.08508334—dc23
LC record available at https://lccn.loc.gov/2018019427

Cover design by LOOK Design Studio
Cover photography by Mike Habermann Photography, LLC

Karen Witemeyer and Sarah Loudin Thomas are represented by Books & Such Literary Agency.
Kristi Ann Hunter is represented by Natasha Kern Literary Agency.
Becky Wade is represented by Linda Kruger.

18 19 20 21 22 23 24   7 6 5 4 3 2 1

Contents

Legacy of Love

A Haven Manor
NOVELLA

KRISTI ANN HUNTER

1

1827
<small>LANCASHIRE, ENGLAND</small>

From a purely rational standpoint, Sarah Gooding should have been ecstatic with her present position. She was wearing a silk gown and playing piano in a grand aristocratic home while more than a dozen people of good family sat within hearing distance. She was more at home behind the keys of a pianoforte than anywhere else and had dreamed of having a prestigious chance to exhibit her talent.

This was nothing like she'd dreamed.

The roughened texture of well-used ivory-covered keys was as familiar as the overwhelming feeling of not quite belonging. Actually, she felt rather unwanted.

That could have something to do with the fact that the enormous vertical cabinet piano designed to crawl grandly up the wall of elegant homes had been turned to create a divide between the player and everyone else. It was difficult to misinterpret such an arrangement.

At least no one could see her yawn as she plunked out the notes to the incredibly simple score of the Italian songbook that had been laid out for her.

Lady Densbury, the current Countess of Densbury, didn't care for ostentatious or distracting music during an intimate gathering such as a family dinner.

Sarah didn't particularly care for Lady Densbury.

As her fingers slowly drifted through a series of plodding arpeggios, Sarah leaned to her left. If she angled her head perfectly, she could see around the tall side of the ornate giraffe piano. Since the top of the piano cabinet stretched at least four feet above her head on the left side there was no way she'd be able to see over it. And while the green brocade panels that decorated the tall cabinet were gorgeous to look at, they wouldn't let her know if the cake had been brought to the table yet.

Since Sarah's employer, the Dowager Countess of Densbury, insisted that Sarah's job as her companion included attending excruciating weekly family dinners, Sarah always focused on the cake. It was the only thing that made the ordeal bearable.

Well, the cake and the hope that Mr. Randall Everard might be home for a visit. Third in line for the earldom and therefore generally ignored by his parents, he'd been raised largely by his grandmother. He didn't come back to the family seat often anymore, much to the dowager's dismay.

But he was there tonight.

If she couldn't get a glimpse of cake, catching sight of Mr. Everard was almost as good.

Unfortunately, even leaning as far to the left as she comfortably could, Sarah couldn't stretch far enough to see anything but the back of the earl's head.

She made a face at his greying hair as she straightened back into her seat.

Sarah didn't particularly like the earl, either. Or his heir. Or even the spare. They were mean and the wives the older sons had procured this past year weren't any better.

Mean probably wasn't precisely the right word. *Overly aware of their heightened position in society and Sarah's extraordinarily lower status* was more accurate, but that didn't quite roll off the tongue as well. It was much easier to think of the family as mean.

Not all the family, of course. Sarah's employer was a dear. The dowager had been a veritable angel to Sarah since hiring her as a companion back in January.

Which meant a few hours of agony once a week was worth it, if it made the dowager Lady Densbury happy.

And then there was the cake.

And if Mr. Everard was home, she got to sit in the corner, eat cake, and make cow eyes at him as he did his best to make his grandmother laugh. Her life wasn't likely to get much better than that.

She turned back to the music. A curl of panic shot through her when she realized she hadn't a clue where she was on the page or even if she was still on the page. Her fingers had been frittering about on the keyboard, playing at whim for who even knew how long. Swallowing hard in an attempt to ease the sudden dryness in her mouth, Sarah picked a line at random and drifted back into the song she'd been requested to play.

It was simple.

Predictable.

Boring.

How long had she been playing for? An hour? Two? The countess enjoyed interminably long dinners. Part of Sarah was convinced it was because Lady Densbury was hoping Sarah's fingers would fall off, or that she'd have some sort of breakdown from being asked yet again to gulp down a plate of plain food in the kitchens before playing sedate, quiet music while the family consumed four courses of elaborate dishes.

What the countess hadn't yet learned was that as long as Sarah got a piece of cake at the end of the night, she didn't care a groat if she missed out on the ruffs and reeves.

After a glance at the music to make sure she played the next several lines generally as they were written, Sarah shifted her weight to lean to the right. That side of the piano cabinet was considerably lower, and it was possible she'd be able to look over it enough to see if the cake had been delivered to the table. At the very least she'd be able to see the dowager, and Mr. Everard seated across from her. If she were lucky, his crooked smile would be visible just beneath his nose, which was a touch too wide to be fashionable but balanced out his features perfectly in Sarah's opinion.

Not that anyone ever asked her opinion.

Her quick stretch hadn't allowed her to see much other than the current countess's eerily emotionless face. Was Sarah sitting closer to the piano than normal tonight? Had they somehow moved the instrument this week to cut her off from the assembly even more?

She flipped the page without missing a note—easy to do when the song never called for more than three notes to be played at a time. Her shoulders sagged a bit as she continued playing. The countess obviously needed more to do in her life since she had time to scour the shops for the most mundane music in existence.

Her gaze drifted from the music back to the lower corner of the cabinet. Normally the dowager made sure Sarah didn't miss the cake, but she was engaged in some sort of entertaining conversation with her grandson about menagerie drawings she'd seen in a recent publication. She might be too distracted to notice the cake.

Sarah nudged the chair back from the keys a bit and leaned to the right once more. There were heads, shoulders, even an elbow, which meant the table was only a little bit farther. If she could shift just a bit more . . .

Her body tilted and started to tumble over the edge of the chair. With a jerk of her arm she caught herself on the piano keys, sending a loud, discordant clang through the dining room.

Everything stopped. There wasn't a clink of utensil against china or even the whisper of clothing. It didn't even sound as if anyone were breathing.

Sarah certainly wasn't.

Her only consolation at the moment was that no one could see around the large piano cabinet to witness her clinging to the edge of the keys, praying her chair didn't slide out from underneath her hip.

A prayer that was actually going to require divine intervention.

A single glance down revealed that the chair was tilted, the far legs inches above the ground. The slightest shift on her part sent the chair sliding a bit farther away. There was nowhere to go but down.

Heat flooded her face and pounded in her ears as breath rushed in and out of her lungs in a panicked race, as if she'd be able to inhale a solution to her horrifyingly embarrassing predicament.

She should drop to the floor. She knew she should. But she couldn't quite bring herself to loosen her white-knuckle grip on the edge of the piano.

"Might I be of assistance?"

The voice was smooth and low and achingly familiar. They'd had a number of short conversations over the past year. One hundred forty-two of them to be exact. Short discussions about nothing and everything. Books, birds, even an occasional examination of the week's sermon if he happened to stay at the estate through Sunday. She never said even half of what she was thinking, of course, but she'd loved hearing his thoughts on the matter, whatever the topic was.

She tilted her head to look up into his blue-grey eyes. That slight adjustment was enough to send the chair skittering across the floor, leaving Sarah to crash down onto Mr. Everard's leather shoes.

One side of his mouth kicked up into a crooked grin as he extended his hand to her. "Are you hurt?"

"No," Sarah choked out as she allowed him to help her to her feet. Once standing she glued her gaze to the keys in front of her. "It wasn't that far of a fall."

He chuckled and reached over to right the chair. "No, I suppose not."

Against her wishes, Sarah's gaze swung to the table. She may not like the majority of the people seated there, but that didn't mean she wanted them to have a reason to think ill of her. In the center of the table rested the most glorious sight. A golden ring of delicious dreams with a thick, white blanket of icing and candied lemon peels dancing across the top.

The cook called it her Madeira Pound Cake because she'd created the cake by blending the two recipes.

Sarah called it bliss on a fork. She'd even been known to wrap a portion in one of the linen serviettes and sneak it out of the house if the evening had been particularly grueling.

If she wanted a piece of it tonight, though, she'd have to face the laughter and disapproval of the earl's family.

"Are you quite well, Miss Gooding?" Lady Densbury's sharp voice cut through the room.

Sarah blinked and forced herself to look at the countess frowning from her position at the foot of the table. "Yes, my lady. Quite well."

She sniffed and nodded. "Then you should probably return to playing. Like getting back on a horse, you know."

Sarah was fairly certain that no one in history had given up playing music because they'd stupidly fallen out of the chair while trying to see around a vertical cabinet piano placed ridiculously in the middle of a room, but it really wasn't worth arguing about. Arguing at the family dinner disturbed the dowager for days, so Sarah simply nodded and dropped back into her seat, making sure to keep her eyes far away from Mr. Everard and even farther away from the tempting cake.

Randall's hand curved into a fist. His grip tightened until his entire arm trembled. Then he shook the tension out and returned to his seat at the table. His mother's treatment of those she deemed socially unworthy shouldn't bother him anymore, but it did. He hated seeing her try to put people in their place, simpering as if she were doing them a favor, reminding them of the way the world worked.

As a third son whose place in the social structure was as questionable as three-day-old milk, Randall found it more than a little disturbing.

Still, she was his mother. And his grandmother's companion seemed the type to let insults slide by like water.

She let nearly everything slide by like water. Oh, he enjoyed talking to her, had enjoyed playing piquet with her when he visited his grandmother, but there was nothing remarkable about her aside from her unusual features. When he'd first met her, the pointy angles of her face that framed wide-set eyes had intrigued him. But when those eyes had spent the entire time staring at the floor, he'd moved on.

Her meekness didn't mean his mother should treat her the way she did, though. He glanced at the piano, the tall back covered by a custom-made painted silk drape depicting St. George fighting a dragon. It was an awful lot of work to go through to make sure the family dinners weren't tainted by the presence of one quiet woman.

"I've an announcement," Randall's oldest brother George said from his place near the head of the table. "Harriet and I have decided not to move back to the London house after the first of the year."

Randall's eyebrows lifted, but it wasn't an announcement that truly interested him. He'd been living at Bluestone for nearly four years, managing the earl's small estate in Yorkshire that was more farm than anything else. George moving back to the family seat in Lancashire wasn't going to impact Randall's life very much.

"That's wonderful," Mother said with a stiff smile. It was her real smile, the one that indicated she was actually happy. Everything Mother did was stiff, so it was difficult to distinguish between the emotions if one didn't know where to look, but Mother's eyes had crinkled at the corners so she was genuinely happy at the prospect of George returning home.

She'd frown if Randall proposed such a thing.

Which was probably why Randall had spent so much time with his grandmother during his youth. They'd suffered Mother's disapproval together, and he'd learned how to follow Grandmother's lead in not letting it bother him—or at least not letting it show. He wasn't sure if his parents' general embarrassment over the dowager countess's less-than-conventional attitudes actually bothered his grandmother or not.

"Well," George said with a smile at his wife. "Harriet is rather looking forward to setting up her own housekeeping somewhere, you know, so we can start our family properly."

And now both mother and father were ecstatic. The potential heir of the heir was on his way.

"Marvelous!" The earl banged one hand on the table and beamed at his eldest.

"You'll want to think carefully about where to set up your own home. You don't want to take on too much in a delicate condition," Mother said, sending her smile in Harriet's direction.

Randall's other brother, Cecil, looked at his own wife with a smile. "Does that mean Beatrice and I can use the London residence?"

Other statements of congratulations drifted up from the occupants of the table—his grandmother, Beatrice, the local vicar who was always invited to these gatherings, and two cousins he wasn't even entirely sure how he was related to.

And behind all the cacophony, a gentle melody trilled from the piano, lending a strange sort of refinement to the noise.

George smiled and nodded his thanks. "It's made me realize I need to take my future more seriously, Father, so I want to be close, learn more about the earldom."

Randall stuffed a large bite of cake into his mouth to stifle the urge to laugh. George had done nothing but learn the earldom since he'd been born. It was Father's obsession, making sure George and Cecil both knew everything there was to know about holding the esteemed title. As a second son himself, the current earl was well aware of the duties of the second in line, so he made sure Cecil was included in any and all teachings.

As the lowly third, Randall had been allowed to learn fun things like fishing.

"I was thinking," George continued, "that perhaps we would set up at Cloverdale."

Another discordant combination of keys had Randall's gaze flying to the piano. Had Miss Gooding fallen again? But no, there were her wide-set icy blue eyes, peering over the lower side of the piano cabinet. Two deep lines had formed between her eyes, and for once her gaze was aimed directly at the family instead of the floor.

Her sudden interest in the conversation made sense. Cloverdale was the dower house where his grandmother—and therefore her companion—lived. Grandmother had resided there for ages, at least two decades. And to his knowledge, he'd been the only member of the family to set foot in the place for at least five years, maybe more, relying on the dowager traveling to these weekly family dinners instead of visiting her themselves.

How could George even suggest living there? How was his father not immediately denying the suggestion?

Randall cleared his throat. Normally he didn't bother entering the family conversations, but in this case . . . "I'm not sure Grandmother wants to live with a new, young household."

Slashes of color appeared on George's cheeks as he looked from his father to the dowager and then finally to Randall. "Of course not. But Cloverdale is a rather large house for one person who doesn't really entertain. I thought Grandmother would be much happier at Stagwild."

Silence fell over the table.

Randall couldn't look at his grandmother, couldn't look at anyone, really. Whether it was because he didn't want to see her hurt by the suggestion or couldn't quite fathom George was actually serious, he didn't know, but he was frozen in his chair, not blinking, hardly breathing.

The earl cleared his throat. "It's not a terrible idea."

Another jangling chord filled the air, making Randall jerk and cover his ears. Miss Gooding stomped around the piano and stood in front of it, chest heaving as if she intended to breathe fire like the dragon in the picture. She stared down the men at the head of the table, eyes narrowing until the pale blue was nothing but a memory.

"This woman has lived through wars, through the death of

her husband and the death of her son, and through the ridicule of people who thought themselves better than her because of their birth." Her gaze swept the table to encompass the countess. Randall squirmed in his seat. His mother had always been a bit condescending toward the dowager.

"And now you want to rip her away from her home, deprive her of the company of her family, and run her off to the wilds of Durham?" Miss Gooding thrust her pointy chin forward, looking like an avenging angel come to put the fear of the Lord into sinners. "You ought to be ashamed of yourselves."

2

Sarah's heart withered to the size of a pea and retreated to somewhere in the vicinity of her toes. What had she just done?

A glance around the room revealed that everyone else was just as shocked as she was. The earl's mouth was still hanging open a bit from his gasp while Lady Densbury's lips were so tightly pursed that they'd turned white and disappeared into her face.

Only the dowager countess looked unruffled by Sarah's outburst. But then, she knew Sarah better than anyone else in the room. It wasn't unheard of for Sarah to express her opinion to the old lady, even if it were contrary to her employer's views on a subject.

Never had she opened her mouth in front of the family, though. She'd meekly accepted her role and retreated behind the piano. But she would not allow them to mistreat the dowager, a wonderful woman who had saved Sarah's pride and independence and had spent the past year demonstrating true strength of character.

She'd been hired as the dowager's companion, and wasn't part of that job seeing to the old woman's comfort? For a woman of her age and severely declining health, moving households to a colder, damper, lonelier climate was akin to a death sentence.

At that moment, the dowager was looking over her shoulder at Sarah, a wide smile on her face and her eyes gleaming with pride.

After a moment, she turned back to her family seated around the large table. "Well, I think that says it better than I could."

The current countess glared at her predecessor. "You can't possibly intend to keep her in your employ after an outburst like that."

"And why not?" The dowager sniffed. "I pay her to look out for my best interests. You shuffling me off to die in some drafty house north of Yorkshire is not in my best interests."

"Mother," Lord Densbury said with affronted exasperation, "no one said anything about wanting you to die."

Sarah's eyebrows winged upward, and a cough sputtered through her lips. Oh the things she wanted to say in response to that cold and callous statement, but she'd done enough damage already.

"No one said anything about wanting me to live in comfort, either," the dowager huffed.

She might have grown slower over the past year and struggled with normal everyday tasks, but her mind was perfectly capable of presenting her own defense. The dowager hadn't needed Sarah's intervention.

Why hadn't she stayed behind the piano in her rightful place?

"Your comfort is all I'm thinking of, Mother. You've mentioned that the stairs in Cloverdale are difficult. A younger family will handle the sprawl better than you."

Silence fell as the dowager tilted her head a bit in consideration. "You've a point, Stuart."

Visible relaxation sagged through the family members at the head of the table. Sarah blinked. Surely the dowager wasn't going to give in on this. Cloverdale was a dower property. No one could make her move if she didn't want to.

But the dowager was smiling, a look on her face that Sarah knew all too well. There would be no concession today.

Giving a nod, the old lady said, "Sarah and I will take up residence in the cottage in Bath."

Desperate to cover the laugh that threatened to emerge, Sarah clapped a hand over her mouth and looked away from the grinning dowager. Her gaze collided with Randall's, and the urge to laugh was smothered beneath his direct gaze.

He stared at her, head cocked to one side, crooked smile tilting his lips up slightly at the corners. What was he thinking?

She fought the urge to fidget, to escape back to the safety of the piano. Around her the conversation raged on, swirling into a murky pit of familial disappointment. She heard the words but couldn't pull herself away from those blue-grey eyes and the curiosity in them.

"The cottage in Bath?" The countess's voice finally cut through the general commotion. She was obviously deeply affronted by the idea.

"Yes, yes." The dowager sounded rather excited about the idea, even though Sarah knew it would take a full team of horses and a royal decree to get the woman to actually leave Lancashire. "I would never have considered it before, you know, being so comfortably ensconced at Cloverdale for twenty-three years, but your insistence that I see to my health has convinced me. The cottage is smaller, and I'll be able to take the waters and breathe the sea air."

"But . . . but . . . you've always declared such things to foolishness and nonsense," the countess sputtered out.

Sarah could almost envision the dowager smiling and mentally rubbing her hands together the way she did when she knew one of the household servants was about to fall victim to one of her harmless pranks.

"Perhaps I've changed my mind," the dowager mused. "You return from your yearly trips to Bath declaring yourself refreshed and feeling five years younger. I have to confess. I wouldn't mind feeling five years younger. It means a terrible lot to me that you would forgo your weeks in Bath so that I can live in health and comfort. And, of course, the sacrifice dear Harriet and Beatrice would be making as well."

Randall's smile widened. He finally broke eye contact with Sarah to look at his grandmother. Blessed air rushed in to Sarah's lungs as she was released from his regard. She couldn't stop staring at him, though, watching the delight on his face as his grandmother maneuvered and guilted his family.

Lord Saunders, who had seemed so confident when he suggested ousting his grandmother from her home, now looked unsettled as he cleared his throat. "Perhaps Harriet and I should return to London for a while. Mother is right. We wouldn't want to take on too large of a task while Harriet is in such a state. Besides, it will allow us to establish ourselves better socially before the children come."

"Yes, yes," the earl rushed to agree. "The connections a man makes in his youth are very important."

"Oh." The dowager heaved a comically large sigh. "I suppose I'll stay at Cloverdale, then. No sense in disrupting everyone's routines just for me."

Another laugh swirled about in Sarah's chest. She needed to get the dowager out of here before it erupted—and before her employer forgot about her vow to stop trying to make her son and his wife drop a bit of their rigidity. They'd called a truce some years ago, but it wouldn't take much for the dowager to renege.

Sarah stepped forward and cast a longing look at the remaining cake before laying a hand on the dowager's shoulder. "Speaking of routines, I believe the hour is getting late, my lady."

The dowager frowned up at Sarah, like a child told he'd have to wait until another day to go swimming in the pond. "Yes, I suppose it is."

It took a few tries for the dowager to rise from her seat, her arm shaking a bit as it braced against the table in an effort to push her way to standing. Sarah bit her lip and resisted the urge to rush forward and help.

Finally the dowager was up. "I want you all to know," she said a bit shakily, "that for all its foibles—and there are many—this is a good family. You're a good son, Stuart, and you've done well with a life you never expected to have. And you've done well with a wife who made that transition better than any other woman could have. I wanted you all to know that."

She nodded around the table at her grandsons. "Cecil, George, Randall, be good. Love the Lord and your family and you'll do well enough." She sniffed. "I bid you all a good night, then. And good-bye."

She turned and left the room, Sarah trailing behind her to the front hall.

Once clear of the dining room, Sarah came alongside the dowager and offered her arm. "That was eventful."

A low chuckle drifted from the older woman as she gave some of her weight to Sarah. A significant bit more than she'd done a month ago. "I'd have thrown myself on their mercies months ago if that's what it took to get you away from that piano."

The butler entered from a side room and waited by the door with their bonnets and pelisses.

Sarah smirked at her employer as she helped ease the finely woven wool over the woman's thin shoulders. "I thought you liked my piano playing."

The old woman's nose crinkled. "I like your piano playing, not that tinkering you do in the dining room."

Sarah reached for her own pelisse. "When we get home I'll—" Sarah's words fell off as the echo of footsteps on marble came from behind them.

With the outer garment half on one shoulder, Sarah turned around. No one ever followed them to the hall after dinner, the meal having more than fulfilled everyone's familial obligations.

Yet there was Mr. Randall Everard, striding through the hall as if he intended to leave as well.

"I had no idea you wished to take the waters, Grandmother. You should have said so ages ago." Mr. Everard's already crooked smile was even more lopsided as one corner lifted in a conspiratorial grin.

The dowager countess laughed as she buttoned her pelisse around her. "Should I ever go, my boy, I'd certainly take you with me."

He leaned down to kiss her on the cheek. "Then who would see to the farms?"

Lady Densbury sniffed. "Perhaps the man who is set to inherit them? You should have gone into the church. No sense hiding your mind and your faith in the dirt. Especially when it's not even your own dirt."

Sarah finished putting her coat on and reached for her bonnet. This was an argument the two had had on many occasions. Randall loved the outdoors and the earth, the challenge of growing things and managing nature, but his grandmother thought it a waste of his sharp mind and love of theology.

The bonnet Sarah took from the butler pulled her arm down with unexpected weight, distracting Sarah from the conversation between the two aristocrats. A peek inside the hat revealed a square parcel wrapped in linen. She grinned.

Cake.

But how was she going to explain not plopping her bonnet on her head to leave the house? Her grin fell as she looked up only to find herself under the scrutiny of both Mr. Everard and Lady Densbury.

"It would seem," Mr. Everard said slowly, "that I am not the only one who has been hiding."

Miss Gooding paled. The angles of her face seemed sharper as her eyes rounded and her mouth dropped open as if she were about to say something but forgot the words.

It was a problem he'd attributed to her the entire year he'd known her—an inability to actually put words together—but her display in the dining room had proven she was anything but inarticulate. It was clear that those moments when he'd glimpsed something more in her personality, something just enough to keep him from ignoring her entirely, had been the edges of her true self poking to the surface.

Why would a young woman so obviously passionate be willing to spend hours every week stuffed behind a piano absorbing verbal barbs of the veiled and not-so-veiled variety?

"May I see you home, Grandmother?"

"Why?" the old woman who'd practically raised him asked with a grin. "You've never seen the need to before."

That wasn't precisely true. He'd seen her home on several occasions before she employed her new companion. He'd even walked her home the first few months of Miss Gooding's employ until he'd become frustrated with the conflicted thoughts and feelings he had about the young woman.

Thoughts and feelings that were once more entering a swirl of confusion. He'd thought he had her figured out, thought he knew her, but as he stood in the front hall now he questioned everything.

He cleared his throat and debated between sounding like a dutiful grandson or teasing his grandmother. In the end, he opted for an honesty his family was all too good at avoiding. "You've never leaned quite so heavily on your companion before."

The dowager's growing feebleness bothered Randall. Yes, his grandmother was old. Yes, he knew, in the way one knows the sun rises in the east, that she would die one day. Until recently he'd been able to easily ignore both of those things. But she looked considerably weaker than she had on his last visit. Thinner. Shakier.

"And you lean too much on your father's laziness," the dowager grumbled, showing him that the spirit hadn't weakened along with the body. "Thought the boy was destined to write sermons and visit parishioners all day so I didn't worry about teaching him when he was younger. Now he's the earl and doesn't even know what crops grow on his farms."

She poked one wrinkled finger in Randall's direction. "You need find your own land to settle on while you've still got the energy to do so."

He hated that she was right, but he also hated that the idea of being completely on his own, starting from essentially nothing, terrified him. "And here I thought my decline and dotage to be years in my future."

"Bah!" She crammed a bonnet on top of her silver curls and lifted her chin to let Miss Gooding secure the ribbons.

Instead of jumping forward to comply, the companion looked from Randall to her employer to the bonnet clutched in her slim-fingered hands. Her delicate throat jumped as she swallowed. Then she stepped forward and . . . handed her bonnet to the dowager? With her hands unencumbered, she set about tying the ribbons. "I am perfectly capable of seeing your grandmother safely home. That is my job, after all."

Something shifted in Randall, making him feel almost off balance. Showing gumption twice in one night? What had come over Grandmother's timid bird of a companion?

"Are you? And what would you do if you encountered a highwayman or wild dog? You won't have a piano with you to soothe them with your melodies."

It wasn't like him to throw such challenging statements at people, but he was curious to see how riled she could get.

"Given that Cloverdale is a mere mile from here, on a well-maintained path that doesn't even require us to leave Densbury lands, I feel confident that I can handle any threat that may come our way." She straightened her shoulders and looked him in the eye with a directness that seared Randall in the chest.

Respect bloomed through him, along with an attraction he thought long dead. There'd been a moment, that one single moment, not long after she'd come to live at Cloverdale, when he'd seen her and wondered what it was about her that had finally convinced his grandmother to get rid of the annoying cousin she'd been talked into hiring. He'd wondered if his grandmother's new companion could shake him from the worn and beaten-down rut he'd been living in.

But then she'd proved herself quiet and timid, and that hope had faded like a candle on the verge of gutting out. But now, with her eyes no longer cast to the ground, it was amazing how different she looked. Not just in appearance, although the sight of her wide eyes seemed to completely change the look of her unique face, but there was a change in spirit. As if she'd seen the more difficult side of life and learned when and how to fight.

Randall shook himself from his frivolous musings.

Whatever fanciful notions he was attributing to the girl, he couldn't possibly connect himself to a woman who couldn't manage to place her bonnet on her head.

Granted, the sun was nearly gone and the hat was no longer a needed accessory, but wouldn't it still be easier to wear it upon her head instead of carry it?

Miss Gooding ran her hand along the brim of her bonnet. "It's getting late," she said quietly, though her pale, icy blue eyes didn't fall from his. "I should get Lady Densbury home."

The dowager shuffled toward the door. "Yes, yes, have to get me home before these old bones decide they've finished creaking for the day."

"I'd be happy to have the carriage brought round." Randall stepped forward and offered his arm to his grandmother. He tried not to frown at how frail her grip felt. Why hadn't his father already started using the carriage to bring her to and from the dower house? Had the earl not noticed the dowager's declining health?

"Nonsense. If I stop walking now, I'll never start again."

"You're wasting your breath," Miss Gooding said in her soft voice. "I've tried everything to convince her to use it more often. If it makes you feel better, though, we do take the carriage if it is especially late or the night is not clear."

That was some consolation, he supposed, and he had no doubt that his grandmother was stubborn enough to refuse the assistance, but he still had to wonder at his father allowing two women to stroll the grounds after the sun had set. As Randall and his grandmother exited the door, Miss Gooding fell meekly into place behind them, still clutching the bonnet in front of her like a basket.

A swirl of impishness fed by the renewed curiosity about the companion drove Randall's tongue. He tilted his head toward his grandmother's ear but cast his gaze over her shoulder to view her companion, who was swiping her curls from her face as the light evening breeze blew them around. "Your companion seems to have an aversion to wearing anything on her head."

27

"Bah." His grandmother waved her free hand through the air. "She doesn't want to smash her cake."

Randall nearly stumbled to a halt. Fortunately the dowager was moving slowly enough that it didn't really matter. He turned his head more fully to look at Miss Gooding, who was now frowning at her employer.

"Best be careful, Lady Densbury," she said, her frown shifting into more of a smirk. "I don't have to share my bounty with you, you know."

"After I asked them to wrap up an especially large piece? That would be a mite bit ungrateful."

"Considering you've given away our secret, this might be the last piece I get to bring home." The sigh that escaped Miss Gooding was exaggerated and long as she lifted a linen-wrapped bundle from within her bonnet and shoved the hat onto her head.

"My dear Randall would never betray my secret, would you?"

Randall had to clear his throat before he could talk. "Of course not."

An inelegant snort came from behind him. "Who, pray tell, are we keeping the secret from, then, if not your family?"

Grandmother gave a matching sound of disgust. "There's family and then there's *family*. Randall here is the second one."

Was he supposed to be flattered by that? He supposed there had always been some distinction between him and his brothers. The knowledge that he would have to make his own way in the world, that his children would not be aristocratic, that his fate was not among the elite, had meant that he viewed life a bit differently.

While his father had trained the elder two boys, Randall had simply been . . . there. His mother had more than once lamented that he'd have been ever so much more useful if he'd been born a girl. Then at least he could have been married off to enhance the family connections. She'd always claimed it was a joke, but Randall never found it funny.

There hadn't even been much of an army for him to join, given

28

that the past ten years had seen an unprecedented peace over the country.

"To prove my loyalty," he said with the intention of getting the lighthearted teasing to continue, "I shall endeavor to sneak an entire Madeira Pound Cake over to Cloverdale before I leave."

He was positive he heard Miss Gooding whimper.

Grandmother shuffled to a stop. "Before you leave? You aren't staying through Christmas?"

Randall looked down into his grandmother's beloved face, accusatory in the light of the bright moon. Desperation had him sending a pleading look back toward Miss Gooding.

He caught the open curiosity on her face before her eyes widened and she dropped her head forward to stare at the ground. No help from that quarter then. "Grandmother, I have to get back to Bluestone."

"For what?" She poked him in the side. "It's the middle of winter. Even your bothersome father knows there's nothing growing right now."

Which made his easy acceptance of Randall's excuse to return all the more painful. "Be that as it may, that is where I belong."

"Bah." Grandmother started walking again, mumbling words he couldn't quite catch.

Miss Gooding obviously had more experience interpreting the dowager because her giggle drifted forward on the light breeze.

"Care to enlighten me on my grandmother's agitation, Miss Gooding?" He turned his head but kept walking. If his grandmother guided him into a tree, they weren't walking fast enough to do any real damage.

Miss Gooding's lips pulled together, making her chin look a bit more pointed and her eyes even more wide set. It was the most unique face he'd ever seen. Somehow, the sharp shape and lines suited her thin arms and narrow body. Like God had assembled her for efficient movement and grace. Like a greyhound.

Probably best not to mention that comparison.

"If I may, Mr. Everard," she said with a bit more firmness to her words and a considerable great deal more amusement, "your grandmother is not happy with your life."

He grinned. "I know. But if I were to change it, we'd have nothing to talk about when I came to visit."

Grandmother grunted. "Of course we would. Because you'd have babies."

"Babies require a wife, Grandmother."

She nodded. "I'd be able to talk about her too."

Randall shook his head and patted the hand resting on his forearm. Thank goodness they had arrived at Cloverdale. This conversation was getting uncomfortable and bordering on ridiculous. "I haven't got a wife, Grandmother."

"And don't I know it?" She stomped up the stairs with as much force as her slightly stooped body could manage. "I went through the trouble of handpicking one for you, and you can't even walk the mile from the estate house to come court her!"

3

Lady Densbury was close enough to death that no one would question it very much if Sarah helped her over the threshold of heaven just a little bit early, would they?

It had been hours since Sarah had fled from the dowager and Mr. Everard. She'd run in the first direction she could think of—which was simply "away"—and had ended up circling the house and coming in through the kitchen.

She'd been so mortified that she went to bed with her head buried beneath her pillow and now, as she rose and prepared for the day, her face still flamed at the merest hint of remembering. If she thought about having to face Mr. Everard once more, well, it was enough to make her want to run in the other direction. Again.

She dressed simply since it was neither Sunday, which meant services at the church, or Wednesday, the day of the torturous dinners up at Helmsfield. When Sarah had started this job back in January, there'd been an excursion of some form nearly every day, but those had quickly tapered off to the occasional visit to the village to shop or have tea. They hadn't even done that in almost two months.

Sarah, who on most days found the reclusive state of the dowager a bit sad, was rather grateful today that she could depend upon staying home. That way she wouldn't chance encountering Mr. Everard.

If he were still in town next Wednesday, she'd plant herself at the piano without even being asked and remain there for the entirety of the evening, not looking his way, even if it meant forgoing cake.

Her last vision of him would be the frozen, gaping features that swung from his grandmother to her with a look of shock and surprise tinged with a bit of revulsion at the idea of marrying a lowly companion who hadn't a single thing to recommend her aside from her ability to play the piano and make an old woman laugh.

Although she wouldn't be making Lady Densbury laugh today. It might be noon before she managed to do more than scowl at the woman.

Sarah trotted quickly down the stairs to avoid the temptation of sliding down the polished curved banister like a four-year-old. A set of drawing rooms near the bottom of the stairs had been converted into the dowager's bedchamber and dressing room, an accommodation the earl hadn't seemed to know about, even though it had been done nearly three years prior. It was a sad reflection on the state of the family.

It was as if the earl was simply waiting for his mother to die.

The fact that Sarah herself had thought such a thing fleetingly this morning was completely different. She'd thought it in exasperated love for the meddling woman.

A look around the room, decorated in soft shades of blue and occasional splashes of deep, vibrant red, revealed the dowager countess was taking her time with breakfast. She was still wrapped in her dressing gown, seated at the small table near the window that curved around the corner of the house.

Sarah nodded at the maid laying out the dowager's clothing for the day and then retreated to the drawing room. When Lady Densbury was ready, she'd come out, settle into the drawing room with a book or other time-passing activity and pretend that she was awaiting visitors who rarely, if ever, showed. The vicar came by on occasion, as well as a handful of ladies in the weeks after they returned from London, but by and large, days at Cloverdale were quiet.

A fire was already blazing cheerfully in the drawing room, filling the area with warmth and light.

Soon the sun would top the trees and the room would be a golden oasis for most of the day. The number of windows meant a great deal of light, but also a great deal of chill, so Sarah set Lady Densbury's black shawl on the back of the chair nearest the fire so it would be warm when the dowager wanted it.

A glint of silver tumbled out of the woolen nest, and Sarah jerked to catch the jewelry before it fell. A smile touched her lips as she ran a finger across the large amethyst heart in the center of the brooch. Silver hearts intertwined around the stone, and a silver crown topped the entire curling mass of shiny nostalgia.

And just that easily, she forgave the old woman for her embarrassing declaration. Lady Densbury was a romantic. She'd loved her husband enormously, and by all accounts he'd loved her, as well—enough to haul her off to Scotland and cause a great scandal when his family had declared her an unfit choice of bride.

They'd spent a year in Edinburgh where he'd bought her this luckenbooth brooch as a token of his unending love for her. It was easily the dowager's most prized possession. Not because of the enormous gem's value, but because of the love it made her remember. Sarah lost count of the number of times she'd heard the story.

It was understandable that the dowager would want such a love for Mr. Everard. He was her favorite relation, and she wasn't loathe to admit it.

It was less understandable that she wanted Mr. Everard to fall in love with Sarah.

Sarah fixed the brooch firmly onto the shawl, then set about preparing the rest of the room for the day.

Book and spectacles on the table to the right of the chair. Basket of embroidery work on the floor beneath the table. Table to the left of the chair empty and ready to hold a cup of tea. Footstool tucked neatly beneath the upholstered wingback chair, ready to slide into use when it was wanted. Drapes pulled just so to let in plenty of light but not cause a glare.

The wrapped parcel of Madeira Pound Cake had been placed on the small table by the window where Sarah and Lady Densbury took their meals. Sarah didn't remember what she'd done with it last night, whether she'd dropped it when she ran or left it with her bonnet and pelisse in the kitchens, but she was happy to see the parcel this morning.

She unwrapped it and took a large bite of cake. Who needed to wait for slices when there were mortifying memories that needed burying?

Still, she couldn't eat the whole thing or she'd be sick, so she wrapped the now heavily divoted chunk of cake back in the linen and set it on the tea table.

With nothing else to do, Sarah made her way to the square piano that took a central place of prominence in the other half of the drawing room.

Sarah loved this old instrument so much more than the modern one she played at Helmsfield. Possibly because it hadn't been situated to remind her that she'd been excluded, but also because it seemed like the piano knew music was loved here. The strings seemed to vibrate more brightly and the keys bounced back more quickly.

A quick flourish of notes seemed to finish waking up the room. Sarah always played in the morning, embellishing simple waltzes or minuets or sending complicated sonatas echoing through the house.

This morning definitely called for more of a loud, echoing sort of song, because while Sarah had found it in her to forgive her employer, she was still more than a little bit miffed.

Making cow eyes at Randall Everard and dreaming he'd notice her was one thing. Having it announced that she'd been chosen for him and found lacking was another.

Randall's horse stood in front of the house, saddled and ready to depart. He'd intended to leave today, having delivered the updated numbers and money to his father. It was two days' easy ride, putting him back at Bluestone in time to celebrate Christmas with the tenants and area gentry. He'd even packed his saddlebags this morning with clothing and food for the journey.

Yet the leather bags were still sitting in a chair in his room instead of being flung across the front of the saddle.

Why was he standing here instead of halfway down the drive?

Because last night he'd seen something in Miss Gooding that fascinated him, something he'd thought was there but never seen evidence of. He would be a fool if he didn't at least see if that glimmer was a flash of momentary sun or an indication of a fine, rare jewel.

"Randall, are you leaving today?" His mother crossed the hall to where he was standing by the front door.

The same place he'd stood last night watching Miss Gooding try to figure out how to get her cake home without making it obvious she had it.

"No, Mother, I was thinking that I might stay through Christmas." Randall didn't know he'd made the decision until the words popped out of his mouth, but as soon as he heard himself say them, he knew it was the right choice.

"Oh." She said nothing for a moment and then gave him a bright, genuine smile. "That's wonderful. It's been a while since we were all actually home for the holiday season."

That was true. Before his brothers had married, it hadn't been unusual for George or Cecil or even both of them to choose remaining in London over making the journey north. Last year it had been Grandmother who had chosen the city over the country, saying her wardrobe needed refreshing and she didn't trust the country modistes. Not only had she returned home with trunks full of clothing, but she'd brought a new companion as well.

"It's a nice idea," Randall said, "the whole family together for Christmas. Perhaps we can convince Grandmother to stay at the main house for the duration of the celebration."

Whether he was ready to consciously admit it or not, this was likely his last Christmas with his grandmother, and he wanted to relish every moment of it.

"I suppose." Mother frowned, deep grooves framing her pinched lips. "She'll insist on bringing her companion."

He rubbed a hand across the back of his neck and tilted his head to consider his mother. "Why don't you like her?"

Dark eyebrows arched over equally dark brown eyes. "Aside from the fact that she cost my cousin a very estimable livelihood? She's entirely too questionable. We've no idea where she comes from or who her people are. We don't even know who she was working for when your grandmother plucked her out of a snow-bank on the edge of the ice-skating pond."

Randall couldn't help grinning. "I thought Miss Gooding plucked Grandmother out of the snowbank."

The countess waved a hand through the air in dismissal. "The dowager had no business ice-skating at all. Emily tried to make that quite clear."

"Which is probably why Emily is no longer Grandmother's companion." Randall slid his hat onto his head. "Grandmother has never taken kindly to being told what to do."

"Yes, I know." Mother sighed. "Your father is still trying to live down her many scandals. It's hard enough, unexpectedly inheriting as a second son. People talk. But to have them question everything he does because his mother was the daughter of a Cambridge professor, well, it's a lot for a family to live down."

"It doesn't seem to have harmed my brothers any." Both of Randall's brothers had married very well. The fact that Randall couldn't see himself married to either woman or even a woman similar to them was part of the reason he was still single at the age of twenty-seven.

"No, it hasn't. We've had to be very diligent about appearances, but it has been worth it."

Had it really? What had truly been gained by his parents' obsession with living down his fun-loving grandmother's scandals? True, Cecil might not have married as well as he had, but George was going to be an earl. An eccentric or two in his family tree wasn't likely to hurt him any.

Even an eccentric brother who considered having a flirtation with his grandmother's companion.

Mother clasped her hands in front of her and sent a questioning look to his horse, still standing on the drive, snuffling his nose at a dry leaf near his feet. "Where are you going if not home?"

"Um, Cloverdale." He did his best to keep his voice as emotionless as possible. He didn't need his mother panicking. "Look in on Grandmother."

"Oh." She was silent for a few moments, but nothing on her face let him know what she was thinking. "We'll see you for dinner, then."

Randall nodded and mounted his horse, feeling more than a little ridiculous. Cloverdale was a mile away. He'd walked there and back last night, and he felt a bit absurd riding the short distance on a horse. Of course, Nero needed to get out and stretch his legs a bit, so Randall soothed his embarrassment by taking the long and winding route to Cloverdale.

The air was cold and wet, biting his lungs if he took a deep breath. Nero's breath puffed around him in icy clouds. It would snow soon, either today or tomorrow.

His prediction came true, with the first fat flakes drifting through the air as Cloverdale came into view. The rounded, elegant lines of the house had always appealed to him, much more so than the imposing stone walls of Helmsfield. It was no wonder that Grandmother had packed up and moved here within days of her son taking up the earldom and residence in the family seat. All of her clothes hadn't even been dyed black when they'd packed them up.

It was a simple matter to care for Nero and put him in one of the two empty stalls in the small shed behind the house. Soon Randall was bounding up the three front steps out of the snow.

Riotous, glorious music could be heard as he approached the front door. Apparently his grandmother already had visitors.

Entertaining ones. Perhaps even two. Surely one person couldn't manage to play all of those notes.

The maid met him at the door and curtseyed before gesturing him toward the drawing room. He usually came to the dower house his first day in town. He'd visit with his grandmother and read or play chess while Miss Gooding embroidered in the corner. She was always embroidering. It was only slightly more boring than the banal piano playing she did when Grandmother brought her to dinner.

Before he reached the drawing room, he heard his grandmother's voice.

"That was mighty peculiar business Sunday, preaching on not caring about the thoughts of others."

Music trilled, the notes rapidly climbing along the keys. "That's not what he said and you know it. He said that it was more important that a person be clean before God than be understood by his fellow man."

Randall frowned. That was Miss Gooding's voice. He was almost sure of it. But it sounded the same way it had been during those moments last night—strong, sure, and without that soft edge of apology he so disliked.

"Bah."

"You can't say, 'bah,' it's in the Bible. He read from Romans." More intricate melodies filled the room. "Besides, you yourself act according to your faith and conscience instead of what is expected of you, even if you won't admit it."

There was a pause where nothing could be heard except the beautiful, captivating piano music.

"Bah," his grandmother said again, although this time there was a distinct note of humor in it.

Randall stepped up to the door and stopped in his tracks once more. There wasn't a guest or two making magic on the piano. There was simply Miss Gooding, playing to rival the masters he'd heard in concert halls while carrying on a conversation well enough to best his sharp-witted grandmother.

And confound it all if there weren't something wildly attractive about that.

He cleared his throat. "One also has to consider the Bible's command to live uprightly in the eyes of man, though. Fearing God while honoring the king."

It was an abrupt way to announce his presence, and Miss Gooding's fingers stumbled to a melodic halt.

Grandmother looked up. "Randall! Perfect. You're just the man I need."

"I am?" he asked.

"He is?" Miss Gooding inquired at the same time.

"Of course." The dowager pointed a shaky, crooked finger at her companion. "You can hardly haul greenery in from the woods by yourself."

Thin golden eyebrows winged upward, and Miss Gooding's mouth quirked. Instead of making her face look angular and pinched, though, it made her look like some sort of fairy or wood nymph Shakespeare would write about. It took Randall a moment to realize it was all in the eyes. She was looking directly at the dowager, not at her toes or the floor. The expression in those pale blue eyes seemed to make all the difference.

"I wasn't aware I was going into the woods today."

"Well, you weren't." His grandmother adjusted her shawl, revealing the silver brooch he'd seen her with for as long as he could remember. "But now that Randall has come, you can."

The companion stood and crossed her arms. "And why am I going into the woods?"

Grandmother covered her mouth with her shawl and coughed several times, taking shuddering breaths in between. After a moment, she swallowed and carried on as if nothing had happened. "I want Christmas greenery."

Silence fell over the drawing room.

Randall stepped forward. "Christmas isn't until next week, Grandmother."

Before the old woman could answer, Miss Gooding stepped

forward, her hands clasped tightly together and held to her chest as if she were an excited young girl. "And why limit the celebration of Jesus's birth to a single day—or even twelve? There's no rule that says we can't extend that a bit."

He frowned. "But tradition—"

"Was made to be broken," Miss Gooding said firmly.

Randall looked at her. He'd found himself doing that quite a bit of late. She wasn't cowering, wasn't keeping to the shadows. In fact, she looked ready to go toe to toe with him over a few twigs and branches.

Apparently he was going to go chop down a holly bush.

4

Sarah pulled her coat more tightly around her and plunged into the woods outside of the dower house. She tried not to think about what she knew to be true, the fate Lady Densbury had obviously accepted, but every branch of greenery she considered, every sprig of holly she yanked sent it screaming into her head.

Mr. Everard pulled a knife from his boot and sawed at a particularly even-looking evergreen branch. "Tell me again why we're doing this five days early?"

"You mean aside from the fact that your grandmother would like you to fall in love with me?"

Sarah slapped one gloved hand over her mouth and felt her eyes widen until the skin around them pulled.

But there was a smile on Mr. Everard's face when he paused his cutting to glance at her over his shoulder. "Yes. Aside from that."

Thankfully he turned his attention back to the branch after his statement because Sarah couldn't think of a single response with him looking at her. She couldn't think of a very good one when he wasn't looking at her, either.

The fact was, Lady Densbury wasn't well. She didn't eat much these days, moved even less. The walk to and from the estate house was taking longer and longer. When Sarah had first started, they'd made the journey in a comfortable twenty minutes. Now they were lucky to walk it in twice that amount of time.

But she couldn't very well tell the man she was afraid his grandmother was dying.

"You know," Mr. Everard said as if he hadn't really expected Sarah to come up with another answer, "if we're destined to be star-crossed lovers or some other such romantic tale, you might as well call me Randall."

"Sarah," she responded, almost automatically. There weren't a lot of people in her life who used her Christian name. The dowager had been the only one in the past three years, and she'd never asked Sarah to return the familiarity. "And if it's all the same to you, I'd rather not be one half of a tragic love story."

He was quiet for a few moments, the rustling of branches and evergreen needles the only noise in the gently falling snow. The dark, waxy leaves of a holly bush pulled her farther into the woods, and she set about removing the prettier limbs and those heavy with tiny red berries.

"Have you already been one half of a tragic love story?"

Sarah straightened and looked at Randall, still turned away from her and seeming to give his attention to the tree. "Why would you ask me that?"

He tossed her a grin over his shoulder. "Because my mother is convinced you have some dark mysterious past that's going to rise up and plummet the family into ruin. As the only unmarried son remaining, my future is the most vulnerable, so I thought I'd try to prepare myself."

"No." Sarah's voice barely escaped her suddenly dry throat. She swallowed. "No, there are no scorned lovers waiting to bring me to my doom."

The holly bush suddenly became the most important thing in Sarah's world as she devoted herself to filling her hands with as many holly clumps as possible. Her past certainly wasn't something any respectable family wanted to be connected with, but it wasn't going to make itself known. She'd been abandoned as a child, left in the care of two wonderful, loving women. Those women would never betray her history, and the unmarried parents who hadn't wanted her twenty-two years ago weren't about to come looking for her now.

Randall came over to her, his arms laden with boughs. "Do you think she's wanting anything other than evergreen limbs and holly?"

"Probably a ball of mistletoe to trap us under," Sarah mumbled. She jerked upright and clapped her gloved hands over her mouth once more, stabbing herself in the face with a handful of spiky holly leaves. "Ow!"

Green leaves and red berries flew everywhere as she wrenched her hands away from her face and waved them about, as if she could somehow fan the stinging pain away. At least the pain would eventually ease. Her mortification wasn't going anywhere. Ever.

Deep, warm laughter filled the wooded area.

Sarah glared at his laughing face as she gingerly touched her fingers to her face. The humor in his eyes and the wide smile made a ribbon of tension curl through her stomach. "Am I bleeding?"

His laughter tapered down to a chuckle. "I don't think so." He knelt to place his bundle of boughs on the ground before stepping closer. "Here, let me see."

Two fingers slid beneath her chin and pulled her face up toward his. She blinked, caught in his grey-blue gaze. It was a bit unnerving, being the absolute center of his attention. She wasn't even certain the dowager had ever focused on her this hard.

"You've a scratch or two, but nothing that bad." One finger slid across her cheekbone and plucked a leaf from her hair. "Does it still hurt?"

There was a particularly sensitive spot on the corner of her lip, but she wasn't about to tell him that. With any luck, her awkward flinging of holly had made him forget the comment about the mistletoe, and she wasn't doing anything to bring it back up.

"I think I was merely startled." Her mouth was dry again, making her words a hoarse whisper. His face was so close, close enough that she could see that the lashes on his left eye clumped together at the edge. She could smell his scent over that of the recently cut evergreens, an earthy blend of leather and moss. When combined with the undeniable scent of Christmas and snow, it made her mind swirl until she couldn't think of anything, couldn't see anything but him.

His hands fell away from her face, and he took a step back. She was left with a dizzy sensation, the feeling of having avoided falling off the edge of a cliff.

He gathered up the dropped holly and piled it with the evergreen trimmings before wrapping his arms around the entire bundle. "This should be enough for the drawing room."

"Yes, yes it should be." She dropped her gaze to the ground and strode past him toward the house. What had just happened?

What had just happened? Randall followed Sarah, arms loaded with greenery. One moment he'd been trying to make basic conversation and with one single comment about mistletoe, he'd been on the verge of pretending he was beneath it. Yes, he'd known he was somewhat attracted to Sarah, intrigued by what he'd learned of her over the past two days, but enough to want to initiate a kiss?

And what was worse was the surprising moment had sent the fun and beguiling Sarah back into hiding.

The walk back to the house was quiet, with Sarah staying three steps in front of him, fluffy white snowflakes dropping gently into her hair, sparkling for a brief moment and then melting away.

In the drawing room, he set his bundle on a table near the large set of windows.

"It smells like Christmas." Grandmother sighed and very slowly pushed herself out of the chair near the fireplace. She took a deep breath and fell into another round of coughs.

For the next hour, as snow fell beyond the windowpanes, the three of them worked to bring the outdoors into the drawing room. Sarah placed sprigs of evergreen into the individual windows while

Randall twisted branches together to form a garland across the mantel. Grandmother wove bits of holly around a candelabra sitting on top of the piano.

Grandmother hummed while she worked until Sarah joined in with the words. Her singing was surprisingly horrific for someone possessing the incredible talent he'd witnessed on the piano when he came in earlier. It made him smile as he lent his own voice to the merriment.

Before long, though, Grandmother was settling back into her chair by the fire, and Sarah was busy straightening the shawl to cover the old woman's shoulders. Grandmother was snoring softly before Sarah had everything situated to her liking.

It didn't seem very festive to decorate while his grandmother slept, so he gathered the remaining greenery into a pile and placed it on the floor in a corner.

A maid appeared at the door with a tray of food. "Oh! She's sleeping already, then?"

"Yes," Sarah said softly before nodding toward the table that had recently been covered in the bundle of plant trimmings. "Leave the food. I'll eat now, and she can eat when she wakes."

Randall glanced at the table where the maid was setting a tray of food that should only have been enough for one person to eat. Did his grandmother ever leave this room?

"Will you be joining them, Mr. Everard?" the maid asked.

"No," Sarah said.

Randall narrowed his eyes at the companion before speaking very slow and deliberately. "Yes. I believe I shall."

Sarah's cheeks puffed out before she blew a stream of air between tight lips.

The maid curtsied. "I'll bring more food straightaway."

Sarah waited until the maid had gone before scooping up a basket from beside the dowager's chair and crossing to the table by the window. After putting a small selection of bread, cheese, and ham on her plate, she settled into her chair and pulled out a small, square piece of fabric from the basket.

Was she honestly intending to ignore him? The idea amused Randall and made him think that her shy withdrawal from his family may not have been fear so much as subtle dismissal. A snubbing of sorts. Not that he'd blame her if it was. There was a reason his trips to Helmsfield had grown shorter and further apart.

A rattled snore drifted from the chair near the fireplace. A halting noise in the middle broke the snore in half before another one started. It didn't sound good, but Randall didn't have enough experience with older people to know whether or not it was something to be concerned about. He left the snoring matriarch to her rest and moved to the chair across the table from Sarah.

He plopped a piece of cheese in his mouth and watched her ply a needle against the fabric. It took him a moment to realize she was removing stitches instead of adding them. "What are you doing?"

She was silent for a moment as a splash of pink covered her cheeks. "I'm removing the stitches your grandmother made this morning."

Randall froze, a piece of ham halfway to his mouth. "Removing?"

"Yes." A few quick tugs pulled another section of thread loose.

Looking at the fabric in her lap, he could see where a small section of stitches were certainly crooked, loose, and out of place, but the rest of the work looked neat and clean, if simple. His grandmother must have been having a very bad day.

Every few moments, Sarah would stop and take a bite of food. Another tray was delivered by the maid, but still Sarah worked in silence, and Randall sat in silence as well, his brain working as he ate, trying to understand the complicated companion.

By the time she'd finished removing all the work his grandmother had so painstakingly done that morning, he had a store of questions to ask her. He waited for her to put the embroidery away, but she didn't. She shifted her hold on the needle and began replacing the work she'd just picked out. Neat, tidy stitches, adding to the picture on the fabric.

Another slew of questions drifted into his mind. There was certainly more to Sarah than he'd ever thought.

He cleared his throat, careful to keep his voice quiet and not disturb his grandmother. "Have you always been a companion?"

The needle stopped, poking out of the fabric like a dagger in wait. Surprisingly, Sarah looked up from her lap, her mouth obviously fighting the urge to grin. "Still trying to determine my dark past, Mr. Everard?" She shook her head and *tsk*ed at him before turning her attention back to the needlework. "No, but I knew I was destined to life in service. A companion is actually a bit better than I could have hoped for."

It was his turn to be surprised once more. Sarah was well spoken, educated, and had obviously had access to musical instruction while growing up. He'd just assumed she was from genteel poverty, someone's poor relation, like some of his cousins were.

Like he was destined to be one day.

"Why?"

"Why?" She glanced up at him and he saw another hint of the vibrant girl his grandmother probably knew. A touch of a smile graced her lips and her wide-set eyes held a spark of mischief. "Because I've never considered dirt and starvation to be something to aspire to."

He felt an answering grin tug at his lips. "Why be a servant? Didn't your parents at least consider marrying you off?"

A shadow crossed her face, and her gaze dropped back to the embroidery. "I haven't any parents."

He sucked in his breath. "They died?"

She was silent for a long time. Too long. Long enough that Randall wondered if she ever intended to answer. Was she deciding how much to trust him with?

With a sharp pull of her wrist, she snapped the thread she was working with. "I really wouldn't know if they're dead or not. I don't know who they were."

She had no one. The idea sent Randall sliding down in his chair. He didn't know what expression he wore on his face, but whatever it was, she glanced at him, and it was enough to inspire her to share a bit more.

"I was raised by a wonderful woman. We write. I know if things became desperate I could go back to her and she'd care for me without question, but that's not what I want for her or for myself. She has a good life, and she's helping other children who have nowhere to go, while I am perfectly capable of supporting myself."

He didn't doubt her conviction, not anymore. She'd proven to have an iron will when it mattered. What he couldn't quite understand was how she'd crossed paths with a dowager countess. His grandmother was known for being a bit eccentric, but . . . "Where did you work before here?"

She grinned at him. "As a parlor maid for a music master. I thought working for someone who loved music would be perfect. I had dreams of learning more by simply being in the same building as he was. And I did. Some. When I managed to press my ear to the door while he was giving a lesson."

Her smile turned conspiratorial as she laid the embroidery in her lap and leaned over the table. "But what you're really asking is how I met Lady Densbury."

Randall couldn't stop the quiet laugh as he nodded and conceded her point with a wave of his hand.

"I pulled her out of a snowbank."

His eyebrows lifted. "That story is true?"

"I'm not sure what story you heard, but yes, she was skating and didn't turn in time and fell into a large pile of snow. I helped her out and held her hand while she skated. On our second trip around the pond she noticed her brooch was missing, so I dug into the snow to find it. When I came back up, she offered me the job. Right there in the park."

"And discharged Emily."

Sarah winced and shrugged. "Emily wouldn't help her skate. That was why she fell in the snow in the first place."

"Well, she is old."

"That's no reason not to live life."

And that was why his grandmother had hired her.

The dowager had no reason to care about references, didn't go out in society enough to care what other people thought or even to really expose her companion to scrutiny. She just wanted to live out her final days instead of wait for them to creep by.

"I'm supremely uninteresting, though," Sarah said as she tied off the thread and dropped the fabric back into the basket. "What is the son of an earl doing spending his afternoon in the dower house?"

"The same thing my grandmother is doing in hiring an un- known companion." Randall leaned forward, not wanting to miss a moment of the expressions that flitted across Sarah's face. He had only a moment to catch them before she hid them away.

"What's—" her voice choked and she swallowed before trying again. "What's that?"

"Living."

And it was true. He didn't feel like he could live in the shadow of his brothers, in the silent doom of his family. There was noth- ing for him there. He was a third son. His parents had nothing to offer him. They didn't speak of it, but everyone knew. Especially George. He'd been separating himself from Randall since he fin- ished school. The only time they talked now was about estate business, or when he and Randall happened to participate in the same conversation at the family dinner.

But here, with Sarah, with his grandmother, that future didn't seem quite so full of imminent doom. He could actually enjoy himself.

She ran a finger along the edge of her teacup. "You don't find yourself living at Bluestone? That is where you spend most of your time, isn't it?"

He nodded. "I like farming. Seeing the actual fruits of my labor. Planning and caring for the soil so that it produces the best crops possible. It's a challenge, and it's never dull. At first it was simply somewhere to go and feel important, but now I actually like it."

It wasn't simply the activity—it was the sense of purpose. If he could convince his father to help him acquire a small farm some- where, just a corner of land where he could grow his own crops and live a simple life, Randall would be happy. It would be enough.

The idea surprised him, but not as much as the fact that Sarah proceeded to provide him with some of her own thoughts about crops and farming. As they drank through an entire pot of tea, they talked of farming, of weather cycles, and of crop rotations.

"I grow a lot of rhubarb at Bluestone. Have you ever eaten rhubarb?"

She shook her head. "I grew up in Wiltshire, then moved to London to work. My palate and experience have been rather narrow."

Before Randall could get the conversation moving again, Sarah caught his eye and nodded toward the fireplace. "She's awake, you know."

"Grandmother?" Randall jerked his gaze in the direction of the chair.

"Has been since we debated the merits of turnips instead of potatoes," she said quietly.

He turned back to Sarah, who didn't look the least bit bothered by his grandmother's antics. "Why didn't she say anything?"

Sarah shrugged. "It amuses her, I suppose."

There was more to it, something Sarah wasn't telling him. Surely Grandmother hadn't been serious the night before when she'd suggested he marry Sarah.

Then again, the idea seemed a bit less preposterous with every passing hour.

5

Randall came back on Friday.

They played chess while the dowager told Sarah everything she was doing wrong. Fortunately the old woman limited herself to correcting the moves Sarah made on the chessboard and left her life choices alone. If Sarah made a few ridiculous moves to keep giving the dowager something to complain about, well, the only thing hurt by that little deception was her chance of winning.

Then he'd stayed for dinner, which sent the poor housekeeper into a frenzy. There hadn't been much need for elaborate cooking or large meals, so the prospect of actually entertaining for a meal was exciting. They'd still eaten at the little table in the drawing room and by the time Randall left to return to Helmsfield, the dowager had been exhausted but happy. She'd needed the help of both a maid and Sarah to get ready for bed, and she'd fallen asleep immediately, a smile on her face and a deep rattle to her breathing.

Sarah had been too overcome by the desire to move and be active to find her own bed, so she'd sat in the drawing room, finishing the last of the embroidered handkerchiefs Lady Densbury wanted to put in the Christmas boxes for her staff. She tucked the completed handkerchief into the last wooden box and slipped into the dowager's room to leave the gift in the basket with the other Christmas boxes.

The labored breathing still filled the room, but it sounded a touch better than it had earlier.

When Sarah did make it up to her own bed, she, too, fell asleep with a smile on her face.

The smile remained as Sarah dressed the next morning and as she came down the stairs. It fell a bit as she realized how very still and quiet the house was at the bottom of the stairs. A peek out the window showed the snow had finally decided to get serious, and the ground was covered in a blanket of glistening white.

Was that the reason everything had a deep sense of calm quiet? Snow had a way of dampening everything. She glanced around. No, it was more than that. . . . It was as if no one was moving, as if Sarah were alone in the elegant rooms.

She moved toward Lady Densbury's chambers, her heart thudding in the morning stillness. Her breath solidified in her lungs as she pushed the door open and didn't hear the same rattle and snore she'd heard the night before.

The dowager was still in bed. A slow but steady rise and fall shifted the blankets.

Sarah's head fell to the side until it was supported by the doorframe, and her breath rushed out so quickly her chest hurt. One day . . . but not today. So Sarah wouldn't think about it.

She moved to the drawing room, looking for something quiet to occupy her time. A few boughs of greenery were still awaiting a home, so she set about weaving them into a decoration for the table where they ate. A clump of mistletoe clung to one of the branches and a quick laugh burst out of Sarah even as a blush covered her cheeks.

Mistletoe was plebeian. Common. Even a little scandalous. All things the dowager was certain to appreciate. She pulled a ribbon from the sewing basket and set about making a kissing ball out of the plant. There were only a few of the kiss-claiming white berries clinging to it, but since it was more for sentiment than actual kissing, that wouldn't matter.

Given the dowager's recent comments and Randall's penchant

for stopping by, Sarah wasn't about to hang her decoration in the doorway. Instead she climbed on the chair she used at the piano and fixed the kissing ball to the drapery rod. It would lend a festive air, but someone would have to be very determined to get caught beneath it.

A bell clanged from the direction of the dowager's room, indicating that the woman had awoken. Sarah moved toward the room to help her employer dress and get ready for the day, trying to convince herself that the amount of sleep the dowager was getting was a good thing. When the doctor had come by last week, he'd said rest was the best thing for her. Sarah could only hope he meant this much rest.

Because one day the dowager wasn't going to wake up from her nap, and Sarah would not only lose her friend, but her job and home as well. She pasted a smile on her face as she greeted the dowager. There was no sense thinking about bad things today. She could worry about them when they finally came.

Randall called himself a fool for coming to visit his grandmother for the third day in a row.

Especially since he knew he wasn't actually coming to visit his grandmother. Not really. He wanted more conversations that both challenged his mind and entertained him. He wanted more enjoyment of simple things. He wanted to see Sarah.

The only problem was, for the first time since he'd completed school and his grandmother had suggested he strike out on his own, he realized what a predicament he'd created for himself by staying tied to the family holdings.

He had absolutely nothing to offer Sarah.

The son of an earl, educated, and at least somewhat decent in appearance, and he could offer her no more of a future than the village chimney sweep. Possibly even less.

But still he came. Because he'd never quite known how to save him from himself.

There was no answer when he knocked this time. Nor was jolly music vibrating through the door. He lifted the latch and let himself into the house.

Laughter met him as he stepped into the hall. In the drawing room, he found his grandmother and her companion seated by the piano and the rest of the staff scattered about the room. One of the maids was standing in the middle of the room balancing a small pillow on her head, holding her breath as she tried to keep it from falling.

All at once the room erupted in cheers, and the maid tipped her head forward and let the cushion fall to the floor.

"Randall," the dowager's voice drifted through the laughter in the room. "You're just in time to take a turn."

Magical Music had always been one of his grandmother's favorite games. Randall was never sure if it was because it involved music—one of the things she loved most in the world—or because it allowed her to make everyone around her drop their dignity and enjoy themselves.

Randall wasn't sure he wanted to drop his dignity in front of Sarah, but she likely cared more about how he treated his grandmother than how distinguished he looked, so he shrugged out of his greatcoat and draped it across a chair before sweeping his arms wide in an invitation for his grandmother to do her worst.

The head of grey curls nodded toward Sarah. "Start playing."

Sarah's eyebrows lifted, but she plunked out a song Randall remembered singing at Christmas since he was a boy. She played softly, watching the dowager for a sign that she should play louder, indicating that Randall had gotten close to whatever task his grandmother had deemed worthy of the game.

He stepped into the room, eyes locked with his grandmother's. She was tucked into a chair beside the piano, blankets wrapped around her and a footstool beneath her legs. She looked small and frail but happy.

Too happy.

His eyes narrowed. What was she up to?

Slowly he worked his way around the room. Slowly Sarah played louder.

He stopped watching his grandmother and started watching Sarah. Her bottom lip was caught between her teeth and a worried frown formed deep grooves between her eyes. As he got closer to her, she played the song a bit louder until suddenly the confusion dropped from her face and her gaze drifted up from the dowager toward the ceiling.

Randall's gaze lifted as well to discover the lone clump of mistletoe hanging from the drapery rod. Sarah wasn't exactly below it, as the piano sat a good two or three feet from the window, but Randall had a suspicion that it was close enough for his grandmother.

Keeping his stride slow and steady, Randall approached the piano, and rounded it until Sarah was practically having to pound on the keys.

Randall looked up at the mistletoe. "You couldn't possibly want to participate in such a tradition, could you, Grandmother?"

The old woman cackled. "I've never been much for tradition, my boy, except when it suited me."

With a grin, Randall reached up and plucked a white berry from the hanging cluster. He let his gaze fall on Sarah, who was watching him with wide eyes, playing the same sequence of notes over and over again. She blinked at him. He couldn't read her face, though. Did she want him to kiss her? Had she thought of him when she'd hung the mistletoe from the drapery rod?

No matter what the answers were, a room crowded with his grandmother's staff was hardly the place to have a first kiss.

So instead of leaning into Sarah like he knew his grandmother wanted, he leaned toward her wrinkled cheek and placed a peck on it instead.

Sarah stopped playing. A collective sigh swept the room. Grandmother looked torn between a smile and a frown. She stared at him awhile and Randall simply stared back. Finally, she nodded and turned back toward the staff. "Elizabeth, it's your turn."

A maid hopped up from the sofa and began traveling the room, searching for what strange task his grandmother had dreamt up for her to do.

Randall found himself a chair and watched Sarah play, rolling the mistletoe berry between his fingers.

The maids soon tired of playing the dowager's parlor games and the dowager soon tired of being awake. Her spells of coughs came closer and closer together until finally Sarah called a halt to the game and settled Lady Densbury into the chair by the fire while the maids returned to their work. The dowager was asleep in moments.

And Sarah was essentially left alone with Randall.

He was leaning against the wall between the large sections of windows, one ankle crossed over the other, still rolling the mistletoe berry between his fingers.

She'd barely been able to play for the rest of the game she'd been so obsessed with watching him fiddle with the berry. All she could think was what if he'd done what his grandmother actually wanted him to?

What if he'd kissed her?

What if she'd enjoyed it?

She cleared her throat. "I didn't think we'd see you today."

He shrugged one shoulder. "There's not a lot for me to do during the day at Helmsfield. Unless Father and George are discussing Bluestone, they don't really need me there."

Sarah had never once considered that it might be a blessing to not have any sort of legacy directing her future. For years she'd been jealous of those who seemed to know where they were going, who'd had a path forged by the generations who had gone before them. Never once had she considered what happened to the people who walked a forged path that concluded in a dead end, or who maybe didn't like the path that had been cut for them.

"When I first came to work for your grandmother, I spent the first two weeks shadowing her about like a lapdog."

Randall's fingers stilled, and his head tilted to the side as he considered her.

Sarah pressed one hand to her anxious middle. Why was she telling him this story? Did she really think she had any sort of advice or comfort to offer? Whether she did or not, she'd started and now she had to see it through. She took a deep breath and continued. "For two weeks I did everything I thought she wanted. I was quiet, only spoke when spoken to and even then tried to say what I thought she wanted to hear. I was terrified that I'd moved so far from London to a place where I had no connections of any variety and I was going to find myself thrown out in the snow."

"Obviously something changed that," Randall said dryly.

Sarah nodded. "Lady Densbury took me to a family dinner."

"One of those torturous affairs up at Helmsfield?"

Again, Sarah nodded. "I behaved there as I had everywhere else. On our way back here she stopped in the middle of the path and jabbed her finger in my chest. She said it was all well and good if I wanted to hide and simper my way through dinners. After all, everyone had their own way of surviving. But I needed to leave that nonsense on the path between the houses because there wasn't anything to be afraid of at Cloverdale."

A light laugh preceded Randall's next question. "And did you stop being a lapdog after that?"

"No," she admitted. Why oh why had she felt the need to tell this story? "I tried even more to be what I thought your grandmother wanted me to be until the day her old companion showed up."

"Emily?"

Sarah nodded, wincing at the memory of that day. "She came to collect some of her belongings. She was livid. She and the dowager yelled at each other, and your grandmother kicked Emily out of the house saying she'd have a maid deliver her things to Helmsfield. After she closed the door, she looked . . . happy.

"It wasn't that she didn't like Emily," Sarah rushed to add. "It was that she'd enjoyed being challenged that much. So then

I stopped trying to figure out how to agree with her and started thinking about whether or not I did agree with her when we talked. Sometimes I do, sometimes I don't, but I know that even then your grandmother knew her body was slowing down and she wanted someone who could exercise her mind."

Silence fell between them as Randall contemplated the small white berry he held. "Why are you telling me this?"

"I don't know," Sarah sighed. "I suppose I'm hoping it will help you find the courage to ask yourself what you want. I know you love Bluestone, but it doesn't actually seem to be making you happy."

Sarah wandered a bit closer to him and walked her fingers down the piano casing. "What do you want to do with your life?"

His chest expanded as he closed his eyes and dropped his head back. "I wish Bluestone were mine," he said quietly. "I wish the farm were mine completely so I could manage it and grow it without answering to my father."

"I don't know much about properties, so having Bluestone may not be an option, but couldn't you find another farm?"

Why was Sarah pushing him about this? Did she really think he was going to throw it all away and take her with him to live on a little farm growing rhubarbs and turnips?

No.

No, she didn't, but wherever she went, she wanted to think that he was happy, somewhere living life the way he wanted.

He brought his head upright and opened his eyes. "When did you get to be so wise, Sarah Gooding?"

She lifted one shoulder. "Must be living with your grandmother."

His mouth kicked up in that lopsided smile she knew she'd take with her when it was time to go, and his eyes angled somewhere above her head. "You're under the mistletoe."

Sarah's eyes widened, and she looked over her shoulder. She was no more under the mistletoe than she had been earlier. "No, I'm not."

He shrugged and reached his hands out so they were clasping hers, keeping her from pulling away. Then he stepped forward, closer to her. "We can fix that."

She took a step back, neck craned so she could keep looking at him. "What?"

"You said I should make my own choices about living my life and right now I'd really like to kiss you." He stopped. "The question is, what do you want?"

Sarah swallowed. "I think . . ."

Could she be brave? Could she take her own advice and live life the way she wanted to?

She took one large step backward until her shoulders were pressed against the window, the cluster of mistletoe directly over her head. "I think I'd like that too."

6

He was going to kiss Sarah Gooding.

The thought thrilled him even as it terrified him.

A single step closed the distance, and he reached out his hand to cup her cheek. Then slowly, he lowered his head toward hers. When their lips finally touched, it wasn't with the heat he'd expected. Instead it was like sliding into the pond at Bluestone in the middle of summer. It was thick and soft, wrapping around him like a comforting, refreshing blanket. If he weren't careful, he could drown.

Her hand came up to clasp his wrist, as if she were afraid he'd step away, and she wanted to keep him there just a moment longer.

He had news for her. He wasn't going anywhere.

Slowly he pulled his head back, relishing the softness of her lips until the last possible moment.

Then he stayed a while longer, staring into her eyes until the dowager woke herself up with a particularly loud snore that sent her into a series of rough coughs.

Sarah let go of his wrist and pushed past him to go to the dowager's side, plying her with tea and rubbing her lightly on the back.

Randall waited until she'd looked up from her ministrations, then he slowly reached above his head and plucked another berry from the mistletoe plant.

She was grinning as he left.

And so was he.

Sunday morning, Randall waited outside the village church, pacing a bit to keep himself warm. Despite the greatcoat he was wearing, the chill was threatening to seep into his very bones. He could only wonder if his grandmother coming out in such weather was actually a good idea, but his father had sent the carriage to Cloverdale, and Randall refused to go inside the church until it arrived.

He hunched his shoulders and watched the road.

Finally, the carriage appeared around the corner. It pulled up to the church and Randall didn't wait for the footman to open the door. He opened it himself to find his grandmother looking pale and weak, wrapped in enough blankets to turn her into one of those mummies he'd seen at the Egyptian museum.

Sarah busied herself unwrapping the dowager enough so that she could descend from the carriage. Randall wasted no time hustling his grandmother into the building, half carrying her over the threshold. He'd have liked to stay and help Sarah out of the carriage, but getting his grandmother out of the cold had to come first.

Instead of making the trek up to her box seat at the front of the church, though, Grandmother sank into the free pew at the back of the room. "This is far enough," she whispered.

So Randall sat with her, ignoring the looks of embarrassed despair from his mother and concern from his father. When Sarah came in, she said nothing, simply slid into the pew and waited for the service to begin.

It was nice, worshiping with Sarah at his side. Everything seemed nice with Sarah at his side.

He wasn't sure if he was really ready to try and buy his own farm and leave the family holdings behind—those sort of decisions took planning, after all—but maybe, just maybe, there was room to start a family at Bluestone while he made the arrangements to move forward.

Getting his grandmother back into the carriage for the ride home was even more difficult than getting her into the church had been. Randall had to actually lift her into the vehicle, and he really didn't like how light she'd felt. While Sarah bundled blanket after blanket around her employer, Randall climbed into the carriage and sat in the backward-facing seat.

Her eyes flew to his, wide in her angled face. "What are you doing?"

"You won't be able to get her into the house by yourself," he said.

She nodded and then turned back to his grandmother, who was coughing again. This time it was more like puffs of air, as if she didn't have the strength to actually cough.

At Cloverdale, he didn't give Grandmother a chance to protest. He climbed out of the carriage and then took her in his arms, blankets and all. While Sarah scurried in front of him to open the door, he gave the coachman instructions to fetch the doctor.

He didn't care if it was Sunday. His grandmother, the woman he'd run to whenever he needed someone, was now the person in need, and he wasn't about to let her down.

Sarah stood outside the dowager's chambers while the doctor examined her. She knew what he was going to say. The same thing he'd said the last five times he'd been to the house.

The dowager countess was old.

Oh, those hadn't been his exact words, but they were the basic idea. He didn't know what was wrong with her or even if there was anything wrong with her. Yes, she was weak and didn't eat much anymore, but that tended to be the way of older people. And everyone did get old eventually.

She had a feeling Randall wasn't going to accept that simple explanation, though.

Right now he was pacing circles in the front hall, making sure the doctor didn't find a way to slip out without talking to him.

Sarah wanted to go help him, hold him. He hadn't been in Lancashire the past month and a half to see the steady decline of Lady Densbury. Even if he had been, Sarah wasn't sure anyone not living in the house would have noticed.

When the doctor emerged, he simply nodded at Sarah before heading towards the door.

Inside the bedchamber, the dowager was sleeping again. The breathing seemed easy, but fast and shallow. Sarah pulled a chair up to the bed and sat, sliding a hand across the cover until she could wrap the thin, gnarled fingers in her own. Then she prayed.

She didn't know how much time had passed, but the next thing she knew, she was awoken by a large, warm hand on her shoulder. She lifted her head from the cover and turned to see Randall standing over her. He wasn't looking at her, though. He was watching his grandmother.

"This is her last Christmas, isn't it?"

"I . . . yes. Probably. I don't think she has the strength to get better even if she could." Sarah blinked and shook her head, not even sure she'd said a sentence.

Randall nodded. "I wanted you to know I'm going back to Helmsfield now. But I'll be back tomorrow."

Sarah nodded and watched him leave the room. Then she took off her dress and climbed into bed next to her employer. If Lady Densbury needed anything in the night, Sarah was going to make sure she got it.

Randall was firmly convinced that his brothers were idiots. Well, perhaps not George. The oldest brother's head was actually screwed on right when it came to most of the business of inheriting an earldom, but he didn't know the first thing about the actual needs of the estates he was going to inherit.

Cecil, on the other hand, was a fool. He sat and discussed politics and estate management with George and the earl as if he would one day have any say in either. It was going to be a rather rude awakening one day when he opened his eyes and realized he actually wasn't any better off in this life than Randall.

Of course, Randall wasn't doing himself any favors. Right now he was doing the work of an estate manager for what essentially amounted to board and a spending allowance. All the money from the crops and rents went to his father. Was that any different than what Cecil was doing? Trying to find a way to be connected to the family business, even though that connection would eventually have to end?

Perhaps all of the brothers were fools.

Perhaps his whole family was. Here they were, discussing business on the day before Christmas. Given the state he'd left Grandmother in the day before and the frivolity of the holiday, one would think they'd have somewhere better to be than in the earl's study discussing crops while snow blew around outside the window.

"What about Bluestone?"

Randall turned from the window at George's words. Finally, a conversation he could actually participate in with a measure of confidence and authority.

"It's producing well," the earl said, running his finger down a line of numbers in the ledger book open on the desk.

Randall's chest expanded a bit. He couldn't help it. This was something he was good at that his father could acknowledge. "We're rotating the fields a bit differently than we used to and reaping at least ten percent more crops."

"Well, that's good, isn't it?" George leaned over Father's shoulder to look at the ledger. "What do we grow there?"

The quill slipped from the earl's fingers as the man turned to stare at his oldest. Randall smirked but stayed quiet. If he answered, George would be in a maddened state for the rest of the day. He didn't like it when he didn't know something and Randall did.

"How is it you don't know what we grow at Bluestone?"

Randall could have answered that one. The earl had kept his two eldest sons close, making sure they knew everything there was to know about being an earl. Unfortunately, the lessons had never covered much of the actual earldom they oversaw.

Of course, given the way his father was talking, Randall wasn't sure the earl even knew what they grew at Bluestone.

With a shrug, George reached over and flipped back a page in the ledger. "I don't think I've ever been there. I don't know much about farming."

"Don't know much . . ." The earl shook his head as his words trailed off, then he frowned in thought.

"The best field for growing rhubarb is going to need to rest next year, so you'll need to plan for that," Randall said when the silence had stretched on long enough that he thought George wouldn't be threatened by whatever Randall had to say.

With a few blinks, the earl came out of his thoughts and focused his gaze on Randall. He nodded slowly. "Good, good. So things will be a bit slower over the next year. A little easier to manage."

Randall nodded and shrugged at the same time. It was part of the nature of farming. He didn't really see it as making things easier or harder. It was just the way it was.

But then his father smiled.

The kind of smile that meant he'd had an idea.

The smile that terrified Randall because it always meant his brothers were going to get another opportunity that he wasn't.

"That's perfect!" The earl pounded one hand on the table and stood up to pace.

Randall's stomach tensed. Smiling and pacing usually meant not only was George about to get something good, but it was probably going to come at Randall's expense. He liked to think the extra agitation the idea caused in the earl was because he hated inconveniencing or hurting his youngest son, but Randall had never had the courage to ask.

When the earl didn't continue, though, Randall ground out, "What's perfect?"

"George and Harriet will go to Bluestone!" Father clapped his hands. "I don't know why I didn't think of it before. They'll get a home of their own to start a family, and we'll have a more official presence on the estate—always good for the tenants to see that. George will get some more experience, and Mother can stay happily right where she is."

The earl was right. It was perfect. Except for one minor detail.

Bluestone was Randall's home.

It had been for nearly four years. And while he knew it would never actually be his, part of him had hoped, just a little bit, that it might be. After all, it was one of the few properties in the earldom that wasn't entailed, that the earl was free to will to someone other than George.

And now it was being ripped from him while his father still lived.

Randall cleared his throat. "I live at Bluestone."

The earl nodded. "Yes, yes, and that all made sense when George and Cecil were looking for wives, but you're unattached and young. There's no need to leave you underfoot on some secluded estate while George and Harriet start a family." He rubbed his hands together and bounced on his toes. "No, no, you'll come back here. You've still got rooms here, after all. Or you could go to London."

"But I wouldn't have anything to do here and even less to do in London," Randall bit out, trying not to be frustrated, trying to remember all the verses he'd studied about God's timing and guidance and how He worked everything to the good of those who loved Him.

Well, Randall loved God, but he wasn't feeling a whole lot of love in return at the moment, and it was taking everything in him to remember to cling to the truth of the matter and not how he felt. The despair and anger welling within him was a powerful beast, though, especially since he knew this moment was his own fault, knew he never should have invested in something that would never be his. He should have started a life of his own the day after he finished his studies at Manchester Academy.

"What are you talking about?" the earl asked. "It's not as if the sun doesn't rise and set the same here as it does at Bluestone. Your day doesn't have to change at all. I'll even tell Richard you can muck about in the fields if you wish to."

Muck about in the fields? Is that what his father thought he'd been doing at Bluestone? That he'd done little more than rest his head there?

As the earl pushed on with his plans, Randall knew the answer was yes. The earl truly didn't know what Randall did every day because he didn't think it mattered to the earldom. Randall could fight for his place at Bluestone, but for what? A chance to pretend he was important?

Randall knew his father and mother didn't wish he was never born, but it was becoming increasingly clear that the only way they knew how to handle the fact that Randall would be on his own when they died was to not consider his life beyond the occasional family gathering.

Which meant there was no reason for Randall to continue this farce of a father-son gathering. Cecil could pretend all he wanted to.

Randall was finished.

7

Randall considered grabbing his saddlebags and leaving then and there, but he couldn't. For one thing, it was snowing. Only an idiot started a long journey into the snow when he had any alternative. As Randall had only minutes ago decided he no longer wished to be an idiot, he left his saddlebags where they were.

Still, he couldn't stay in this house, couldn't pretend everything was well.

He didn't even want to wait for someone to bring his horse around to him.

All he had to do was cut through the kitchens and he'd be a short, brisk walk away from the stables where he could saddle his own horse like he did at Bluestone.

On his way through the kitchens, which were fortunately fairly empty at the moment so he didn't have too many servants to shock with his presence, he saw a cake. Golden and round and waiting to make its grand debut at the family dinner table. He wasn't sure if it was intended for tonight's meal or for tomorrow's Christmas dinner, but it wasn't going to make it to either.

He was taking it with him to Cloverdale. While the earl had been moving his sons around like chess pieces, Sarah had been caring for the earl's ailing mother. She deserved cake more than anyone else.

Within moments, he'd acquired a basket from a slack-jawed

kitchen maid, wrapped the cake, and padded it with cloths to keep it from sliding too much, and was making his way toward the stable. Riding through the snow with his basket was tricky, but he'd rather take a horse through the snow than walk in it any day.

White puffs of fresh powder flew from beneath Nero's hooves as the horse pranced down the lane.

The closer Randall got to Cloverdale, the more conflicted he felt. There was worry, of course, a bit of dread over what condition he'd find his grandmother in, but there was also excitement. Would Sarah be excited about the cake? Would she play for him again? Maybe allow him to pull her beneath the mistletoe once more?

Whatever lay ahead of him, it had to be better than what was behind because it would be real. He'd be able to feel and talk without putting on an act, without pretending he had no problems.

The house was still and dark as he rode out of the woods. He made himself take care of Nero, making sure the horse was well settled since he hadn't any idea how long he'd stay here.

He heard music as he approached the front door. Light, lively music that lifted the weight from his shoulders even before his hand touched the latch. Until that moment he hadn't realized how afraid he was that he'd arrive today and find his grandmother had passed on.

With that worry gone, now the only thing his mind could focus on was how wide Sarah's smile would be when she looked inside the basket he carried.

Yesterday, Sarah was convinced that the dowager was on her way to meet Jesus. She'd prayed all night for the strength to say good-bye—for even the chance to say good-bye. The dowager hadn't rested well, had been even more fitful with Sarah in the bed, so she'd pulled a chair over and spent the night curled up in it.

But when the sun had pierced through the window, the old woman had woken with a smile. She'd eaten a few bites of ham and drank an entire cup of tea. There was no question that she was incredibly weak. Sarah had all but carried her into the drawing room to settle her into her favorite chair. But the dowager's spirits had been high.

She'd acted all day as if it were Christmas morning and no one had the heart to contradict her. Sarah had convinced her that yesterday's visit to the church had actually been today's. Then she'd distracted her by playing as many Christmas carols as she could think of.

"I got you something," the dowager said as the final notes of "Bring a Torch, Jeanette Isabella" faded away. "I tucked it away at the bottom of your music pile."

Sarah hopped up from her chair and crossed to the shelf where she kept her stacks of music. At the bottom of one of the stacks she found music for a brand-new song. "'God Rest You Merry, Gentlemen'?" She looked over at her smiling employer. "I've never heard of this one."

"It'll be a challenge then. About time that instrument gave you one."

An excited grin stretched across Sarah's face as she settled at the piano to decipher the new tune. New music was almost as good as the dowager's joyous mood.

She'd made her way through the tune once and was playing around with embellishments when Randall walked in, snow dusting the waves of his brown hair and a basket in his hand.

"Happy Christmas," the dowager called.

Randall sent Sarah a questioning look, and she simply shrugged. Did it really matter if Christmas came a day early?

"How are you, Grandmother?"

The sigh she gave was happy. "I don't think I'll be making it to Helmsfield for dinner today."

He held up his basket. "Then I guess it's that much better that I snuck something special out of the house for you. Although I'm not sure I should give it to you now. Sarah might eat it all before you get a chance."

Sarah's gaze flew up from the keys. He couldn't possibly mean . . . She sniffed the air, but the cut evergreens overpowered any hint of lemon that might have existed. Did he really have what she thought he did?

"I would never steal cake from a little old lady," she teased.

He smiled at her over his shoulder. "And what about from a twenty-seven-year-old man?"

"I make no promises."

"Well, I stole the whole thing, so I'm sure there's plenty to go around."

She smiled back at him as she played through the new tune once more with the chords and additions she liked the best.

And that was how the day went. Sarah left Randall—and the cake—in the drawing room with the dowager while she went to see about creating something resembling a Christmas feast. The servants had, of course, assumed Sarah and Lady Densbury would eat with the rest of the family. But given that Lady Densbury wasn't likely to eat much of whatever they prepared, it was more important that things appeared grand and festive than anything else.

When she returned to the drawing room, Randall was covered in a fresh layer of snow, and he wore a grim look on his face while the dowager appeared even more happy and peaceful than she had earlier.

While the servants bustled into the room, bringing furniture and decorations from elsewhere in the house and laying out food so that it looked like a grand feast, Sarah pulled Randall to the side of the room. "What happened while I was gone?"

He looked down at the toes of his shoes, and Sarah finally understood why that habit of hers had always irritated the dowager. "Randall?"

"Grandmother had a task for me, that's all." He looked up and his eyes were as bleak as the sky when it snowed. "One final request."

Randall watched Sarah contemplate his words, saw the sadness that drooped her shoulders. As one they looked over to the dowager, smiling brightly as Christmas exploded around her.

"She's doing better today," Sarah whispered.

Randall nodded. "But for how long? We have to accept that she can't go on like this forever."

It was more than just his grandmother's imminent death that he had to accept. *He* couldn't go on like this forever. Grandmother had been right all along. It was time for him to find something that was his. It was time to take what little money he had and leave Bluestone.

Convenient, since he was being evicted from the property anyway. Maybe this way he could feel like he was leaving of his own volition.

"No, she can't go on like this." Sarah turned a stern look his way. "But dying is not dead. So put a smile on your face and come learn this new Christmas carol. She went through the trouble of having it delivered, and I mean to play it until she's humming it in her sleep."

A smile tugged up his lips before he even realized it was coming. Randall followed her over to the piano without protest, but part of him mourned this moment as well. Because if he was leaving Bluestone, he really had nothing to offer her. And if she would soon be leaving Cloverdale, he'd have no way to keep her in his life while he changed his situation.

They'd eaten more than half the cake. Sarah didn't even want to think of how many slices she'd eaten, but every time she'd stop playing music or conclude some game with the servants for Lady Densbury's amusement, Randall had been there with a plate decorated festively with a sliver of cake and a sprig of evergreen.

Sarah's fingers were actually a bit sore from the amount of piano playing she'd done that day, and her side definitely hurt from the amount of laughter.

All in all, it had been a surprisingly good day.

"Come here, my boy," Lady Densbury called as the servants took the last of the food and dishes from the room. "I wish to see the snow."

Randall carefully eased his grandmother from the chair, and Sarah came over to help, though there wasn't much she needed to do. The dowager had grown so thin over the past few months that a child could have supported her out of the chair.

The black shawl slipped off of the dowager's shoulder, and Sarah rushed to replace it. Where was the brooch that always held the shawl together?

Sarah frowned as Randall guided Lady Densbury to the window. Now that she thought about it, she hadn't seen the brooch in a couple of days. She pushed the blankets around in the chair, felt between the upholstered edges, even crawled on the floor to search beneath the nearby furniture. It was nowhere to be found.

"Come look at the snow, Sarah," the dowager called.

Sarah gave up her search and went to Lady Densbury's side. Randall smiled at her over the old woman's grey curls.

"It's beautiful," Sarah said.

Lady Densbury nodded. "I've always loved the snow. It covers up all the ugly. Makes the whole world clean. I like that. I like to think that's how God sees me, covered in a blanket of snow just like it is out there. Not a blemish in sight."

Tears pricked Sarah's eyes. She'd been raised by people who loved the Lord, who taught her to love the Bible and its teachings. It was something she never really expected to be surrounded by again after she'd left home to make her own way in the world. Living for nearly a year with Lady Densbury's steady faith had been a blessing.

"I like that," Sarah whispered. "I don't think I'll ever look at snow the same way again."

They stood there, watching the setting sun glint off the pristine white snow, until the dowager started to tremble. "I think I'm ready to go back to my chair now," she whispered.

Randall didn't even ask. He simply scooped her up in his arms and carried her to the chair, carefully wrapping the shawl around her shoulders as she settled back into the cushions.

"I'm going home now," Randall said. "But I'll be back tomorrow."

She nodded and placed one shaky hand on his cheek. "You remember your promise."

He closed his eyes and swallowed hard. "I will."

Sarah walked Randall to the door. "Happy Christmas," she said with a light laugh.

He shook his head. "I always wanted more Christmas when I was a boy. More candy, more games, more singing. Now that I finally got two of them, it's not everything I'd hoped for."

"No, I would imagine not." Sarah smiled sadly. "But it was a good day."

"It was." Randall paused, staring down at his shoes once more before looking back into her eyes. "Sarah, I . . ." He sighed. "I'll see you tomorrow."

Then he was gone. Sarah traced the grooves of the closed door, warring with hope but losing. Between the holiday and the way her heart beat faster when he appeared in the drawing room door, it was a futile effort to resist hoping that what had been a distant attraction and infatuation to fill a void in her life had bloomed into something real and mutual.

Perhaps he would stay awhile. Through the new year. Maybe longer. It was winter, wasn't it? Was there really that much to do on a farm in the winter?

The hopefulness lightened her step as she returned to the drawing room and the dowager's side. A peaceful smile still curved Lady Densbury's lips, but her eyelids had fallen closed, the pale blue veins showing starkly against the paper-white skin.

"Shall I help you to bed, my lady?"

Her eyes drifted open, and she sighed. "I'd rather stay here, if you don't mind. Perhaps you could play? There should be music when a woman finally gets to see Jesus."

"I . . . I . . ." Sarah pressed her lips together as her chin trembled and water filled her eyes until she could no longer focus on the dowager. A deep breath in through her nose steadied her enough to speak in a shaky, choked voice. "Of course, I'll play."

Then she moved to the piano and played. The tears spilled over and ran down her cheeks in a steady river that soon dampened the neckline of her dress. Still she played. She played every song she knew and some she made up as she went. She played until the skin of her fingers dried out and started to crack. She played until the labored breathing that had consistently rattled her ears for months gave way to a silence that felt heavier than any shroud.

Then she curled up on the floor beneath the piano and wept.

8

Randall stood in the middle of Helmsfield's front hall on Christmas morning, mouth agape at the chaos surrounding him. Servants were running everywhere, carrying bundles of evergreen boughs and holly out to a wagon that had been pulled up in front of the house. More servants were loading food into the wagon and still another was placing hot bricks in the carriage waiting in front of the wagons.

In the midst of the vehicles stood his father, directing everyone where to go.

Randall stepped out of the way of a scurrying footman and crossed the drive to his father's side. "What are we doing?"

"Taking Christmas to Cloverdale, of course. Mother will hardly be in any condition to make the journey after her state of health on Sunday. I've even asked the vicar to come join us after the service at church."

Randall thought about the simple celebration at Cloverdale the day before and then looked around at the elaborate trimmings his father had collected. The casual genuine atmosphere of the impromptu early Christmas was certainly the type of gathering his grandmother would enjoy more, but for his father to pack up the entire family, the servants, and a wagon full of food, well, it was more thoughtfulness than Randall had realized the man possessed.

His mother came down the steps and made straight for the coach and the hot bricks. "Do grab your greatcoat, Randall. The men have to ride up top."

With a shake of his head and a smile nudging at one side of his mouth, Randall returned to the house to collect his greatcoat and hat from one of the servants. As he bounded up on top of the coach next to the driver, his partial smile turned into a grin. For once his family would encounter Sarah somewhere she was comfortable being herself. He couldn't wait for them to see the woman he'd come to know.

Cloverdale was still and dark, just as it had been the past few days when he'd arrived. All the life in the house happened between the drawing room and the kitchens, so it wasn't too surprising that it looked nearly abandoned at first glance.

He jumped from the top as the coach was still rocking back on its springs. The front door opened before he could even make it to the steps.

One look at the housekeeper's face and Randall stumbled to a stop. "No," he whispered.

Her eyes widened as she took in the wagons and the coach and the finely dressed family piling out into the snow. She looked terrified, her eyes wide over deep purple shadows.

"I'm so sorry, my lord," she said, "I'm so sorry."

Randall rushed forward, getting to the front steps at the same time as his father. "When?" he choked out.

"When?" the earl repeated. "When what?"

The housekeeper sniffled. "A little after two in the morning, I suppose. We all kept vigil outside the drawing room while Miss Gooding played. It was as peaceful a moment as I've ever seen, my lord, if that be any consolation."

The housekeeper gestured behind her to a servant who was partially bundled up in an unbuttoned coat, bonnet and scarf in hand. "We were just about to send word over to Helmsfield, my lord."

The earl's hat fell from his fingers. "She's dead?"

"Where is Sarah?" Randall found the strength to move his feet as he considered how Sarah must be feeling at that moment. He pushed his way into the front hall. "Where is she?"

"In the drawing room, sir. None of us had the heart to wake her."

Randall strode into the front hall but stopped as he came even with the open door to his grandmother's rooms. He could see the bed from this angle, see where the servants had done what they could to begin the necessary preparations. If he didn't know better, he'd think she was sleeping.

But she wasn't. And he didn't think he could face the final proof of that by himself. His family was behind him, shock rippling through the group, but none of them had known Grandmother like he had. Like Sarah had.

He needed to find Sarah.

It took him two full looks around the room before he found her, curled in a ball, asleep in his grandmother's chair.

In four strides he crossed the room and knelt in front of the chair, gathering her into his arms.

She blinked her eyes slowly and then looked up at him, tears already shimmering on her lashes. "I played," she whispered. "I played her home."

He ran one hand down her arm to pull her fingers free of her lap. Her hands were curled, the skin dry and rough in places. She flexed them slowly and winced.

A noise of agony echoed from the hall into the drawing room. Sarah rose, and Randall tucked her close to his side as he crossed the hall to face the truth.

His father was already there by the bed, shock and dismay on his face. The rest of the family ranged behind him, all somber. George placed a hand on the earl's shoulder and then stepped away from the bedside. He laid his coat on a chair and began directing servants. He passed out instructions so quickly that Randall couldn't even catch them all, but soon there were people moving forward with all the funeral preparations. Some were sent to gather snow to pack around the body while it was prepared for burial, others were to lay out the food in the dining room so that everyone would be able to retain their energy for the day ahead. A footman was even sent to the church where everyone in the area would be gathered for Christmas services. It was a blur of activity that Randall couldn't begin to comprehend.

George might not know that Bluestone grew rhubarb, but he obviously had the makings of a competent earl.

Not knowing what else to do, Randall moved to the bed, looking down on his grandmother, who looked as peaceful as she had looking out across the snow. Maybe more so as she wasn't fighting for breath anymore. And he stood there, with his father on one side and Sarah on the other, and together they cried.

Sarah lay in bed, blinking at the ceiling. What was she going to do with herself now?

Yesterday had been busy, with everyone preparing for a funeral instead of a Christmas celebration. She'd helped the countess and the other ladies prepare the body. Then there'd been plenty to do in the kitchens to feed all of the extra people roaming around the house.

But today? There wasn't much for her to do today.

The funeral would be in two days. It was possible the family would keep Sarah in their employ for a while longer to go through the dowager's things, but there really wasn't anything for her here anymore.

Not unless she considered Randall, and after they'd cried together, he'd been just as caught up in the hectic day as she had, and they hadn't had a moment together since.

He'd even left with his family without telling her good-bye.

With a sigh, she pushed herself out of bed and got dressed. A breakfast tray had been delivered, recently based on the temperature of the tea. The entire routine was normal. So normal she could almost convince herself the past two days hadn't happened.

She went down the stairs and turned toward the dowager's

chambers out of habit, but the room was silent and dark, the drapes still pulled against the morning sun.

Making as much noise as possible, Sarah crossed the room and wrenched the drape back. Seeing the bed perfectly made and nothing out of place made the entire thing real.

Lady Densbury was really gone.

She'd said her good-byes as she'd lived her life, in her own personal way. Oddly, the one regret Sarah had was that the old woman hadn't gotten to give out the Christmas boxes she'd put together so very carefully for all her staff.

Wanting to make sure that one last thing happened for the dowager, Sarah moved to the dressing room to collect the basket of boxes. But it was gone. For months the basket had sat in the corner of the dressing room, slowly filling with boxes. Now all that sat in the corner was a piece of paper.

Sarah bent down to retrieve it.

Don't worry.

She flipped the paper over, looking for a signature or an indication of who had written the note, but there was nothing. The handwriting looked masculine, but there'd been an awful lot of men in the house yesterday. Could one of them have taken the basket? Why?

Noise from the front hall drew her from the room, note still in hand.

Half the staff stood in the hall along with Randall, who was holding the large basket of Christmas boxes. He cleared his throat and smiled. "I'm here to fulfill Grandmother's final request."

Randall shifted the basket to his hip and tried to guess what Sarah was thinking. She looked rested, which was good. He was glad she'd been able to sleep.

He hadn't.

He'd spent the whole night thinking about his grandmother, the way the day had rolled out, the look on his father's face. And he'd come to one conclusion.

He didn't want to miss out because he'd planned too much and waited too long.

No, the timing wasn't perfect and the opportunities weren't the best, but if Sarah was willing, when they'd finished doing everything that needed to be done here, he wanted to start over with her.

But first he had to hand out Christmas boxes.

The small wooden boxes had been carved with names of each staff member, and Randall handed them out as if it were a solemn duty. In a way, it was. It was the last thing his grandmother had asked of him. Oh, she'd given him some sort of excuse about wanting Randall to deliver the boxes because she wanted Sarah to be part of the festivities instead of handling them, but part of Randall had known that she didn't expect to be here this morning to do it herself.

There were exclamations from the maids as they found their embroidered handkerchiefs folded around a year's worth of wages.

His grandmother certainly knew how to leave her mark.

One by one, the staff disappeared, boxes in hand. Off to celebrate with their own families or simply take the day to try to relax from the tension of the day before.

Finally, it was only him and Sarah left in the hall. He handed her the box with her name carved on the top.

She opened it with a smile that quickly turned into tears as one hand lifted to cover her mouth. The hand holding the box trembled so much that he was afraid she would drop it, so he placed his hands around her own to stabilize it.

A glint of silver from the depths of the box drew his attention. Nestled inside the velvet lining was his grandmother's silver-and-amethyst luckenbooth brooch. Her most prized possession. Beneath it was a note Randall was desperately curious to read, but he didn't know if it was something Sarah would share.

He lifted the brooch out, though, and slid the silver straight pin into the fabric of her dress, fixing the brooch on Sarah's shoulder. "It looks good on you."

"Why would she do this?" Sarah whispered.

Randall nodded to the box. "It's probably in the note."

Sarah set the box on a table and unfolded the paper to reveal a note written in shaky scrawl and dotted with blots of ink.

"'My dear Sarah,'" she whispered, reading the note aloud. "'My husband gave me this brooch as a sign that our love was stronger than whatever the world could throw at us. Every time I saw it I knew it was no concern whether anyone else thought I wasn't good enough for him. He thought I was and that was all that mattered.'"

One of Sarah's hands lifted to graze across the purple stone in a gesture that was achingly similar to the way his grandmother would touch the jewelry. She sniffled and then went back to the note.

"'I'm giving it to you so you remember the same thing. Ran—'" She stopped reading with a gasp and then slapped the note shut.

"What?" Randall took her hand in his, the note crinkling between them as he rubbed a thumb along her wrist and felt her pulse pounding. "What does it say?"

"I . . . um . . ."

Randall grinned, having a suspicion his astute grandmother had seen things much sooner than he had. "Was it about me?"

Two slashes of pink spread across Sarah's cheekbones.

Randall's grin widened. "Did she say that I love you and want to build a life with you no matter what my family thinks of your mysterious past?"

Sarah bit her lip and blinked away a few more tears. "No." She hiccuped. "She said Randall's an idiot if he doesn't realize how much you love him and that he should tell his family to . . . to . . . well, let's just say she doesn't think you should be very nice about putting them in their place."

One curl had drifted down from Sarah's pinned-up hair, and Randall reached a hand out to rub the golden strands between his fingers. "I happen to agree with her."

The smile Sarah gave him was a bit watery as the tears spilled down her cheeks, but it was all the more beautiful because of it. Randall leaned down and pressed his own smile to hers in a kiss that was as awkward as it was joyous.

"From this moment on," he said, "we live life the way my grand-mother did. We love Jesus. We love each other. And we let everyone else come along or get out of the way."

"I'd like that." Sarah pushed up on her toes and brushed a light kiss across his cheek. "Happy Christmas."

Randall smiled. "Christmas was yesterday."

Sarah shrugged. "I don't see why we have to limit the celebra-tion."

As he laughed, Sarah peered into the basket. "Wait. There's one more box."

Randall looked down to see that there was indeed one more box hidden among the folds of fabric that had been used to line the basket.

He slid it out, surprised to find his own name on the top.

There was a letter in his box as well, though it sat on top of the other contents. He set the box down and opened the letter, reading quickly over the handwriting that was considerably neater than Sarah's had been. Whatever his grandmother had planned for him, she'd been at it a while.

"What does it say?" Sarah asked.

Randall groped for the wall and leaned against it before looking up at the love of his life. "She bought me a farm." He swallowed. "In Virginia."

Sarah's eyebrows drew together. "That's in America."

He nodded, already feeling his heart pound at the excitement and adventure that awaited him. This was starting over, a new beginning, the kind that rarely came a person's way.

And he couldn't wait to seize it.

"Charles Thomas, the son of a friend of Grandmother's, owns the farm next to it and has been seeing to the land, but he's ready for me to take possession of it as soon as I can get there."

Randall held his breath, waiting for Sarah's reaction. It was very possible that going to America meant never seeing England again, at least not for a very long time. He wanted it, though. He wanted it badly, but only if Sarah would come with him.

After a few moments in which Randall had very serious worries for the condition of his heart, she said, "I've never been on a boat before." She swallowed and smiled. "It's quite something that my first time will be across the ocean."

He laughed and grabbed her up in his arms, twirling her about the hall before setting her back on her feet.

Breathless, she pushed her mussed hair out of her eyes. "Was there anything else in the box?"

He lifted the lid back up and glanced inside. Shock had him dropping the lid shut just as quickly. Inside the box was money. More than enough to let them start their life in comfort and begin their new farm right. How long had his grandmother been saving it? Stashing it away in this box so he would have no excuse but to live his own life?

His arms wrapped around Sarah once more, and he buried his face in her hair, letting all the emotions of the past week roll through him. He'd have never asked for his grandmother to die, never thought he'd be ready to leave his family and venture out on his own, never imagined that the woman who would make him feel strong enough to take on the world would be found hiding behind a piano.

And yet here he was. With everything he had ever dared to want and more. No, he'd never imagined getting here this way, but he knew one thing for sure.

The family he built with the new life and opportunity he'd been given would know what it meant to love fully and love truly. It was his grandmother's legacy.

And like the brooch, like the farm, like his wife-to-be's love of lemon-flavored cakes, he intended to pass it on.

Epilogue

I t's a girl!" the midwife declared joyously as hearty cries filled the room.

Sarah huffed in and out through an exhausted smile. A girl. Finally. Five sons were all well and good when one was running a farm, but it was awfully nice to have a little girl to raise.

In short order, the baby was cleaned up and nestled at her mother's side. Randall stood next to her, running a finger along the soft down on the baby girl's head. "She's beautiful," he whispered in awe. "Just like her mother."

It was a blissful, peaceful moment, and Sarah let her head sink into the pillow as her eyes slid shut, relishing the rare quiet.

Her eyes snapped open and sought Randall's gaze. It was never quiet in their home. "Where are the boys?"

Randall grinned. "Teaching their Uncle Cecil how to properly dig a field drainage ditch. Our youngest has very interesting theories on the proper way to hold a shovel."

Shortly after Sarah and Randall had made the move to America, Cecil had begun corresponding with his younger brother over farming plans and the details of handling a small parcel of land.

The dowager had left him a small estate in Cambridgeshire, one that everyone had assumed was part of the earldom, but was in fact Lady Densbury's, according to all the paperwork the solicitors had scurried to go through. Her Cambridge professor father hadn't been quite as poor as some people had assumed.

It was a blessing from God that Cecil had brought his family to visit now as Sarah had been nearly bedridden for the past month. But now her little girl was here, and it was all worth it.

The baby groped across Sarah's chest, tiny fist bumping against the amethyst brooch at her shoulder. Sarah didn't wear it often. It wasn't the sort of thing that was very practical for a farmer's wife. But when she was feeling especially nervous, it was a wonderful reminder of the love and support that surrounded her.

"What should we name her?" Randall asked.

Sarah had staunchly refused to discuss girl names because she'd been afraid to get her hopes up that this time she would finally get a little girl. Besides, she'd already known the perfect name. "Rosemary."

Randall's eyebrows winged upward. "Rosemary? You know we don't grow rosemary here, don't you?"

The farm had been incredibly successful. They'd had a tough year or two, but it had been the perfect place for two people looking to start a brand-new life. They'd married soon after Lady Densbury's death and packed up to come to America immediately, hoping to set up house before the spring planting. But they needn't have worried. Lady Densbury had the house ready for them, complete with a piano in the front parlor.

The old woman had been meticulous and thoughtful, making sure that her family was taken care of, knew they were loved. And she'd done it all because it was right. She'd gained nothing from it. Nothing tangible and earthly, anyway.

And that was a wonderful legacy to pass on.

"Rosemary was your grandmother's name," Sarah said.

The look on Randall's face was rather comical. "It was?"

Sarah nodded and ran a finger along the curve of her sleeping daughter's cheek. "Hello, little Rosemary. I can't wait to tell you about your great-grandmother. I hope you'll be as loving and determined as she was. And one day I'll pin this brooch on you so that no matter where you go, you will know that love is more important than anything else. Love God. Love family. Love life."

Then she kissed her baby's head and shifted so Randall could lay on the bed and hold them both. Then together they slept, each dreaming of a future wrapped safely in the arms of love.

Gift
of the Heart

KAREN WITEMEYER

To my Posse.

Without you, there would be no Theodore,
and this story really needed a Teddy.
You're the best!

Who can find a virtuous woman? for her price is far above rubies. The heart of her husband doth safely trust in her, so that he shall have no need of spoil. She will do him good and not evil all the days of her life.

Proverbs 31:10–12

1

R uth Fulbright held her sleeping seven-year-old daughter snugly on her lap in the middle of the stagecoach seat while the passengers who considered themselves her betters exited the conveyance. The pomaded dandy sitting to her left jostled her with his elbow when he tried to stand. She leaned right to get out of his way, and a plume from the hat of an exiting matron nearly took out her eye.

Gracious. Who knew stage travel could be so hazardous? She'd thought bandits would be the worst peril she might face on the twenty-mile trek from the train station in Weatherford. She'd never imagined pitying glances, snobby sniffs, and pointed plumage could inflict such damage. Not that they'd done more than scrape a few sore places on her pride. A woman raised in the South after the devastation of war learned how to hold her head high in any social arena.

Her dress might be threadbare, her shoe leather paper-thin, and her wedding ring missing from her finger, but she was clean, respectable, and had no reason to feel shame.

As the dandy to her left shuffled past, his hunched form bumped Ruth's daughter.

"Pardon," he mumbled, though his glare seemed to blame her daughter for being in the way. A true gentleman would have waited for Ruth and Naomi to exit first, thereby clearing his path, but he obviously viewed her as an obstacle and not a lady.

"Mama?" Naomi roused, her head lifting from Ruth's chest and her lashes fluttering upward to reveal the soft brown eyes that were so much like her daddy's.

A pang hit Ruth's stomach, though it didn't jab as deeply as it once had. Stephen had been gone two years now. Two years, three months, and nine days. She really ought to stop counting. Stop marking time by her losses instead of her gains. But it had been so long since she'd had a gain. . . .

Enough of that. Ruth straightened in her seat and smiled at her daughter. "Mornin', sleepyhead." She brushed Naomi's bangs back and kissed her forehead. "We're here."

Naomi's eyes widened, and her lips curved upward. "At our new home?"

Ruth nodded. Her daughter immediately pulled away from her and jumped down to the coach floor.

Praise the Lord for the optimism of youth. Ruth didn't know how she would have endured the last few months without Naomi's ability to see sunbeams shining through every cloud. Heaven knew there'd been enough clouds to support a league of rainmakers in her life lately. It was hard to remember that, however, with her daughter pulsing with excitement directly in front of her.

"Let's go!" Able to stand at her full height inside the stage, Naomi rushed toward the exit, nearly colliding with the pomaded dandy climbing down. She halted at the last moment and spun around, urging her mother to her feet with an impatient wave. "Come on, Mama. Hope is waiting for us!"

"Hope *Springs*," Ruth corrected, even as her daughter's misspoken words filled her tired soul with cautious expectancy.

Hope had to be waiting for them here. Ruth had no place else to look.

As soon as the dandy reached the ground and stepped aside,

Naomi bounded out of the coach like a rabbit eluding a snare. Ruth grinned and shook her head. Let the girl run and play. She'd been cooped up in train cars and stuffy stagecoaches the entire day. If Ruth weren't nearly a quarter of a century old, she'd join her. Heaven knew her legs could use a good stretching. Too bad society frowned on such displays by grown women.

Yet as she grasped the handle to balance her exit from the stage—no gentleman, pomaded or otherwise, was apparently available for the duty—all urge to play was consumed by a sudden onslaught of locusts swarming through her belly.

What if Mrs. Lancaster had grown tired of waiting and hired another cook? Dorothea had assured Ruth that her cousin would hold the job for her, but Ruth had been delayed a week finding someone to give her a fair price on her ring so she could afford the train fare from Clarksville to Weatherford and then stage fare to Hope Springs. What if her employer viewed that as a breach of contract?

She rubbed the bare place on her finger where her wedding band used to be, mourned its loss for a heartbeat, then stiffened her shoulders and went in search of her luggage. She'd done what needed to be done to carve out a new life for her daughter. Regrets made a poor foundation for building a future. She preferred to rely on faith.

God had led her to Hope Springs. She was certain of it. Too many pieces had fallen in just the right places at just the right time for there to be any other explanation. And if God had led her here, He wouldn't abandon her.

Be content with such things as ye have, Ruth quoted to herself as she patiently waited for the driver to hand down the last of the trunks and hatboxes of her wealthy travel companions, *for he hath said, I will never leave thee, nor forsake thee.*

Hope was springing, and she aimed to catch it.

A tan object hurtled down toward her head. Ruth gasped and threw her arms out just in time to snatch it from the air. Good grief. She'd been so busy preparing to catch hope that she'd nearly been flattened by her valise.

"Sorry, ma'am." The shame-faced driver drew his hat from his head and dropped to his knees atop the coach roof. He grabbed the railing and leaned over the side. "I thought you were Old Tom. Are ya all right?"

It wasn't exactly flattering for a lady to be mistaken for a grizzled coachman, but to be fair, the man who'd ridden shotgun and had been catching the luggage *had* been standing in her position the moment before. The other passengers had drawn him away with their complaints over how their belongings were being treated, and Ruth had stepped into the space he'd vacated.

Ruth set her valise on the ground, then brushed the front of her dress to wipe away the worst of the travel dust that had exploded across her chest when the valise hit. That done, she aimed a smile in the driver's direction. His apology had been sincere, and the kind words buoyed her spirits. "No harm done. If you hand that last bag down a little more slowly, I'm sure I'll be able to manage it with more finesse."

She lifted her arms above her head to receive the next bag, and the driver reared back. Ruth swore she could hear the question running through his mind. What was the greater sin, arguing with a lady or subjecting her to physical labor?

Ruth wiggled her fingers in an effort to absolve him of any perceived wrongdoing. "I'm stronger than I look," she assured him. "Besides, you have a schedule to keep."

The driver glanced over at the passengers on the boardwalk who were waiting to board. "Tom!" he yelled, clearly looking for a third option. Old Tom, however, was either hard of hearing or his ears were already filled to capacity with the haranguing he was receiving. He didn't so much as flinch at the driver's call.

Muttering under his breath, the driver slapped his hat back on his head and pivoted to reach Ruth's carpetbag. He let it dangle from one arm as if weighing it, then grudgingly handed it over the side, leaning far enough down to ensure the bag touched her hands before he released his grip.

Knowing precisely how heavy the bag would be—not very, since

her store of dresses numbered only two beyond her current ensemble—Ruth handled the bag with ease. "Thank you, sir."

He tipped his hat, admiration shining in his eyes and infusing
Ruth with confidence that she could, indeed, manage whatever
challenges came her way. Picking up her valise, she marched past
the well-dressed crowd and scanned the area for her daughter.

Naomi spotted her first. "Mama, look! A kitty."

"Oh my." Ruth tried not to think about muddy paw prints on
Naomi's best dress, or fleas or rabies, as she bent forward to examine the stray cat dangling from her daughter's arms. The poor
thing looked half strangled, its white belly exposed and back legs
stretched long.

She'd never seen a stray cat react to capture with such calm.
Most hissed and scratched or fled before being scooped up. This
black-and-white tabby must belong to someone. Or at least had
in the past. Maybe he'd been left behind by a resort guest.

"Better let him go, sweetie. He doesn't belong to us."

Naomi let out a loud sigh, then kissed the animal atop its head
and gently set him down. "Bye, kitty."

The beast zoomed away, making a beeline for the three-story
resort hotel that stood directly across the street. With a scrabble of
claws, it climbed the tree that shaded the walkway. Ruth watched its
impressively speedy ascent until the oak's branches hid it from view.
Another movement slightly above the tree caught her attention.

A man stood on a balcony. Dark hair. Dark suit. *Expensive*
suit. Even from here she could see the tailored lines. The fingers
of his left hand tapped idly at the wooden railing as he surveyed
the goings-on beneath him like some kind of overlord. An overlord
who happened to be looking directly at *her*.

Ruth ducked her chin. Whoever he was, she wouldn't stand and
gawk as though she had no manners, even if that was precisely
what *he* was doing. He was probably another stuffy resort guest.
The wealthy loved to look down their noses at poor peasants.
When they deigned to notice them at all.

"Here to take the waters, miss?" A young lad of maybe sixteen or seventeen approached, a warm smile on his face. He wore a dark green uniform with *Hope Springs Resort* embroidered in gold on his jacket front. "I'd be happy to help you with your luggage."

He reached for her valise, but she shook her head. "Thank you, no. I'm not a guest of the resort." Though it soothed her prickles a great deal to have him treat her with the same courtesy he would have treated her better-dressed companions. Whoever had trained him had done an admirable job. "I'm Mrs. Lancaster's new cook. Could you point me in the direction of the Homespun Café?"

"Glad to." He beamed at her, his cheerfulness so contagious that the weight of her insecurities and doubts lifted, leaving a giddy excitement in their place.

He steered her around the other travelers, then pointed down the street to a modest structure at the end of the block. "The café's the last building on the right before you get to the courthouse square. If you don't find Myrtle Lancaster inside, check around back. She keeps chickens and a garden out there. Might be tendin' to those."

"Thank you." Wishing she had a spare coin to reward the kind young man for his thoughtfulness, Ruth settled for a bright smile. "You've been very helpful."

"My pleasure, miss." He tipped his hat, then turned to resume his duties at the resort.

"Come, Naomi," Ruth said with a lift of her chin. "Time to see where Mama's going to work."

Naomi skipped along beside her mother, brown braids bouncing. "Did you hear what he said, Mama? They have chickens! Do you think they'll let me help gather the eggs? I'm super good at it. 'Member?"

"I do remember." Naomi had loved tending to the chickens on their farm. Scattering their feed, collecting the eggs. She'd followed her mama out to the coop every morning before the bank had foreclosed on them. Naomi had only been five, but even at that young age, she'd handled the eggs with extreme care, never breaking a single one. "We'll have to see what Mrs. Lancaster prefers."

Ruth prayed her employer would be a kindhearted soul who

enjoyed children, not a termagant who expected them to be seen and not heard. Naomi was a darling child. Well-behaved. Obedient. But silent, she was not. Her inquisitive nature and exuberant spirit didn't lend themselves to a reticent demeanor.

Ruth needn't have worried, for the instant they stepped inside the welcoming atmosphere of the Homespun Café, they were overwhelmed with the whirlwind that was Myrtle Lancaster.

At the sound of the door, a middle-aged woman wearing a ruffled apron in the most extraordinary shade of fuchsia jumped up from a seat near the side window, abandoning a cup of tea and a fashion magazine. "Hello!" She bustled forward, her blue eyes twinkling. "Welcome to the Homespun Café." Her canary-yellow calico skirt swished back and forth beneath her violently pink apron, giving Ruth the impression that she had fallen inside a kaleidoscope. "I'm afraid I can only offer a limited menu of sandwiches and lemonade until my new cook arrives, but I have an assortment of quilts and other locally crafted items that can serve as wonderful mementos of your visit to Hope Springs." She waved an arm toward the west side of the room where an assortment of items adorned strategically arranged tables and racks. Quilts. Cloth-lined baskets finished with lace and bows. Milking buckets decorated with hand-painted flowers.

"I hope my stay will be longer than a visit." Ruth set down her valise and extended her right hand. "I'm Ruth Fulbright. Your new cook."

Mrs. Lancaster squealed in glee, then completely ignored Ruth's outstretched hand and swooped in for a hug.

Ruth froze at the effusive greeting, not quite sure how to react, but her hostess didn't seem to care. She released her hold as swiftly as she had engaged it, leaving Ruth to teeter unsteadily like a weather vane in a gust of swirling wind.

"Oh, Mrs. Fulbright, you've no idea how happy I am to see you!" Mrs. Lancaster bent slightly and slapped her hands on her knees. "And this little ladybug must be Naomi. Dorothea told me all about you."

Naomi grinned. "The man at the hotel said you have chickens. I'm a real good egg-getter."

"Are you, now? Well, it just so happens I'm in need of a skilled egg collector. Can you start work tomorrow? I pay a penny a week."

"You don't have to—" Ruth's declension died when Myrtle gave her a wink that clearly stated she was not welcome to participate in this negotiation.

Naomi clapped her hands and turned pleading eyes to her mama. "Can I, Mama? Please?"

"Only if you follow Mrs. Lancaster's instructions to the letter."

"I will, I promise." Her vow lisped a bit through the gap of her missing front tooth, but the sparkle in her eyes warmed Ruth's heart.

"That's settled then," Myrtle said, straightening. "Why don't you go out back and say hello to my feathered ladies while I show your mother around?"

Naomi cast Ruth a quick look asking for permission. The instant Ruth nodded, she took off like a shot.

"Reminds me of my little granddaughters, Edna and Ethel. Twins, if you can believe it." Myrtle swept up her teacup in one hand, magazine in the other, then trounced toward the back of the building, presumably toward the kitchen. Ruth followed, hoping that was what her employer expected. "They'll be nine this year. Live two counties over, so I don't get to see them nearly enough." Myrtle tossed a mischievous grin over her shoulder. "I'll have to spoil that girl of yours in their stead to make sure I don't get out of practice."

"That's very kind of—"

"Here's the kitchen," Myrtle pronounced as she pushed through a swinging door. "Cookstove was new three years ago, water pump at the sink, pantry at the back. I got a gal who comes in at night to clean the front of the shop, so you're only responsible for this area. Make a list of whatever supplies you need, and Mr. Lancaster will run them down for you. You can set your own menu, but I don't want anything fancy. People who want fancy eat at the hotel dining room. People who want good old home cooking come to the Homespun Café. Locals too. Having pie on hand for menfolk who drop by of an afternoon has proven popular, and flapjacks tend to bring 'em in in the mornings."

Ruth made furious mental notes. Stephen had always bragged about her cooking, and her dishes were among the first emptied at the church socials, but she'd never cooked in any kind of professional capacity. What if she made too much or not enough? What if customers didn't like her food? What if—

"Now, I've arranged for a lovely little cottage for you on the outskirts of town. It's rustic, I'm afraid, but sturdy. Dorothea mentioned that money is a little tight, so I avoided the rooming houses. With all the tourists coming in for the mineral baths and specialized treatments, prices have shot through the roof. They charge four dollars a night at Azlin's resort. Can you believe it? Scandalous. But the people keep coming." Myrtle shook her head as she circled around to the small table at the back of the kitchen. "You and Miss Ladybug can take your meals here, of course, after the customers have been served. We're open seven to seven Monday through Saturday, with Sundays off. I run the gift sales and have a gal who will wait tables for you. In between meal services, you're welcome to escape the heat of the kitchen to tend to personal errands."

Ruth's vision blurred at all the information being thrown at her. The most glaring of which was the four-dollar-a-night hotel room. Her wages had been promised at eight dollars a week. Even with meals included, she'd be hard-pressed to pay even a quarter of the going town rate for lodging.

"This cottage you mentioned," Ruth inserted when Myrtle paused for breath, "how much is the rent?"

Myrtle waved a hand as if the number was not significant, but *every* number was significant when all one had to her name was a dollar and twenty-three cents left over from her train fare.

"There's a down payment of the first month's rent in advance, but after that it's only twenty dollars a month."

Ruth's knees nearly gave out. Twenty dollars a month? How would she manage to keep Naomi in clothes and shoes? And with winter coming, they'd need a good supply of coal. Not to mention schoolbooks, kerosene, and essentials to set up their home. They didn't even have a dish to eat off of. And that was after Ruth earned a month of wages. Paying upfront would be impossible.

"Is there somewhere else? Someplace smaller, perhaps. Naomi and I don't need more than a room, really."

Myrtle's expression turned sympathetic. "I'm afraid not. Most folks here with space for boarders are already renting to the tourists for higher rates. Mr. Lancaster even rented out our spare room. It's booked for the next three months. Perhaps I could speak with him about offering it to you at a lower rate after that, but we use that extra money to visit the grandchildren. . . ."

"Of course you do. Precisely as you should." Ruth would *not* beg on this sweet woman's door. She'd find a way to make this work. "I'm sure the cottage you spoke of will do nicely. It was kind of you to make inquiries for me." Perhaps she could convince the owner to take weekly installments instead of a lump sum. Surely *something* could be worked out. "Whom should I see about the arrangements?"

Myrtle's face bloomed in relief, her ebullience restored. "That would be Mr. Palmer, Mr. Azlin's business manager. You can ask for him at the hotel."

"Mr. Azlin owns the cottage?" Dread hardened Ruth's stomach. Wealthy men didn't tend to be the sympathetic sort.

"Of course, dear. Mr. Azlin owns nearly everything hereabouts."

2

Ruth sat in a hard wooden chair in front of a hard wooden desk atop hard wooden floors. The warning could not be clearer. *Don't expect anything soft from the man who belongs to this room.* The very walls made her feel like prey with their hunter green paint and oak wainscoting surrounding her on every side, pressing in. Even the mountain landscapes hanging around the room seemed to taunt her about reaching above her station.

Ruth frowned. Since when had she become a melodramatic ninny? The chair was just a chair. No harder than any other.

Get a hold of yourself. Mr. Palmer will be here soon, and you need your wits about you.

Deciding to distract herself, Ruth opened her reticule and extracted the only item of value she had left. Her mother's heirloom brooch. Housed in a cloth bag Ruth had sewn as a lavender sachet for her trousseau when she was fourteen, the small luckenbooth brooch felt heavy in her hand. She turned the sachet pouch over, hiding the embroidered lavender blooms on the front, and ran her finger along the initials and dates she'd stitched into the backing after she'd married Stephen.

LD 1768
SGE 1827
REH 1859
RHF 1882

Such a legacy of love handed down from mother to daughter. A legacy that now belonged to Naomi. Ruth recalled the stories her mother had shared of how a great English noblewoman, Lady Densbury, had gifted the amethyst brooch to Ruth's grandmother, Sarah Gooding, a mere servant, when Sarah married the lady's grandson. Sarah and her beloved Randall left England to start a new life in America, and the brooch was handed down to their daughter, Rosemary. Ruth's mother had met and married a cotton plantation owner in Tennessee, and even through the horrors of civil war and the loss of their land, their love remained true. When Ruth inherited the brooch, she already knew who she'd be marrying. Stephen Fulbright had owned her heart since childhood, and at sixteen, she'd married her true love and followed him to Texas to make a life of their own farming cotton.

Only their love story had ended with harsh abruptness. A fever. A failed crop. A bank foreclosure. Yet she harbored no regrets. Stephen had been her best friend and her greatest joy. Ruth's chance at lifelong love might be gone, but Naomi had an entire future ahead of her. A future that deserved a love story and a family brooch to hand down to her own daughter someday.

Ruth loosened the ribbon that held the sachet bag closed and tipped out the brooch. Two interlocking silver hearts supported a large amethyst topped with a silver crown. The Scottish symbol of loyalty and love, connected hearts that could endure all manner of hardship without being torn apart. The deep purple jewel symbolized the rarity and preciousness of such love, a reminder not to join oneself to a man lightly but only to one of noble character and devoted heart.

Please don't force me to give this up, she prayed as her fingers traced the outline of the jeweled pin. *Soften Mr. Palmer's heart. Help him have pity.*

Sharp, efficient footsteps clicked outside the office door. Ruth scrambled to get the brooch back in the bag and the bag back in her reticule before the door opened. She was still fiddling with the drawstring when a polite voice sounded behind her.

"Mrs. Fulbright. I'm sorry to have kept you waiting."

She turned in her seat to smile at the short man with round spectacles and a tidy mustache who closed the door and crossed to the desk.

"I understand you're here to make rental arrangements for one of Mr. Azlin's properties." He took a seat behind the desk and pulled a thin stack of papers and a small brass key from the top drawer. "Mrs. Lancaster made the initial arrangements on your behalf, so I have the rental agreement drawn up. All I need from you is your signature and the first month's rent."

He smiled as though he hadn't just requested a feat as impossible as walking upon the ceiling. With brisk professionalism, he turned the papers to face her and slid them across the desktop. Then he handed her a pen and moved his inkwell to within easy reach.

Heart racing, Ruth bit her lip and considered the paper before her. She scanned the agreement, finding nothing objectionable in the wording. Fair price. Fair terms. The owner even included a caretaker's name to contact if she should have any issues with the structure or any of the workings therein. More generous than she would have expected. Or perhaps an indication that the owner didn't want to be bothered with any petty problems regarding his property.

Ruth had walked past the cottage on her way to the hotel, knowing it would be irresponsible to sign an agreement on the word of a stranger, even one as kind as Myrtle Lancaster. The two-room cabin sat on the far side of town, past the courthouse, well out of the way of the resort and the majority of town traffic. When she'd peered through the windows, she'd been thankful to spy a bed and a bureau in the bedroom, as well as a small cookstove in the main chamber along with a table, two chairs, and a small cabinet. No rugs or curtains or even paint on the walls, but it was serviceable and sturdy, just as Myrtle had promised.

Yet Ruth couldn't sign. Not yet. She set the pen on the desk with a soft tap.

Mr. Palmer's smile slipped. "Is there something amiss?"

With her tongue maddeningly dry and insides trembling, Ruth met the solicitor's gaze. "I'm sure you're aware that I'll be working as Mrs. Lancaster's cook. I'm not here for a short medicinal stay. I'm to be a permanent resident of the community."

His brow crinkled. "I fail to see how that impacts the rental agreement."

Ruth sighed. Dancing around the issue wasn't helping. She needed to spit out the facts. "What I'm trying to say is that I'm a good investment. One that perhaps warrants a bit of leeway in the manner of payment. I don't have the money you require now, but as soon as I draw my first week's wages, I'll put half of my earnings toward the rental cost. I'll do so each week, so that by the end of the month, the rent will be paid in full."

Mr. Palmer's frown deepened, and he tugged the papers back toward him, pulling her hope of a home out of reach. "Actually, you'll always be a week behind." He shook his head and put the key back into the desk drawer. "I'm sorry, Mrs. Fulbright, but our policy is firm. Rent must be paid at the beginning of the month. It's a standard agreement. Without it, there's nothing to stop an unscrupulous person, or a person who falls on hard times," he allowed, showing at least some sympathy for her plight, "from living rent-free for a month and then skipping out without payment. As much as I would like to help you, I don't actually know your character, do I? What kind of manager would I be if I let every young woman who batted her lashes at me twist the arrangement to her liking? Mr. Azlin would be taken advantage of, and I'd soon be out of a job."

Batted her lashes? The condescending toad! She'd done no such thing.

"Why don't we let Mr. Azlin decide for himself?" Ruth jutted out her chin. "Keep you out of the precarious middle?" Her daughter needed a roof over her head, and Ruth wasn't about to let this man refuse her without a fight. If he didn't have the authority to change the policy, then she would just have to address the man who did.

Mr. Palmer sniffed. "I assure you, Mr. Azlin is no more likely to accept your terms than I am. He designed the agreement, after all."

"Even so, I wish to discuss it with him." She lengthened her neck and stiffened her spine. She'd not be dissuaded or intimidated. Not when her daughter was counting on her. "If you'd be so kind as to let him know that I await his convenience?"

"Mr. Azlin is a very busy man." He let the insinuation hang in the air.

Ruth didn't falter. She met Mr. Palmer's gaze without blinking. "I'll wait."

Beauregard Azlin massaged the muscles of his right forearm in an attempt to dull the jabbing pinpricks radiating along his nerve endings. A particularly sharp jolt shot to his wrist, causing Bo to wince. He supposed he'd better arrange for a mineral bath in his personal chamber tonight.

The waters hadn't cured what ailed him during the last five years that he'd resided in Hope Springs, but regular doses did seem to minimize his symptoms. Well, minimized the pain, anyway. The paralysis of his wrist and forearm had seen no improvement. His arm still hung useless past his elbow, just as it had since he broke it when he'd been a lad of ten. It didn't even hang straight. He had a permanent crook that announced his crippled state to all and sundry.

Which was why he secluded himself on the top floor of the hotel. Those used to the finest things in life were easily unsettled by the less than perfect. A crippled host didn't inspire confidence at a resort promoting health benefits. Rather the opposite. So Bo sequestered himself and relied on his staff to keep him well-informed. He oversaw every detail of the resort, from the food served in the dining room to the temperature of the baths to the décor in the guest rooms, ensuring every aspect met his demanding standards. Whether the guest was a wealthy industrialist from New York or a humble farmer from three counties over, they were all to be treated with the greatest courtesy and respect.

No one came to Hope Springs without some kind of ailment weighing on their body and mind. Rich or poor didn't matter when sickness hit. And if the mineral water from his wells could bring relief and hope to the people who visited, he'd thank God for the provision.

It was harder to thank God for the paperwork that accompanied said provision. Bo smirked as he released his arm and reclaimed the pen he'd set aside. The pastry chef he'd hired required the finest blackberries for his tarts, and apparently the fruit that arrived in this morning's delivery had been less than adequate. A telegraph had already been sent to the supplier, but Bo had discovered that personal correspondence, allowing for greater explanation of the problem along with appreciation for past efforts, went a long way toward establishing healthy relationships with vendors that led to more *fruitful* results in the future.

A tiny snort of air escaped his nose at the bad mental pun. He really needed to get out more. Unfortunately, that would leave his correspondence uncorresponded, so abandoning his duty was not an option.

He clasped the pen in his left hand and dipped it in the ink. After more than two decades of practice, he'd become proficient at writing with his non-dominant hand, yet it still required more concentration than he would prefer. There was no such thing as scribbling for him. Every word had to be meticulously crafted.

A knock sounded on his door.

"Enter," he called without looking away from his penmanship. Once he completed the sentence he was working on, he glanced up at his business manager and best friend.

Cornelius Palmer strode forward, his eyes full of mischief.

That didn't bode well. Bo set down his pen and straightened. Cornelius was a genius at managing employees, but he had a rather strong meddling streak.

The manager rocked up on his toes, a touch of glee oozing around the corners of his professional stoicism. "It seems a situation has arisen that demands your personal attention."

Bo leaned back in his chair and gave Cornelius his most quelling stare. "Oh?"

"A Mrs. Fulbright has requested to see you regarding the rental property on Third Street. She would like to arrange weekly payments once she starts earning wages, since she does not have the capital to pay the monthly rate in advance."

Bo hardened his jaw. Mrs. Fulbright. The new cook at the Homespun Café. A widow with a young daughter. And most likely the self-sufficient lady he'd spied from his balcony this morning, collecting her luggage from the stage driver. Bo hated turning people down, especially those in need, but his innate sense of fairness demanded that he treat everyone the same. He'd turned down others who wished to rent his property when they couldn't make the payment. Therefore, he couldn't bend his rule now just because the person asking was a woman with a certain pluckiness he admired.

"I'm sure you explained my policy on the matter." Bo waved his left hand, shooing Cornelius from the room. "If she cannot pay, I cannot rent her the house."

"I told her precisely that, but she insisted on appealing to the owner himself." Cornelius's lips twitched, clearly fighting down a grin, causing instant dread to well in Bo's gut. "Said she'd wait." He paused for effect. "For as long as necessary."

Bo scowled.

"So unless you want to have her bodily removed from the premises—which, as your business manager, I must recommend against; not good for the resort's image, I'm afraid—I suggest you meet with her."

"You're enjoying this, aren't you?" Bo grumbled as he gained his feet.

Cornelius bounced on the balls of his feet and gave his grin full reign. "Immensely."

The little traitor. *Little* being quite literal. Bo stood a full head taller than his manager. Not that it mattered one whit when it came to changing Cornelius's mind about anything. Cornelius wasn't intimidated in the slightest by Bo's size or bearing. Not even Bo's wealth could cow him.

Which was why the two of them got along so famously.

"Fine." Bo strode for the door, reaching for the latch with his left hand. "In your office, I suppose?"

"That, she is." Cornelius followed him to the door. "Oh, and Bo?"

Knob in hand, he paused to glance over his shoulder. "Yes?"

"Better take some armor for that soft heart of yours. She's got a fire in her that will turn you into a puddle if you get too close."

Bo eyed his friend. "Don't you know by now? I never get too close."

3

Determined to get the meeting over with as quickly as possible, Bo swept into his manager's office with a single-minded purpose—to get rid of the woman who had presumptuously glued herself to Cornelius's chair.

Only the chair was empty.

Losing steam, he chugged to a halt halfway across the floor. Had she left?

"Mr. Azlin?"

He swiveled to the left. The minx had positioned herself behind the door, giving her the advantage of taking his measure before he could take hers. Clever tactic.

He turned toward her and offered a small bow, more in admiration of her strategy than in gentlemanly politeness. "Mrs. Fulbright."

She had remarkable bearing. Fierce almost, yet feminine at the same time. Her dark hair, not quite as black as his own, had been pulled into a simple knot that accentuated the fine bones of her face. Her gray-green eyes glowed with resolve even as the fingers at her side trembled.

Bo took three strides, placing himself directly before her and forcing her to crane her neck back slightly in order to make eye contact. She wasn't the only one who understood tactics.

"Let's be candid, shall we, Mrs. Fulbright?" He didn't wait for her to respond, just continued on as if her agreement was tacit. "My business manager has informed me of your situation. I'm afraid I have no better news to impart. I will not rent the property to you until I receive the first month's payment. So if you have nothing else, I'll let you be on your way."

"Actually, I do have something else." She met his gaze square on, held it, then deliberately turned away from him and walked over to the desk. "A business proposition."

Bo followed, frowning that she'd just reclaimed the upper hand.

She rounded the corner of the desk before facing him. "Having a long-term tenant is in your best interest in regard to stability and income. Providing a home for my daughter is in my best interest, yet you require payment in advance. So the only way for both of us to get what we need is to find those funds." She set her purse on the desktop, opened the drawstring, and pulled out a small pouch with purple flowers stitched on the front. A hint of lavender wafted from the bag. "If you are amenable, I think I have a way to solve that dilemma."

The tremble in her fingers became more pronounced as she unfastened the little pouch. She tipped it upside down, and a silver pin tumbled out. The piece looked old. Moderately valuable too. Yet she'd chosen to hold on to this trinket longer than anything else, judging by the pale circle of skin on the ring finger of her left hand that indicated she'd already sold off her wedding band.

The scripture about taking care of widows and orphans abraded his conscience even as the one condemning favoritism urged him to hold his ground.

Bo shook his head. "I'm not going to buy your jewelry."

She turned on him, her expression vehement. "Good, because it's *not* for sale. It's a family heirloom that will be handed down to my daughter when she's of age."

"Then why are you showing it to me?" He speared her with his most intimidating glare.

She broke eye contact, and for a moment Bo felt the thrill of victory. Until her gaze found his again, her eyes filled with so much regret that he had to fight the urge to wrap his good arm around her shoulders and spout platitudes about how everything would be all right. Yet the fact that she was offering up her family treasure told him that things hadn't been all right for this young woman in a long time.

Mrs. Fulbright was no helpless damsel in distress, though. She'd met him with a battle plan and the fortitude to see it through to the end. Even as he watched, she blinked away her regret and focused her eyes into twin dagger points. "I propose a loan, Mr. Azlin, with my family's brooch serving as collateral. It's handcrafted Scottish silver with an amethyst stone. Worth far more than the twenty dollars you require for the rental fee."

"So you expect me to play the role of pawnbroker."

She lifted her chin but did not argue his assessment. "I'll make weekly installments, including interest, until the debt is paid. Then I'll reclaim my brooch and you may retire from the brokerage business, having made a modest commission. Your policy is upheld, I have a roof to place over my daughter's head, and you make a profit. A mutually beneficial arrangement, wouldn't you say?"

What he would say was that she'd neatly maneuvered him into a corner, managing to appease his sense of justice while giving him an opportunity to extend mercy. He was tempted to applaud that fine bit of negotiation but restrained. She was entrusting him with her family's greatest treasure, and he wouldn't make light of that sacrifice.

Keeping his features impassive, he took the pin from her and examined it, holding it up to the light to inspect the gem. Genuine. Not that it mattered. Even if it were paste, he'd still give her the loan. She deserved it.

"I'll give you fifty dollars for it."

She shook her head. "I only want twenty. That way I can earn it back more quickly and pay less in interest."

He raised a brow. "I saw your sparsity of luggage, Mrs. Fulbright." Her eyes widened, but he pressed on, uncaring that she knew he'd been watching her. He watched everyone. It was how he kept apprised of all the goings-on in town. "You'll need linens for the bed, food for the pantry, coal for the stove. It's October, and the weather here is unpredictable at best. Seasonably warm one day, snow the next. I'll not have you moving into my cottage only to freeze to death."

She hesitated, her gaze rolling upward as though she were making mental calculations. Then her mouth tensed, and her eyes found his again. "I can make do with forty."

In all his experience, Bo had never had a client attempt to talk him into fronting *less* capital at the outset of an investment. Ruth Fulbright was an original. Quite the most fascinating woman he'd ever encountered.

"Deal?" She thrust her right hand toward him.

He stared at her, heat rising up his neck. He couldn't shake on their deal. Not unless he wanted to do some kind of awkward left hand to right hand thing that made him look like an imbecile.

Her cheeks reddened slightly, but she held her ground and did something no one had ever done before. She dropped her right hand and extended her left.

Bo straightened, set the brooch atop the desk, then fit his hand to hers, an entirely different type of admiration sparking to life inside his chest.

"I'll, uh, draft an agreement and fetch your money," he said as his hand slid from hers.

Then he made a sharp pivot and left the room before she made a complete puddle out of him.

Later that evening, Ruth tucked her daughter into the bed the two of them would be sharing—a bed sporting new linens, an all-purpose wool blanket, and two hen feather pillows, thanks to Mr. Azlin's generosity.

He hadn't been what she'd expected. Gruff and stern, certainly, but a spark of compassion had warmed his ice-blue eyes when she'd offered up her brooch. As if he understood the pain of loss and regret. And when he'd shaken her hand? Well. Her skin still tingled a bit when she recalled that moment. Which meant she must stop recalling it at once.

She scraped her palm down the side of her skirt before sitting on the edge of the bed.

"The water tastes funny here," Naomi said, guiding Ruth's thoughts away from a wealthy man with hidden vulnerabilities to the more grounded topic of everyday reality. "It smells funny too. Like old eggs." Naomi crinkled her nose.

Ruth smiled. "You'll get used to it in time." She pulled the covers up to her daughter's chin. "The minerals that make the water taste funny also help people feel better. That's why so many visitors come to Mr. Azlin's resort."

Naomi nibbled her bottom lip. "Maybe we should have brought Daddy here."

The unintentional ambush slammed into Ruth's chest with all the force of a mule's hind leg. It took several heartbeats for her to recover enough to answer. "The kind of sickness your daddy had couldn't have been cured by mineral water, sweetie." She stroked Naomi's hair back from her face. "But if we had come here back then, I think he would have liked this little house. Don't you?"

"He probably wouldn't have liked the funny water," Naomi said, her nose crinkling, "but I think he would have liked the rest. Especially the chickens."

"The chickens?"

Naomi nodded, her hair splayed over the pillow behind her head. "Mrs. Lancaster has even more chickens than we did. And there's a fat brown one that likes me already. She followed me all around the coop today."

"She did?" Ruth grinned, thanking God for the resiliency of youth.

"Uh-huh. She even let me pet her feathers."

"That's wonderful." Ruth kissed Naomi's head. "Time for prayers, dear heart."

Naomi squeezed her eyes closed. "Dear God, thank you for our new home. Thank you for Mrs. Lancaster and the chickens and the black-and-white kitty. Help Mama to like working at the café. Help me to like my new school. And help the water not taste as funny tomorrow."

Ruth bit back a smile.

"Oh, and help Mr. Azlin take good care of my brooch and not lose it. In Jesus's name . . . amen." Her eyes popped open. "'Night, Mama."

"Good night, sweetie."

Ruth rose from the bed and padded from the room. It had been hard to tell Naomi about the brooch, but Ruth didn't believe in hiding painful truths from children. Growing up in the South after the war, she'd learned that accepting reality and dealing with it did more to make a person happy than denying the truth and wishing for what couldn't be. Yet in telling Naomi about the brooch, she'd also made her daughter a promise: that she would get it back, sooner rather than later. A promise she fully intended to keep.

Bo left the resort a couple hours after dark and began the quarter-mile walk home to the modest two-story structure he'd built after completing the resort nearly five years ago. With all his duties at the resort, he spent very little time at home. Nevertheless, he longed for it every evening. For the quiet, the peace. No judging eyes or pitying glances. No one making demands on his time or his money. No guests to appease or staff to guide. No staff at all, really. He had a housekeeper who came in once a week to tidy up, and a gardener who showed up every now and then to keep the weeds from overtaking the hedges, but other than that, the place was strictly his own. His retreat. His sanctuary. His place to be alone.

Alone.

Bo frowned. That descriptor had always carried a positive connotation in his mind, a sense of relief, of freedom. Tonight, however, the promise of being alone didn't offer the same attraction.

Something else tugged at him, something that made his feet veer from their practiced route to take a detour down Third Street, across the road from a small, nondescript house.

He slowed his pace. A dim light shone from the front window of the house he'd rented to Mrs. Fulbright and her daughter. Had they settled in? Found what they needed from the mercantile to make the place livable? He hoped so. Hoped they were comfortable. Warm.

A silhouette moved from the back room into the front and passed the uncurtained window. A slender silhouette with gentle curves. Bo's gaze arrested on the window, his steps faltering to a halt before he realized what he'd done and immediately set his feet back in motion. Then something furry tangled his stride and nearly sent him sprawling onto his face.

Bo lurched sideways to avoid stepping on the creature and barely managed to keep his balance. "Listen, you." He shook his finger at the unrepentant tabby that sat directly in Bo's path, licking a white paw as if he hadn't just tried to fell an innocent man on his walk home. "The tripping of unsuspecting pedestrians is strictly prohibited in this town."

The cat set his paw down, blinked in denial of any wrongdoing, then sashayed across the street, black tail swishing. He paused halfway and looked back at Bo with narrow green eyes that seemed to say, *Spying on innocent ladies is prohibited too, big man. Just letting you know I'm on patrol.*

Apparently the little girl had found a protector. Bo would have expected the stray to flee a child who had nearly strangled it in her efforts to carry it around earlier in the day, but he should have known better. If the girl's mother could inspire the protective instincts of a hardened entrepreneur to the point that he willingly lowered himself to pawnbroker status, her daughter could surely win over a recalcitrant tomcat.

Bo fetched his handkerchief from his inside jacket pocket. Peeling back the top layer of the folded square, he revealed the heart-shaped brooch he'd pinned to the linen. He'd had women try to gain his affection in the past, women willing to look past his crippled arm in order to gain access to his bank account, but this was the closest he'd ever come to actually owning a woman's heart.

He ran his thumb over the stone in the center, then glanced back across the street. "I'll keep it safe for you," he vowed softly, then folded the handkerchief again and tucked it into his breast pocket, where it rubbed against his chest all the way home.

4

Ruth opened the oven door and pulled out her second apple pie of the afternoon. Cinnamon sweetness filled the café kitchen as she set the golden dessert on the towel-covered windowsill to cool. The lattice top had come out rather well, if she did say so herself. She closed the oven door and flapped her apron in an effort to dissipate the heated air. It might be November outside, but in this small kitchen, it felt like the middle of July.

"Oh, that smells heavenly!" Myrtle Lancaster pushed through the kitchen door, her jade- and ginger-striped skirt flapping against her legs as she tossed aside her canary-yellow shawl, marched straight for the fresh pie, and inhaled deeply. "Mmm. Friday is my new favorite day."

Ruth laughed. "You say that about every day."

Myrtle tilted her head. "Not about Wednesday." She turned away from the window and wandered toward the work counter where Ruth had a giant roast potted and ready to go into the oven. "I know the customers love your sweet potato pies, but I just can't get past that texture. I want to chew my food, not have it squish through the cracks."

"That's why I keep a jar of peanut brittle on hand." Ruth grinned. This woman was a constant delight. Her bright clothes and cheerful disposition made it impossible to dwell in the doldrums while in her presence. The Lord could not have blessed Ruth with a better employer. "Wouldn't want your teeth to get out of practice."

"And that's why I keep you and the ladybug around." Myrtle winked. "To keep my chompers in shape and my hens laying. I swear their production has increased since you got here, despite the cooler weather. That girl of yours has a way with critters." Myrtle lifted the roaster's lid and inspected the meat and vegetables within. "Where is Naomi this afternoon? You usually bring her here after school."

"She's playing with the Marshall girls down by the pond." Ruth had bought a secondhand coat for Naomi but had not yet finished knitting the scarf and mittens she'd need for winter. There was a definite November snap in the air, but the sun was shining, so Ruth had agreed to the outing, much to her daughter's delight. "She and the youngest girl, Millie, have become fast friends." Ruth bent to adjust the stove's dampers, then hefted the large roasting pan into the oven.

"Those Marshalls are good people," Myrtle confirmed. "Hardworking. Responsible. Though they do have the odd habit of giving all their young'uns monikers that start with *M*. Makes it near impossible for a body to remember which is which. Especially since there are five of 'em. Thank heavens they got a boy in there. At least I know which one to call Michael."

After living in Hope Springs for nearly five weeks, Ruth knew most of the local families, at least those who lived in town. Between church services and the steady stream of café customers, she'd interacted with most of them at some level. But she wouldn't really call any of them *friends*.

Except Myrtle, of course. The older woman chatted the day away with her when business was slow. Ruth knew all about Myrtle's grandchildren, Mr. Lancaster's habit of collecting old wagon wheels, and the fancy porcelain bathing tubs the resort had special ordered all the way from Chicago. Myrtle was a wealth of information.

Which was why Ruth pulled out a chair at the small table in the corner and invited her employer to join her.

"Ah." Myrtle's mouth quirked up at the corners as she slid into her seat. "You're finally going to ask me about him, aren't you?"

Ruth banged her knee against the table leg. "Who?"

"Bo Azlin, of course."

How had she known? Had Ruth been acting in a way that revealed her . . . curiosity?

Myrtle chuckled. "Oh, don't look so alarmed. He's the most mysterious thing about Hope Springs. I'd think you odd if you *didn't* ask about him. In fact, I'm surprised it took you this long. Though you have been busy with the café, so I suppose the delay is understandable."

Ruth relaxed slightly as she adjusted her skirt and gave her sore knee a rub. "Why does he hide himself away all the time? Even at church, he arrives late and leaves early. I would think the man who basically built this town would be a more active part of it."

"Some of it's his nature," Myrtle confided. "He's a bit of a hermit. Probably due to that useless arm of his. I'm guessing he's a might touchy about it."

Probably because people used terms like *useless* to describe it, Ruth thought, her dander rising, even though she knew her friend didn't mean anything unkind. Mr. Azlin *did* suffer from some paralysis, making his arm less than useful, but still. One could refer to it in a more delicate manner.

"Beauregard Azlin came to town five years ago, after hearing about the healing waters in Obadiah Smith's well. Back then, Hope Springs was nothing more than a handful of homesteads, no town to speak of. Obadiah and his wife Ethel came here in '81. Obadiah had lingering malaria symptoms, and Ethel had the rheumatism real bad. The well they dug in '83 turned up some funny-tasting water, but it didn't hurt the stock, so the Smiths started drinkin' it too. Lo and behold, after a few weeks, they started feeling better and figured it was the water that done made the difference. Word spread. People started coming from miles around to drink from their well. The mister and I were among them.

"Clyde suffered from horrible dyspepsia. It got so bad he could hardly eat anything. The poor man shrank down to skin and bones. I thought I was gonna lose him." Myrtle bit her lip and sniffed, then gave her head a shake and slapped her palm on the table. "But the Good Lord led us here, and after only two weeks, Clyde was able to keep simple foods down. After a month, he started putting on weight. I told him he better get comfortable, 'cause we weren't never leaving. Been here ever since. I opened my café, figuring the folks coming for the water had plenty to drink, but they'd need some vittles to keep them going. Made a decent profit too. Until Azlin showed up."

Thinking of the stern man with the intelligent, icy blue eyes and brisk, businesslike manner, Ruth could easily picture Beauregard Azlin recognizing the opportunity the small settlement represented. "I suppose he saw the potential for profit."

"That he did." Myrtle leaned forward across the table. "But he wasn't looking for an investment when he first came." She glanced around the kitchen as if checking for any eavesdroppers who might have snuck in. She lowered her voice. "He was looking for a miracle."

Ruth's image of the shrewd businessman gave way to the vulnerability that had been exposed when she'd stupidly stuck out her hand to shake on their deal her first day in town. Since then, she'd frequently tried to imagine what it would be like to have full use of only one arm. Something as simple as putting on a coat or pulling on trousers became exponentially harder. She knew because she'd tried it—tried pulling on her drawers with only her left hand one day. As soon as she'd made any progress up one leg, they'd slide down the other. It had taken her five minutes to manage a task that took mere seconds with two functioning hands. And she'd completely given up on tying the drawstring. For Mr. Azlin's sake, she hoped suspenders were more easily accomplished than waist ties.

"He took the waters for weeks," Myrtle continued. "Drank them, bathed in them. They must have offered some level of relief, because he decided to stay. And once he decided to stay, he bought up land, platted a town, and started advertising the medicinal benefits of mineral water. Gave us the name Hope Springs and built the resort with its fancy drinking pavilion, on-site doctor, and steam generator to provide guests with heated mineral baths in six bathing chambers. It took Clyde and me a while to adjust, until we realized we didn't need to compete with Azlin. There were plenty of plain folk coming to take the waters too, and they preferred simple food at a fair price."

"You make Mr. Azlin sound rather mercenary." Ruth traced the edge of a knothole in the tabletop. Apparently he truly did own the entire town. And here she'd been feeling . . . well, not sorry for him, exactly. Just . . . sad, she supposed. A man who constantly hid himself away must be lonely.

"Mercenary?" Myrtle's brow furrowed for a moment then cleared. "No. Azlin's a sound businessman. I got nothing but respect for him. From what I hear, he treats his employees well. Demands quality performance but pays handsomely for it. Doesn't overwork them, neither. He donates to the church, built a school as soon as we had enough kids to fill a classroom, and offers the same level of service to the farmer as to the fancy folk. He's a good man. Just doesn't like being around people much outside of the ones who work for him." She shrugged. "Guess he figures the folks at the resort have to be nice to him, since he pays their wages."

Ruth stiffened. "I'm sure he has genuine friendships among his staff." At least she hoped so. "He and Mr. Palmer seem rather close."

Myrtle leaned back in her chair. "I suppose they are. Cornelius Palmer is his right-hand man." A chortle burst from her. "Ha! I just realized what I said." She slapped the table edge with her fingertips. "His *right hand*."

Ruth didn't laugh. Mr. Azlin's preference for solitude was beginning to make more sense.

Myrtle noticed Ruth's lack of amusement and cleared her throat. "Yes, well . . . if Mr. Azlin has any close friends in Hope Springs, I would wager Mr. Palmer is among them."

"Quit butting your nose in where it doesn't belong, Cornelius," Bo groused as he lengthened his stride down the third-floor corridor in an effort to outdistance his interfering business manager. Unfortunately, Cornelius Palmer had the speed and tenacity of a terrier. Bo half expected his friend to latch on to his pant leg and wrestle him down the street to the café.

"It's just a piece of pie, Bo. What's the harm?"

"If you want me to try the pie so badly, order it yourself and bring me a slice." But, of course, they weren't really talking about pie.

Cornelius spun past Bo before he could reach his office door and planted himself directly in front of the handle. "What are you so afraid of?"

Bo scowled, not that it had any effect on his friend.

"Order a piece of pie," Cornelius said. "Compliment the cook. Strike up a conversation. You're an educated man. The concept's not that difficult."

Was Bo's regard for Ruth Fulbright really so obvious? He'd only commented upon her impressive determination to pay her debts once or twice. She made payments every week. Sometimes only a dollar or two, other times as much as five. She'd nearly repaid half the loan already, which spoke well of her integrity and proved how valuable she considered that brooch.

And if Bo happened to be on his balcony every weekday at three o'clock when Mrs. Fulbright strolled down to the schoolhouse to fetch her daughter, it was merely coincidence. Though he had to admit the two were a delight to watch. Ruth would hold the girl's hand and listen patiently as Naomi recounted a dozen stories about her day. Sometimes that infernal cat would show up and prance close enough to let the girl pet its fur, then dash off with a superior smirk.

One time about two weeks ago, the rascal had bounded up the tree next to the resort, just as it had the day the Fulbrights had arrived in town. It drew Ruth's attention, leading her to spot him on the balcony. Yet instead of hurrying her daughter away or pretending she hadn't seen him, she'd lifted a hand in greeting. Naomi noticed and followed suit, waving with a grin so big that even from three floors up, Bo could see the gap from her missing tooth. He had waved back, and that had begun a new daily routine. He would wander out onto his balcony. They'd wander back into town. And they'd all share a wave. Bo hadn't thought anyone else had noticed, but apparently Cornelius's network of staff had developed espionage skills.

"As essential as you are," his manager said, "I'm pretty sure I can keep the resort from collapsing if you take an hour of personal time to meander down to the café for a slice of apple pie."

"Apple?" His favorite. Which Cornelius knew. No doubt it was the reason he'd waited until today to press his case. If Bo protested too much, it would only confirm Cornelius's suspicions regarding his interest in the young widow. It was either eat pie or eat crow, and Bo suspected the pie would taste better.

"Fine. I'll visit the café and get a piece of pie. Happy?"

"Yes," Cornelius said as he stepped sideways to clear Bo's path to the door of his office, "but it's *your* happiness I'm campaigning for." His expression grew serious. "Not all women are shallow, Bo. There's a handful out there who are actually worth knowing. My gut tells me Ruth Fulbright is one of them."

"Your gut or your network of spies?" Nothing happened in Hope Springs without Cornelius Palmer learning about it.

His friend's eyes danced. "Both. The locals praise her cooking, the merchants report that she refuses credit and pays for everything up front, the Lancasters have practically adopted her as a second daughter, she attends church every Sunday and tithes despite her reduced circumstances, she's won the admiration of the schoolmarm with her daily visits, and she even volunteered to help with the school's Christmas program. She's a woman of character, Bo. Not only that," he said with a wink, "but she waves at you every day when she walks her daughter home from school. The most recent occurrence being less than an hour ago." Cornelius lifted his chin in masculine acknowledgment. "A fellow would have to be blind not to notice that, and you, my friend, might be as hard-headed as a buffalo, but you're not blind."

Bo glowered at his friend. "Enough with the salesmanship."

He lightly shoved Cornelius farther into the hall, then wrenched the doorknob and pushed into his office. "You're not crafting one of your advertising pamphlets. Besides, I already said I'd go." He crossed to his desk and pretended to organize the papers lying there, though in truth his eyes didn't absorb a single written word.

Cornelius leaned against the doorjamb. "Just thought I'd make sure you didn't forget."

"You won't quit hounding me unless I go this very minute, will you?"

Cornelius shook his head, a completely unrepentant gleam in his eyes. "Nope."

"I should dock your pay for meddling in your employer's private affairs," Bo grumbled as he set the unread papers aside and stomped back toward the door.

"Are you kidding?" Cornelius scoffed as Bo passed. "After today, you're going to owe me a raise."

Bo used his longer stride to outdistance the smug look on his friend's face, but once he reached the cold air of the outdoors, the heat of his temper dissolved. Ruth Fulbright was everything Cornelius had said and more. The love she had for her daughter and the passionate way she fought for Naomi's future did odd things to his heart, soothing old wounds he'd thought long healed. Or at least forgotten. But then, a boy never fully recovered from the loss of his mother's favor.

As a child, he'd been her pride and joy, the darling boy who was so handsome and bright and charmed all his mother's friends with a smile and a witty comment. But when the doctors proved unable to restore the use of his arm after the broken bones knit together, Mother no longer trotted him out to make pretty with her friends. He was hidden away. Given over to tutors and private nurses to help him adjust to his *difficulty*. She still stopped by his room at night and kissed his forehead, but she never called him her darling boy. Never praised his achievements as he learned to compensate for his disability. He was damaged goods. Her dreams for him had died, and with them, his ability to trust in a woman's regard.

Yet Ruth was different, Bo thought as he strode down the alleyway behind the buildings on Main Street. If anything happened to Naomi, Ruth would be at her side, fighting for her, picking her up when she stumbled, and cheering every forward step.

When he reached the end of the block, he crossed the street, the welcoming front porch of the Homespun Café inviting him closer. But his feet slowed. Then stopped completely.

His breathing shallowed. His palms grew moist.

For pity's sake, it was just a piece of pie!

Maybe he should go by his house first. Change . . . or something. None of the other patrons would be wearing custom-tailored suits. Yes. A change of clothes. That was what he needed.

Bo veered away from the café and headed east, his steps carrying him off the road, away from town. Away from anyone who might witness his cowardly retreat.

For that was what this was. The act of a coward. It was no use lying to himself. No one cared about his clothes. The truth was, if he showed up in something other than his usual business attire, it would only draw *more* notice. And questions. Questions he couldn't even answer for himself.

Bo drew to a halt and took stock of his surroundings. He'd managed to walk halfway to the local fishing hole before reason had caught up to him.

He shook his head at his ridiculous behavior, then turned to start the hike back to town. Cornelius would never shut up if he didn't—

A sound interrupted Bo's mental castigation and brought his head around. He searched the landscape around him but saw nothing more than a few oak trees and some brush. He closed his eyes, trying to hone in on the soft sound. Identify which direction it had come from. Because it had sounded like . . .

His eyes flew open.

Little girls.

Crying.

Targeting the sound, he took off at a dead run.

5

Bo skidded to a halt behind a trio of girls huddled near the pond. The Marshall girls, by the looks of them. All blonde, wearing matching red coats. All hunkered at the edge of the bank. The oldest was down on her knees, reaching toward the pond, the other two on either side of her.

"Come on, Naomi! Grab hold," Millicent cried before turning to her big sister. "*Please*, Margaret, you gotta pull her up. You *gotta*!"

Naomi? Bo's heart stuttered. Ruth's Naomi? Was she in the water? God help her!

Bo surged forward. "What happened?"

The girls startled at the boom of his voice. Millie took one look at him and started bawling. Her sister, Madeline, the one closest to him, just stared wide-eyed. They would be no help. Bo steered the gaping one aside and dropped to his knees beside Margaret, the eldest. Looking down toward the water, he saw a familiar pair of doe-brown eyes peering up at him in panic instead of their customary cheer.

"M-M-Mr. Azlin. Help m-m-me."

Bo's stomach sank. *Naomi*. She stood chest-deep in frigid water, mud streaking her arms and face as she clung with one hand to a three-foot stick the oldest Marshall girl had lowered.

"She fell in," Margaret said, "and the bank is too steep for her to climb out. I tried to reach her with this branch, but her feet are stuck in the mud, and her wet clothes make her too heavy for me to pull out."

Bo turned and pointed at the wide-eyed moppet who wasn't bawling. "You. Go to the café and fetch Mrs. Fulbright. Now."

Madeline launched to her feet and sprinted toward town.

He turned back to Naomi, the girl who'd warmed his heart the last few weeks with her smiles and playful antics. "I'll get you out," he vowed. "Don't be afraid."

"I'm n-n-not," she insisted between chattering teeth.

She might not be afraid, but *he* was. Terrified. Her eyelids drooped. She seemed to be having a hard time keeping them open. How long had she been in the water?

Bo rolled onto his stomach, dead prairie grass crunching and jabbing at his belly as he stretched his good arm down to Naomi. She released the branch and grabbed for his hand. Their fingers touched, but the distance was too great for him to get a good grip. Her arms splashed back down into the water, then immediately clawed at the muddy bank as she lost her balance.

"I c-can't reach!" Her gaze met his, pleading with him to save her.

Never had he imagined such capacity for protectiveness lurked inside his callused heart. Yet in that moment, it sprang forth like a lion ready to do battle with any foe that threatened his cub. "I'm coming in."

She nodded and seemed to calm at his words. A brave little thing for only seven years old. Most girls her age would be sobbing or screaming.

After yanking his shoes from his feet and shucking his coat, Bo used his good arm to balance against the pond's bank and dropped over the side into the water beside Naomi. Cold slammed into him as the water covered his belly. He sucked in a breath. *Lord, have mercy.*

Bo bent down, wrapped his left arm around Naomi's waist,

and heaved her upward. The mud, however, did not want to relinquish its prize. Naomi groaned. Bo wiggled closer and pressed his stockinged feet as close to the girl's boots as possible, shifting around her heel until the mud took on his larger feet and loosened around her smaller ones.

With a prayer for strength, he hefted again, and this time her boots pulled free. She twisted into him, latching her arms around his neck and her legs around his waist. She laid her face against his chest and clung to him like a barnacle to a ship's hull.

Bo's heart swelled with something oddly paternal. Her small arms felt good around his neck. Her cheek pressed against his shirtfront in complete faith, as if she had no doubt that he would rescue her.

Unfortunately, childlike faith wouldn't get them out of this pond. Not together, anyhow. With only one good arm, there was no way he could safely climb out of this mire carrying a passenger. His spirit was more than willing, but his flesh was frustratingly weak. Never had he hated his injury more than at this moment.

The bank was more like a cliff than a slope at this end, and stood nearly the height of his head. Getting himself out was going to be challenge enough. He'd have to slog down to a shallower exit point. He could take Naomi with him, but the faster he got her out of the water, the better. Already her hold on him was loosening, her strength waning.

He glanced up at Margaret. The sensible girl had regained her feet and stood on the bank, awaiting instructions. Her sister, Millicent, watched and hiccupped fading sobs from behind Margaret's skirt.

"I'm going to hand her up to you," he said. "Can you manage?"

Margaret nodded. "Yes, sir."

Bo turned his face toward the little girl curled against his chest. "Naomi?" He nudged her head with his chin.

"Uh-huh?" She sounded only half awake. He jostled her a bit with his arm, his pulse thumping in his veins. He needed to get her out of here and warmed up as quickly as possible.

"Naomi." He sharpened his voice, demanding her attention. "Listen to me."

She roused a bit and pulled her head back to look him fully in the face.

"I'm going to push you up to my shoulder, but I need you to help me. When I lift you, grab my head and scoot onto my shoulder. Got it?"

Her eyes focused. "Got it."

"One . . . two . . . three!" Clasping a fistful of her coat near her waist, he grunted and lifted her as high as he could.

Her hands tore free from his neck and grabbed at his head, pulling his hair. Water from her soaked clothing ran down his front. The mud shifted beneath his feet. He compensated, doing all he could to keep his stance secure while Naomi sought purchase. Finally, she found her way onto his shoulder and wrapped her right arm around his skull like a turban.

He kept his hand at her waist to ensure her safety, then called up to Margaret. "Ready?"

The girl moved her younger sister away from her, then nodded.

Bo craned his neck to peer up at Naomi. "I need you to let go of me and reach for Margaret."

"But w-w-what if I f-fall?" Her grip tightened on his head as her small body shivered uncontrollably.

"I won't let you fall. I promise." Even if he had to toss her onto the bank, he'd make sure she didn't go back into the water.

Margaret held her arms out, shortening the distance. "You can do it, Naomi. You're the bravest girl I know."

"I am?"

Bless that Marshall girl's hide. Years of getting younger sisters to do her bidding was paying dividends now. Naomi's grip eased. Her left hand let go of his shirt to reach tentatively toward the fifteen-year-old girl on the bank.

Margaret bent down and clasped Naomi's hand. "Give me your other arm too," Margaret urged.

Bo twisted slightly, aiming his left side closer to the shore as silent encouragement. As Naomi reached, Bo moved his hand from her waist to her seat to give her a boost. Margaret latched on with both arms and dragged Naomi up the side of the bank and onto dry ground.

The instant she was out of danger, Bo turned and charged through the water toward the oak tree about twenty yards away. Its roots would offer hand- and footholds. He managed to scramble out with only a few slips and ungainly lurches along the way, and hurried back to the girls.

Running footsteps and a glimpse of a familiar dark blue skirt with a great deal more exposed petticoat than usual informed Bo of Ruth's arrival, but he didn't allow that to sway him from his purpose. He scooped Naomi into his good arm and marched for home.

The girl needed to get warm, and he owned the fastest means of doing so.

"Naomi!" Ruth rushed to his side and reached for her daughter. "Mama's here, sweetie." She stroked the back of the girl's head. Bo marched on.

Naomi lifted her head slightly, her movements alarmingly sluggish. "I fell in the pond, Mama, and c-couldn't get out." Tears laced her words, the trauma finally catching up with her. "Mr. Azlin s-saved me."

Ruth jogged slightly to keep up with Bo's lengthy stride. "Yes, I saw him. He's quite the hero, isn't he?" Her voice carried a false lightness, hiding her own worry from the child she sought to comfort.

"Mm-hmm." Naomi's head lolled back down to Bo's chest as if she were too weary to hold it aloft.

"Naomi?" Fear cracked into Ruth's tone. She grabbed at Bo's arm. "Give her to me."

Bo clenched his jaw. "No." The girl would be heavy for her mother, her sodden clothing adding to her weight. They'd make better time if he carried her.

He kept moving, sticks and stones stabbing the tender bottoms

of his feet, since he hadn't taken the time to put his boots back on.
A gust of wind blew down from the north, sending a shiver over
his wet skin. He twisted slightly to shelter Naomi from the chill,
but that same movement pulled her away from Ruth.

He turned to her, a look of apology in his eyes. "She's chilled
to the bone and is having a hard time staying conscious. We need
to get her warm, and the fastest way to do that is at my house."

Margaret ran up behind them and handed something to Ruth.
Bo didn't see what it was, nor did he care. Not when Naomi's little
arms were loosening about him again.

He jostled her. "Stay awake, kitten. You hear me?"

"Kitty?" she mumbled, lifting her head a little, thank God.

A loud *meow* echoed directly behind Bo. That infernal cat was
back, but at least it wasn't tangling itself in Bo's feet. And if the
creature managed to keep the girl alert, he just might find himself
beholden to the mangy thing.

At least Ruth had ceased trying to pull her daughter from his
arms. Not that he blamed her. He felt like an ogre, keeping her
child from her, even if it was the most expedient course. If Naomi
was his and out of reach, he'd likely be going mad about now.

An acorn shell stabbed his left arch. Bo winced but didn't slow.
His house was in sight. The two-story colonial-style home was
small compared to his parents' Chicago estate, but its stalwart
brick walls and sturdy columns promised stability and protection
from the elements, exactly what Naomi needed.

He hurried up the path only to halt as he reached the front
steps. He couldn't fetch his key while holding the girl. He turned
to Ruth, surprised to find her carrying his coat and boots.

"Drop those," he ordered impatiently with a glance down to
the porch, "and take her."

Ruth did as bid, though she took an extra second or two to
hang his coat neatly over the railing before opening her arms to
her daughter. "Come here, sweetie," she crooned as Bo assisted
with the transfer.

Her gaze met his and nearly stopped his heart. Fear. Gratitude.

Determination. Love. They all bombarded him. Her walls had been demolished by her concern for her daughter, leaving nothing to stem the flow of raw emotion streaming through her. But it was the trust and hope shining above the rest that stole his breath, because those were for him.

He shoved his hand into his trouser pocket, the wet fabric combating his efforts. His fingers closed around the brass key, and he pulled, turning his pocket inside out in the process. A few coins pinged onto the ground. He ignored them, fitting the key into the lock. It clicked, and he swung the door inward.

"Follow me to the bathing chamber." Usually a gentleman would insist on the lady entering first, but Ruth didn't know where to go, and time was critical.

The accursed cat dashed inside too and ran circles around Bo's feet. "Shoo! Little miscreant."

But as Ruth crossed the threshold, Naomi beckoned to the infuriating creature. "Come, kitty."

Bo didn't have the heart to argue, though he did glare a warning at the beast not to get in his way. Thankfully, the tabby kept to the walls as Bo strode down the hallway to the bathing chamber. He and that cat might not like each other, but one thing was clear. They both adored the little girl shivering in her mama's arms.

6

Ruth followed Mr. Azlin down the corridor, clutching Naomi to her chest. Her baby was so cold. She'd follow him anywhere if it meant getting Naomi warm. Hadn't Myrtle said something about him bringing in steam generators to provide heated baths at his resort? She prayed he had a similar operation set up in his home. He must. Why else would he bring them here instead of the hotel?

Mr. Azlin banged open a door and marched into the largest water closet Ruth had ever seen. Geometric tiles in blue, green, and beige lined the floor. A chain-pull toilet stood in one corner, a basin with actual spigots on the wall beside it. Towels on a rack, a shaving mirror large enough to show Ruth from the waist up, even a padded chair in case one simply wished to sit and admire the luxury. Or remove one's boots. Probably the latter, though Ruth certainly couldn't fault anyone for engaging in the former.

Yet as awe-inspiring as the chamber was, Ruth's fascination rested on the mud-covered, dripping man tinkering with some sort of stove between the commode and the giant, claw-footed porcelain tub that encompassed the remainder of the far wall. A water tank sat atop the stove, and in remarkably little time, he had the contraption hissing with steam.

Next, he turned on the spigot above the tub, glanced back at

Naomi as though judging her size, then let the tap run until about a foot of water filled the bath.

"I don't want to scald her," he said as he began adding the heated water. He stuck his hand in and stirred. "After being half-frozen in that pond, even lukewarm water will feel hot." He glanced back at them, frowned, then looked at the boiler contraption. He shut off the hot water pipe. "It might be best for you to get her in the tub now, then add the hot water a little at a time to help her warm up gradually. I'll bring you an ewer. You can fill it halfway with heated water, then add cool from the sink. Turn this valve here to release the hot water," he instructed.

His entire manner was so intense, so *protective* toward Naomi. Ruth's heart warmed faster than the water hissing in the steam generator. Not only had he forsaken his own safety and health to rescue her daughter, his clearheaded, decisive advice now, in the aftermath, soothed Ruth's frayed nerves. They had a plan, and they had the means to accomplish it. Now it was up to her to see it through.

With Naomi's weight growing uncomfortably heavy in her arms, Ruth moved toward the tub and nodded. "I'll get her in the bath." Her gaze melded with his, and she prayed he heard her heart in her words. "Thank you, Bo."

She wanted to tell him so much more—that her whole life was wrapped up in this child, and she never could have borne losing her; that he was heroic and wonderful, and the first man she'd trusted with Naomi's welfare since Stephen died; that his hair was standing straight up in stiff spikes all over his head and made him look adorable. Which was probably why his Christian name had slipped from her lips.

Not that he seemed to mind. His icy blue eyes lost a layer of frost as he focused on *her* and not the problem he was so valiantly attempting to solve. "She'll come out of this, Ruth. I swear."

"I know." And in her heart, she did. The certainty of it had settled over her soul sometime between the sight of him thrusting Naomi out of that pond and his clipped instructions about valves and proper bathwater heating.

He held her eyes for a long moment, then gave a crisp nod and strode toward the hall. He paused in the doorway, then marched back to her side. "You sure you're all right with the generator?" His focus shifted to Naomi, concern etched into the lines of his face.

"We'll be fine," Ruth assured him around the lump in her throat.

This man had most certainly saved her daughter's life, yet it was the tenderness in his demeanor toward Naomi that was quickly turning her knees to jelly. Or maybe it was the weight of holding Naomi that caused the weakness. Either way, she'd be better off getting this far-too-handsome Good Samaritan out of the room before her heart forgot that he was her landlord and not her suitor.

Ruth cleared her throat, though that failed to dislodge the lump of emotion clogging the passage. It swelled like a ball of yeast dough as Bo reached out his hand to stroke Naomi's wet, bedraggled hair.

"I'm good with stoves, remember?" she blurted. "No need to worry."

He drew back his hand as if she'd rapped his knuckles. Ruth's stomach clenched. Why had she spoken so sharply?

"I'll fetch that ewer," he said, then left before she could utter an apology.

The door closed, and the fog clouding her mind dissipated. Naomi wasn't out of the woods yet.

"Time to get you in the bath, sweetie." Ruth sat on the chair and stripped a groggy Naomi out of her wet clothes. She had just lowered her daughter into the lukewarm water when a knock sounded on the door.

"Are you all right, Naomi?" The water wasn't deep, but Ruth still fretted over turning her back.

"Uh-huh." Naomi's eyes were open but not terribly focused.

"Here," Ruth said, fitting Naomi's fingers over the side of the tub. "Hold on to the side until I get back. All right?"

Naomi nodded.

Ruth hurried to the door, keeping her eyes on her daughter with every step. Angling her body sideways, she cracked open the door.

A black-and-white cat streaked in, ran to the tub, reared up on its hind legs, and batted at Naomi's fingers.

"Kitty!" Naomi grinned, a touch of clarity returning to her eyes. A good sign.

Confident her daughter would be all right, Ruth turned to address the man shifting awkwardly from foot to foot in the hallway. He'd changed his clothes and brushed his hair. He'd even found some shoes not caked with pond silt to put on.

"Your cat seems to have made a new friend," she said.

"Not my cat." He thrust a pitcher in her direction, his face carefully turned away from the doorway.

Ruth opened the door wide enough to collect the ewer from him, but as she reached for the handle, she caught a glimpse of her damp bodice in the mirror on the wall. Her white shirtwaist, once starched and proper, now clung to her corseted chest like egg wash on pastry, highlighting instead of hiding what lay beneath. She angled herself more fully behind the door.

"Thank you," she murmured.

He nodded without looking at her, then lifted something that had been draped over his shoulder and handed it to her as well. "A shirt," he said, his voice gruff, "for the girl. I figured she'd need something dry to wear when she got out of the bath."

The white flannel was soft to the touch, well broken-in, yet much plainer than what she usually saw him wear. This was a comfort shirt, not a work shirt. Odd that she'd never pictured him in anything but starched linen. But then, the developer of Hope Springs only presented the starched version of himself to others. Until today. Today he'd forfeited appearances altogether to save a child of no connection to himself, and exposed the soft places inside the starched shell as he continued to worry and fuss and provide.

"I'll fetch the resort doctor to take a look at Naomi and let Mrs. Lancaster know what happened. Plan to stay here tonight. You and your daughter can use my room. It's just down the hall. I'll stay at the hotel."

"You don't have to—"

138

"It's already decided." He might like to spout orders left and right, but they came from such a kind place, Ruth couldn't find fault, only appreciation. "Get her warm," he said. "Keep her warm. Stay as long as you need. Make use of anything you find."

He turned to go, but she reached out a hand and clasped his arm. Finally, he looked her in the eyes.

Ruth blinked back the misty gratitude that threatened to blur her vision, overwhelmed by the extravagance of his care. He'd thought of everything, his mind three or four steps ahead, anticipating their needs before they even materialized.

"You're a good man, Bo Azlin," she said. "One of the best I've had the privilege to meet. Thank you for all you've done. If you hadn't been there . . ." No. She wouldn't let her mind go to that dark place. Ruth gave her head a little shake, then straightened her spine, trying not to melt at the compassion she saw glowing in his sky-blue eyes. "You have my most heartfelt appreciation and deepest respect. I thank God for the day He brought you into our lives."

Ruth's words replayed in Bo's head the next morning as he made his way back to his house. All right, they'd been replaying in his head all night, stealing his sleep and conjuring dangerous dreams. Dreams of a family. Of a woman who saw him as a hero instead of a cripple. Of a little girl falling asleep tucked against his chest as he carried her home. Even of a stupid cat getting underfoot yet making a young girl laugh, thereby justifying his inclusion.

I thank God for the day He brought you into our lives.

Bo did too. Though not for the same reasons. Ruth had spoken out of gratitude, and truly he was glad to have helped her. First with the loan, then with Naomi. But he wanted more than appreciation between them. Something deeper, more lasting. Something he'd convinced himself he didn't need because he believed it out of reach. Women didn't want men like him, after all. They might want his money or his position in society or even his friendship, but they didn't want *him*.

On the other hand, what if Cornelius was right, and Ruth was different than most women? Could Bo build on her gratitude, her respect, to create a more personal connection? The idea tantalized as much as it terrified. Yet as an investor, he understood the concept of risk and reward. The Hope Springs Resort wouldn't exist today if he hadn't taken chances. Calculated chances, but chances nonetheless. He'd recognized the value of the mineral waters not only for making a profit, but for ministering to the sick and hurting, and he'd gone to work to obtain them and make them the best they could be.

Who can find a virtuous woman? For years, Bo had quoted that verse in Proverbs as a remedy for self-pity. Virtuous women were a rare commodity; therefore, there was no shame in not having one. Only a handful of lucky fellows got that privilege. He simply wasn't among them. After all, the law of supply and demand dictated a poor probability. Why would a woman settle for a man with a bum arm when a plethora of whole men were available for her choosing?

Who can find a virtuous woman? for her price is far above rubies. But what if he'd stumbled across one of those rare gems? Shouldn't he take action? Poor probability didn't equal zero probability. Jesus himself taught that any man fortunate enough to find a pearl of great price should make whatever sacrifice was necessary to obtain it. All one needed was a little boldness, a little courage, and a little faith. Surely Bo could scrape up a mustard seed's worth.

His step slowed as he reached his front walk, his pulse thumping for no reason. They weren't here, after all. Ruth was back at the café, Naomi with her. Cornelius might be the one with spies, but Bo had his way of keeping tabs as well. The main one being Dr. Ross. The resort physician had examined Naomi last night, then visited again this morning to make sure the child had suffered no long-standing effects from her ordeal. He'd reported to Bo after breakfast, assuring him that except for a little sniffle, the girl was fine. Between the warm bath, a healthy dose of honey-laced tea, prayer, and the beef broth Mrs. Lancaster had insisted on bringing over the night before, Naomi's health had been fully restored.

So why did Bo's hand tremble as he reached for his door latch?

Just because a woman he admired had slept in his bed last night, perhaps even worn one of his nightshirts, didn't mean his house was changed. It was simply brick and mortar. Same as always.

Only it wasn't. As he pushed the door open and crossed the threshold, memories assailed him. Of Ruth. Of Naomi. In his home. Walking his corridors. Following him. Trusting him. Relying on him. He swore he could feel their presence still.

Bo paused at the bathing room and peeked inside. Ruth had rigged some kind of clothesline between the windowpane and the steam generator. There hung the clothes he'd worn and discarded yesterday. He stepped closer and fingered one leg of his trousers. A slight dampness clung to the fabric, yet the mud stains were nowhere to be seen. Even his filthy stockings, the ones he'd planned to toss in the garbage, hung from the line—a bit dingier in color, perhaps, but not even a magician could have removed all that ground-in grime. The fact that she had exerted the effort humbled him.

This was a woman who had no extra funds, who no doubt stretched every ounce of wear she could from her garments out of necessity. Yet she'd laundered his clothes not out of necessity but out of appreciation and kindness, even knowing that a man of his privilege would simply take his clothing to a laundress. She must have been exhausted from worry over her daughter, yet she'd taken the time and effort to give him this gift. And not only his clothing, but his floors too. He glanced at the tile. Immaculate. He strode back into the hallway and examined the floorboards. Clean. No muddy footprints anywhere to be found.

Ruth Fulbright gave of herself with a generosity of spirit that couldn't be measured in decimals and ledger lines. Far above rubies, indeed.

With almost reverent care, Bo took the clothes down from the line, folded them, and set them on the chair. Then he refilled the steam generator's tank and lit the boiler. If he was going to the café for lunch to check on his ladies, he needed to shave. He rubbed a hand over the dark stubble furring his jaw as he leaned close to the mirror above the sink. He frowned. Piratical whiskers didn't recommend a man as an honorable suitor. It had been bad enough that he'd conducted his interview with Dr. Ross in less than pristine condition this morning on account of being too distracted last night to remember to grab his razor and mug when he'd left for the hotel, but he wouldn't subject Ruth to a slovenly appearance.

While the water heated, Bo strolled down to the kitchen to put on some coffee and discovered one final surprise. On the table sat two giant wedges of apple pie on one of the white china dinner plates from his cabinet. His mouth watered, yet it was the sheet of paper sitting beside the plate that he reached for first. He recognized the monogrammed stationary but not the childish scrawl sweeping across the page.

> *Tank you for saving me, Mr. Azlin,*
> *and for leting me sleep in your big bed.*
> *Sory your cat ran away when Mama*
> *went to the cafay to get your pie.*
> *I'll try to find her for you.*
>
> > *Your frend,*
> > *Naomi*

Then, in a more elegant hand at the bottom, Ruth had added a postscript.

> *I heard apple was your favorite. It's a day old, but hopefully it will still meet with your approval.*
> *Naomi and I would like to invite you to join us for dinner at the café this evening. 7 o'clock. Casual attire.*
> *There might even be some chocolate cake in it for you.*

As if he needed any additional incentive. His intended lunch date had just been promoted to a dinner date. And at the lady's request.

Bo straightened.

Hope was a dangerous thing to give a man, and Ruth Fulbright had just served him up two ridiculously large slices.

7

Clad in clean clothes, freshly shaven, and delightfully stuffed with apple pie, Bo stepped outside and fought the absurd impulse to whistle. As he reached behind him to pull the front door closed, a young voice called out to him.

"Mr. Azlin! Mr. Azlin! Wait!" Naomi Fulbright ran toward him, huffing slightly, a smirking ball of black-and-white fur dangling from her crossed arms. "I found Miss Creant!"

Miss *who*? Bo didn't know any Creants in Hope Springs. But he did know a little girl who shouldn't be running so hard less than a day after surviving a taxing ordeal.

"Whoa there." He quickly tugged the door closed and jogged down his porch steps to meet her. "Slow down, tadpole."

She stuttered to a stop, looked up at him, and laughed. "Tadpole. That's a funny name. Are you calling me that because I fell in the pond?"

She didn't look the least bit offended, thank heavens, but Bo eyed her in all seriousness. "It seemed appropriate. Do you like it, or should we choose something else?"

Naomi grinned and gave a decisive nod. "I like it." She leaned down to nuzzle the cat's head with her chin. "What do you think, Miss Creant? Is tadpole a good name?"

Better than *Miss Creant* for a tomcat. Of course, the beast didn't seem to mind the misnomer. It nuzzled her right back, claws fully retracted. No hint of the villainous nature he reserved for Bo. The cat hung there, purring, completely infatuated. Not that Bo could blame him.

"Miss Creant likes it too." Naomi lifted her face and, without warning, shoved the cat at him. "Here you go. She came right up to the back door of the café like she knew I'd promised to find her for you."

The cat squeaked, and Bo lurched backward, both apparently unprepared for the sudden change. Bo held out his hand to ward off the feline. Its purring had ceased, and its claws were making an appearance.

"I don't want him." Bo shook his head and stepped back.

Naomi frowned, still holding the animal out at arm's length. "Why not? She's your kitty."

"She's my . . . ?" Bo closed his eyes for a second, then opened them. "First off, she's not my kitty. Secondly, she's not a she. She's a boy cat."

"Then why did you name him Miss Creant?" Naomi's freckles winked at him as her nose crinkled.

"I didn't." What was she talking about?

"I heard you," Naomi insisted, "last night. In your house. She . . . *he* ran past you down the hall, and you called him Little Miss Creant."

Little Miss . . . all at once the pieces clicked together. Bo chuckled, then full-out laughed. Naomi started laughing too, despite the fact that she could have no idea what was so funny.

Bo wiped at his watering eyes, then gestured for Naomi to follow him to the front steps. "Come here, tadpole." He lowered himself to the top step and patted the spot beside him. She plopped down, settling the tabby on her lap. "That cat likes you far more than he likes me. All he does is tangle up in my feet when I'm trying to get somewhere. I called him a little miscreant out of frustration last night. Do you know what a miscreant is?"

She shook her head.

"A miscreant is a troublemaker. A rascal."

Naomi stroked the cat's head and back, setting him to purring again. He looked quite smug about the affection she lavished on him. "But he's not a troublemaker. He's sweet. See?" She grabbed Bo's hand—thankfully the left one was closest to her—and helped him stroke the tabby's back. The miscreant in question opened one green eye in warning, but once the stroking ensued, he quit his protest and settled back into a deep purr. Naomi giggled. "He likes you."

Bo was doubtful, but he played along. Naomi released her hold on his hand and peered up at his face with a look that clearly expected compliance with her less-than-subtle hint. She was certainly her mother's daughter. Feisty, sweet, and determined to win. Those soft brown eyes of hers turned his insides to mush, and before he'd even given the idea conscious thought, he found himself rubbing the cat behind his ears and under his chin. The soft fur was actually quite soothing. Hmm . . . If he could get a demon cat to like him, maybe he had a chance of convincing a particular café cook that he could be more to her than a pawnbroker or a landlord.

"Well," Bo said as he pulled his hand away with a reluctance that surprised him, "we can't call him Miss Creant. He needs a boy name. What do you suggest?"

Naomi's gaze moved upward, and her brow furrowed. She shifted from side to side and twined her legs beneath her. He guessed sitting cross-legged was reserved for occasions of deep pondering.

She made some thoughtful little *hems* and *haws* and tapped her finger to the corner of her mouth, but Bo barely paid attention, too distracted by the condition of the exposed sole of her shoe. The leather had been worn down to nearly nothing, and he swore he could see the black of her stocking along the edges where the stitching had been stretched out of proportion. As if her foot had grown too large for the boot and was squeezing out the sides. No wonder her feet hadn't pulled free from her shoes when he'd tried to yank her out of the mud yesterday. Her boots were probably two sizes too small.

Why hadn't Ruth used some of the money he'd loaned her for new boots? Was she really so set on earning back that scrap of jewelry that she'd let her daughter suffer? Bo eyed the coat Naomi wore over her dress. It wasn't the snug-fitting brown thing that had swum with her in the pond—that was probably still drying out somewhere—but a too-large pale blue bodice with puffed sleeves that he recalled fitting rather nicely on another woman of his acquaintance when she'd pestered him for a loan, a jacket she only wore on Sundays with her traveling suit, one of only three ensembles she owned. He had them all memorized.

No, Ruth Fulbright was not stingy when it came to her daughter. She'd literally given Naomi the shirt off her back to keep her child warm while the girl's coat dried. So as dire as the need for new shoes was, other needs must be even more pressing.

Needs a man like him could meet with a snap of his fingers. Needs a woman like Ruth would be too proud to have fulfilled through charity. Needs a child like Naomi deserved to have met no matter the method.

"I can't think of any good names," Naomi said, yanking him back to the conversation at hand. "I tried to think of black-and-white things to name him after, but *cow* and *skunk* and *chocolate cake with vanilla icing* just don't seem right."

The mention of chocolate cake immediately inspired thoughts of dinner tonight, but Bo forced his mind back to cat names.

"Black-and-white is a good place for inspiration," he said, trying to compliment the girl. After all, *skunk* seemed a perfectly sound name for the frustrating feline eyeing him with bland disdain while he groomed his front paw. "I have an uncle who loves to dress up in a fancy black suit with a white shirt and cravat. The black jacket even has tails hanging down." The uncle in question was a pompous dolt who enjoyed looking down on his younger male kin while making nice to all the ladies, ensuring his spot on the more desirable guest lists remained secure. "His name is Theodore."

The cat stopped licking his paw and glanced up at Bo, his head tilted as though trying the name on for size.

"Theodore is perfect." Naomi clapped her hands. "I'll call him Teddy." She picked up the newly dubbed beast and hugged him against her cheek.

Whether the squeeze was too much or Theodore had finally reached the end of his domesticity reserves, the cat squirmed out of Naomi's hold and scampered away.

"Teddy! Come back!" She moved to give chase, but Bo stopped her with a gentle touch to her arm.

"Let him go, tadpole. He'll come back when he's ready." She seemed fully recovered—cheeks pink, energy abundant—but he'd hate for her to relapse because she was determined to chase down a cat he didn't even want. Besides, he rather liked sitting with her. Talking. Getting to know her. Maybe even learning a bit more about her mother. "So, are you feeling better today?" he asked.

"Oh, yes." Her eyes glowed with enthusiasm as she resumed her seat. "I've never slept in a bed so big or so soft. Mama said I slept so hard, I didn't kick her even once, and usually I'm a big ol' wiggle worm."

Bo grinned, her joy infectious. "I'm glad you slept well."

Her face turned serious as she glanced sideways at him. "I do have a question I've been wanting to ask you, though."

"Oh?"

She nodded. "Mama said it wasn't my place, but now that we're friends, my place has changed, right? I mean, we are friends, aren't we?"

Those eyes. How did Ruth ever resist anything this girl requested?

"We're definitely friends," Bo said, his voice ringing with authority, ensuring there would be no room for doubt in her mind. "You can ask me whatever you like."

Her smile nearly blinded him. "Good." She twisted around to face him. "Because I want to know if you still have my heart. You haven't lost it or anything, have you? It's small and can fall into hidey-holes real easy. *I* know. Mama scolded me good when I played with it one day without asking and forgot where I left it." Her voice dropped to a whisper. "She actually cried when we found it under the bureau, and Mama *never* cries."

There must be one powerful story behind that little brooch, Bo thought as he pulled the folded handkerchief from the inside pocket of his coat. He didn't admit to the panic he had experienced when it occurred to him last night that he had flung his jacket aside with no thought to the jewel in his pocket when he'd jumped into the pond. He'd snatched the coat up from his porch on his way to fetch the doctor, breathing a sigh of relief when his fingers encountered the pin right where he'd left it. He'd been carrying it around like a sentimental fool and could have lost it. Yet when it was time to dress this morning, he'd put it right back in that pocket. Where he'd gotten used to carrying it. Next to his heart.

Holding the handkerchief out to Naomi, he flipped back the top layer of cotton with his thumb. "Here it is," he said. "Safe and sound."

Surprisingly, she made no move to take it. She just nodded and shot him an approving glance. "Just wanted to make sure."

The purple amethyst glinted in the sunlight as Bo rested it on his leg. Instead of stashing it back in his pocket, he rubbed the curved edge of the silver brooch with the pad of his thumb. "Why is this piece of jewelry so important to you and your mama?"

"Because it brings true love to whoever it belongs to."

Bo's thumb slipped off the silver edge. "What?"

Hardworking, practical, no-nonsense Ruth treasured this piece of jewelry because of its fairy-tale properties? He shook his head. That couldn't be right. Maybe it was just a story she'd told her daughter as a bedtime ritual.

"Don't worry." Naomi gave his knee a patronizing tap. "Mama says it's more of a tradition than anything magical. It's not going to zap you with a cupid arrow or anything." She grinned, the gap in her front teeth on display.

"What a relief." Though he was pretty sure that arrow had already found its mark.

Naomi grabbed her crossed ankles and rocked back and forth.

"It all started with great-great-grandmother Densbury. She was a fancy English lady who eloped to Scotland with her sweetheart. He bought her that pin as a token of his infection."

Bo smothered a laugh. "Affection, I believe. A token of his affection."

She shrugged as if one were the same as the other, then continued on with her story. "Lady Densbury gave the brooch to her servant, Sarah, when she married the fancy lady's grandson. Great-grandmother Sarah gave the brooch to Grandma Rosemary, who fell in love with Papa Alexander even though he was a southerner and war was fixin' to break out. Then Mama got the brooch and married my daddy. Four ladies with the brooch, four love matches. Mama says I'll be number five."

Bo forced a smile as he folded the handkerchief over the pin, hiding it from his view. Four love matches. Ruth and her late husband. Not exactly a man he could compete with. And if Naomi was to be number five, did that mean Ruth had given up on ever finding love for herself again? If she'd closed her heart off to love, his courtship would be a much more arduous endeavor than he'd originally speculated. Unless . . .

Technically, *he* owned the brooch at the moment. Maybe it would lead him to true love and bump Naomi down to love match number six.

And maybe magic lamps really produced genies to grant wishes.

Get your head out of those fairy stories, man. If you want to win Ruth, you need a plan rooted in reality, not fantasy.

Bo eyed Naomi's worn boots again, then turned a thoughtful look to the path where a child-sized footprint marked the ground.

Life didn't get more real than shoe leather.

8

Ruth checked the table for the fifth time in as many minutes. She nudged one of the forks a touch closer to its plate. Scooted the bread basket sitting in the center of the table a hair to the left. Smoothed the fabric of her second-best shirtwaist and tried not to wish she had something prettier to wear.

Bo was used to elegant ladies. Society ladies. She glanced at the café stove, where her fricasseed chicken over rice sat in the warming oven, green beans in one pot, skillet gravy in another. He was used to fancy chefs and fine dining too. What had she been thinking, inviting him to dinner? She couldn't possibly impress him with her ordinary offerings.

Was that what she was trying to do? Impress him? Her stomach fluttered at the inescapable answer. She laid a hand on her abdomen to still the sensation.

Good heavens. She was actually trying to impress a man. She hadn't gone to such lengths for anyone but Stephen, and even then, she and her late husband had grown up together, so there had never really been a need to gain his attention. They had just transitioned from playmates to sweethearts with the passing of time.

Her attraction to Beauregard Azlin had snuck up on her without warning. In a single day, through a series of remarkable kindnesses, he had gone from a man who stirred her curiosity to a man she admired with such esteem that she actively sought ways to spend time with him.

She waited for the guilt to hit, for a sense of disloyalty to Stephen, but beyond a bittersweet twinge of residual grief, nothing reared its head to torment her. Nothing but the fluttering in her stomach that had spread to her chest, her heart now beating an erratic rhythm and threatening to throw her breathing into disarray.

Stop fretting like a ninny and do something.

Ruth marched over to the stove, grabbed a slotted spoon, lifted the lid on the first pot she came to, and stirred the beans. Then she pried back the coffeepot lid and gave it a sniff. Yep, it still smelled like coffee. The contents hadn't changed to tea while she'd been woolgathering. She shook her head at her foolishness and had just grabbed the gravy spoon when Naomi threw the back door wide.

"He's coming!"

Thank heavens. She was running out of things to stir.

Setting the spoon aside, Ruth reached behind her back to untie the apron she'd left on until the last possible moment. She handed it to Naomi to hang on the hook, as was their usual habit at the close of day, then patted her hair to ensure all her pins remained in place.

"You look pretty, Mama." Naomi grinned at her, and the knot in Ruth's belly loosened just a tad.

"She certainly does," a male voice echoed, and that knot immediately tightened back up.

Heat that had nothing to do with the stove flushed Ruth's cheeks as she lifted her eyes to greet their guest. "Mr. Azlin. I'm so glad you could join us. Please, come in." She gestured, and he crossed the threshold. The room immediately felt smaller. More intimate, leaving her nowhere to hide. "May I . . . take your hat?"

"Only if you call me Bo for the remainder of the evening."

Gracious. Who knew the stern businessman could be such a charmer? Smiling and flirting. Her stomach would never settle at this rate. "All right." Her voice didn't quiver, but her fingers trembled as she reached for his hat. "I hope you like chicken . . . Bo."

His blue eyes lit up when she said his name. How had she ever thought them icy? They might be pale in color, but they had the richness of a blueberry compote—warm, sweet, and rather addictive.

"Love it."

It took her a moment to recall that they were discussing chicken and not his eyes. She smiled, then retreated behind the most comfortable presence in the room. "Naomi, would you show our guest to his seat?"

"Sure!" Without an ounce of the shyness afflicting her mother, Naomi bounded forward, grabbed Bo's good hand, and dragged him toward the table. "Mama and I usually just sit at the work table when we eat supper after the café closes, but we wanted tonight to be special, so we carried in one of the tables from the main dining room. It was a little tricky getting it through the doorway," she jabbered, "but we turned it on its side and squeezed it through."

"I'm impressed," Bo said, giving his full attention to Naomi, seeming to actually care about what she was saying. Ruth's heart warmed a little more. He was good with her. Not just in emergencies, but in the little things—the things that made the biggest difference in the long run.

She hung his hat from the same hook that held her apron, rather liking the sight of the two items together, then retrieved the chicken from the warming oven and moved to serve.

Bo stood as she approached, but she motioned him back down. "Please. No need for formality."

"'Cause we're all friends. Right, Mr. Bo?" Naomi bounced in her chair, her face glowing with admiration for the man taking his seat beside her.

His eyes lingered on Ruth for a long heartbeat, then swiveled to her daughter. "Right, tadpole."

"Tadpole?" Ruth queried as she dished out a healthy portion of chicken and rice onto Bo's plate.

He reddened slightly. An adorable effect on one so starched and proper.

"It's 'cause I fell in the pond," Naomi announced, pride lacing her words. "Isn't it great?" She beamed, her adoration of her rescuer obvious. Bo probably could have dubbed her *goose liver*, and she would have been equally pleased.

Ruth spooned a much smaller portion onto her daughter's plate. "It fits you perfectly, with all your squirming. Sit still in your chair, please, young lady."

Naomi darted a sideways glance at Bo, mouthed something that looked like *wiggle worm*, stifled a giggle, then straightened in her seat. "Yes, ma'am."

With Naomi's chatter serving as a buffer, Ruth eventually relaxed and enjoyed the evening. Bo complimented her cooking and ate every bite she placed before him, including two thick slices of chocolate cake—he apparently had a sizeable sweet tooth. He even dragged the table back to the dining room for her while she washed the dishes, a notable accomplishment for a man with only one good arm. He credited his young assistant for their success, claiming her steering of the table legs made all the difference as he navigated the doorway, but Ruth knew he was being modest.

Mostly because she'd been watching him out of the corner of her eye. It was hard not to appreciate such a masculine display.

Afterward, he lingered in the kitchen as if waiting for something. What, she wasn't quite sure. But she wasn't about to shoo him away, not when she enjoyed his company so much. But once all the food was stored and the dishes were back in the cabinets, she had no reason to delay bringing the evening to a close.

She retrieved his hat and handed it over with regret. "Thank you for joining us tonight."

His fingers brushed hers beneath the brim. An accident, or had it been intentional? Heavens, but she wanted it to be intentional. Even if that made her the biggest fool in Texas.

"I had a most enjoyable evening." He glanced down at his shoes, then slowly cranked his chin back up to meet her gaze. "May I have the honor of walking you ladies home?"

Ruth's heart pounded as a shy smile curved her mouth. "That would be lovely. Thank you."

By the time Ruth closed up the café, Naomi had claimed Bo's good hand and was already dragging him around the building toward the main road with some excuse about wanting to see if Teddy was about. He allowed Naomi to lead him away, a grin of pleasure softening his features as he cast an apologetic glance over his shoulder.

Ruth didn't mind. Not really.

All right, maybe a little.

It didn't seem very mature to be jealous of her seven-year-old daughter monopolizing the attention of the man she had just cooked and, yes, primped for, but the twinges in her chest could be explained no other way. Perhaps she should be alarmed by how quickly Naomi was growing attached to Bo, but Ruth's practical nature shoved the worry aside. After losing her father, Naomi needed a positive male influence in her life, and the more Ruth learned about Beauregard Azlin, the more positive attributes she uncovered. Besides, trying to protect Naomi from the pain of loss should Bo grow weary of his friendship with a child would only steal the girl's current joy. Pain might come later; it might not. Life held no guarantees, a fact of which both Ruth and her daughter were acutely aware. So when friendship or the hint of something more presented itself, one faced two options—either hide away from the possibility of pain or stride forward with the hope of discovering joy.

Ruth had always been more of a strider than a hider. Which was why she quickened her pace to catch up to Bo as he chatted with her daughter about cats and their penchant for tree climbing, then slipped her left hand into the crook of his right arm.

His face jerked toward her, his eyebrows shooting upward. Did no one ever touch his right arm? Perhaps it caused him discomfort. No, her action had startled him, but she saw no evidence of pain in his face. Perhaps the discomfort belonged to others, people afraid they might somehow catch his affliction. Well, *she* wasn't afraid, and he shouldn't be, either. Not about what others might think when they saw him or about what they might do. He was a good man. A strong man. And she was proud to be on his arm tonight.

She curled her fingers lightly around his bicep to secure her hold and wondered if he could feel her touch. The spark of heat in his eyes said yes. Then he did the most remarkable thing—he squeezed her hand closer to his side. He might not be able to move his right wrist or hand, but he could move his upper arm. At least a little.

His lips curved into a smile that sported none of the playfulness or indulgence he'd showered on Naomi. No, this smile exuded something much warmer and masculine, the kind of smile a man gave a woman whose company he found pleasing.

"Shall we?" he asked.

She returned his smile in equal measure. "We shall."

9

I noticed a certain reclusive resort owner lingering after services yesterday to speak with a lovely young cook," Myrtle said as she sashayed into the café kitchen, her tangerine- and teal-striped ensemble only half as bright as her eyes. "Wonder what was going on there?"

"I can't imagine," Ruth said, her arms elbow-deep in soapy water as she washed the dishes from the Monday breakfast service. She was surprised it had taken Myrtle this long to say anything. She'd half expected her employer to be waiting on the back stoop when she got in this morning, ready to quiz her on how things went on Saturday evening.

Myrtle snorted in disbelief as she shuffled over to the sink, took up a dish towel, and started drying. "You can imagine better than anyone else in town."

Ruth glanced over at her friend. "He spent more time talking to Naomi than to me. Or being talked *to*. Naomi carried most of the conversation."

"The little ladybug might have been the one doing the talking, but it was her mama who dominated Bo Azlin's attention. He couldn't take his eyes off you!" Myrtle crowed like one of her roosters and elbowed Ruth in the side. "And I ain't the only one to notice."

Wonderful. Now Ruth had become the topic of town gossip. Not exactly her aim when she'd rushed out of the service to catch Bo before he could sneak off to his house. Her thoughts had been for him. Hiding away from the town only made him more of a curiosity. He needed to live among them, give them the chance to grow accustomed to him. And it had worked. After she effectively delayed him, several others approached to speak to him as well. Most already knew him from the resort, but not all. It had been a good start.

And if her eyes had met his more than once across the churchyard as she conversed with other, less interesting people, well, that couldn't be helped. When a man entered one's thoughts every thirty seconds, glancing his way only every two minutes demonstrated admirable restraint, in her estimation.

"You're good for him." The teasing vanished from Myrtle's voice, leaving only sincerity ringing through the kitchen.

Ruth handed the last dish to her friend and wiped her hands on her apron, not quite sure how to reply. "I want to be," she admitted. "Heaven knows he's good for us. Naomi glows when she's around him, and after the episode at the pond . . . well, he's more than earned my respect. But we come from such different backgrounds. He's high society, and I'm . . . backwoods."

"All that's window dressin', Ruth, and you know it. Strip them society folks of their money, and they'd be just as backwoods as you or me, only with snooty airs that would make them harder to get along with. On the other hand, put you in a fancy gown and throw you into a society gathering, and you'd fit in with no problem. You're educated, refined, and I'd bet the farm you know the difference between a salad fork and a dessert one."

Lord love Myrtle for her unique way of putting things into perspective. Ruth couldn't help but grin. "Yes, ma'am. My mama made sure to pass down the essentials of navigating a properly laid table before I left Tennessee."

"I figured as much." Myrtle winked, then tossed her towel onto the counter before placing a motherly hand on Ruth's shoulder.

"Don't let the numbers get in the way, darlin'. If you find value in the man himself, that's what matters. If he finds the same value in you, that'll balance the ledger. Your lack won't matter, and his abundance won't neither. A prairie fire could sweep through town tomorrow and destroy everything Azlin has built, leaving him as poor as you are now. But his character, his heart, would remain. If that's the treasure you seek, then quit thinking about how you don't measure up and start thinking about how you can give him something that's beyond measure altogether."

Myrtle's words lingered in Ruth's mind throughout the week, leading her to change her routine. Instead of simply waving to Bo as she walked Naomi back to the café from school, she stopped and engaged him in conversation—not the most private exchange, with him being on a third-floor balcony, but by Wednesday she'd lured him down to the main floor. He even strolled with them all the way to the café. The first time he did so, she had rewarded him with pie. After that, the pattern was set. He waited for them at the corner, they walked and talked, she fed his sweet tooth, and each day she fell a little deeper in love.

"Mama, what's that?" Naomi pointed a mittened hand toward their house as they hurried home that Friday evening after closing up the café. They huddled close for warmth against the chill of the first truly frosty evening of the season.

"I don't know." Their little cottage sat beyond the reach of the streetlamps lighting the downtown area, and with dark falling so early this time of year, Ruth couldn't discern anything beyond a shadowy square near her door. "Shall we investigate?"

Naomi grinned, detached from Ruth's side, and sprinted ahead, leaving her mother smiling at her enthusiasm. The north wind might be stinging their cheeks and freezing their fingertips, but it couldn't dull the excitement of a mystery waiting to be solved.

"It's a box!" Naomi called from her hunkered-down position on the porch. "With our names on it. Can I open it? Please?"

Ruth reached the front stoop, removed the mitten on her right hand, and retrieved the key from her coat pocket. "Let's get inside first and stoke up the fire in the stove before our noses turn blue."

Only, when they got inside, the fire had already been stoked. When Ruth pushed open the door, warmth from the front room enveloped them like a welcoming hug. *What on earth?*

Naomi bustled in behind her with the unwieldy package, bumping Ruth aside and reminding her to close the door again before all the delicious heat escaped.

Bo. It had to be. No one else had a key.

Her pulse flickered. Her practical side warned against reading too much into the gesture. He was a kind man. A landlord looking out for the well-being of his tenants. Yet her heart scoffed. A considerate landlord might repair a wobbly step or seal a leaky window. Not warm a room in anticipation of her arrival. Such an action spoke of intimacy. It left her feeling cherished, pampered. Loved?

A glow filled the room as Naomi lit the lamp on the kitchen table, where the mystery box now sat. "I've got the scissors," she crowed, snatching Ruth's sewing shears from her knitting bag. "Can I cut the string?"

Still in a bit of a daze, Ruth nodded as she moved toward the kitchen table. While her daughter struggled with the string, Ruth fumbled with the buttons on her coat. She managed to strip the outer garment off at the same time Naomi severed the twine and tugged the lid free.

She yanked the packing paper aside like a pirate clearing sand from atop a buried treasure. A folded sheet of ivory stationery fluttered to the floor, and Ruth bent to retrieve it. Before she could do more than note the existence of handwriting on the inside, Naomi gasped and brought Ruth's attention back to the box. Her own breath sucked in at the sight.

Shoes. Two pair. Both brand new. The smaller pair in beautiful black leather, a sturdy design with low, flat heels, double soles, and box-tip toes. Perfect for an adventurous girl as likely to climb trees as to pick wildflowers. And the larger ones? Ruth ran a hand over the chocolate-brown Dongola leather, soft and pliable even before being worn. No fancy heel to make a lady's feet hurt after standing all day, but a practical low heel that managed to be stylish even as it promoted comfort.

"Can I try them on, Mama?" Naomi asked in a hushed voice, wonder infusing her tone.

"I . . . I'm not sure." An unmarried woman of good character didn't accept gifts of clothing or other costly items from a man not related to her by blood or marriage. She supposed a widow might be permitted more latitude, but she couldn't afford to be careless with her reputation. However, Naomi desperately needed new shoes—shoes Ruth had been saving for yet hadn't figured out how to purchase while still reserving enough funds to buy back her brooch before Christmas. "Let me read the note first." Both to confirm who the shoes were from—though she was pretty sure she had that figured out—and to buy herself time to decide whether or not she could accept the gift. "Why don't you hang up your coat, scarf, and mittens? Mine too, please."

That should give her a couple minutes, though knowing Naomi, she'd rush through the job in seconds in order to come stare at the shoes some more. Not that Ruth could blame her. She was dying to see if the brown pair fit. How he had estimated their sizes, she had no earthly idea, but they looked to be nearly perfect.

Forcing her gaze away from the shoes, Ruth lifted the folded sheet of fine stationery and opened it.

Ruth,

I know it is a bit irregular for an unmarried man to offer a lady of his acquaintance a gift such as this, but I pray you will accept. It pains me to think of my two favorite ladies walking into winter with inadequate footwear.

His two favorite ladies.

Ruth pressed her lips together in an effort to contain her delight, but a smile stretched across her face anyway as she forced her eyes back to his slightly lopsided penmanship.

Please don't view this offer as charity, but as a gift between friends. No, that's not completely accurate. If I am to be honest, I must admit that something more than friendship prompted this gift.

Ruth's heart pounded in her chest, the beats so strong that she began to feel a little light-headed.

I've come to care for you, Ruth, a great deal. Naomi too. And while a gift of clothing is not quite proper for an unattached lady to accept from a gentleman of no connection to her, I believe social etiquette would permit such a gift to be exchanged should there be an understanding between the parties involved.

So allow me to officially declare my intentions. I would like very much to pay my addresses to you, Ruth.

The paper trembled in her hand as she read the words. Was this really happening? Or had some cruel trick of the flickering lamplight changed completely ordinary words into a reflection of her hopes?

Forgive my cowardice for writing of such personal matters in a note instead of speaking them in your presence. However, I wanted to grant you the freedom to consider my request without any pressure to accept. The shoes are yours to keep, whatever you decide. I ordered them from an out-of-town shop, so no one will know their origin. Your reputation is safe. All I ask is that if you decide not to accept my suit, you wait until Monday to wear the shoes. I'll drop by the café for a piece of pie tomorrow afternoon. If you are not wearing the shoes, I will have my answer and save us both the embarrassment of speaking of such things.

Whatever you decide, know that you will continue to own my respect, and Naomi will always be welcome to visit Theodore at my home. (The furry miscreant has moved in despite my objections.)

Sincerely,
Bo

Ruth fumbled for the back of the chair closest to her, scraped it backward, and toppled into the seat as her knees buckled.

"Mama?"

Ruth, her mind sluggish due to the fantastical ideas swimming about her with dizzying speed, slowly lifted her head to regard her daughter. Naomi had returned to the box, her old shoes stripped off to reveal stockinged feet wriggling with anticipation. Her little hands clasped the edges of one of the black boots as her eyes pleaded for permission.

Trying them on couldn't hurt anything, could it?

"All right."

Naomi squealed and snatched the boot from the box.

"But we'll need to have a discussion before we decide if we keep them," Ruth cautioned, her sensible nature finally reasserting itself and clearing some of the fog from her befuddled brain. Accepting a suitor would affect not only Ruth, but Naomi as well.

"Yes, ma'am." The answer came quickly and without true understanding, but explanations and decisions could wait.

They had shoes to try on.

Ruth reached for the buttonhook Naomi had dropped on the floor beside her discarded shoes, and began loosening the fastenings of her worn boots, the cracked leather and paper-thin soles offering no resistance. Yet her mind drifted from her task.

Instead it lingered on the man who knew her well enough not to court her with flowers or candy, or even shoes with fancy stitching and fashionable heels. He'd chosen practical items of high quality. Shoes that would last. That would offer protection and comfort. Much like the man himself. A chivalrous man who went out of his way to bless her with a warm home on a cold night. A man who spoke of affection for her and her child, yet offered his gift not as a bribe to win her affection in return but simply to meet a need he'd cared enough to observe in the first place.

As her left shoe hit the floor, Ruth's heart demanded she accept him as her suitor. But how would that affect their business relationship? If things didn't work out between them, she would be completely at his mercy. He owned the house she and Naomi lived in. And her brooch—what if he refused to sell it back to her? She could find another place to live, but nothing could replace the heirloom that meant so much to her family.

Even as that fear reared its ugly head, her heart and common sense smacked it back down. Bo wasn't petty. He was a good man, honorable and trustworthy. Why, it was *she* who would be dishonorable if she accepted his addresses simply to ensure the return of her brooch.

By her accounting, she still owed him $8.75. If she paid him $1.75 a week, a figure she should be able to manage if no unexpected expenses arose, she'd have her debt paid off four days before Christmas. Giving her plenty of time to gift the heirloom to Naomi as she'd planned. And perhaps she'd prove to Bo in the process that the value she saw in him wasn't found in his wealth but in his character.

Her resolution solidified, Ruth pried off her right shoe and reached for the beautiful chocolate leather boot closest to her in the box. She slid her foot inside, but instead of instant comfort, something pointy jabbed the ball of her foot. Frowning, she pulled her toes from the shoe and turned the boot upside down, expecting a rock or cobbler's tack to tumble free.

Instead, what hit her hand was a familiar silver pin, the intertwined hearts bringing an instant tear to her eye.

10

The following morning, not long after dawn, Bo stood outside in the freezing air, his attention glued to the cottage door across the way.

Theodore meowed at his feet, grumpy at being roused from his cozy new bed in Bo's kitchen even though he seemed equally invested in the outcome of their reconnaissance. Bo had told Ruth he'd visit the café that afternoon, which he would, but after an agonizing night of guessing and second-guessing and quadruple-guessing what her answer might be, the torment had driven him from his bed and out into the cold.

He hunkered farther into the upturned collar of his coat, his right arm throbbing in the frigid temperatures. Gloves were nearly impossible for him to manage without assistance, so the best he could do was have his tailor line his coat pockets with fur. It worked well enough for short periods of time but became less effective the longer he remained outdoors. He'd passed the point of effectiveness about fifteen minutes ago. Bo lifted his left hand to his mouth and huffed warm breath onto it, his exhalation visible in the cold. Theodore leaned against Bo's ankle, his tail wrapping around Bo's leg.

"We're a couple of fools, aren't we? Hiding behind trees and freezing our toes off. All to catch a glimpse—"

The words died as if lopped off by a butcher's cleaver. For at that moment the door of the cottage opened and two young ladies bundled in coats, mittens, and scarves stepped outside.

Bo ducked more fully behind the tree sheltering him from sight even as his attention focused on the feet traipsing toward him. Feet frustratingly obscured by feminine skirts. Thanking God for the shorter skirts worn by children, Bo shifted his focus to Naomi, his pulse thumping when he recognized the new shoes he'd selected. Surely that meant Ruth wore hers as well.

But what if she misinterpreted his intent in the note and allowed Naomi to wear her new shoes while holding her own back as a silent refusal? What *exactly* had he written? Bo scrubbed at his forehead. He'd rewritten the letter so many times, he could barely recall. He'd told her he would see her at the café. He knew that. But had he only mentioned *Ruth* waiting on wearing the shoes until Monday? He couldn't be sure.

Yeowl!

A feline screech rent the air. Theodore clawed halfway up the tree trunk and sprang at the females scurrying past.

"Teddy!" Naomi called in delight, but it wasn't the girl the troublesome cat targeted. He dove straight for Ruth, launching himself beneath her petticoats as though a mouse hid within the flannel ruffles.

Ruth gasped and sputtered, but most importantly, she lifted her skirts to extricate herself from the black-and-white menace. A menace that had just earned himself a heaping pile of filet mignon scraps. For beneath those petticoats were a pair of lovely, trim ankles encased in unscuffed brown leather boots that were undeniably new. Undeniably *not* sitting in a box waiting for Monday.

Suddenly light-headed, Bo closed his eyes and pressed his head into the trunk of the tree, his mind no longer cognizant of the cold, the scratch of the oak's bark against his skin, or even the sound of footsteps continuing down the street.

He had capacity for only one thought.

She'd worn the shoes.

"All right, what's going on?" Cornelius dropped his pencil and stared across his desk. "I know you enjoy these accounting meetings more than the average employer, Bo, but I fail to see a reason to smile when our reservations have dropped by ten percent."

Bo brushed off his manager's concerns, the day far too fine to worry about a few flagging numbers. "They always dip in December, Corny. You know that. People want to be with their families during the holidays."

Family. A picture rose in Bo's mind of he and Ruth sitting in his parlor—*their* parlor—a fire in the hearth, Naomi playing with Theodore on the floor, Ruth knitting something soft and warm, him sitting beside her on the settee, rubbing her neck with fingers that were supposed to be turning the pages of the book in his lap but were more interested in her skin and the shy smile on her lips.

"*Corny?* Since when have you ever called me . . . Oh, ho. I see how it is. You've gone and done it, haven't you? You've fallen in love with the Widow Fulbright."

Bo scowled. "You make her sound like a doddering old hag."

"Yet I hear no denials regarding the more significant portion of my observation." Cornelius crossed his arms and leaned back in his chair, the grin creasing his face annoyingly smug. "Have you told her?"

Bo fidgeted. "I've made my intentions clear." In a letter.

"Intentions are one thing, but a woman wants to know how a man *feels* about her."

"And you're such an expert on women." Bo rolled his eyes and pushed out of his chair. "If we're not going to finish the accounting, I might as well return to my office and work on the inventory orders."

"*I* wasn't the one staring off into space like a lovesick puppy, ignoring the reservation numbers."

Bo pivoted and leveled a stare at his manager, who had the audacity to smirk. "You can be replaced, you know."

Cornelius chuckled, not an iota of remorse in sight. "Uh-huh. About as easily as you can work the inventory without being distracted by thoughts of Mrs. Fulbright."

"Impertinent scoundrel."

"Lovesick puppy."

Bo dismissed the manager's rejoinder with a wave of his hand. "You already used that one. It doesn't count."

"Maybe not, but that doesn't make it any less true." Cornelius eyed him as he tapped the reservation lists into a tidy pile.

Bo was saved from making a reply by a knock on the door. Not that he would have rebutted his friend's claim, anyway. Cornelius, as usual, was utterly correct.

"Pardon the interruption," the resort clerk said as he stepped halfway into the room, "but there's a Mrs. Fulbright downstairs to see Mr. Azlin. I know I'm supposed to direct all inquiries to you, Mr. Palmer, but since it's Mrs. Fulbright . . ."

"You did the right thing, Donaldson," Bo said before Cornelius could make some vexing comment about how his feelings were obvious to everyone else, so why not just come out and admit them to the one person who really mattered. "Give me a minute to conclude my business with Mr. Palmer, then show her to my office."

Donaldson nodded and backed out of the room.

Cornelius shot Bo a wry look. "Sure you don't need me to act as your go-between?"

"Keep that up, and you'll go *between* my fist and the floor."

Cornelius laughed, full and loud. Bo chuckled too, then grabbed the papers he still needed to review and strode out of the manager's office. The moment the door closed behind him, his stomach clenched.

She was here. Coming to see him. Now. Mid-morning. A delightful surprise, yet one that inspired uneasy thoughts. What had precipitated her visit when she knew he'd be coming by the café later this afternoon? Had she changed her mind?

Bo strode down the hall to his office, his heart rate ticking up much higher than the short jaunt warranted.

167

And Donaldson, frustratingly efficient man that he was, didn't afford Bo much time to recover. He'd barely been in his office a full minute before the clerk's sharp knock rapped on the door.

"Enter," he called.

And she did. Her coat folded over one arm, her dark blue skirt swishing just enough for him to catch sight of a chocolate-brown boot toe that nearly made him sigh in relief.

She still wore the shoes.

Though she also wore an expression that he couldn't classify as lovestruck. It was more a look of cautious optimism mixed with determination, not unlike the one she'd worn when they'd first met, only this time a depth of personal connection lingered beneath it, bringing Bo across the room to her side without conscious thought.

He nodded to Donaldson, and the clerk backed away, closing the door behind him. Once alone, Bo placed his hand at Ruth's back and steered her deeper into the room. "It's good to see you. I, ah, like your shoes."

Pink tinted her cheeks, making Bo smile and relieving a bit of the nerves jerking his insides back and forth like a tug-of-war rope.

Her green eyes found his. "Can we talk for a minute? About . . . the shoes?"

The tugging rope in his gut snapped taut in an instant. "Of course." He led her toward the pair of chairs in front of his desk, but she balked, tossing her coat into the first seat and spinning toward him. She placed her palm on his chest. Paralysis hit his lungs at the delicate pressure.

"Bo, if we are to court, I think we need to make a few things plain right from the outset. To ensure there are no misunderstandings."

"All right," he managed, his lungs firing again now that he knew courtship hadn't been removed from the negotiation table.

At the same time, he braced himself for what she might want him to understand. That her heart wouldn't be part of the bargain, that it would always belong to her first husband? His chest constricted. Could he agree to such an arrangement? He loved her, yes, but he wanted her love in return, not just an amiable companion.

She stepped back from him and retrieved something from her coat pocket. Then she reached for his left hand, opened it, and carefully placed a familiar silver pin into his palm.

"Returning this to me was a generous gesture," she said, her eyes slowly lifting from the brooch to his face, "and it assured me of your honorable nature, but I need you to take it back."

"Why?" Bo kept his hand open, giving her the option to change her mind. The heirloom meant the world to her. He wanted her to have it.

Ruth folded his fingers over the pin and wrapped both her hands around his. His skin warmed at her touch, as did his heart.

"Pride plays a role, I suppose," she said, her lips twitching in a self-deprecating smile. "I want to accomplish what I set out to do. But there's more to it than that." Her face softened as her eyes held his with a tenderness that made him want to forget all about jeweled pins and just hold her tight against his chest and never let go. "I want to make it clear to you, and to anyone else who might feel the need to speculate, that I am not accepting your suit because of any financial benefit such a connection might bring me."

Mouth suddenly dry, Bo rasped out the question attempting to claw through his rib cage. "Then why *are* you accepting my suit?"

Her hands still cupping his closed fist, she lifted it between them. "Because, Beauregard Azlin, you are strong and capable, good to my daughter, kindhearted, and a man a woman can rely on."

Was it wrong for him to feel disappointed by such a flattering answer?

"But most of all," she continued, and his pulse ratcheted back up, "I'm accepting your courtship because every time I look at you, something comes to life inside me, something I thought dead and beyond resurrection." She brought his hand up to her lips and brushed a kiss against his knuckles, a kiss so sweet and soul-stirring, he felt it travel up his arm, through his chest, and directly into his heart. "You make me believe that love might actually find me twice in one lifetime, and knowing what a blessing love with the right man can be, I can't let that chance slip away without reaching for it."

"Neither can I." And to prove it, he reached for the amazing woman before him.

He tucked the brooch into his vest pocket as he moved, wrapped his good arm around her waist, and tugged her close. "I love you, Ruth," he murmured as her arms twined about his neck. "With all that I am."

His lips found hers, and when she lifted up to return his kiss with the same passion surging in his veins, all doubts fled. The wounds his mother had left on his soul, his contempt for the weakness of his injured arm, the haunting memories of social climbers who'd been willing to settle for a cripple with a healthy bank account—they all vanished when Ruth's fingers tangled in the hair at his nape and her mouth melded with his in a way that made him feel stronger, more whole, and more confident than ever before.

If this woman loved him, nothing could hold him down.

The kiss lingered, deepened, and built a hunger inside him he had to fight to contain. But contain he did, for her sake. Loosening his hold, he leaned back, watching as her lashes slowly lifted. He smiled at her, tenderness welling up inside him as he gazed at her. Unable to help himself, he stroked the side of her cheek. So soft. So . . . perfect. Just like the woman herself.

Neither spoke for a long moment, perhaps afraid to banish the magic. But eventually Ruth's practical nature shone through.

"I should get back to the café." Yet her feet didn't move.

"And I should get back to work." Though he made no attempt to do so.

Silence descended again until Ruth blurted, "Naomi approves." She glanced away, that lovely pink returning to her cheeks. "Of our courtship. She's rather fond of you, you know."

Bo grinned. "I'm rather partial to the little tadpole, myself."

"She's singing in the school program on Christmas Eve. Will you come?"

"Of course." He might not be partial to social gatherings, but his regard for Ruth and her daughter overrode minor discomforts.

"Good, because I don't want you to hide away anymore, Bo. This is your town, your people. You should be among them." She vibrated with a fervor on his behalf that shocked him. "Your injury is part of who you are and nothing to be ashamed of. Small-minded folks might whisper about it, but even they will get bored once the mystery wears off."

"You don't understand," he explained. "My clients come to the resort for healing and relief from pain. It's not good business to be a walking advertisement for the limitations of the available treatments."

She poked a decidedly non-affectionate finger into his chest. "Do you advertise that the waters will heal muscular or nerve injuries?"

"No, but—"

"Do the mineral baths you take offer relief of any kind?"

Bo shook his head. "They help with the pain and stiffness, but—"

Another poke. "Have you ever considered that some of your clients might be encouraged to know that the owner of the resort isn't just an entrepreneur looking to make money off their poor health, but a man who uses the waters himself and finds benefit in the treatments?"

He had no reply to that, which apparently satisfied his little champion.

His champion. How had that happened? He was supposed to be her defender, her protector, yet here she stood, bristling on his behalf and pushing him to be a better version of himself. A version he wanted to be . . . for her. A version he suddenly believed he could be *because* of her.

He stood a little straighter and nodded in what he hoped was a serious vein—hard to manage when he wanted to grin like an idiot. "I'll make an effort to be more visible," he promised.

"And involved?"

She was a bulldog. And, oh, so kissable when she was crusading on his behalf.

"And involved."

She smiled, and the light of it filled the room. "Good. Then I only have two more requests."

He raised a brow. "Oh?"

"First, no official proposals until the brooch is paid off."

He shrugged. "All right." Easy enough. Proposal or not, he'd staked his claim, and she'd agreed. He could hold off on the formality. "And second?"

"Would it be all right if I came by to visit you around this time a few days a week? The café is slow after breakfast, and Myrtle has given me permission to run errands. It's just . . . I love my daughter, don't get me wrong, and I enjoy the times when all of us are together, but it's hard to conduct a proper courtship with a seven-year-old chaperone."

Memories of the kiss they'd shared swarmed his mind and fueled his imagination. "Come every day, if you like," he said, his voice a tad husky. "I'll be here."

11

CHRISTMAS EVE

Bo waved to a pair of resort guests out for a little shopping as he hurried down Main Street toward his house. He had a luncheon appointment to keep, and not even the haughty sniffs of the well-dressed man and his mother could dim his mood.

True to his word, Bo had ceased avoiding situations that placed him in the path of others. No more back staircases, alleyways, or side entrances. If he needed to go somewhere, he just went and made a point to be friendly with the people he encountered along the way. He still allowed Cornelius to handle the daily management of the resort, but he no longer dodged the clientele. The locals had accepted him quite readily, just as Ruth had predicted, and many of the resort guests had proven tolerant as well. Some even expressed genuine interest in his personal experience with the mineral waters. But in truth, their reactions simply didn't matter as much to him as they once did. He had the good opinion of the woman he loved. All others paled in comparison.

A snowflake caught in Bo's lashes as he strode past the courthouse, leaving the last-minute Christmas bustle behind. It had been snowing off and on all morning. Not hard enough to accumulate, but enough to give a powdered-sugar dusting to the trees and rooftops. A beautiful setting for an indoor picnic with a beautiful lady. A picnic he'd gone to great lengths to ensure would be a private affair.

When he reached his house, he stomped his shoes to knock off the worst of the snow and mud, then pushed the front door wide and stepped inside.

"Hello?" he called.

A female whirlwind rushed through the parlor doorway with a welcoming grin that tightened Bo's chest in the best possible manner. She launched herself at him, and he caught her easily with his good arm, the two of them having fine-tuned the maneuver over the last few weeks.

He jiggled his nose against her neck until she laughed.

"Stop, Mr. Bo," she protested between giggles. "That tickles!"

"That means I'm doing it right, tadpole." And just for good measure, he jiggled again before taking pity on the girl and letting her down.

As soon as Naomi's feet touched the ground, she grabbed his hand and dragged him toward the parlor. "Come on, Mr. Bo. Teddy and I set everything up."

Sure enough, a blanket lay spread on the floor near the large front window, which offered a stunning view of the snowy holiday landscape.

"Teddy! That's Mr. Bo's lunch, not yours." Naomi released his hand and ran forward, valiantly tearing an egg salad sandwich away from the transgressing cat, splattering bits of egg across the blanket in the process. She turned and handed Bo the squished remains of what had no doubt been a work of culinary art when Ruth had packed it. "Sorry about that. Teddy's still learning his manners."

Bo smiled at her and accepted the gift, trying not to look at it too closely. He'd eat a few bites on the crust side to circumvent any feline contamination before he declared himself full. "That's all right. I'm here more for the company than the food anyway." He winked at her, and her grin grew wide enough to expose the half-grown tooth working to fill the gap in her smile.

"Mama said you had something 'portant to talk to me about."

He nodded. "I do. Shall we sit?"

She plopped down next to a second sandwich, one completely unmolested by cat slobber, and crossed her legs while she waited for him to sit.

He settled himself across from her on the blanket and leaned slightly toward her. "I love you and your mama very much, Naomi."

She grinned. "We love you too, Mr. Bo."

His heart warmed, as it always did when on the receiving end of this sweet girl's esteem. She lavished her affection with generous abandon. Having her as a permanent part of his life . . . well, he could only guess at the richness such a blessing would bring.

"When a man wishes to marry a woman," Bo pontificated, wanting to give the occasion a fitting level of solemnity, "he typically approaches her father or other family member to seek permission for her hand."

"Why just her hand?" Naomi frowned, her nose scrunching up as she held her right hand up for inspection. "Doesn't he want the rest of her too?"

Bo fought down a chuckle. "Yes, of course. The hand is symbolic. A woman goes from holding her father's hand as a little girl to holding her husband's hand when she marries. The husband takes over the responsibility for her protection and well-being. The man and woman become partners, walking through life side by side, hand in hand."

Naomi nodded, then angled a glance up at him. "And you want to marry my mama."

"Yes, I do." More than anything. "And since her father is not around for me to ask, I thought I should seek permission from another member of her family." He tapped her knee. "You."

Naomi sat up straight, her brown eyes widening.

"Do I have your permission to marry your mama, tadpole?"

"Oh, yes, Mr. Bo. Yes!" She jumped across the space between them, grabbed him about the neck, and bowled him over.

He hugged her tight, then rolled them back up to a more dignified position.

Naomi scooted from his lap, knelt beside him, and rose up so she was nearly eye-level with him. "Does this mean you're going to be my new daddy?"

His heart squeezed. "I'd like to be, yes." His voice clogged as he answered, so he coughed a bit to clear his throat. "It doesn't mean that we forget your first daddy, though. Your mama has told me how much he loved you."

Naomi's eyes misted slightly. "He was a good daddy. I remember him chasing chickens with me and kissing my forehead at night when I went to bed. I miss him." Her small hand patted his knee. "But when I'm with you, Mr. Bo, the lonelies don't hurt quite as much."

He might have missed the first seven years of her life, but with that simple touch of her hand, she had sealed their connection. Naomi was his daughter now, belonging to him as completely as if his blood ran through her veins. He silently vowed to love, protect, and guide her to the best of his ability and pleaded with God to grant him wisdom for the task.

"When you're my daddy, will I still call you Mr. Bo?" Her nose was back to scrunching.

"You can call me whatever you like," Bo said. "Maybe if you called your first father *Daddy*, you could call me something different, so we keep Stephen's memory special."

"What did you call *your* daddy?"

Sir, most of the time, but Bo didn't want that distant formality between him and his tadpole. "My father liked everything to be proper, so I called him *Father*, but I think you and I are less stuffy than that." He winked at her, then grew thoughtful. "I had a friend at school who called his father *Papa*." There had always been a lot of open affection between Charlie and his father. Laughter, backslapping, mutual respect. Mr. Welch might not have had the social pedigree of most of the boys' fathers, but Bo had envied the relationship he'd had with his son.

"Papa," Naomi said, trying it out.

Bo's heart stuttered.

Then she scrambled to her feet, bent at the waist, and bussed his cheek. "You have my permission to take my mama's hand, Papa Bo."

Bo took Ruth's hand that night as they sat in the Hope Springs church, listening to the schoolchildren perform Christmas carols. His thumb caressed the back of her hand, and shivers pirouetted up Ruth's arm all the way to her nape.

He'd actually taken her hand. In public. In the second row of the church building. Surrounded by townsfolk on all sides. Granted, their clasped hands lay on the pew between them and not noticeably displayed, but still—for a man who until recently had avoided drawing attention to himself, he was proving to be the opposite of shy when it came to courtship. Sunday dinners in the fancy resort restaurant, evening escorts home with her on one arm and Naomi on the other, sitting beside her in church with his legs close enough for her to feel the warmth radiating from him. She might be a humble cook, but he wooed her as though she were a queen. Was it any wonder she was head over heels in love with him?

With the brooch paid off and back in its embroidered bag, waiting for Naomi to unwrap it later tonight, nothing stood between her and Bo moving forward with their relationship. Nothing but a proposal that remained unspoken.

Ruth had quizzed Naomi about what she and Bo had talked about during their private picnic lunch earlier today, but her usually gregarious daughter offered no explanations, only eyes dancing with secrets.

Now those eyes glimmered with apprehension as Naomi stepped forward for her recitation. Throughout the concert, the schoolchildren had taken turns reciting verses and a scripted narrative chronicling the nativity story. Now that the last notes of "Hark! The Herald Angels Sing" had faded, it was Naomi's turn. The last recitation of the evening.

Ruth squeezed Bo's hand as her daughter's nervousness became her own.

"She'll do fine," he whispered.

All she could manage was a nod, her full focus aimed at her daughter. She smiled in encouragement as Naomi's eyes found her, and breathed a sigh of relief when her child's voice rang loudly through the sanctuary.

"After the angels told the shepherds about the birth of baby Jesus, the shepherds hurried to Bethlehem to worship the Savior. But the story didn't end there. For they spread the word of all they had seen, and everyone who heard their story was amazed." She paused and bit her lip, her gaze curling up to the rafters.

Oh no. She'd forgotten the next line. Ruth mouthed the words, having memorized them herself while helping Naomi practice, but her daughter wasn't looking. Naomi's cheeks reddened, and her feet fidgeted until her teacher came to her rescue.

"The joy of Jesus . . ."

Naomi's face cleared in an instant, her smile stretching wide. "The joy of Jesus," she recited, her voice ringing with renewed confidence, "is not just for the shepherds or the Magi, it is for the whole world. 'Make a joyful noise unto the Lord, all the earth: make a loud noise, and rejoice, and sing praise.' Psalm 98:4. Please stand and join us in singing our final song, 'Joy to the World.'"

Ruth wanted nothing more than to break into thunderous applause at her daughter's triumph, but no other parent had interrupted the program with such a display, so she restrained the impulse. Barely. She glanced to her right to share the moment with Bo, and the pride etched into his features stole her breath. The pride of a father watching his child succeed. His eyes met hers, and something profound passed between them, a connection made of not only two strands, but three.

Blinking to keep the surging sentiment at bay, she turned her attention forward again and began to rise. Bo released her hand, but as they sang along with the school choir, his rich tenor blending with her soft alto and the soprano voices of the children, she couldn't imagine her world being filled with any more joy than it currently contained.

But apparently her imagination was stunted, for more joy was indeed in store.

After visiting with the Marshalls and their lovely, alliterated daughters and consuming enough cookies and mulled cider to make her pleasantly sated, Ruth finally managed to navigate Naomi and Bo away from the townsfolk and back to her cottage, where she'd planned for the three of them to exchange gifts.

Despite the fact that they'd been away for nearly two hours, the house exuded warmth when Bo unlocked and pushed open the door.

Ruth slanted a glance at him. "How did you . . . ?"

He waggled his brows. "I have my ways."

And his minions. He'd probably tasked one of his employees from the resort with stoking her fire. Not that she was complaining. Courting a man with connections definitely had its advantages.

However, Bo's loyal minions had done more than stoke the stove. They'd laden the top of her small cabinet with Christmas bounty. A mincemeat pie, winter squash, oranges, dates, persimmons, and a half-dozen iced hot cross buns perfect for breaking one's fast on Christmas morning.

She turned to him. "There's so much."

"I didn't want you to have to cook on Christmas."

The thoughtfulness of the gesture combined with the adorable little-boy grin on his full-grown man's face demanded a kiss in gratitude. Rising up on tiptoes, she touched her lips to his slightly stubbled jaw. "Thank you."

His arm wrapped around her waist and held her close. "You're welcome," he murmured, his light blue eyes anything but icy as they peered into hers.

Unaware of the growing intimacy between the adults, Naomi grabbed her mother's hand and tugged her away.

"Look, Mama, there's more presents!"

"I see that. It seems Mr. Bo snuck some extra treats in here when we weren't looking."

Bo came up behind them. "Well, I thought that big one there would look funny sticking out of my coat pocket at the program tonight."

Naomi giggled as she pointed to the large rectangular box covering half the kitchen table. "That box wouldn't fit in your pocket, Papa!"

Papa?

Ruth's chest constricted as her eyes sought Bo's. Silent communication passed between them.

I hope you don't mind.

I adore you for taking my daughter as your own.

"It has my name on it, Mama. Can I open it?"

Ruth forced herself to turn her attention to her child. "Of course."

There were only two chairs, so Ruth settled Naomi on her lap and gestured for Bo to take the seat across from them.

Naomi untied the string and opened the lid. Inside was a beautiful wool coat, peacock blue and as stylish as anything Ruth had ever seen. Naomi's indrawn breath exuded awe.

"Here," Bo said, getting to his feet. "Let me help you try it on."

Together, they worked the buttons on her secondhand, far-too-small-but-good-enough-in-a-pinch coat and peeled it off. Her arms slid easily into the sleeves of the new blue coat with jet buttons.

"It's perfect! Even a little big, Mama, so I have room to grow." She spun around in a circle, pure rapture painted upon her face. "Thank you, Papa. I love it!"

Bo smiled, and Ruth's heart throbbed with such joy that she didn't trust her voice.

Naomi grabbed two small packages wrapped in brown paper, handed one to Bo, and laid the other on the table in front of Ruth. "Open mine next!"

Inside the crumpled paper was a large flat rock with a blot of red paint in the center. Ruth had no idea what it was supposed to be, but Naomi had made her and Bo a matching set.

"It's lovely," she exclaimed. "Did you paint this yourself?"

Naomi nodded. "Uh-huh. It's a love rock. You can put it on the bureau or on a shelf, and every time you see it, you'll remember that I love you."

"Because of the heart," Bo said, figuring out the identity of the amorphous paint blot.

"Exactly!" Naomi beamed at him.

Ruth shared an amused glance with Bo before getting up and wrapping her daughter in a hug. "Thank you, sweetheart." She kissed Naomi's forehead. "I know precisely where I will put it." She strode across the room to the bureau in the corner and placed the love rock prominently in the center, scooting her hairbrush and pins aside. "There. Now I'll be sure to see it every day."

Not one to let any present sit unopened for long, Naomi grabbed up the next present and thrust it at Bo. "This one's for you. From Mama."

Ruth slowed her steps as she made her way back to the table, her stomach fluttering. He unwrapped the paper and pulled out the royal blue scarf and mittens she'd knitted.

"I know mittens aren't terribly stylish," she said, "but I thought these might be easier to manage. I've never actually seen you with gloves, so if you don't care for them, don't feel obligated to wear them."

Bo stopped her prattle by coming to stand directly in front of her, the scarf already draped around his neck despite the warmth of the room. "They're perfect," he said, his voice low and rumbly and so wonderfully appreciative that all her insecurities vanished. "Thank you, Ruth."

His attention shifted to her mouth, and she lifted her chin slightly, eager for his kiss, but a giddy voice behind them ensured they stayed on track with their current endeavor.

"My heart!" Naomi had opened her next gift while Ruth and Bo had been preoccupied with each other. "Oh, thank you, Mama! I'm so glad to have it back." She ran up and threw her arms around Ruth's waist, hugging her tight. "I knew Papa would take good care of it, but I'm glad it's mine again."

Bo patted Naomi's shoulder as she gave him the same hug

treatment she'd lavished on her mother. "It was always yours, tadpole. I just held it for you for a little while."

Naomi smiled up at him, then pulled away. "There's one left, Mama. For you." She dashed back to the table and returned with a small box clutched in her hands. She thrust it toward Ruth. "Open it!"

Ruth took the box and lifted the hinged lid with trembling hands. Inside lay a chain made of the finest silver, sparkling against the black velvet background. A silver pendant hung from the chain, nearly identical in design to the luckenbooth brooch Naomi had just received. This one, however, didn't have a large gemstone in the center of the interlocking hearts. No, this one had small gems embedded at the tops of the hearts themselves. The heart on the left had aquamarine stones, and the one on the right boasted a grayish green gem she couldn't name.

"Green onyx," Bo said, seeming to read her mind. "The jeweler I wired in Chicago said it would best match my description of your eyes."

Of course. And the light blue aquamarine for Bo's eyes.

"It's lovely." And so meaningful. She'd told him the symbolism behind the brooch's design: loyalty, love, and an unbreakable connection. The very elements he offered her now.

Bo stroked her hair, his touch tender, precious. "I'm giving you my heart, Ruth. To bind with yours for all eternity. Will you have me?"

Tears welled in her eyes as her answer formed on her tongue. Unfortunately, Naomi jumped into their circle, startling the words right out of her.

"I already gave my permission, Mama, so you're allowed to say yes."

Bo laughed, and Ruth couldn't help but join in. The moment might not be the most romantic in human history, but it was perfect for their little family.

Joy overflowing in her soul, Ruth met her future husband's eyes and gave the answer that had been pounding in her heart from the moment he asked the question.

"Yes, Bo Azlin. I'll have you. For now and forevermore."

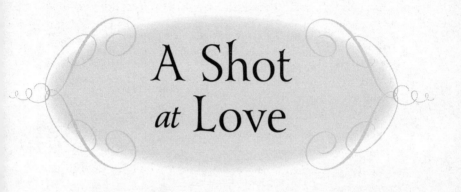

A Shot
at Love

A Sound of Rain
NOVELLA

SARAH LOUDIN THOMAS

The LORD God is my strength; He will make my feet like deer's feet, and He will make me walk on my high hills.

Habakkuk 3:19 NKJV

1

Fleeta hunkered low, careful not to rattle the crisp fallen leaves all around her. She didn't want to be seen or heard.

Albert was meant to be coming around the crest of the hill, pushing deer toward the spot where she waited. Fleeta wished her oldest cousin would still hunt with her, but he was too interested in girls these days. Had his eye on that prissy little Rebecca Howard. Fleeta sighed and flexed her right hand, keeping alert and ready. The family needed the meat. Especially if she was going to take Bud Lyons up on his offer to buy out his business. She needed to make sure her family was taken care of, so she could focus on making her dream come true.

She heard leaves crunching off to her right. If it was a deer, it was coming slow and easy. That was good. Best if Albert didn't scare the deer and send it running. She examined the terrain and the scattering of hardwood trees. The forest was more mature here, offering plenty of room between trunks, another blessing.

Movement caught her eye and she saw a stout buck step out of the shadows. Her breath caught. He was pale, almost white with a spray of brown across his rump, and his rack was immense. Could this be the ghost deer the men spoke about in reverent tones

185

every fall? The one that seemed to escape even the best hunters? He was coming easy, browsing the nearly leafless branches of sassafras and maple trees, one ear cocked in the direction Albert was surely coming.

Fleeta exhaled and lifted her rifle, careful not to attract his attention. She took aim, breathed a prayer of thanksgiving, and applied pressure to the trigger.

"Fleeta, Albert—come quick." The shrill voice pierced the perfection of the moment.

Both the deer and Fleeta froze, and then the buck bounded away, his white tail flashing. Fleeta eased off the trigger and hung her head. She saw Albert coming, his posture clearly showing his disgust even at a distance.

Fleeta stood slowly, her knees stiff from crouching for so long. She glanced back toward the dirt road and saw Elnora standing there, one hand shading her eyes against the morning sun, the other waving for them to hurry. Something about the way she stood put Fleeta on alert. Although only three years older than Fleeta's twenty-two, her cousin had behaved like an adult since she was old enough to speak. She'd done more to raise Fleeta than Aunt Maisie ever had, and that was little enough.

"What is it?" Fleeta watched Elnora try to pick her shape out from among trees.

"Fleeta, for heaven's sake come to the house and bring Albert with you. I need you to drive Momma to the hospital—I'm afraid the baby's coming early."

Elnora refused to learn to drive, while Fleeta had begged her aunt and uncle until they relented and let her learn. Uncle Oscar drove the farm truck to work in the mines most days, leaving a rusty sedan at the house "for emergencies."

Fleeta slung her rifle over her shoulder and broke into a jog, knowing Albert would catch up fast. He was nearly thirteen and taller than she was with longer legs. She glanced back to make sure he was coming and saw a bright blue jay hopping from branch to branch after him. Fleeta supposed it was Jack, the bird Albert had half tamed. It often followed him at a distance, hoping for treats and looking for anything interesting to steal. You sure enough didn't want to lose a button or anything shiny while that bird was around. He'd once stolen the key to the front door, and they hadn't locked it since.

"What's Elnora yammering about?" Albert asked as he caught up. "You had that deer, easy. Now we're stuck with squirrel for supper. Again."

"She says Aunt Maisie needs to go to the hospital." Fleeta glanced at Albert without breaking her stride. "Did you get a good look at that deer?"

"Not really, just saw he had a nice rack, but I couldn't count the points for branches in the way." Albert made a face. "Why's Ma need to go to the hospital? Is it the baby?" His eyes slid away from hers. "Seems like Papa ought to leave her alone so she'll stop having babies." He flushed and stumbled over a rocky patch.

"What do you know about having babies?" Fleeta hoped it wasn't much.

"Enough to know Papa needs to leave her alone." His eyes flicked to Fleeta and away again. "Won't she be too old soon?"

Fleeta wasn't sure if he meant too old for babies or too old for . . . something else, but she decided not to ask. "She's not fifty yet, but I guess she might be too old before long."

Fleeta tried to tuck her hair deeper under her hunting cap as she hurried along. Elnora was already halfway back to the house, nearly running. Her cousin's urgency frightened Fleeta. Though Aunt Maisie had made light of her unexpected pregnancy, Fleeta had seen how it wore on her. Now, six months along, she'd been "resting" more and more. Fleeta whispered a prayer that Elnora was fretting over nothing and that the ghost deer hadn't been a sign of anything bad. There were rumors about him.

2

As she stepped through the front door, Fleeta thought the sprawling farmhouse felt cooler inside than out. Fifteen-year-old Simeon was supposed to keep the fires up in the kitchen and sitting room, but he preferred to read and dream. At the moment, he was nowhere to be seen.

Elnora darted up the stairs to the second floor where it was even colder. "Hurry, Fleeta."

Fleeta exchanged a worried look with Albert, handed him her rifle, and scurried after her cousin. At the top of the stairs she met Simeon, who was wide-eyed with his red hair sticking up. He was clearly in a hurry to get away.

"There you are—the fires need stoking." She expected a fight, but he just nodded.

"Yes'm. I'll take care of it." He swallowed convulsively. "Momma . . . she's . . . I've never seen her cry like that. And there's blood. . . ."

Fleeta suddenly found it hard to swallow too. She gripped Simeon's arm and gave it a quick squeeze. "Don't worry. I'll get her to the hospital."

Feeling like her hunting boots were weighted down with concrete, she crept toward her aunt's bedroom door. Now she could hear the crying—more of a keening really. Rounding the corner, she saw Elnora bent over her mother, a mass of toweling in her hands. The sharp scent of blood hit her, like when they butchered meat. The bedding was stained red, and Aunt Maisie was curled in against herself, as if she were trying to keep from flying apart in pieces.

Elnora looked over her shoulder. "It's too late for the hospital. Send Albert for Dovie and right quick. Momma's losing the baby."

Fleeta flew down the stairs, flinching when she heard Elnora call out, "And hurry right back to help me."

By the time Albert fetched Dovie from the next farm over, Fleeta thought she might collapse. She'd carried water and bloody linens, held Aunt Maisie's hand, and bathed her face with cool water that seemed unnecessary in the chill room. But still her aunt sweated and groaned. Dovie, who'd likely delivered more babies than the doctor in town, stepped in and soon had the situation in hand.

Aunt Maisie finally quieted, and Dovie's gentle voice filled the room as she said, "It's a girl. Looks like the cord got in the way."

Aunt Maisie bit her lip and closed her eyes. "Can I see her?"

"Of course you can."

Dovie wrapped the infant in a clean cloth and laid her in her mother's arms. Aunt Maisie traced a finger along the soft bluish cheek. "Would have been nice to have another baby girl after all these boys."

Fleeta struggled against hot tears that made her eyes feel gritty. It wasn't right—Aunt Maisie suffering so. And for what? An armload of sorrow. Maybe that deer had been a bad omen after all.

Elnora sat on the side of her mother's bed and pulled the cloth back from the infant's face. "Will you name her?"

"Marion."

Fleeta stiffened. She choked on the sentiment, telling herself it was only fitting that a dead child be named for her own dead mother. She didn't suppose her mother wanted to leave her to be raised by her aunt and uncle, but sometimes she felt abandoned all the same. She'd been too young to remember, but the story was that after her father died, her mother soon followed, laid low by grief. Maybe if she'd loved her own, very much alive daughter more . . .

"Do you want to see her?" Aunt Maisie asked through tears.

Fleeta ran from the room.

3

Later that evening Aunt Maisie lay on the sofa, a quilt she'd stitched with her own two hands tucked up to her chin. She smiled weakly and drew one of those hands from beneath the cover to beckon Fleeta over.

"Have any luck hunting today?"

Fleeta flicked a glance toward Elnora, who stood in the doorway looking grim. She'd wanted her mother to go on to the hospital, but Aunt Maisie refused.

"Saw a nice buck, but he got shut of me." She couldn't help but feel that the deer and the day's tragedy were bound up together in some strange way.

Her aunt laughed softly. "You mean someone or something spoiled your shot. Once my Fleeta takes aim . . ." She grimaced and closed her eyes.

"Aunt Maisie, you won't get pregnant again, will you?" Fleeta grasped her aunt's cold hand, hoping her words weren't too impetuous.

"I hope not." Tears slid down her cheeks. "But things like that are best left up to the Lord."

Fleeta wanted to cry out at the sorrow in her aunt's voice. How could she talk about the will of a God who would let a baby die? Especially since Aunt Maisie had lost so many before. The last one had barely taken root before Aunt Maisie lost it. They didn't even know if it was a boy or girl—just made a wooden marker that said *Baby Brady*. Well. She would never let herself be in such a position. After growing up with four boy cousins and her uncle, she'd had her fill of men. She'd take care of herself and never look to a husband for anything.

"I'm going to start supper, Mother. Fleeta will sit with you for a while." Elnora spoke softly from the doorway, her own three-year-old son clinging to her skirt.

Fleeta had to confess that her only girl cousin had done tolerably well in the husband department. He was good to her and the sweet little boy they'd named after his grandpa. And as best Fleeta could tell, there wasn't another baby in the offing yet. Maybe they had more self-control than Uncle Oscar did. Fleeta blushed at the very thought. Another reason to avoid marriage.

Aunt Maisie squeezed her hand. "Fleeta, it's high time I gave you something. How old are you now?"

Fleeta raised her chin. "Twenty-two."

"That means it's been twenty years since your sweet mother died of grief after losing your father when that log truck turned over." Aunt Maisie shook her head. "They were so in love. . . ."

Fleeta was grateful her parents had loved each other, but she hated when her aunt talked about Mother dying of a broken heart. It made her seem weak and unwilling to suffer so she could stick around for her only child.

"Before she died, your mother asked me to give you something."

Fleeta perked her ears. Something from her mother? Aunt Maisie could be dramatic, but she'd never mentioned this before.

"Go to my room and get that pasteboard box down off the top of the armoire."

Fleeta scurried to do her aunt's bidding. She dragged a chair over to the armoire and climbed on it, wishing for the umpteenth time that she was taller. She peered over the dusty top of the furniture and saw a box shoved all the way to the back. She hooked it and dragged it forward, then took it to the front door and blew off as much dust as she could, sneezing at the cloud she made.

"Here you go, Aunt Maisie." She tried not to sound too eager.

"Take the lid off and see if you can't find a cloth bag tucked in there somewhere."

Fleeta set the lid aside, breathing in the scent of old paper and . . . lavender maybe. There was a stack of letters tied with pink ribbon, some loose Valentine's cards, a few official-looking documents, an old pair of eyeglasses, and there—at the bottom—a cloth pouch with a spray of purple flowers on it. She pulled it out and handed it to her aunt, who curled her fingers around it and seemed to look off into space—or time maybe.

"Your mother married Eb when she was twenty-seven—practically an old maid. But she always said she was waiting for her true love like your grandma Naomi had with her Harper." Aunt Maisie grimaced as she shifted on the sofa. "I always thought that kind of romance only happened in books, although Naomi and Harper did seem happier with each other than anyone has a right to be. And when Eb came home from the city after the bank he worked in failed, well, it was like your mother had been waiting just for him." Aunt Maisie closed her eyes and drew her quilt tighter. "And maybe she had been."

Now this was the kind of story Fleeta liked. Not the mushy part, but the story about her father learning the timber business after being forced out of banking. The story of how her parents got married two months after laying eyes on each other and how her mother was a terrible cook, but her father just smiled and ate what she gave him. She hoped Aunt Maisie would tell one of those.

Instead, she handed Fleeta the little pouch, still warm from her palm. "Open it."

Hank Chapin didn't usually enjoy traveling so far from home, but this timber surveying trip could be just the break he needed. Judd Markley, his employer and his friend, had come along to visit his family in Bethel. Which meant Hank wasn't having to sleep in a tent or a trailer—he was bunking with a nice family—and best of all, it was deer season. Judd had been telling him tales of the mighty bucks he'd be sure to see in West Virginia, and Hank was itching to try his new Remington 740 Woodsmaster rifle. Hank was generally conservative with his money and his resources, but he considered his gun collection an investment. And when he'd seen the Remington .30-06, he couldn't resist. It was light, and his favorite scope fit perfectly. Yup, this work trip could be just the thing he needed to get his mind straight so he could decide what to do with his future.

Hank dressed quickly and started for the privy out back. A lack of indoor plumbing was something he'd grown accustomed to on trips like this one. At least the Markley family had a hand pump in the kitchen to bring in water.

He reached for the back door and heard a giggle on the other side. Pushing gently so as not to startle anyone, he peered through the opening. Blue eyes and gingery curls greeted him, along with a shriek of laughter, as a sprite of a girl scampered behind a boy only a little older. The boy sized him up, and Hank halfway expected him to spit.

"You must be Uncle Judd's right-hand man," the boy said in a way that made Hank think he was aiming to sound grown up.

"I like to think so."

"Heard you'uns get in last night. Me and Gracie were in bed, but I was still awake." He puffed his chest out a notch. "If you need anyone to show you around the place, I'd be glad to do it."

Hank grinned. "Let me get ready to face the day and I just might take you up on that."

The boy nodded as though making a lifelong commitment.

"James—Grace—get on in here and leave Mr. Chapin alone." A woman's voice came from the same direction as the aroma of sausage and coffee.

The pair scampered off, and Hank finished his morning ablutions undisturbed. As he stepped up onto the back porch, Judd appeared around the corner, carrying a bucket of foamy milk. His brother Abram, whom Hank met the night before, walked a few steps behind, although his voice carried on up ahead.

"George swears he saw that big ole piebald buck out on the hogback last week. Says he aims to bag him this year. I said, 'Yeah, you and every other feller with a rifle in southern West Virginia.'" Abram paused midstep when he spotted Hank. "Mornin'—hope you slept hard enough to work up an appetite. Lydia aims to spoil you and Judd rotten while you're with us."

Hank found himself liking Judd's family almost as much as he already liked Judd.

"I could eat something. And then I think I'm expected to go on a tour of the farm with James."

A huge smile bloomed in the depths of Abram's beard. "Fancies himself a man, and I don't see any reason to tell him otherwise. Leastwise not yet. I know touring you around would just about make his year."

"Then I'll try not to founder at the breakfast table."

Abram's laugh rolled from deep inside and settled into all the tired places in Hank's spirit. He felt tension he didn't realize he'd been holding slide off his shoulders. He'd been feeling an itch he wasn't quite ready to examine for a while now. This trip might be an opportunity to think about whether or not he wanted to scratch that itch. Whether or not it was time to leave Waccamaw Timber and strike out on his own in an entirely different direction. With Judd at the helm, he wasn't exactly feeling squeezed out, but neither was he likely to ever rise any farther in the ranks. He smiled and slapped Abram on his broad back.

"Now what was that you were saying about a deer?"

Abram's eyes lit even brighter. "Ah, he's half deer, half ghost, and the rest of him's just tall tales. Supposedly, there's a twelve-point buck somewhere out in them hills." He made a sweeping gesture with his arm. "He's mostly white with brown spots like a piebald pony—leastways that's what the ones who claim to have seen him say. As the story goes, he's been roaming around here for at least ten years, growing a bigger rack every summer. And when someone sees him, something big's supposed to happen to 'em. Good or bad depends on who you ask." He wrapped a muscled arm around Hank's shoulders. "Amos—the feller who claimed to see him last—swears he shot him through the neck last fall, but somehow that ole buck survived. Maybe if you've brought some Southern luck with you, you'll get a shot at him while you're here."

Hank laughed. "I'd hate to rob y'all of the chance to tell those same tales next year. Still, he sounds like just the prize Judd's been promising me since we first talked about hunting up here."

Judd shifted the milk bucket to his left hand and stepped up onto the porch. "Watch it, Abram. I promised him a deer, not a legend."

4

Fleeta examined the little bag, creased and with a pale stain in one corner. She worked the string in the neck loose and pried the top open. She turned it up and tilted what was inside out into the palm of her hand. A piece of jewelry glinted back at her. Two overlapping hearts were joined with a purple heart-shaped stone, the whole topped with a crown. It was pretty, but Fleeta wasn't sure what to make of it. She'd never been overly fond of jewelry, and the family couldn't afford such things anyway.

"Did it belong to my mother?"

"It did. And to her mother, and her grandmother, and so on all the way back to England if Marion's tale is true, and I don't see why it wouldn't be." Aunt Maisie took the bag and turned it over, showing Fleeta initials embroidered there. "These are supposed to be the initials of each woman who's had it along with the year each one married. There's your mother, MEB for Marion Evans Brady. I can't remember your grandma Naomi's maiden name— her momma married twice." She tapped the brooch. "Probably valuable with that amethyst in it, but the main thing is, Marion wanted me to give it to you when the time was right for you to find true love."

Fleeta choked and nearly dropped the bauble. "True love? You mean like in romance novels?" She slid her eyes toward a bookshelf with a dozen or so well-worn paperbacks. Aunt Maisie claimed to have few vices, but reading tawdry romances was definitely among them. Fleeta had tried to read one with a picture of a woman being swept into the arms of a man who looked like a pirate, but couldn't stomach all the roiling emotions and breathless embraces. She preferred *The Spirit of the Border* by Zane Grey or *The Count of Monte Cristo* by Alexandre Dumas.

Aunt Maisie blew out a little puff of air. "Oh, I suppose more like your parents had—they just doted on each other, and although I saw them get mad a time or two, they never stayed that way for long."

"So why are you giving this to me now?" Fleeta held the brooch as if she were afraid it might bite her.

"Because you're a young woman, and it's high time you found a young man. This last . . . illness has made me realize I won't be around forever and I need to see you settled. I don't know what Marion had in mind as far as timing goes, but it feels right to give this to you now."

"What am I supposed to do with it?" Fleeta heard her voice rise with emotion.

"You could wear . . ." Aunt Maisie looked Fleeta up and down, from her scuffed boots to her flannel shirt and dark hair in a messy braid down her back. She laughed. "No, I don't suppose you would. Put it on your dresser in your room. Look at it and remember your mother wanted you to fall in love one of these days." She slid lower on the sofa. "Now let me rest. I'm about wore in two. I'd tell you to go on in there and help Elnora with supper, but I expect you'll be on kitchen duty for a while. We can't expect Elnora to keep up two households, and I'm afraid . . ." She closed her eyes and exhaled long and slow. "Well, this is the weakest I've ever felt. I'm afraid I may not be up and about as quickly as I'd like."

Fleeta slid the brooch back in its pouch, trying not to look at the initials of all those women who must have been content with finding true love instead of pursuing some other dream. She slipped out of the room as silently as she would slip up on a turkey the day before Thanksgiving. She blinked back tears, a wild mix of emotions disturbing her spirit. She wanted to be a gunsmith. To take care of her family. And now she was supposed to fall in love too?

Aunt Maisie didn't mean to mess up her plans by losing the baby, but how could she follow her dream and take over Bud's business while she was so desperately needed at home? And this falling in love business was absolutely out of the question. Her mother supposedly died from grieving over her lost love, and Aunt Maisie was surely suffering for loving Uncle Oscar. What was her aunt thinking? Obviously, all these plans were incompatible. She had to choose. And for now, that was simple enough. She would have to put her dreams on hold until Aunt Maisie was well again, and she would not fall in love. Ever.

5

"What should I call you?" James asked Hank after showing him every inch of the barn.

Hank started to suggest just his first name, but then thought better of it. Abram and Lydia had clearly taught their children to be mannerly, and he didn't want to undermine that. "How about Mr. Hank?"

James mulled it over. "That'll suit me fine. I was thinking we might call you Uncle Hank, but Ma might think that's too familiar." He nodded his head. "Want to get a closer look at the cattle?"

Hank agreed and ambled after the boy as he headed out to the pasture. He admired several red-and-white Herefords as well as an Angus bull, then only half listened as James rambled on about the pleasures and challenges of farm living. Mostly he was thinking about that itch of his. For almost a year he'd had a notion that it might be time for him to give up his position with Waccamaw Timber. Once upon a time, he'd thought he might be in line to run the company, what with George Heyward's children not being interested in the job.

Then Judd came along, married the boss's daughter, and stepped into leadership. No, Hank had to be honest—Judd didn't just step in. He'd earned his place at the top in more ways than one. And he didn't begrudge his friend in the least. But it did change his long-term outlook on things. Going from heir apparent to second banana was tough no matter how much he liked and admired Judd Markley. He supposed they could continue on indefinitely, yet Hank had a few buried dreams of his own that had been stirred up like silt in a pond. Hank gazed at the trees beyond the edge of the field—good timber, and good cover for deer. Yes sir, this place was heaven for a woodsman, especially one with long-dormant dreams.

James fell silent, and Hank paid closer attention. The boy was staring off into the distance like he, too, was taking the measure of the fields and forests. Hank smiled. He and Judd needed to head out soon to survey the stands they were thinking of purchasing, but for now he was glad to enjoy spending a little time with a delightful boy on a delightful morning. The thought ran through his mind that he might like to have a boy of his own one day. He'd stepped out with a girl or two, but he'd been so focused on work, his romances withered from lack of attention. And that right there was another buried dream rising to the surface.

"You gonna enter the turkey shoot on Saturday?"

"What's that?"

"There's a turkey shoot over at the Smallridge farm this week-end. Seems like Pa and Uncle Judd will want to enter. You aim to give it a try?"

"Don't believe I've ever been to a turkey shoot, but I might come along and see how it's done." He winked at the boy. "You gonna enter?"

James kicked at a tuft of winter brown grass. "Aw, I ain't good enough." He bit his lip. "I'm not supposed to say *ain't*. What I mean is, I'm probably not good enough. Uncle Judd and Pa stand a chance, but that ole Fleeta Brady usually wins. I heard Pa say Fleeta could shoot a gnat in the eye."

"Well then, I'll come along just to see this Fleeta shoot. Sounds like a good show. Now I'd best round up your uncle Judd and cruise some timber while the day's still young."

On Saturday morning, Fleeta sat muttering to herself as she scratched a design into the stock of Vernon Howard's favorite deer rifle. She'd placed her mother's brooch where she could see it every time she went into her room. But while she loved having a connection to her mother, she didn't much like being reminded of Aunt Maisie's words, which had been eating at her all week.

True love. How foolish does Aunt Maisie think I am? Why would I tie myself down to some man who'd only want to boss me around and saddle me with young'uns? If I'm ever going to smith guns, I need to keep my focus on what matters most.

She finished roughing out her design and sat back to see how it looked overall. She'd begin carving soon, but she liked to make sure everything was balanced before she jumped into the real work. She'd been carving wood since she was big enough to hold a penknife, although it was only in the past few years that folks realized she was pretty good at it and began bringing her work. At first it was toys and purely decorative stuff, but then she did Uncle Oscar's shotgun with a grouse taking flight, and he swore he hadn't missed a bird since. Now everyone and their brother were after her to work something up. Of course, they wanted her to do it for free, but once she realized there was money in it, she started charging.

Vernon's wife was paying her plenty to carve her husband's favorite hound dog into the stock. She'd hinted that he thought somehow the dog, getting up in years, would hunt better once Fleeta carved its likeness onto the rifle. Fleeta was more than skeptical about that, but if she somehow won the dog another chance, that was fine with her. Plus, unfounded rumors and superstitions allowed her to charge more.

She'd almost saved up what Bud Lyons was asking to buy out his gun shop over in Hanson, the nearest town with more than a post office. While it wasn't enough to buy everything outright, he'd let her live in the room upstairs and make full use of all his equipment. Admittedly, his tools weren't quite up to snuff, yet she figured it was the best she could do for now. Once she started making real money, she could upgrade item by item. Except, of course, Aunt Maisie couldn't spare her yet. She was better, but Fleeta was still doing the bulk of the housework and cooking—not that anyone appreciated it. She was a poor maid and a worse cook. Still, she guessed she was doing better than the boys would on their own, and still finding time to keep up with her woodwork.

Fleeta ran her hand over the smooth, curly maple, picturing how she was going to make the dog practically leap off the surface. She smiled as she examined the forestock. She'd added a raccoon, looking over its shoulder at the dog pursuing it. Leaves and acorns swirled between the two animals. Satisfied with the overall effect, Fleeta set the rifle aside. It was time to head on over to the turkey shoot.

Stowing her favorite squirrel rifle in the rack behind the bench seat of Uncle Oscar's truck, Fleeta slid in next to her uncle, who was going just for the fun of it. The whole family had conceded that Fleeta was their best chance at a turkey, so she'd do the shooting. As large as the family was, they'd need two turkeys for Thanksgiving dinner, and she'd be sure to get at least one today. She hadn't lost a turkey shoot in years. For the second turkey, she and Albert could always hunt one up. They could probably get two or three, except she liked winning shoots like this one—showing up the boys was just about the most fun she ever had.

They parked in Merle Smallridge's pasture, lining the truck up with several others already in place. Looked like a good crowd, which meant an extra fun time. Every now and then a stranger would show up and Fleeta would play the timid female. The local fellas let her get away with it for laughs.

Slinging her Winchester 1890 over her shoulder, Fleeta made her way around the house to the back of the barn, where competitors were already sighting down the firing line. Merle had nailed hand-drawn targets to fence posts about fifty yards out. A lot of folks had gone over to shotguns for turkey shoots, but Merle liked to keep to rifles. Which suited Fleeta just fine. She caressed the forestock of the rifle that once belonged to her father. A .22 caliber, it didn't have a ton of firepower, but it was accurate and felt like an extension of her own body. She kept thinking she'd carve the stock—it would be good advertising if nothing else—only she couldn't decide what to put on there. She supposed she was a little bit afraid of spoiling this last connection to her father.

An image of her mother's brooch flashed through Fleeta's mind. Now she had a connection there as well, although it felt tainted by silliness with all that "true love" nonsense coming from Aunt Maisie.

"Fleeta, I didn't know you were coming." Merle ambled over with his rolling gait, the result of a steer breaking his left leg. The leg healed crooked, and Merle always looked like he was either drunk or on board a ship at sea.

"You know how much I enjoy a good shoot," Fleeta said. She eyed the men fiddling with their rifles and testing the air for a breeze. "Any competition today?"

"Well, as it happens—"

"Ho there, Merle! You willing to let a Southern boy get in on this shoot?"

Fleeta turned to see who had interrupted their conversation. Judd Markley was striding toward them. He too had a hitch to his gait, but only someone who knew about his getting trapped in a mine collapse was likely to notice it. Judd was something of a legend around these parts. He'd not only survived a cave-in, but he'd gone off to South Carolina, gotten married, and come to be a bigwig in a timber company down there. Fleeta didn't much know him, but Uncle Oscar thought the world of him and his brother, Abram.

"Who you got there?" Merle asked.

Fleeta noticed a second man catching up to Judd. He was shorter and thicker, though not heavy by any means. His hair was sandy—almost blond but not quite. More the color of honeycomb. Fleeta thought he looked pleasant enough and started to smile. Then she froze as she got a good look at the rifle slung over his shoulder. Sure enough, it was a Woodsmaster—a Remington 740, and a .30-06 caliber. And if she wasn't mistaken, the gun was brand new. Her breath caught in her throat, and she forgot to blink. It was the finest rifle she'd ever seen and a semiautomatic at that. She wanted to reach out and touch it so bad she could almost feel the silk of the wood and the ice of the steel.

Someone elbowed Fleeta in the ribs. "I said, this here's Fleeta Brady. Fleeta, you know Judd, dontcha?"

Fleeta choked on the spit she'd failed to swallow. "I do, but it's been years since I last saw him."

Judd looked at her with serious eyes that let her know he wished her to be at ease. She gentled under his gaze and shifted her focus back to the second man. Apparently she'd already been intro-duced, but she had no idea what his name was.

"It's short for Henry," he said with an easy smile. "Folks started calling me Hank before I could talk, so I didn't get to have any say in the matter. Fleeta, though, that's unusual. Is it a family name?"

Fleeta finally blinked. "I have no idea. My parents died when I was a baby. Is that a Remington seven-forty?"

Hank blinked back. Twice. "It sure is. Just acquired it over the summer and thought I'd bring it to West Virginia and see how good it is at getting me a deer."

"The gun won't have any trouble. Only thing that could get in its way is the one firing it."

Judd made a sound that might have been laughter. Fleeta ig-nored him, her eyes riveted to that beautiful rifle of Hank's.

Hank cleared his throat. "Would you, uh, like to take a closer look?"

Fleeta handed her own rifle to Judd and held out her hands. Hank settled the gun into them, and she sighed involuntarily. She ran her hands over the stock, examining it from every angle. She opened the breach and furrowed her brow. "It's not loaded."

"No, I generally don't drive around with a loaded gun."

Fleeta shook her head. "An unloaded gun isn't much more use than a stick." She closed the breach, fitted the rifle to her shoul-der, and sighted out across an open field away from the gathering crowd. She moved her finger inside the guard and squeezed the trigger until it clicked. Like cutting warm butter.

She exhaled slowly and handed the gun back to Hank before she could get any more attached to it. "A fine piece of workmanship," she said.

"I agree. I'm a bit of a collector, and this is my latest prize." He tilted his head to one side, considering her. "Maybe you'd like to shoot it before the day's out?"

Everything in Fleeta screamed yes, but instead she took a steadying breath. "Oh, well, I'd hate to waste your ammunition."

"I've got enough to spare a few rounds." A look of surprise crossed his face. "Wait a minute—James mentioned someone named Fleeta he said is a crack shot. Is that you?"

Fleeta felt her cheeks flame. She was a crack shot, but she didn't like knowing folks were talking about her skill. Not even little boys and strangers.

Before she could answer, Merle jumped in. "That's her all right, and I was just about to tell her she's disqualified from this match."

A bucket of well water dumped over her head couldn't have surprised Fleeta more. "What do you mean 'disqualified'?" she asked, pinning Merle with her sternest look.

"I mean you win every shoot every time and it ain't fun no more. Me and the boys agreed, you have to sit this one out and give somebody else a chance for once."

Fleeta spun toward Judd. "Give me my rifle." She snatched it from him. "If you *men*"—she said the word with a sneer—"are afraid to shoot against a girl, then I don't have any use for you. I can get my own turkeys anyhow." She stomped off, but before she got more than three steps away, someone snagged her arm and stopped her.

"Hey now." It was Hank with that funny drawl stretching his words out. "That doesn't seem right."

Fleeta wanted to tear away from him, but she also wanted to shoot that rifle in his other hand. She waited, quivering with anger, frustration, and the unexpectedly pleasant shock of his touch against her arm.

"What if you make the contest a little harder for whoever won the last shoot? Put the target farther out or something like that?" His grip eased, and still Fleeta waited. "If you think she's that good, then challenge her with something worth her trouble."

Fleeta wanted to smile at that—it was the nicest thing she'd ever heard someone say about her. She'd relish a challenge. She half turned to see how Merle was taking the suggestion. He was scratching at his scraggly beard and eyeing Judd.

"What do you think, Markley?"

"I think it would be a pleasure to see Fleeta do some fancy shooting. And I don't think there's a one of those boys over there who wouldn't be game for putting Fleeta to the test." He glanced at her. "So long as she doesn't mind."

"I can outshoot anyone here or in the state of West Virginia, for that matter," Fleeta said, throwing her shoulders back. "You make it just as hard as you want and I'll still win that turkey."

Hank grinned. "This is shaping up to be an entertaining afternoon."

6

Merle had two live turkeys penned near the barn—a fat hen and a tom that looked like he could whip a dog in about sixty seconds. Fleeta wanted the tom. The hen was up first. Everyone who wanted a chance put up their money and got three tries to hit an X drawn on a piece of paper gently flapping in the breeze. There were at least two dozen men ready to try hitting one of the three targets already in place. Merle would change them out as they got riddled with holes, although there was much laughing about how the targets would last longer if the poor shots went first.

"I'll sit this one out," Fleeta said, leaning against the side of the barn.

Hank decided to plant himself nearby. When James mentioned a fine shot named Fleeta, he'd assumed it was a man. He'd been thoroughly unprepared for this dark pixie of a woman who might be wearing men's clothes but wasn't fooling anybody. She was clearly unaware of her femininity, which made Hank assume she was equally unaware of anyone else's masculinity—his own included. But she'd struck a chord in him, and he had to admire anyone who appreciated a fine gun as much as she clearly did.

"You're not trying for the hen?" Fleeta asked him.

Hank hoped he hadn't been staring. "Judd's gonna try for the hen, and I'll go for the tom if he loses. Lydia said one turkey would be more than enough for Thanksgiving dinner."

"You planning to stick around that long?"

"I am. We came up to check out some timber the company might buy, but we timed the trip so we could do some hunting and spend the holiday with Judd's family."

"What about your family? Won't they miss you?" Fleeta kept one eye on the first round of shooters while she talked to him.

"I have a sister who says she wishes I were there, but I think that's mostly because I keep her children out from underfoot when I'm around." He shifted his Winchester, cradling it in his arms. "My parents were killed in a boating accident when I was sixteen. My sister practically raised me, but I'll spend Christmas with them, so it's all right."

Fleeta's eyes jerked to his face, raw with sudden emotion. "You lost your parents? Both of them?"

"I did, but it's been a long time now." He missed them, sure, but he'd made peace with the loss in his twenties after a few years of hard rebellion. He was thirty-four now and liked to think he'd matured at least a little.

"Do you remember them?"

Hank quirked a brow. That was an odd question, but then again, he had her full attention now and found he liked it. "Well sure."

"My parents died before I was old enough to remember. Aunt Maisie and Uncle Oscar were good to raise me, but I sure do wish I could remember even one thing about my parents." She had a wistful look. "Sometimes I think I can remember a song, maybe one my mother sang, but it's probably just wishful thinking."

"Do you have any brothers or sisters?"

"Naw. I've got more cousins than I can count, though. Mostly boys except for Elnora—she's the one raised me more than Aunt Maisie did. Aunt Maisie was too busy—" She stopped abruptly and flushed pink, making a beauty spot stand out near the corner of her right eye.

"We have a winner!" The shout came from Merle at a makeshift table where he'd been examining targets.

"What?" Fleeta stomped her foot. "I wasn't paying attention to that last round of shooters. Looks like Eddie got it the way he's dancin' around over there. He's using his daddy's Stevens over-under." She looked thoughtful. "I'm surprised he did that well with an open sight."

"Could have been luck," Hank said.

Fleeta nodded slowly. "Judd's a good shot and so is Marsh Wilson." She pursed her lips. "Might have something to do with Eddie's daddy being laid up, and Eddie losing his job when the two railroads merged." She rolled her neck as though preparing for battle. "Bet they won't go easy on this next round."

Merle approached, listing to one side like a drunken sailor. "All right, Fleeta. Here's the deal. We're gonna let everyone who wants a chance shoot, and then you go up against the winner. 'Cept you have to shoot from seventy-five yards out."

Hank stepped forward. "Here now, that hardly seems fair."

Fleeta held up her hand. "Hank's right." She flicked a look at him. "I'll shoot from a hundred."

Hank watched her walk over to the scoring table and lay down her money. She nodded at the other men, who treated her like she was one of them. He thought about the girls he knew back in South Carolina and decided they might could learn a thing or two from Fleeta Brady.

Fleeta pulled a soft rag from her back pocket and rubbed her peep sight with it. Lots of folks used scopes, and a few still had open sights, but she preferred her aperture sight. When she looked through it, everything else faded away, and that one little bead in the center of the target was all she could see. Sometimes she wished the world could be like that, fading into the background so she could focus on the one thing that was important—becoming a gunsmith.

Carving stocks was pure pleasure, yet it was just one step in the process, and a last step at that. She wanted to shape a rifle from the very beginning. Which meant she needed not only to be able to work wood, but steel as well. Bud let her come into his shop and watch and even tinker a little now and then. She'd rifled a barrel or two with his help, and he said she had a knack for it. But the equipment was expensive, and while her nest egg was growing, she wasn't sure she'd be able to leave the family with Aunt Maisie taking so long to recover from losing the baby. She felt like she owed it to the family who had taken her in to stick around for as long as they needed her.

"Stand clear." Merle waved at the men lined up ready to shoot, and Fleeta turned her attention to the competition. Hank was in the second row, behind Marsh. Since Judd wasn't shooting this round, Fleeta figured Marsh was the one to beat. He was shooting with a Winchester 94, .30-30 caliber. Fleeta had carved mountain laurel blossoms into the stock. Marsh's wife was named Laurel, and when he commissioned the carving, Fleeta guessed it was as close as she'd ever come to thinking there might actually be such a thing as true love.

She grunted under her breath, remembering Aunt Maisie's words: *"Your mother wanted you to fall in love one of these days."* But why in the world would her mother want that for her? As best as she could tell, her mother died of grief because she loved Fleeta's father so much that she couldn't live without him. Why then would she want her daughter to sign on for that same kind of heartbreak?

Fleeta lifted her rifle to her shoulder and sighted at the target Marsh just shot. He'd come ace of splitting the X in two. He'd be tough to beat, but she thought she could do it. Hank stepped up next and handled his rifle as if it were an extension of his hands and arms. He moved carefully, methodically, and with purpose. Fleeta hadn't thought to admire him as a man, but she could certainly admire him as a shooter. He clearly respected and cared for his firearm.

Hank fired three times in rapid succession. Fleeta sighted through her aperture again to get a better look, and by golly it appeared he'd bested Marsh. Merle sent one of his boys out to bring the targets in. There would be two more rounds and then she'd learn whom she was going to shoot against.

A nervous tickle stirred in Fleeta's belly. She laid a hand there, feeling puzzled. She'd never been nervous about shooting. She thought back to her lunch of ham and an apple. Surely that hadn't upset her stomach. And yet butterfly wings fluttered.

Hank held his breath each time another man fired. He wasn't sure why he wanted to win so badly, but he did. He was a crack shot, having handled and fired guns since his arms were long enough to reach the trigger. Though he owned some outstanding collectors' pieces, his rule was that if a gun couldn't be fired, he didn't want it. He'd shot each and every gun he owned multiple times and could hit just about anything he aimed at with all of them.

Today, however, his hands shook as he waited for the final shots to be fired. He tried not to look over at Fleeta, where she stood with her back straight and tendrils of hair grazing her cheeks in a way she obviously didn't realize was lovely. As a matter of fact, he'd bet none of the men here realized just how pretty she was. They just saw the competition.

Merle sent his boy out for the last of the targets as everyone stood waiting, trying not to look like that was what they were doing.

"Appears our friend from the South has shown us up today, boys." Merle held the target Hank and Marsh shot so that everyone could see it. "I think this is the closest I've ever seen, but looks like Fleeta's going to have to try somebody new today."

Hank felt a grin lift his cheeks, and he risked a glance at Fleeta. She was looking back with narrowed eyes and an intensity that made Hank a little uneasy. He thought he knew how a deer caught in her sights might feel.

Merle sent out new targets and pointed to the spot Fleeta would stand, well back from Hank. He felt small, shooting from fifty yards closer in. Even so, he stifled the urge to protest. He suspected Fleeta's pride was at risk even more than the turkey.

"You'll each have one shot," Merle said. "Closest to the X wins the turkey."

Hank shot first. He sighted through his scope, his very expensive scope. He exhaled slowly, squeezed the trigger like he didn't want to bruise it, and took the recoil without flinching. He was pretty sure he'd hit the X dead center. Hank felt something like pride rise up in his own breast and started to turn to see what Fleeta thought when he heard a sharp crack split the air. She'd already fired. No fiddling about, no hesitation, just boom and done.

"All clear," Merle hollered, and Hank had to lift his muzzle before he could look at the target through the scope. Tension hung in the air as they waited for the target to be brought in. Fleeta was the only one who looked cool. She cradled her rifle, barrel pointed into the dirt, a half smile giving her a Mona Lisa look.

Merle laid the square of paper on his makeshift table and took his time examining it. Hank's nose itched, but he resisted scratching it. Merle waved Judd over and pointed at something on the paper. Finally he stood and looked around at the men who seemed to be holding their collective breath.

"It's a tie."

"What?" The cry came from Fleeta.

"Look for yerself," Merle said. "They's little more than one hole in this target. Might be one's a hair's breadth closer than the other, but I double-dog dare you to tell me which is which."

Fleeta strode over and snatched up the paper, squinting at it. Hank approached more slowly and looked over her shoulder. Merle was right. There was no way to tell who'd made the winning shot.

"Fleeta, you shot from farther away, so you made the harder shot. Go on and take the turkey," Hank said, feeling gentlemanly about it.

"Doggone if I will. We'll shoot again, but both from seventy-five

213

yards." Her cheeks flushed pink, and he feared the sparks flying from her eyes might set the barn on fire.

Hank opened his mouth to demur, but the look on Fleeta's face shut him up.

"How about you shoot each other's rifles this time?" The suggestion came from Judd. Hank eyed his friend and thought he saw a sly smile playing around his mouth.

Fleeta suddenly looked shy. She eyed the Woodsmaster, then looked Hank full in the face. "I'll understand if you'd rather not."

Hank felt something swell in his chest. This woman was willing to sacrifice her pride out of respect for . . . him? He blew out a breath. No, he suspected she just didn't want to presume to handle his prized rifle.

"Fine with me," he said. "Anything tricky about that gallery gun I ought to know?"

Her eyes narrowed. He didn't think she'd like him calling her .22 by its nickname. She set the rifle down on the table between them. "The only trick to shooting is knowing how to do it."

He let a lazy smile spread across his face. "Sounds right to me," he drawled, extending his own rifle toward her. "She kicks a mite."

Fleeta took the gun and tilted her nose toward the sky. "Uncle Oscar says his shotgun kills at both ends, and I've never minded shooting it."

Hank chuckled and picked up her .22. He could still feel the warmth of Fleeta's hands on the stock, which was worn to a silky smoothness. The rifle felt good, like it had been well cared for and appreciated. He realized he no longer cared who won the contest. Instead he just wanted Fleeta to feel good about the outcome, whatever it turned out to be. Which meant he could neither try too hard nor throw the match. He'd just have to do his best and let the cards fall where they may.

7

Fleeta tried not to caress the gun in her hands. She'd never seen anything quite so beautiful. The balance was perfect, and she wanted to touch every part of the rifle, to take it apart and fit it back together again. She wanted to make one just like it.

She'd watched Hank shoot and thought his gun pulled ever so slightly to the left. She'd give her eyeteeth to shoot it just one time before trying to hit the mark. Every gun had its own personality, and she wanted to learn a little more about this one. Yet that was what made this particular shot so difficult—shooting with a strange gun. Of course, her little .22 was zeroed in perfectly, so Hank didn't have a thing to worry about. She glanced at him as he reloaded her rifle. He didn't look worried either.

Merle set out two new targets about fifteen feet apart and lined Fleeta and Hank up at the seventy-five-yard mark. "You'uns shoot at the same time. I'll call it." He watched to make sure each shooter was ready.

Fleeta nestled Hank's rifle against her shoulder and found the target through the scope. The setup was obviously expensive, but she wished for her own peep sights nonetheless. She rolled her off shoulder and relaxed her finger against the trigger guard. If the rifle pulled left, she needed to sit just a smidge . . . there.

215

"Ready, aim, fire." Merle said the words with something like glee. He was clearly enjoying himself.

Fleeta pulled the trigger, and sure enough the Woodsmaster gave her a solid kick. Still, it was nothing compared to her uncle's shotgun. She kept her eye open and stared through the scope, trying to see how close she'd come.

"Rifles up," Merle said and sent his boy out to fetch the targets. Fleeta had time to see her own mark but hadn't gotten a look at Hank's. She gnawed her lower lip as they waited.

Merle and Judd bent over the targets, then looked at the circle of men gathered around. Merle waggled his eyebrows. "The turkey goes to . . . Hank Chapin."

Fleeta gasped and then caught herself before clapping a hand over her mouth. She lifted her chin and turned to shake Hank's hand. "That's some good shooting. Congratulations."

Hank took her hand, and his was warm and dry. It felt oddly comforting as he pressed his palm against hers. "I think I had the better gun."

Fleeta felt her cheeks pink. "It is a good gun, but not near so fine as yours. I wouldn't mind shooting it again sometime." The pink flushed deeper. That was a forward thing to say.

"My seven-forty might have cost more, but I don't think I've ever fired a piece of equipment so finely tuned as your rifle. Mine still needs some adjusting, some breaking in. This gun"—he held it out to her—"won the match more than I did."

Fleeta exchanged his rifle for hers. She guessed if she had to lose to someone, it was just as well she'd lost to a gentlemanly fellow from out of state. At any rate, after this she'd probably never see Hank again. She found that thought to be both comforting and disappointing.

Elnora and Aunt Maisie were downstairs in the kitchen, fussing over Thanksgiving dinner. Aunt Maisie, still puny, mostly gave directions and flapped her hands. Fleeta had been right there in the thick of it with them until Elnora suggested in her usual over-bearing way that Fleeta should put on a dress and act like a lady for once in honor of the holiday. As if it wasn't insult enough that she'd had to stay back from that morning's hunting party to help prepare the meal.

Fleeta snorted and stomped upstairs to try to do something with her hair. Women's work indeed. Simeon for one would much rather hang around the kitchen than do anything outside. He'd come back from hunting early, then spent the rest of the morning reading *Twenty Thousand Leagues Under the Sea*. He probably would have been more help in the kitchen than she was. Hadn't it been enough that she and Albert provided the two wild turkeys that were even now roasting side by side in the oven?

Giving up on her hair, Fleeta dug out a circle skirt Aunt Maisie had made for her a few years back. She shook out the wrinkles and slipped it on, feeling as though she were drowning in the dark green fabric. At least the color wasn't terrible. She found a cream-colored sweater she was pretty sure belonged to Elnora, but if her cousin wanted Fleeta to dress up, she'd just have to sacrifice her sweater. And it probably would be a sacrifice, since Fleeta knew she couldn't be trusted to keep it clean.

Looking at herself as best she could in the dressing table mirror, Fleeta thought the skirt hung limp, but no way was she putting on petticoats or crinolines. And she most certainly was not wearing a girdle. Making a face, she brushed out her hair again and plaited it in its usual braid. If Elnora wanted something more than that, she'd have to do it herself. Fleeta turned to abandon the room when a sparkling gleam caught her eye. The brooch sat on her dresser nestled against its cloth bag. Should she wear it?

She picked up the bit of jewelry, feeling the cool weight of it in her hand. She pinned it below her left shoulder and looked in the mirror again. It was pretty against the cream of the sweater—she was enough of an artist to recognize that. But Aunt Maisie's comments about finding true love echoed in her ears, and Fleeta curled her lip, practically growling. Enough of this nonsense.

She snatched the pin off, snagging her—no Elnora's—sweater in the process. Oh, she wished Aunt Maisie had never given her this thing. Except it had belonged to her mother. Fleeta let her head drop back, the silver of the brooch growing warm against her palm. She couldn't throw it away or even give it away, and yet the amethyst felt like an accusing eye threatening her with this thing called love.

Tucking the pin inside its pouch, she grabbed a gun cleaning cloth, wrapped everything in it, and buried it in a drawer behind her underthings. Maybe if she kept it out of sight until she was a confirmed old maid with her own gunsmith business, it wouldn't trouble her so. She spun on her heel in the ridiculous slippers she had also borrowed from Elnora and headed back downstairs.

Hank expected to miss being with his sister Molly and her family for Thanksgiving, but the Markley clan was keeping him well occupied. After a quick breakfast of biscuits with molasses, they set out through a skiff of snow with James intent on getting his first deer. When they spotted a four-point buck, Judd and Hank fell back while Abram led his twelve-year-old son in taking down the animal with a single shot.

James looked like he'd won the biggest prize at the county fair. Abram tousled his hair. "Good job, son. Quick and certain, that's the way to do it. Don't take the shot if you're not sure you can make it. Few things are worse than wounding an animal and having to track it down."

James nodded. "Yes, sir. Can I dress it out?"

Abram hid his smile. "We might help some, but any hunter worth his salt dresses his own deer."

James pitched in, and the four of them had the deer ready to drag home in short order. Hank was grateful there were several of them to take turns dragging it out over rough and rocky terrain. Once they got to the house, they hung the deer from the limb of a massive pine to let it cool in the chill November air. There was plenty of work to be done yet, but for now it was time to join the ladies for the Thanksgiving feast.

The turkey Hank won at the shoot was set as the centerpiece of a laden table. Lydia and her mother, Rose, had toiled for two days preparing fluffy yeast rolls, sweet potato soufflé, fried cabbage, mashed potato and rutabaga, corn-bread dressing, creamed onions, something called leather breeches, which appeared to be a sort of bean, and three kinds of pie. Hank couldn't imagine who would eat it all until he saw Judd and Abram tuck in. He hoped they wouldn't think less of him for not eating half a pie all by himself.

"And now, in long-standing Markley tradition, it's time for an afternoon nap," Judd announced after they'd helped the ladies clear away the remains of the meal.

Even James, who had likely slept little the night before in anticipation of their hunting trip, was more than happy to sprawl in front of the fire and close his eyes. And Grace, although nearly nine and prepared to fight napping, didn't argue near as hard as she might have on another day.

Hank settled with the family in the front room where lazy conversation gradually gave way to soft snores. And yet he found he wasn't the least bit sleepy. The pleasures of the day filled his spirit in a way that made him want to simply spend time appreciating being invited so fully into the bosom of this good family living in this beautiful place. Finally, he stood and tiptoed to the back door, letting himself out into the bracing air. He'd see if he couldn't walk off at least a little of the huge meal he'd eaten. He also wanted to ponder those life changes he'd been carrying around in the dark corners of his mind.

Thirty minutes later, Hank realized he'd let himself become so lost in thought that the roll and sway of the mountain land had lured him into . . . getting lost. It was a hard thing to admit, and he wasn't quite prepared to consider his cause hopeless, but when he crested this most recent hill the view wasn't at all what he'd been expecting. He thought he'd be able to see a curl of smoke from the Markleys' chimney beyond the next rise, but instead there was a mountain looming that really shouldn't have been there. A blue jay sat on a bare limb, cocking its head at him and jeering in that coarse way jays do. For a minute, he had a notion to follow it when it flew, but decided not to grasp at straws.

He peered around in all directions, unsure of where to go next and wondering if maybe he should just stay right where he was until someone came along. This surely looked like a path that would be used regularly. It wound through the edge of a field near the tree line. A cow stepped into his field of vision. Or it might just be a cow path. Still, where there were cattle, people couldn't be too far off.

Still weighing his options, Hank sat on a fallen log to give himself time to think. The tree had gone down years ago, and its stump was almost hollow—rotted from the inside out. It was the sort of timber that looked good from the outside but failed to produce. It made Hank ponder what his life would amount to if it were measured in board feet. He'd been feeling a bit hollow lately, like the heart had gone out of him. If he were honest, he'd have to admit it had something to do with seeing Judd and Larkin so happy. They had a child now—the main reason Larkin hadn't come along on this trip. Little Lavonia was barely walking, and the young parents agreed traveling with a child not yet two would be a trial for them all. Sweet Lavonia had wormed her way into his heart just like James and Grace were quickly doing. Maybe there was more in this world for him than playing second fiddle for the Waccamaw Timber Company.

The jay he'd noticed earlier landed on the punky stump and dipped his head as though peering inside. The bird snatched a fallen leaf in its beak and flew to a low branch, tilting its head to consider Hank. He'd known jays to be curious, but he'd never known one to take such an interest in him.

"You act like you're after something," he said aloud.

The bird dropped its leaf and bobbed along the branch, eye now focused on the stump. Hank turned his attention back to the hollowed wood and noticed that the leaves inside didn't look natural. They looked more like someone or something had piled them there—stuffing them in. Could it be a nest of some sort? Hank wondered if they had critters in these hills he didn't know about. He poked at the mass with a stick, finding the leaves formed a sort of cap that came away revealing . . . what appeared to be a gun cleaning cloth. He fished it out, and something tumbled onto the ground at his feet. He picked the lump up and found it to be an embroidered cloth pouch with a weighty something inside. Tipping the bag, a piece of jewelry—really beautiful jewelry with intertwined hearts and a glinting purple stone—dropped into his hand. Well now. Had he stumbled upon someone's secret cache?

Distracted, Hank didn't notice the soft sound of footsteps approaching until they were nearly upon him. He startled and caught himself before toppling off his log as Fleeta Brady hove into view, head down and muttering to herself.

8

Fleeta realized she should have at least changed her shoes. Not that she cared about ruining Elnora's slippers, but the dratted things didn't offer any traction. She'd been in such an awful hurry to get out of the house that she hadn't thought this through. She said a word under her breath she knew wasn't fit for a lady—or a respectable man, for that matter—but she didn't care. Aunt Maisie had been relentless all day. Instead of being pleased that Fleeta had made an effort to dress appropriately and act like a girl, she kept harping on about that brooch. Why wasn't Fleeta wearing it? Was true love such a terrible thing? Look at how happy she and Uncle Oscar were—didn't she want the same?

"Ha," Fleeta said, startling a squirrel.

"Hello." The unexpected voice made Fleeta jump a foot.

She jerked her head up and looked all around. There, in the edge of the woods off the trail, sat Hank Chapin—looking awfully at home for a stranger.

"Where in the world did you come from?" she asked without thinking. Oh, she needed to start thinking.

Hank's lips twitched. "I've been walking off my Thanksgiving dinner and settled here because I'm not altogether clear on which way is home."

Fleeta stared at him like he had two heads. "The Markley farm

222

is right over yonder, on the other side of those hills." She narrowed her eyes. "Are you really turned around or are you just funning me?"

Hank held his hands up in surrender. "Guess I'm a flatlander through and through. Will you point—?"

Jack the blue jay dove between them, squawking. He seemed intent on Hank's hand as he waved it toward the fields and trees. Fleeta gasped and pounced at him, grabbing the hand that held . . . her brooch. "Where'd you get this?"

Hank blinked rapidly. "Found it."

Fleeta felt as if she'd been breathing the vapors from Merle's corn mash. Had Hank been in her room? Impossible. "Where did you find it?"

"I have the impression that you recognize this bauble," Hank said. "Is it yours?" He offered it to her, along with the embroidered bag. She took the items like they might suddenly disappear if she moved too fast.

"Sure looks like the brooch that belonged to my mother." She pinned him with a glare. "Now where did you get it?"

Hank pointed at a half-rotten stump. "Tucked in there under some leaves."

Fleeta examined the stump from every angle and poked around inside it. "Yes, I see where it was nested in here. And this"—she held up the bit of fabric Hank had let fall—"is the cleaning cloth I wrapped it in. But just this morning I hid it with my . . ." She felt heat rise to her cheeks. "In my dresser. Now, how in the world?"

She almost forgot about Hank as she circled the stump, examining the ground all around. Finally she found what she was looking for—a boot print with one heel worn way down. She tightened her mouth and stood, contemplating how to punish Simeon. Sure as shooting, the boy had stolen her brooch and hidden it here. She couldn't think why he'd do such a thing, but she aimed to find out.

"Have you discovered the culprit?" Hank asked.

Fleeta spun toward him. "Maybe. You don't need to trouble yourself about it, though."

Hank's eyes softened, and he tilted his head to one side. "I get the feeling that pin is special to you."

Fleeta looked at the jewelry in her hand. "I guess it is."

"You should be wearing it," Hank said in that same soft voice. He stepped close, took the brooch, and pinned it near her right collarbone, in the softness of Elnora's sweater. "There. That looks awfully nice." His eyes flicked to hers, and Fleeta felt heat spread throughout her body and rise to her cheeks. "Pretty girl like you ought to have nice jewelry."

Fleeta felt the weight of the pin against her shoulder. The sensation was strange and wonderful at the same time.

"Never have been much for feminine frills," she said and grazed the gemstone heart with her fingertips. "This belonged to my mother. It's supposed to come to me when . . . well, it's special. My aunt Maisie gave it to me recently."

Hank beamed at her. "I knew that was no run-of-the-mill jewel hidden in a stump. Now what cad spirited it away and hid it from you? I'll trounce him for you if you'll but name him."

Laughter burst from Fleeta's throat before she even knew it was there. Hank probably could trounce Simeon, but she wouldn't betray her family. "Oh, I'm pretty sure I know who, but I guess he won't do it again once I talk to him about it."

"Well, if you're sure, I suppose I can let it go this one time. But if he does it again, you'll have to let me challenge him to a duel." He paused and cocked his head the other direction. "Or maybe a wrestling match—that seems more suited to these parts, although I do have a dandy set of antique dueling pistols."

Fleeta realized her earlier foul mood had lifted completely. Hank Chapin was all right. She granted him a smile. "Do I need to escort you home? Seems like you mentioned being a mite turned around."

Hank stuck his arm out toward her, and she linked her hand through his elbow without hesitation. "I'd be a fool to turn down such an offer from such a lady," he said.

And for maybe the first time in her life, Fleeta really did feel like a lady.

Hank was sorry when they arrived back at Abram's farm. His walk with Fleeta Brady had been much too brief. The woman wanted to be a gunsmith of all things, and Hank had no doubt she'd accomplish it.

"I've been jabbering on long enough," Fleeta said, slowing her pace as they approached the barn. "What about you? Is being a timberman what you've always wanted to do?"

Hank stopped and leaned against the weathered boards of the barn. He hoped to stretch the conversation out a bit longer. "No, not really. I guess I just fell into it. Started working for George Heyward when I was still in high school and worked my way on up to management."

"Didn't you ever have any dreams?" She sounded genuinely puzzled.

"Well, I guess when I was younger. With my parents gone, I mainly wanted to earn my own money. Might be George Heyward became like a second father to me, and then after I was with him for so long, I kind of adopted his dreams. But now . . ."

Fleeta looked at him with her lips slightly parted, as though truly curious to hear what he would say next. "Now what?"

Hank felt his normal reserve melting away in the light of her warm golden-green eyes. "Now George has an honest-to-goodness son-in-law to carry on Waccamaw Timber, and I'm thinking I might could turn my favorite hobby into a business."

"And what hobby is that?"

A smile spread across Hank's face unbidden. "Guns."

Now she looked more than curious; Fleeta looked downright eager. "Guns are your hobby?"

"I'm a collector. I have everything from that modern Remington you fired to antique Civil War pieces that are pretty valuable. Mostly I collect guns for my own pleasure, but here lately I've tracked some down for friends looking for a particular firearm." He felt his smile widen. "Now that's some kind of fun."

"And you figure people would hire you to find guns for them?"

"That, and I'd continue collecting pieces for sale. I think there's good money in it if you do it right."

Fleeta opened her mouth as though to speak, but it seemed they'd been spotted. James whooped and lit out across the yard, coming to an abrupt halt in front of Hank. "Who's your lady friend?"

"Don't you know Miss Fleeta Brady?" Hank asked.

James did a double take and squinted his eyes. "Why sure, I just ain't never seen her in a dress."

Grace followed her brother at a more sedate pace. "Don't say 'ain't.' Momma will tan your hide." She too eyed Fleeta, from the pin at her shoulder to her scuffed and dirty slippers. "You look awful pretty. Why don't you dress like that all the time?"

Hank looked at Fleeta out of the corner of his eye. She was the nicest shade of pink, clearly flustered by all the attention.

"'Cause she can't hunt and shoot in a getup like that," James said as though nothing could be more obvious.

Grace wrinkled her brow. "I bet she could if she wanted to."

Hank decided it was time to rescue Fleeta. "Y'all sleep off that Thanksgiving dinner?"

James rubbed his belly. "And I'm about ready to eat again. A man gets powerful hungry after bringing down a big ole buck."

"You weren't hardly gone long enough to have worked over-much," Grace said. "And I bet the grown-ups did most of the work hauling that deer home anyway."

Now it was Fleeta's turn to rescue James. "You got a deer this morning? I didn't get a chance to hunt, what with all the cooking. How big was his rack?"

James's chest puffed out a good two inches. "Four points and this wide." He held his hands a bit farther apart than was strictly accurate.

"You'll make some lucky girl a fine husband, providing like that," Fleeta said.

Grace pushed into the conversation, clearly feeling left out.

"But you do your own hunting. Does that mean you don't need a husband to do it for you?"

Fleeta considered the question. "I guess there's more reasons than that to have a husband, but it doesn't really matter since I don't ever aim to marry."

Hank felt a stab of concern, but Grace saved him from asking the question.

"Why wouldn't you want a husband?"

"My mother died of grief not long after my father passed. And Aunt Maisie's never had time for anything but taking care of kids. I want more than that."

Grace looked as thoughtful as Hank felt.

"Like being a gunsmith," Hank said.

Fleeta smiled. "Exactly. As soon as I save up enough money to take on Bud Lyons's shop, I know I can get work. Everyone around here knows I'm good with guns, and they already come to me for carving."

Hank perked his ears. "Carving?"

"Yeah," chimed in James. "Come see Dad's over-and-under. Momma got it done for him for Christmas last year." He grabbed Hank's arm and hauled him toward the house.

Judd and Abram were still splayed out in the sitting room when they burst through the front door.

"Dad, can I show Hank your over-and-under?"

Abram stretched and stood. "Sure. Go fetch it for him."

Fleeta and Grace entered the room.

"Why, Fleeta, don't you look nice," Abram said. "James been bragging about your woodwork?"

Seemingly in a perpetual state of rosiness, Fleeta nodded. "He was. Guess it's better than me bragging on it."

"I don't think anyone who's seen your work would accuse you of bragging," Judd said.

James reentered the room more slowly than he left it. Hank supposed he'd been taught—rightly—to take more care when holding a firearm. He handed the Browning to Hank. It had a 12-gauge shotgun barrel over a .22 caliber rifle barrel, and the walnut stock was a thing of beauty. An incredibly detailed apple tree had been carved there, with two children beneath it. An older boy held a bucket brimming with fruit, while a girl stood with an apple in her hand. The design continued toward the barrel with a swirl of apple blossom.

"Most folks get pictures of the animals they hunt or their dogs, but Dad got us," said James. "Some folks think Fleeta's carvings give 'em good luck hunting. Why, Merle Smallridge said he had to quit using the twenty-two Fleeta carved squirrels on. Said it wasn't sporting anymore."

Fleeta was absolutely scarlet now. "That's pure nonsense," she said.

Abram grinned. "I don't know. That apple tree out back sure did produce an abundance of fruit this past fall." He tousled James's hair. "And these young'uns sure are coming along fine." He winked at Judd. "Might be you should get Fleeta to carve a stand of timber into your rifle stock."

Fleeta swatted at the air, dismissing Abram's teasing, while Hank ran his fingers over the contours of the carving. He couldn't come close with pencil and paper, much less a carving knife. He glanced over at Fleeta, who watched him with a slight frown. "A remarkable likeness." The frown relaxed. "This boy looks like he could step right off this rifle stock and get his second deer of the season."

James grinned, and the corners of Fleeta's mouth finally tipped up.

Hank handed the gun back to James. He was getting an idea. "Say, Fleeta. You think you could carve a magnolia blossom into one of my rifle stocks?"

Fleeta pursed her lips. "I don't think I've seen a magnolia. I guess I'd have to look at a picture first."

"That can be arranged," Hank said.

"Hold on," she said. "You're not wanting me to cut on that Remington, are you? That's too fine a gun. I don't think I'd have the nerve to take that on."

"I've got a double-barrel shotgun with me as well. Twelve gauge. I'm thinking one of your flowers would dress it up nicely."

Fleeta's shoulders relaxed a notch. "Oh. Well, I expect I could handle that."

"Question is, how quick can you get it done?"

Her eyes sparked, and he noticed they were the green of a meadow in late summer when the grasses start to turn gold. He decided a description like that was exactly the sort of thing that would get him in trouble with Fleeta Brady.

"How quick do you need it done?"

"I'm leaving next Wednesday."

Now her shoulders sagged. "I can work fast, but not that fast. Plus, I ought to finish Vernon's rifle before I start something new."

"Well then, guess I'd better leave it with you and plan on coming back before Christmas."

Fleeta gave him a sharp look. "You'd drive all that way just for a carved stock?"

Hank leaned in close. He could tell Fleeta was steeling herself not to pull away from him. Stubborn. He liked that. "Might be I'd have another reason for coming back this way."

She swallowed hard and maybe leaned in a fraction. "What might that be?"

"Timber," Hank said, stepping back. "We'll make some offers to buy before we leave this trip, but I'll need to come back and finalize any deals and get a timbering plan in place so we can get started before the ground goes soft in the spring."

Fleeta's mouth tightened. "Of course. I could have the work done in a few weeks if you find me a picture of that flower you want carved on there."

"Y'all got a library?" Hank was enjoying himself.

"Not close by, but the bookmobile comes 'round on Mondays."

Hank nodded. "We'll give that a try."

"Can we come?" Hank had nearly forgotten about the children standing with them.

"Miss Pearson lets me borrow three books every week," Grace

said. "So long as I take real good care of them." She beamed at her brother. "And James has taken out every book of poetry at least five times apiece."

James turned ruddy and ducked his chin. "That's not worth bragging about."

"Oh, but it is," Hank said. "I don't read near enough poetry. I should probably try some. What would you recommend, James?"

Grace hopped on one foot. "Tell him the cat feet poem—I can almost remember that one."

James looked put upon, but squared his shoulders nonetheless. "It's by Carl Sandburg—he's real good. It's about the fog, but I guess Mr. Sandburg lived in a city instead of the country like we do." He cleared his throat.

"The fog comes
on little cat feet.

It sits looking
over harbor and city
on silent haunches
and then moves on."

James gazed absently out the window. "That's how the fog is too. Can't you just see it?"

Hank was surprised to realize he could. He looked at Fleeta and saw that she was watching him. Maybe to see if he'd poke fun at a country boy quoting poetry, which he would never do. He was a country boy himself, just from a different part of the country. He thought the poem could describe Fleeta as well as the fog. She kind of snuck up on a man, soft and quiet, although he had the definite sense he could no more hold on to her than he could a gossamer cloud of mist.

"Yes. I can see it," Hank said, looking into those summer-green eyes. They widened, and then she looked away.

9

On Monday morning, Fleeta woke well before dawn. She planned to meet Hank at the post office, where the county bookmobile parked from ten until two every Monday. She often went—Mrs. Pearson made it a point to get books about gunsmithing or the history of firearms for her—but today felt different. For the first time in her life, she found herself giving more than a passing thought to what she should wear to visit the bookmobile.

She finally settled on a clean pair of denim pants and a plaid shirt. She'd seen some of the girls around town turning the cuffs of their pants up, so she tried that and decided she could stand it. She tied on her serviceable Sunday lace-up shoes, wishing for half a moment that she had a pair of saddle oxfords. Instead of braiding her hair, she pulled it back at the crown with the bulk of its dark mass hanging down her back. The weight of it made her feel self-conscious, but Hank was probably used to girls being way fussier. She drew the line at lipstick, which she would have had to borrow from Elnora or Aunt Maisie anyway.

She started out of her bedroom, then at the last moment turned and scooped up her mother's brooch. It didn't look right against her everyday shirt, but she wanted her mother close, so she pinned it to her undershirt. No one else would know she was wearing it.

"Not for some man's love, but for yours, Momma," she whispered as she left the room.

Slipping downstairs, Fleeta was determined to get away without anyone seeing her. Uncle Oscar was out in the barn with the boys, Aunt Maisie tucked up in a chair near the fire and reading one of her romance novels. Fleeta moved to the front door, which was hardly ever used, and held her breath as she slowly turned the doorknob.

"Going to the bookmobile?" Simeon appeared as though from thin air.

Fleeta was proud that she didn't jump. "Maybe."

"I'll come too. I want to see if Mrs. Pearson has any more books by Jules Verne."

"Fine. I have a bone to pick with you anyway." Fleeta opened the door, making extra noise now that her solitude was ruined.

"With me? What'd I do?"

Fleeta noticed her cousin looked uncomfortable in spite of his protest. She'd been waiting for the right moment to confront him. They set off down the road, Fleeta turning the collar of her coat up against the coolness of the first day of December. There was a crispness to the air that invited deep, cleansing breaths. It tasted good, and Fleeta was so pleased to be meeting Hank that she could almost forgive Simeon for taking her brooch. Almost.

"You stole the pin my mother left me and hid it in the woods over near the Markley place." Even now she could feel the brooch resting just above her heart.

Simeon, who had been scuffling along with his hands in his pockets and head down, jerked around to look at her. "How'd you—?"

"How'd I find it?" Fleeta considered how much to share. "Maybe I tracked you to that ole stump out there off the cow pasture."

"Hunh. You probably could." Simeon looked at her sideways. "Hidden away in the back of a drawer the way it was, I didn't think you'd miss it for a while. Whatcha gonna do about it?"

"I ought to tell Uncle Oscar and let him tan your hide, but I'm feeling too fine to see you suffer. I just want to know why you did it. Did you think you could get money for it?"

Simeon dropped one of the books he carried under his arm. "I had my reasons and money wasn't any part of it." He stuck out his lip as he picked up the book and dusted it off.

"Got a girl then? Thought maybe you'd give it to her?" Fleeta didn't think that was the real reason, but she hoped to nettle Simeon into spilling the beans.

"Shoot, no." The boy's ears turned red, and he started walking faster. "That's pure crazy. I just don't want you to go and get a man."

"You don't want me to what?"

"Momma keeps talking about how you're supposed to find true love now that she's given you that ole pin." He lifted his chin higher. "I read books. I know how that stuff works. If you keep that thing, you'll find some man who'll carry you off and we won't see you anymore."

Fleeta stopped in the road. "Simeon. Is that really why you did it?"

He stopped too, half turning but not quite looking at her. "I like having you around, and if you go, Daddy will make me take up where you leave off. I'll have to hunt and earn money and I don't know what all." He looked miserable. "I just want to read books and maybe write them one day too."

Fleeta, not prone to shows of affection, reached out and wrapped one arm around her cousin's shoulders. "Oh, Simeon. I'm not letting any old piece of jewelry decide what I do with my life. Don't you worry. The only reason I like that pin is because it belonged to my mother, and there's not much left of her."

Simeon leaned into her shoulder. "So you're not afraid you'll fall in love and have to go off with some man?"

"I am not." Fleeta squeezed him and continued down the dirt road. "Now, once I have my own business and make my own way, I might look around a little. Although I'll probably be awful busy, so it'll have to be a man who can take care of himself."

Simeon looked thoughtful. "Maybe you'll find one who takes care of you."

Fleeta threw her head back and laughed. "That would suit me just fine."

Hank watched Fleeta and a lanky boy with books under his arm approach the post office. He'd had to plan carefully to get away from the house without two little shadows following him, and he was disappointed to see that Fleeta was not equally alone. He supposed the boy must be one of her cousins. Where Fleeta was all dusky skin and sinew, the boy was pale and clearly not used to his long legs yet. There was a protectiveness in the way Fleeta watched the boy—a fierceness. Or maybe that was just Fleeta.

Mrs. Pearson stepped out of the bookmobile van and smiled. Hank had expected a gray-haired lady of a certain age, but the librarian was middle-aged at most, with a full figure garbed in a bold, flowered dress topped by a bulky sweater and scarf. She'd already made Hank's acquaintance and had a book ready for them to examine.

"Why, Simeon, have you finished those books already?"

"Yes, ma'am. I read this one twice." The boy held up his copy of *Twenty Thousand Leagues Under the Sea*.

"Excellent." Mrs. Pearson clapped her hands. "I have here *The Mysterious Island*, which I think you will simply adore."

Simeon's eyes lit up, and he darted into the bookmobile behind the librarian.

Fleeta watched him go with fondness. "He surely does love books," she said, shaking her head.

"Seems like a fine thing to love," Hank said.

"I suppose, but he takes grief over it at school. The other boys would rather hunt and fish, and Simeon gets left out."

"Is he happy?"

Fleeta flicked a look at Hank. "Mostly I guess. Might be he's what you'd call content."

"Then I wouldn't worry too much. Lots of people go a long way looking for contentment without ever finding it."

Fleeta furrowed her brow and rubbed the back of her neck. "Are you content?"

"I used to be, but here lately I've started to think I might want to aim for something more. Like my own business." He paused and looked into her eyes. "Maybe other things too."

Fleeta gave him a sharp look. She took a breath and opened her mouth, then seemed to change direction midstream. "Let's get on in there and see if we can find a picture of this flower you're wanting to have carved."

"Mrs. Pearson has the picture awaiting your perusal." Hank made a sweeping gesture toward the door. Fleeta tightened her mouth and practically leapt over the steps into the van.

Inside, the space was tight with all four of them. Simeon stood in the rear, already reading a book open in his hand. Mrs. Pearson watched him with a bemused expression. There was a small book stand with a book of botanical prints open to a picture of a magnolia drawn by Georg Dionysius Ehret. Fleeta moved forward and smoothed the page, tracing the petals with her fingertips.

"Sure is pretty."

"That it is, and you should smell it. The aroma of summer as far as I'm concerned."

Fleeta nodded, clearly concentrating on the picture. "Can I check this out?"

"I'm sorry, Fleeta, but this is a reference book."

Fleeta worried her lower lip. "I don't suppose you have a piece of paper and a pencil?"

Mrs. Pearson moved to the front of the van and pulled out a sheet of typing paper and a freshly sharpened pencil. Hank smiled. Of course she'd have such supplies at the ready.

Fleeta took the items, propped a children's picture book on the edge of the stand, and began making quick, deft strokes across the paper. Hank wanted to move closer, but he was afraid he'd distract Fleeta. Everything else seemed to have dropped away for her as she captured the lines of the flower. He finally edged closer as her drawing slowed.

"I believe you've got it," he whispered, almost in her ear.

She jerked and swiveled her head to look him in the eye. It was the same look he'd seen in the eyes of a startled deer. For those moments Fleeta had been drawing, she'd forgotten about him.

Her eyes roved his face, and then she stepped back, banging an elbow against the shelves. "Yup. This should do it."

Hank smiled, but didn't give her any more room. For some reason, he liked unsettling her.

Fleeta looked all around the van, her focus landing on Simeon. "You ready to go? This is all I need."

Simeon grunted and looked up from his stack of books. "You might wanna see this one," he said, extending a book toward her. "I wanted to know more about Sir Walter Scott after reading that *Ivanhoe* book of his, and Mrs. Pearson found me this history of Edinburgh, Scotland." He pointed with his chin. "This picture sure looks like that pin Momma gave you."

Fleeta took the volume while Simeon stuck his nose back inside one of his books and wandered outside. Mrs. Pearson beamed after him. "I can't wait to see how that boy turns out," she said to Fleeta. "Anyone who loves books that much will surely do well in life."

Fleeta paid her no mind, though, her attention riveted to the page in front of her. She read aloud but softly. Hank thought she was mostly reading to herself. He couldn't make out all the words.

"'. . . crafted of silver and set with gemstones . . . two intertwined hearts with a crown . . . Scottish love token . . . betrothed . . . luckenbooths were often passed down from mother to daughter in Scottish families.'"

Her head came up, and she looked at him, tears glistening in her eyes. She closed the book, clasped it to her heart, and staggered out of the van. Once they were outside, it was as though Fleeta finally got a full breath. He could see her push her shoulders back and lift her chin.

"Are you all right?" he asked.

She nodded and reached inside her jacket, fiddling until she pulled out the pin he'd found in the stump on Thanksgiving Day. "I think I told you this belonged to my mother. Seems it's something called a luckenbooth—a traditional Scottish pin given as a love token that mothers would then pass along to their daughters." She tilted the pin so that the weak winter sun made the heart-shaped stone flash. "I wonder . . ."

Hank waited a moment and then quietly asked, "What do you wonder?"

"About all those mothers and daughters who have worn this. The little bag it came in has initials sewn into it for each bride who owned it." One tear escaped, and she scrubbed it away. "What were they like? Who did they fall in love with? Were they happy? All that history and I hardly know any of it."

Hank reached out and curled his fingers around Fleeta's so that the brooch was concealed in both their hands. "Seems to me the history isn't the main thing; it's the love that pin represents. Mothers' love for their daughters as well as—" he paused and swallowed hard—"a woman for the man she marries."

Fleeta turned damp eyes on Hank. "I suppose she did love me. Just not enough to live for me when my father died."

Hank wanted to draw her into his arms and comfort her. Saying her mother hadn't chosen to die was no comfort at all. Who could know? Maybe she had let grief for her husband steal her from Fleeta. All he knew was the fierce surge of love he was feeling right at that moment. "I don't know anything about your mother, but I do know you're worth living for."

Fleeta closed her eyes and inhaled as though breathing in his words. The hint of a smile touched her mouth. Her incredibly lovely mouth. "Do you really think so?"

"I do," he said and gave in to the urge to wrap her in his arms ever so briefly. He released her. "Now, as to the business at hand. Can you capture my magnolia in wood?"

She finally gave him a full-on smile. "I can. The petals are nice and big, and it's not as fussy as, say, apple blossoms or violets. Although I do wish I could see the real thing."

Once again she was all business, and while Hank was happy to have distracted her from her pain, he wouldn't mind comforting her some more.

"We'll just have to get you down south sometime. In the summer, of course, when the magnolias are blooming." Hank said the words without really thinking. Fleeta looked at him as though he'd suggested she run off to China. "Have you traveled much?" he asked.

Fleeta's eyes shuttered. "Not much cause to go gallivanting around. I'm happy right here."

Hank looked around at the fields, forests, and mountains stretching out beyond the post office and the two-lane road. "I can see why."

"Really? Sometimes I wonder if folks don't think we're backwards."

"If they do, it's clearly because they haven't met you." Hank wanted to reach out and touch Fleeta's cheek, but figured he'd already touched her more than she was used to. "Walk you home?" he asked instead.

Fleeta laughed. "I guess I can find the way."

Now it was Hank's turn to flush. "I'm not quite the helpless flatlander you think I am. And where I come from, a gentleman sees a lady home."

Fleeta tilted her head to one side and furrowed her brow. "You might be the first person to accuse me of being a lady."

Hank smiled. "Well then, I sure am glad God gave me eyes to see it."

Fleeta ducked her head and called out for Simeon to come on, handing him his book about Scotland when he caught up. Soon the boy lagged behind them, nose still in a book, stumbling now and again as they set out. After they'd walked in silence for a while, Hank reached in his breast pocket and fished out an envelope.

"Here's the down payment on your work."

"I usually get paid after I've finished the work," Fleeta said, not touching the envelope. "I've got your gun—that's collateral enough."

Hank pushed the envelope toward her. "I'd feel better if you took this."

She reached out for it and accepted the money like it might poison her. She tucked it in the back pocket of her pants.

"Aren't you going to look? We never did discuss an exact fee."

Fleeta heaved a sigh like he was a great deal of trouble and pulled the envelope back out. She stopped and lifted the flap, peering inside. She thumbed through the bills, then turned sharp eyes on Hank. "This looks more like full price to me."

Hank tapped her hand with an index finger. "Half. I'll give you the same again once it's done."

"No sir. I don't feel right about that. This is too much."

Hank stopped and turned to face her while Simeon strolled on, oblivious. "'The labourer is worthy of his hire.' That's from the book of Luke, tenth chapter. Jesus said it, so I'm willing to believe it's true."

Fleeta was clearly fighting an internal battle. Hank laid a gentle hand on her shoulder. "Honestly, Fleeta, you do exceptional work, and I'm proud to offer you what I think is an honest wage."

She pursed her lips and studied the ground for a minute. "All right. But if it's not absolutely perfect, you don't owe me another penny."

"Deal," said Hank, holding out his hand. She grasped it in a firm shake and finally graced him with a smile. Which, Hank thought, was worth ten times what he'd put in that envelope.

10

Fleeta was itching to get to work on the magnolia carving. When a piece particularly captured her imagination, she often found herself mentally lining out the design even as she went about daily tasks. While she stacked and hauled firewood, she'd imagine how a petal might curve across the swell of the stock. As she milked the cow, she'd envision a woody stem disappearing into the trigger guard. But before she could start on Hank's shotgun, she had a few final details to work into the carving of Vernon's hound dog, and she wouldn't rush one job just because she was eager to start another.

She did take enough time to draw a rough sketch, so that Hank could give his approval before he left for South Carolina. He and Judd had finished scouting timber and were stopping by before heading back the following day. Fleeta wasn't used to feeling nervous, but somehow this project had her on edge. She washed the supper dishes while Aunt Maisie sat nearby, dish towel in her hand, trying to be useful. Fleeta supposed it was hard on her not being hale and hearty. Lost in thought, Fleeta let a plate slip and almost broke it.

Aunt Maisie stood and shooed her out of the kitchen. "Go on in the sitting room and wait for your company before you make a mess. You're nervous as a cat in a roomful of rockers. I'll finish this."

Fleeta tossed her dishrag onto the counter and gladly abandoned the kitchen. She'd never enjoyed anything related to food preparation anyway. She sat on the sofa and glanced at Simeon, who sat sideways in an armchair, nose buried in his new book. Uncle Oscar sprawled across the floor in front of the fire, hands resting on his chest, softly snoring. The man could sleep anywhere. The other boys had gone out to the barn after supper. Supposedly they went to fix the hand plow, but Fleeta knew they had a pack of cards out there. She pulled out her magnolia drawing and tried to focus on it while she waited for Hank.

About the time Fleeta became fully absorbed in her drawing, there was a shuffling and then a knocking at the back door. Judd had known the family for years, so of course he would come to the back door. Fleeta jerked her head up and suddenly wondered if she looked presentable. She'd been so worried about her artwork that she hadn't given even a passing thought to her appearance. She jumped up and looked in the small glass over the mantel. Her hair had worked loose from its braid, and there was a smudge of something on the front of her shirt. She looked around wild-eyed as she heard Aunt Maisie greeting their visitors. She darted into the hall and quickly redid her hair, then lifted the spot on her flannel shirt to her mouth and licked it. Yup, jelly from supper. She sucked at it and hoped that would do the trick.

Uncle Oscar must have awakened, because she heard him greet Hank and Judd.

"Fleeta was right here a minute ago," he said.

"She's in the hall," Simeon said, and Fleeta wished for once the boy really had been as oblivious as he seemed.

She lifted her chin and reentered the room. "Good evening," she said. "Won't you gentlemen have a seat?"

Uncle Oscar knit his brow, and Judd smothered a laugh. Simeon just stared, then shrugged and resumed reading. Hank smiled and sat on the sofa, much to Fleeta's relief.

"I have your drawing right here," she said, offering the paper to Hank, who took it and gave it his full attention.

"I like the balance," he said at last. "Will the carving affect the grip at all?"

Fleeta sat beside him—although not too close—and pointed out where she had added a seedpod with its natural hash marks to improve his grip.

As they talked, Uncle Oscar pulled out his knife collection and began showing it to Judd. The other two men drifted into the dining room, where Oscar could lay out his collection more easily.

"You're quite an artist," Hank said, turning admiring eyes on Fleeta. She flushed. He was much too close, but she didn't know how to move away without it being awkward.

"It comes natural, I guess. But what I really want to do is make a gun from start to finish, not just decorate one."

"What's stopping you?"

"Tools mostly. Gunsmithing tools are expensive, but with what you're paying me I'm a heck of a lot closer than I was." She didn't want to mention that she couldn't leave Aunt Maisie and the rest of the family while they were in earshot.

"Glad to be of help," Hank said. He looked into her eyes, and for a moment Fleeta forgot to be uncomfortable. "You're not like other girls."

"I should hope not. Girls wear me out." Fleeta widened her eyes. "I mean . . . what I meant to say is . . ."

"Oh, it's all right," Hank said. "Girls wear me out too. But then I've never met one who could shoot, hunt, carve a gunstock, and rescue lost flatlanders, all while looking equally fetching whether wearing a flannel shirt or a green skirt the color of pines in winter."

Fleeta moved her arm to hide the spot on her shirt, too flustered to think straight. "Elnora says I should be more ladylike, and Aunt Maisie says I should be thinking about marriage and children, but I'd rather be a gunsmith."

Hank touched the end of her braid where it had fallen over her shoulder, and Fleeta could swear she felt electricity shoot into her scalp. "Are those things mutually exclusive?"

She shrugged, using the motion to shift away a little, trying to get room to breathe. "Maybe not, but I don't have time for everything, so I've decided to prioritize. Starting my own business is at the top of my list."

Hank tapped the drawing in front of them. "Well, you certainly have a knack for this, and if my contribution helps you get started in business so that you have time for . . . other things, then I'm glad."

Fleeta felt like he was saying something more but didn't dare ponder what exactly that was. She settled for saying, "I'm grateful for the work."

Hank nodded. "We're leaving tomorrow at first light. We'll be back the week before Christmas. Think you'll have my stock carved by then?"

"I'm planning on it."

"Good. Good." He took a deep breath and shifted closer. "Fleeta, I've been thinking—"

"Hank, you ready? We need to get a good night's sleep." Judd strode back into the room, looked at the two of them, and cocked his head. "Or maybe you'uns need a minute more?"

"No, I think we've settled everything," Fleeta said, releasing a breath she hadn't realized she was holding. "Unless you have any changes?" She looked at Hank.

Hank ran a hand through his hair and shook his head. "No, I guess not." He glared at Judd. "I suppose we'll be back soon enough."

Judd looked as though he was trying hard not to laugh. "That we will. Or maybe even sooner." He winked, and the two men headed out.

One afternoon the following week, Fleeta found herself elbow-deep in the family's laundry when Albert stuck his head inside the doorway.

"I was over at Bud's shop this morning, trying to trade for that shotgun he's had on the wall for a coon's age, and he said for you to come by soon as you can."

"Did he say what for?"

Albert shrugged. "Nope, just said he wanted to talk to you."

It was all Fleeta could do not to drop everything and run over there that minute. But it was a good hour on foot, and she hated to ask Uncle Oscar or one of the boys to take her, especially since Albert had just been. Of course, she knew how to drive, but Aunt Maisie—who swore she'd never learn—wouldn't let Fleeta go anywhere in a car by herself. Not to mention the fact that she was supposed to get this blasted laundry done today.

Fleeta sighed and cranked another work shirt through the wringer. She knew some folks had electric wringers, but Elnora said having a machine at all was a luxury. Fleeta hadn't paid much attention to such *luxuries* until Aunt Maisie's latest downturn. It seemed like she'd never get well and truly better—she stayed so pale and got tired so quick. Fleeta certainly wasn't going to abandon her family when they needed her, yet the longing to know what Bud wanted was about to drive her crazy.

Finally she finished wringing out the last shirt, dumped it in a basket on top of the others, and braced herself to hang it all out on the line. Though it was December-cold outside, at least the sun was shining. She glanced at the clock and frowned. Even if she left for Bud's right now, walked the five miles as fast as she could, and didn't stay but five minutes, it would be dark before she got halfway back home. It just didn't pay to be a girl.

The wind bit at her fingers as she pegged out shirts and pants, her mind turning over and over as she pondered how to get to Bud's. As she picked up her empty basket and headed toward the house, Albert's pet jay swooped past her. She followed Jack's flight until he landed on the seat of Albert's beat-up old motorcycle out in the barn and snatched up a silvery bolt left lying there. Her cousin had finally gotten the machine running and had been riding it madly up and down the dirt roads since Thanksgiving. Uncle

Oscar complained that it scared the livestock, and Elnora said he would surely break his neck. But to Fleeta, it looked like freedom.

She wondered . . . Stashing the laundry basket inside the house, Fleeta piled on another layer of clothing—a pair of Albert's pants over her own, another flannel shirt, a heavy coat, wool mittens, and a scarf wrapped around and around her head. She lumbered out to the barn, eye out for any stray family members.

Albert had shown her—with great pride—how to work the motorcycle, and she'd gone for a brief and tolerably sedate ride on the back with her arms around Albert's waist. It had been exhilarating and a little bit terrifying. Could she do this by herself? She thought about Bud and her dream of smithing guns. Yes. She could do this.

Fleeta straddled the banged-up motorcycle, noting how Albert had polished the teardrop-shaped gas tank with the word *Indian* across it. She mentally traced her way through the start-up sequence before setting her foot on what looked like a bicycle pedal to the right of the machine. Thank goodness all her gun work had made her mechanically inclined. Satisfied that she knew what to do, Fleeta braced her foot against the pedal and thrust down with all her might.

Nothing.

She frowned and tried it again. Still nothing. Clearly she'd missed a step. Frustrated and a little bit intimidated by what she was attempting, she decided this must be a sign that God didn't want her taking Albert's motorcycle.

She felt like kicking something.

But instead of getting off the motorcycle and kicking a tire, she kicked that pedal one more time and the machine roared to life. She revved it using the right handlebar control, which was a little awkward with mittens, and felt a grin spread across her face. It was pure bliss to be in control of a powerful rifle, but this—this was heaven. She giggled and then laughed aloud, put the motorcycle in gear, and flew out of the barn like Jack chasing after one of Albert's treats.

11

W hat in tarnation did you ride in on?" Bud asked, squinting
through the dirty window at the front of his shop.

Fleeta took a deep breath and clasped her hands hard in front
of her. She was shaking from the cold and the sudden realization
that she had basically stolen her cousin's motorcycle. The exhila-
ration of setting out on the machine had given way to worry as
the wind bit her cheeks and cut through her mittens, making the
motorcycle even harder to handle. She'd wobbled a time or two
and it had taken her longer to get here than she'd expected. But
here she was. She released the air pent up in her lungs and held
her hands out toward the wood stove that seemed to do little more
than keep the frost off the insides of the windows. Her hands still
shook, but she didn't think Bud was paying close attention.

"It's Albert's motorcycle."

"Hunh. Albert trusts you more than I would. 'Course you ain't
exactly a typical female."

Fleeta tried to take the comment as a compliment, even though
it bit almost as deep as the wind had. She shrugged the words away
and turned to the older man. "Albert said you wanted to see me."

Bud grinned as wide as a barn door. "That I do. Seems like we
might be able to move our timeline up for you taking on this here

business." He said the last word as if it were three words—biz-e-ness.

Fleeta felt her heart flutter and her stomach clench. "How's that?"

"My sister down in Florida wants me to come live with her. I can't stand the cold like I used to, so it's sounding awful good to me. Sunshine and oranges all winter long."

Fleeta didn't even know he had a sister, but that was beside the point. "So you're leaving?"

Bud rubbed his chin and got a cagey look. "I'm thinking awful hard about it, although I'm not quite ready to turn all the way loose of what I have here. Plus, you seemed pretty sure you wouldn't be able to buy me out anytime soon. That right?"

Disappointment tamped down the happy flutters Fleeta was experiencing. "No sir, but I'm closer than I was." And once Hank gave her the second half of his payment, she'd be closer still.

"That so? What if you gave me what you've got as a sort of down payment, then you can use the place while I'm in Florida. I'll come on back around May or June, and if I decide to make this change permanent, maybe you'll have saved up enough by then to buy me out."

Fleeta realized she was shaking again, only this time it wasn't the cold. "That might work." She didn't want to sound too eager, but the thought of her dream being within reach made her feel faint.

"How much you got?" Bud drummed the fingers of one hand on the counter in front of him. He seemed to realize what he was doing and stopped.

Fleeta did some quick calculations in her head. She didn't want to give him every penny she had, but neither did she want to offer too little. She wrapped her arms around herself and looked at the floor. Of course, Hank was going to pay her a fair amount when he returned before Christmas, and she could use that for the basic supplies she'd need. Swallowing hard, she offered up almost all her savings.

Bud pursed his lips and looked toward the ceiling. "Hmmm." He counted on his fingers. "Not counting December, you'll have five months to earn some more." He scratched his head and let tobacco fly into a spittoon near his feet. Fleeta eyed the places where he'd missed and thought cleaning that up was the first thing she'd do if this all worked out.

"All right then. You bring me that amount by day after tomorrow and we'll have us a deal." He stuck out his right hand. Fleeta shook it as though the strength of her grip alone would hold her dreams together. She'd figure out how she was going to do this and take care of her family later.

The air was even colder and the evening heading rapidly toward dark as Fleeta made her way home. She'd had an even harder time starting the Indian the second time around, and she feared it might be out of gas, but it finally caught. Now she was riding as slow as she dared over the dirt roads. She was ecstatic over the deal she'd just struck, yet at the same time she was pretty sure Albert would skin her alive when he found his motorcycle missing. Never mind what Uncle Oscar and Aunt Maisie would have to say.

Still, she managed to spend most of the trip home imagining how she'd fix up Bud's shop. There was a small kitchen in back and a bedroom upstairs. Of course, she'd never been up there, but Bud assured her it was a spacious sleeping room. She'd been in the back room and saw how it needed lots of work. The sink with its hand pump was stained with iron, and the stove looked like it might fall apart if the wind kicked up, but she was plenty handy, and her cousins would help. She made a face. Well, they would if they ever forgave her for running off with Albert's motorcycle and planning to abandon them.

Almost home, Fleeta wished she could remove one hand from the grip long enough to tuck her nearly frozen fingers under her arm. But she was already shaky with both hands firmly grasping the handlebars and she was afraid to attempt it. She squinted down the road, not knowing how to turn on the motorcycle's headlamp. It was more than a little dark.

Making the last turn onto the road that led to the farmhouse, Fleeta let out her breath and relaxed as much as she dared. She'd have to face the music tonight, but she'd get someone to run her back over to Bud's with the money she'd promised, and just like that she'd have her own gun shop. More or less.

Lost in thought in the darkness, Fleeta caught a glimpse of a deer bounding through the woods out of the corner of her eye. The animal was huge, even larger than the motorcycle she was riding, and suddenly filled the road in front of her. Fleeta liked to think she was trying to avoid hitting the deer, but she supposed it was mostly instinct that caused her to twist the handlebars and lay the machine down in the rocky roadbed. There was a terrible sound of scraping metal, roaring engine, and maybe her own screaming. Then just the sputter of the dying motor.

Fleeta lay in the road and looked off to the left where a massive buck stood watching her. He had at least eight points on his wide-spreading antlers. He was dappled with a white underbelly and chest and brown spots cascading across his back. With a start, Fleeta realized it had to be the same buck she'd missed shooting the day Aunt Maisie lost her baby. The ghost deer. Even in the gloaming she could see his eyes—warm, brown, and with an expression of . . . pity? With a flick of his ears and a snort, he turned and ran off, leaving Fleeta to shake off the impression that a deer felt sorry for her.

"What in the name of all that's holy is going on out here?" Uncle Oscar's unmistakable voice accompanied the bouncing light from his Big Beam flashlight.

Fleeta flinched, almost hoping she was hurt badly enough to avoid her uncle's wrath, not to mention Albert's.

"Fleeta, darlin', is that you?" Her uncle set his light down so he could lift the motorcycle, which Fleeta realized was pinning her leg to the ground.

Uncle Oscar knelt beside her and winced when he saw her leg.

Fleeta looked too and blanched at the sight. She never had trouble with blood—unless it was her own. And in spite of having two pairs of pants on, she could see blood soaking her calf. A wave of dizziness made her lay her head down in the grit of the road.

Albert appeared over her uncle's shoulder. "I think you're in worse shape than the motorcycle, Fleeta."

She marveled that neither of the men seemed angry, just concerned. For her.

"I'll be all right." Her voice cracked, and she bit her lip to keep from crying. "Did you see that deer?"

"Let's get her inside," Uncle Oscar said. "She's talking nonsense."

Albert wheeled his precious Indian over into the yard and came back to help Fleeta to her feet. With the help of both men, she hobbled to the back door and into the brightly lit dining room. The whole family—even Elnora with her husband and son—sat around the empty table, watching her. Fleeta noted that Simeon's book was lying in front of him, closed.

Aunt Maisie stood and braced herself against the table. "Thank God you're still in one piece. I've never been so worried in my life. Oscar, is she all right?"

"Looks like a pretty good cut on her left leg there. See if you can't get her britches off."

Aunt Maisie and Elnora shooed the boys from the room and began stripping Fleeta's extra layers off like they were handling a newborn. Once they'd exposed her bare leg, Fleeta refused to look at it. She stared at the ceiling instead, steeling herself for how bad it must be. They might even need to stitch it up. What if she lost her foot?

"Well if that isn't the luckiest thing I ever saw." Aunt Maisie stood back, hands on her hips. "Sweetheart, it's more motor oil than blood. You just have a little ole cut there. Let me dab some Mercurochrome on it and you should be fine." She headed out of the room at her usual slow pace.

Fleeta blinked back tears, trying to take in this latest news.

"Does anything else hurt?" asked Elnora.

Fleeta couldn't stand it anymore. "Why is everyone being so nice? I stole Albert's motorcycle so I could go meet with Bud Lyons and make plans to leave here." She grabbed Elnora's arm. "I'm going to run off and abandon you all. And I've been underhanded about it. Why isn't Uncle Oscar yelling at me?"

Elnora laughed and shook her head. "Oh, Fleeta, Albert loves you more than that silly motorcycle, and no one expects you to stay here and carry the load that's this family. You have dreams and plans of your own." She pursed her lips. "I'm still pretty skeptical about this business of making guns, but if that's what you want to do, then I'm proud of you."

Now the tears did flow. "But I ruined Albert's motorcycle."

"I only hope you did, but I suspect he'll have it up and running again before tomorrow's out. And even if you did spoil it, you're far more important than some piece of machinery."

Fleeta choked on a sob. "I don't deserve"—she gasped—"I don't deserve . . ."

"None of us do," Elnora said, tears glinting in her eyes now. "But you're family, and one mistake isn't going to change that. We love you." She smiled. "*I* love you. And if you feel like you need to be punished, well, Mother with Mercurochrome will likely prove sufficient."

Fleeta smiled as well and hugged her cousin, whom she realized was more sister than she had any right to expect. "I love you too."

"I'm going to pay you whatever it costs to fix that thing," Fleeta told Albert two days later as he tinkered with the Indian. She was sore, and her bruises were worse than the cut on her leg, but she was grateful it hadn't been worse.

"I thought you were sinking your savings into Bud's place."

Fleeta squirmed. "Not all of it."

"Aw, it won't cost me anything. I just need to figure out how to trade for a new frame. This one's bent too bad to straighten back out. Merle says he can rustle one up for me, and you know he loves a good trade almost as much as cash."

"What will you trade him?"

Albert wiped his hands on a rag. "Might let him have my bone-handled knife."

Fleeta jerked up straighter and flinched as pain shot through her bruised shoulder. "That's your favorite. You use it all the time."

"Yeah, well, sometimes you have to shift your priorities."

"Surely we can come up with something else."

Albert laughed. "Here he comes now—if you can come up with something he'd like better than my knife, I won't stop you from offering."

Fleeta's hand went almost involuntarily to her mother's pin, where she wore it under her sweater and coat. Ever since that day at the bookmobile, she'd continued to wear it pinned to her underthings—it made her feel as though her mother were close by.

"Howdy, young'uns," Merle hollered. He always talked too loud, probably because he was usually talking over gunfire. "Only way I could get you a frame was to go ahead and buy the whole motorcycle. Figured if you didn't want it, I could fix it up and sell it to somebody else. 'Course it's gonna be a mite pricier than we originally talked about."

Fleeta saw her cousin's shoulders sag. "How much pricier?"

"Weeell," Merle said, dragging out the word, "enough that I'm gonna need more than a shoat or a speckled pup to trade for."

Albert reached for the knife he wore at his waist. Fleeta grabbed his arm. "What about cold, hard cash?" She'd thought to offer him her brooch but just couldn't bring herself to do it.

"Well now, that's about my favorite thing to trade for—just the right color and always fits."

Fleeta could see Albert squirming, but he let her go ahead. "How much do you think would be a fair price?"

The two of them went back and forth a few times, until Merle finally agreed to a number that was going to make it impossible for Fleeta to give Bud the amount they had agreed upon. Even so, Fleeta went to her hiding place, leaving the men to talk, and retrieved the money. While it pained her to hand it over, making things right with Albert was more important than anything else right now.

Merle tucked the cash in a jacket pocket and almost jogged back to his truck, where he brought out a motorcycle that looked to be in even worse shape than Albert's. He waved them over.

"Check it out real good." He ran a hand along the motorcycle's frame. "It's seen better days, but the frame's as straight as a Baptist preacher, and I reckon you can get other parts off'n here."

Albert walked all around the machine, then peered into the back of Merle's truck. "Hey, is that a sidecar?"

"Sure is—you can have that too. Don't have much use for a sidecar without something to drag it around."

The look of utter delight on Albert's face made Fleeta's sacrifice feel almost worth it. Almost.

12

Hank was beyond frustrated. He'd planned to head back to West Virginia no later than December eighteenth. Now it was the nineteenth, and the men on the Wateree job were making his life a misery. He'd tried to chalk up men missing work as well as deadlines to the holidays, but his Christmas cheer was about to run out.

He stomped into the main office in Myrtle Beach and headed straight for Judd's desk. George Heyward was technically still in charge of Waccamaw Timber, but he'd been leaving more and more of the actual timbering up to his son-in-law, with Hank as his right hand and no hope of ever advancing beyond that. Though Judd hated being in the office, he recognized it as a necessary evil if he was going to keep up with all the timber tracts—including the one they'd just agreed to purchase in West Virginia.

Hank hit Judd's door with the butt of his hand and burst into the room. "How am I supposed—?" He stopped talking as Larkin leapt from her husband's lap, her cheeks gone rosy.

"Why, Hank Chapin, didn't your mother teach you to knock?" She smoothed her skirt with one hand and tucked hair that had come free of her ponytail behind her ear with the other. Judd just grinned.

Hank snorted. "Well, I know your mother taught you never to make out in a place of business."

Larkin made a face at him. "I'll kiss my husband wherever and whenever I want."

Judd tilted back in his leather chair. "And I'm sure not going to try to talk her out of it." He hooked a hand around Larkin's waist and drew her to his side. "Sweetheart, based on the steam coming out of Hank's ears, I think we're going to have to talk business for a few minutes. While Hank knows I prefer your company to his, I'm guessing I'd better give him some time."

Larkin flipped her ponytail and gave Hank a sassy look. "Oh, all right, but only because I'm due to pick Lavonia up from Mother's." She bent down and gave Judd a final kiss. As she passed Hank on the way out, she reached over and squeezed his arm. "Don't let the world get you down, Hank. God has everything worked out already." She winked at him. "And I've told Him more than once what I think those plans ought to be."

Larkin gone, Hank slumped into a chair across from Judd's desk. "You have your hands full with that one. I always figured she'd marry a doctor or a lawyer, but I sure am glad you showed up."

Judd rubbed a hand across his mouth, looking thoughtful. "I am too, and you know, finding a girl and getting married was just about the last thing on my mind that day you met up with me on the Greyhound bus." He leaned forward, his arms on his desk. "Larkin's got a point about God having plans."

"Yeah, well, I don't doubt it. But in the meantime, I've got to get that crew down on the Wateree to do more than talk."

"Why?"

Hank loved Judd like a brother, but at that moment he thought he might boil over. "Why? Because we have a quota to meet, a deadline coming up, timber to get to the mill. What do you mean, *why*?"

"I mean, why do you have to do it?"

Hank felt the fire go out of him. "It's my job."

Judd nodded. "So it is. And it's my job and it's the job of that Leroy fella we hired back in October."

"Aw, Leroy's still learning the ropes."

"I learned 'em by jumping in with both feet and paddling as hard as I could. Might be Leroy could do the same." Judd settled back in his chair and crossed his hands over his middle. "Seems to me you're a man who doesn't know whether he wants to cut bait or go fishing and so you're trying to do both."

Hank rubbed at a headache starting right between his eyes. "You could be right. It's just . . . what if I wanted to get out of timbering?"

"You're a right handy fella. I reckon you could do whatever you put your mind to."

"But it would mean leaving Waccamaw Timber."

Judd nodded. "In order to do something else, I can see where that would be necessary."

"You wouldn't be upset?" Hank gripped the arm of his chair. He hadn't planned to have this conversation until after Christmas, but here it was, out in the open.

"Well, I hope you might stick around to make sure ole Leroy doesn't go under before you leave, but following your heart—and God's leading—seems like the right road to take." He rerolled the cuff of his work shirt. "And it's occurred to me that when Larkin hitched her wagon to a mountain man, it might have put a crimp in your plans. Seems like if neither Ben nor Larkin stepped up to the plate, you might have been in line to sit in this chair." He thumped its leather-wrapped arm. "I'd be glad to run this business with you as partner, but it'll be a while before I'm in a position to offer that. You always struck me as the sort of fellow to know what you want—if it's something other than Waccamaw Timber, I'll help you any way I can."

Hank's mind was racing. He could stay on with the timber company while he lined up some customers for guns. He figured six months would be enough time to train Leroy and to make sure he wasn't jumping off a cliff. And while Judd's hint at a future partnership was tempting, it also clarified the idea that what he wanted was to run his own show—not someone else's.

"Hank, I can smell that engine in your head burning oil. Slow down, take some time, and think things over." Judd found a piece of paper on his desk and ran a finger down a list. "You've got some holiday time coming, plus we'd planned on you heading back to West Virginia to tie up any loose ends on that new tract. How about you get that done and then take some time for yourself. Hunt some more." He grinned extra wide. "Check and see if Fleeta's got that gunstock carved for you yet." He winked. "I won't be expecting you back until after Christmas."

"But what about—?"

Judd held up his hand. "I'll handle it." He smiled. "Or maybe I'll put ole Leroy to the test. I think that boy's got grit."

Hank started to protest again, but then thought better of it. He felt lighter, freer than he had in a long time. Judd had just given him room to decide about his future. It was the best Christmas gift he could ask for. He pictured Larkin snuggled in Judd's lap, and his thoughts turned to a certain dark-haired beauty with a smudge of gun oil on her cheek. There was a lot of future to think about.

He reached across the desk to shake Judd's hand, but his friend got up and came around to him, grabbing him in a bear hug.

"You're my best friend in South Carolina," Judd said. "I hope that will never change."

Hank thumped Judd on the back. "Can't see why it would."

"Oh, and if you need a place to stay up there in West Virginia, I know Abram and Lydia would be proud to have you."

"Sounds like just the medicine I need," Hank said.

Fleeta pulled an old candy tin out from underneath the grain bin in the barn. She'd first found the hiding place when she was six years old. For years it had been her special spot for stowing pretty rocks, a broken pocketknife, bits of ribbon, or other treasures. Recently she'd started keeping her savings here. Elnora had been after her to open an account at the bank, but Fleeta liked to keep her money where she could see and touch it. She counted it all for the third time, coming to the same total. She'd take all of it to Bud and hope he'd be willing to wait until she got her next payment from Hank for the rest.

Her heart beat like a moth against the glass of a lantern. She rarely spent money, much less the entirety of her savings. She wished her parents were around to guide her. Surely they would know if she was making a wise decision or not. She pressed her hand to the place just above her heart where she could feel the outline of her mother's brooch. Maybe, in a way, they were with her.

Impatient with her own useless wishing, Fleeta stuffed the cash in her pocket and turned toward the door. Albert had finally gotten his motorcycle running again and offered to take her to Bud's in the sidecar. Fleeta would have preferred riding the motorcycle on her own, but she didn't dare suggest it.

She bundled up and jogged out into the farmyard, where Albert was revving the Indian. He'd folded an old blanket in the sidecar, and Fleeta burrowed underneath. Albert had rounded up a pair of riding goggles from who knew where, and he grinned at Fleeta from behind them.

"Ready?" he hollered over the coughing roar of the engine.

Fleeta nodded and held on tight as Albert unleashed the motorcycle. She saw Jack the blue jay swooping through the air after them.

They got to Bud's much faster than Fleeta had on her own. She climbed out of the sidecar, her knees weak and her hands sweaty. She told herself it was a combination of Albert's driving and her excitement over seeing her dream come true, but her dry mouth felt more like fear than excitement. Bud met them out front, a duffel slung over his shoulder.

He didn't waste any time on howdies. "My aunt Gertie's sick— I've got to get on over there and see what I can do to help. I'll be gone about a week. You want to do this when I get back? I'm not quite ready to hand her over today."

Fleeta counted the days. "I was hoping to sign the papers before Christmas so I could open up on January first."

"I know—you mentioned something about that. We can take care of business right now, and I'll send Aunt Gertie's girl over here to clean it up and let you know it's ready before the week's out. How's that sound?"

Fleeta fidgeted and glanced at Albert, who shrugged his shoulders. He was no help. "All right, let's get our business done and I'll be looking for—what's her name?"

"Mary. You probably ain't met her before."

"No, I don't think I have, but I'll be looking for her before Christmas. Let her know I'll be glad to help with whatever needs doing."

Bud nodded and whipped a piece of paper out of his back pocket. "Got the paper work right here. Says you'll pay me the sum we agreed upon and then you'll have full use of all my equipment and this here building for the next six months at which time we'll revisit the agreement."

"About that." Fleeta shifted from foot to foot. "Turns out I had"—she darted a look at Albert—"an unexpected expense. I don't quite have the *full* amount we discussed."

Bud spat a stream of tobacco juice. "Doggone it, how much do you have then?"

Fleeta told him.

"No, no, that ain't enough."

"As soon as I get the final payment on a job I've been doing, I'll be able to give you the rest. Probably as soon as you get back from your aunt Gertie's."

Bud heaved a sigh. "I'm gonna need some kind of assurance you plan to pay the rest. Don't you have anything else of value you can give me for collateral?"

Fleeta felt the weight of her mother's pin and slowly reached for it. She noticed Jack fly over and land on the far corner of the porch roof. He peered at them with those hard, black eyes of his, and Fleeta felt almost as though the bird was accusing her of something. She reached a trembling hand inside her shirt and pulled out the luckenbooth. The sharp point pricked her flesh as she removed it.

Bud's eyes lit up for just a moment, but then he got a cagey look. "That a real jewel there in the middle?"

"It's an amethyst." Fleeta tilted the brooch in the sunlight so that it glinted. "I'll want it back as soon as I bring you the rest of the money."

Bud reached out and took the brooch, turning it around and around in his hands. The stone caught the sun and looked almost alive. Fleeta swallowed hard. She hated to part with the pin even for a week, but she'd get it back just as soon as Hank gave her the rest of the payment he'd promised.

Bud tossed the brooch high, caught it as it tumbled through the air in a glittery flash, then flipped it again. This time, as the pin tumbled through the air, Jack swooped down and snatched at it.

"Whoa there. Dadgum bird." Bud tucked it in his pocket. "I reckon this'll do. Now if you'll just sign that paper, I can be on my way. Aunt Gertie's not going to get better while we stand here jawing."

Fleeta took the paper and began reading—it looked fine, but she knew she should read every word. "Can we step inside while I look this over?"

"Already locked her up and I got to get on the road." He reached for his pocket. "If'n you need more time, we can do this after Christmas."

"No, no, that's all right." Fleeta took the ink pen Bud offered and scrawled her signature at the bottom of the page, then handed over the cash.

Bud took the pen and paper, tucked them back in his pocket, and thumbed through the roll of bills Fleeta gave him. He nodded his head once, shook Fleeta's hand, and trotted toward his truck, tossing the duffel in the back with a thud. "I'll send a copy of that paper back with Mary." He climbed in the truck, rolled the window down, and leaned his head out. "Good doing business with you." He waved toward Jack, still sitting on the porch roof. "And watch out for that dumb bird—he'll steal anything shiny you leave lying around. Stole a perfectly good punch just last week."

Fleeta raised her hand in a wave. "Hope your aunt's better real soon."

"Thank ya," Bud said and drove away.

Albert turned to Fleeta. "Thought there'd be more to it than that."

"So did I." Fleeta stared after the truck, then looked back at the ramshackle building. "Think you can help me fix this place up?"

"Don't see why not," Albert said. "Probably not half so hard as getting a motorcycle to run."

Fleeta went over to the porch, which was badly tilted. Leveling that up would be the first order of business. She peered in the front window, but the shade had been drawn. She tried the next window and found the same.

"Guess Bud didn't want anyone to see what kind of mess he left the place," she said. "Good thing he's sending Mary over to red it up."

Albert stomped his feet and slapped his hands together. "Let's head on home. I'm freezing out here, and the ride back isn't going to warm me up any."

Fleeta felt reluctant to leave. This was her place of business now, and she longed to go inside and start setting it to rights, but she supposed there would be time enough for that later. With a last, longing look, she tucked herself back into the sidecar and dreamed all the way home about the guns she'd shape.

13

Hank rolled up in Abram's front yard on December twentieth. Although it was a sight colder than in South Carolina, he supposed this was mild weather for being almost Christmas. He thought his sister would be put out with him for missing two major holidays in a row, but when he said he was heading back to West Virginia, she got a dreamy look in her eye and wished him a Merry Christmas. He strongly suspected Larkin had been talking to her.

"Mr. Hank!" The voice emanated from a blur of a boy rocketing toward him from the front porch of the house. Hank braced himself against James crashing into his side. "You're just in time to go with us to cut some pine and holly for the banister and the mantel."

"Let the man sit a minute," Abram said from the front door. "That greenery isn't going anywhere in the next hour."

James let his head fall back in exasperation.

Hank leaned forward and whispered in his ear, "Might be I won't need to rest as long as your daddy thinks."

James brightened and took Hank's suitcase, hauling it toward the house with only a little listing to one side. That boy would be a man before long.

"Judd sent word to expect you," Abram said. "Lydia's thrilled clear down to her toes to have company for Christmas. Gives her an excuse to dress the place up extra nice."

"Not for my sake," Hank said.

Abram shook a finger at him. "Now, don't you go ruining it by being polite. It's the happiest I've seen her in a month of Sundays. Just say how nice the decorations look and she'll be content till next December."

Hank smiled. "That I can do."

James lugged Hank's suitcase inside while Abram lingered on the front porch. He leaned on the railing and eyed Hank. "I'm thinking it's more than my wife's good cooking and a parcel of timber that's brought you back so soon."

Hank shrugged and rolled his eyes skyward. "Could be, although Lydia's a mighty fine cook."

"That she is. I hear Fleeta Brady can't cook a lick."

Hank narrowed his eyes at his new friend. "What's that got to do with the price of eggs?"

It was Abram's turn to shrug, but his eyes sparkled. "Nothing. Just thought I'd mention it. Now come on in—supper's about ready."

Fleeta couldn't stand this much longer. Mary still hadn't come around by the twenty-first of December. She'd been assuming Bud's niece would stop by to tell her when the shop was ready, but then again maybe she'd just tidy it up and go on home. Might be Fleeta should mosey on over there and see if anything had been done. She couldn't hardly stand all the holiday fuss Aunt Maisie and Elnora were stirring up anyhow. Too much baking and decorating and acting all mysterious about gifts. She'd found peace working on Hank's magnolia carving, but that only went so far. What she really wanted was to scrub every inch of Bud's old shop and get it ready to open at the first of the year. She'd put word out that she'd be operating out of that space soon, and if folks lived up to their promises, she'd have a fair amount of business right away.

So, on a mild morning just three days before Christmas, she packed some cleaning supplies, laced up her work boots, and set out to walk to town and the shop that was now hers. She had her head down, picturing how she'd display rifles on the back wall, when a car eased up beside her. She nearly jumped sideways, but controlled herself, feeling embarrassed that she'd been snuck up upon. Especially when she glanced to her right and saw it was Hank Chapin.

"Thought I'd better come check on that carving you're doing for me."

Fleeta felt a surge of happiness that she credited to being on her way to her very own smithing shop. "It's purt near done, although I still have some fine-tuning to do. You in a hurry to have it?"

Hank shut off the car and got out to talk to her. "Not especially. Although I might like to see you finishing the work if an audience wouldn't trouble you."

This time Fleeta felt something clench low in her stomach. It wasn't unpleasant so much as unnerving. He wanted to watch her work? "I don't guess anyone's ever asked that of me before."

"It's fine if you'd rather not. I'm just curious to see what tools you use and how it's done."

Fleeta warmed at the idea of someone being that interested in her carving. "It'd be all right, I suppose. You could come to supper one evening and I'll finish it up after. That way you'll have it before Christmas."

Hank nodded and considered the bucket she was holding. "Where are you toting that bucket of cleaning stuff?"

"I'm on my way to check on my new gunsmith shop." She delighted in his raised eyebrows.

Hank cocked his head at her the way Jack did when he thought Albert had a treat. "You found a shop?"

"I did," she nearly crowed. "Bud Lyons is moving south, and he's letting me rent his place, along with all his tools for six months, then hopefully I'll have made enough money to buy it outright."

Hank let out a whoop, grabbed her, and twirled her in the air, nearly sending the bucket flying. When he set her back down on her feet, one arm stayed around her shoulders as he looked into her eyes with such warmth that she forgot it was December. "I knew you could do it, I just didn't think it would happen this fast." He squeezed her shoulder and reached down for the bucket.

She almost wished he'd left that hand right there, warming her back so that it sent heat all through her. The thought made her want to shake herself like a dog and run off, but she willed herself to simply reach for the supplies he'd taken.

"Oh no," he said. "You just march right on around this car and climb in. I'm driving you to your new shop."

Hank hurried around the car and opened the door with a flourish. Fleeta hesitated, then grinned and slipped into the spotlessly clean sedan. Hank stowed the bucket in the trunk, then climbed back behind the steering wheel.

"You must be thrilled, and your family too," he said as they started down the road.

Fleeta laughed, but it sounded breathy and unnatural. She cleared her throat. "I sure am, but the family doesn't pay me much mind."

"Well, that's a shame."

"Aw, it's not that they don't care. There's just so much to keep up with, and Aunt Maisie still isn't right after losing her last baby." She flushed. She hadn't meant to mention that. "They're glad for me—they just don't show it too much." She felt her cheeks get even warmer. They certainly didn't grab her up in their arms and spin her around.

"I'm glad I'm here to celebrate with you then," Hank said. "Can I help you set the place to rights?" She opened her mouth to reply, and he hurried to add, "Not that you need me, but I find a joy shared is often doubled."

"All right then," she said with a slow smile. Then Fleeta relaxed and let herself enjoy his easy company.

Hank felt like a schoolboy. But instead of carrying a girl's books or lunch sack, he was helping her with a bucketful of cleaning supplies. He'd thought a lot about Fleeta in the weeks since he'd seen her and wondered if he was building her up too much in his mind. But the moment he laid eyes on her, obviously woolgathering as she walked along in her worn boots, denim pants with a patch over one knee, and overlarge man's coat, he knew if anything he'd underestimated his feelings. There was definitely something about how unfussy and how independent she was that drew him in like the tide. And he knew that even if she ran him off, he'd roll in again and again until she let him stay.

"There it is," she said, pointing to a ramshackle building on the edge of town.

Hank schooled his expression. The two-story structure sure didn't look like much. He hoped the rent wasn't too high. But then it likely wouldn't be since it wasn't exactly on the main thoroughfare.

"Do you have a key?" he asked.

"No, but Bud's niece is supposed to be around. Should be unlocked."

Hank didn't say so, but he would have expected a gunsmith shop full of tools to be locked up tight. Maybe folks were more trusting around here.

Fleeta stepped up onto the rickety porch and tried the front door. No good. "Come on around back," she called.

Hank followed her through knee-high dead weeds until they came to a back door. It too was locked. Fleeta made a face and began working her way around, trying the windows.

"Maybe we should wait until this niece turns up," Hank suggested. "Someone might think we're trying to break in."

Fleeta grunted and heaved open a window. "Aw, folks know I'm taking this place over," she said, scrambling through the opening. She poked her head back out. "Come around to the front door and I'll let you in."

Hank wasn't sure this was the best protocol, but the look of utter delight on Fleeta's face stifled any protest. He shook his head and walked back around front, tripping over an old tire on the way. The door was still closed when he stepped up onto the porch, but he could hear scuffling inside. Then the door flew open, and he froze at the look on Fleeta's face.

"I must have misunderstood," she said, turning back and raising the shades on the windows.

The room was dim and dusty and, to all appearances, empty. Hank breathed in the musty closed-up smell and finally set the bucket down on a sort of wooden counter that ran half the length of the wide front room. Fleeta was now behind that counter, running her hands over a shelf. She stood, cobwebs in her hair and a smudge of dirt on her cheek. "There aren't any tools here." Her eyes were blank, staring off into the distance.

"Maybe they're in another room," Hank said.

Fleeta snapped her fingers. "He hid them in case anyone broke in. Of course. Help me look. You take the first floor and I'll take the second."

She was off and up the stairs before Hank could say anything more. He began a thorough search of the three rooms on the first floor. The main room ran the width of the building with a small kitchen and what appeared to be a storeroom behind it. The front room was profoundly empty. The kitchen included a chipped sink with a hand pump and drain board, a stove he doubted worked now if it ever had, and a Formica-topped table with a three-legged chair. The storeroom featured shelves with some dusty jars of canned goods and a wooden crate that, based on the smell, contained rotten potatoes.

No tools or anyplace to hide them.

Hank headed back out to the main room just in time to see Fleeta descend the stairs and plop down near the bottom. "I don't understand it. I paid him for the use of the shop and the tools, and it's obvious no one's been here to clean." She turned hurting eyes on Hank. "You don't think he'd . . ."

Hank did indeed think Bud might have taken Fleeta's money

and run, but he wasn't going to put that into words. "I'm sure there's an explanation," he offered instead. "In the meantime, we can air this place out so it's ready when we find out what happened to the tools."

Fleeta shook her head. "I can't believe what a fool I've been." She leaned forward until her forehead rested on her knees. "And you're here to witness my shame."

Hank stood, the emptiness of the room yawning around them. He needed words but couldn't think what they should be.

"And the worst of it is, I gave him Momma's pin."

Fleeta's shoulders began to shake. Hank braced himself for the wails, but she was silent, tears dripping to the floor with her whole body curling in on itself. He took a step toward her, not sure what to do. Finally he sank down on the stairs beside her and laid a gentle hand on her back. He could feel the muscles there even beneath her coat. She was strong, but at this moment weakness had overcome her.

He quoted one of his favorite verses, without even thinking about it. "'And he said unto me, My grace is sufficient for thee: for my strength is made perfect in weakness. Most gladly therefore will I rather glory in my infirmities, that the power of Christ may rest upon me. Therefore I take pleasure in infirmities, in reproaches, in necessities, in persecutions, in distresses for Christ's sake: for when I am weak, then am I strong.'"

The shaking beneath his hand stilled, and Fleeta raised her face, blotchy and red. "I don't feel the least bit strong."

"Maybe that's because you aren't," Hank said softly. "But God is. And maybe He has a plan to use this for His glory."

Fleeta released a stuttering sigh and leaned her cheek against Hank's shoulder. "I can't see how. All I know is that my dream is gone, along with my mother's pin, and I'm not sure which one hurts more."

Hank slid a tentative arm around her shoulders and found she didn't resist. He held her, whispering a prayer that God would show them both the good is this terrible turn of events, because for the life of him he couldn't see it either.

14

Two days after finding Bud's shop empty, the mix of emotions running through Fleeta was still more than she could sort out. The horror and disgust that she'd let Bud cheat her out of his equipment and her mother's brooch kept swamping her. She hadn't told anyone but Albert about her discovery. Albert scuffed his boot and looked solemn, finally saying, "Maybe he took it all with him to keep it safe."

Fleeta didn't believe that for a second, although it was nice of Albert to try to make her feel better. She told herself she'd just have to face up to her mistake and learn this very hard lesson. Storming around and crying—which she could very easily do—were altogether too female a reaction, one she'd already let Hank see. From here on out she'd just have to bear up and take it like a man.

But even as the agony of her mistake began to sink in, she also felt nervous and maybe even excited about Hank coming over to watch her finish his gunstock. He'd been so kind to her, so comforting, and that Scripture he spoke—while it didn't change her situation, it had soothed in a way she couldn't quite explain. And in the midst of her pain she was looking forward to seeing the man she'd come to think of—only in the quiet of her own mind—as her Southern gentleman.

Aunt Maisie got supper going and then turned the meal over to

Fleeta, which was a good thing since she could hardly fry an egg and hadn't improved much with practice over the last weeks. There was stewed rabbit—she'd got the rabbits herself—fried cabbage with potatoes, and now she was supposed to make corn bread while keeping everything else from burning. As she mixed buttermilk and eggs into cornmeal, she marveled that wood seemed to just shape itself under her hands while bread felt downright contrary. Once she thought the batter looked like Aunt Maisie's, she poured it into a skillet with lard that had been heating in the oven. The batter bubbled and hissed in the fat, sending up the sweet smell of corn. She slid it in the hot oven thinking maybe she wouldn't ruin the meal for once.

She heard voices in the sitting room. Wiping her hands on her pants, she hurried out of the kitchen to see if Hank had arrived. He stood inside the front door talking to Uncle Oscar, which gave Fleeta a moment to look him over. She'd noticed before that he wasn't especially tall, but he was broad-shouldered, and she itched to push down a piece of his sandy hair sticking up in back—probably because he'd taken his hat off like gentlemen do.

She decided he looked . . . solid. She'd known handsomer men, yet Hank's looks soothed and unsettled her all at once. A sudden thought shook her—what if Aunt Maisie had given her that blasted brooch because Hank was about to enter her life? Not that she wanted to fall in love with him, but if she had to love someone, he might do. What was it Aunt Maisie said? She should look at the pin and remember that her mother wanted her to fall in love one day. The idea that seemed so awful that day suddenly didn't feel quite like the death sentence she'd imagined.

Except, of course, the brooch and any influence it carried was now lost to her. She'd as good as thrown it away.

Hank turned, and there was that warmth in his eyes again. Fleeta felt her insides flutter and spin. She started to speak, then rushed from the room back to the kitchen to make sure the cabbage wasn't burning.

The meal proved as much a success as Fleeta could hope. The

corn bread was a little dry, and the cabbage stuck to the pan in places, but nothing was burnt or ruined.

"Ma, you must be feeling better," Albert said.

"I have been some," Aunt Maisie answered. "What made you notice?"

"I figured you must've cooked supper since it ain't ruined."

"Isn't ruined, and Fleeta did a fair amount of the cooking."

Albert feigned shock. "It's a miracle." He looked at Hank, wide-eyed. "I thought we might starve or die of poisoning the way Fleeta cooks." He then yelped, thanks to Fleeta's well-placed foot.

"Albert, don't tease your cousin so," Aunt Maisie said. "You know she's a . . . tolerable cook."

Fleeta almost wanted to kick her aunt as well, but instead she stood from the table. "Hank, you want to see your gunstock now?"

Looking like he was trying to hold in laughter, Hank nodded and followed her into what Aunt Maisie liked to call the parlor. It was a little-used room, especially in winter when it wasn't worth the trouble of keeping up another fire. Fleeta had cleaned the room from top to bottom that morning, telling herself she was doing it to distract herself from thinking about throwing her dream away. She added coal to the fire she'd built before supper to keep the cold at bay. She'd set out Hank's shotgun and her tools on a towel laid over her aunt's tea table. She preferred a sturdier worktable, but it would do.

Hank already had the gun in his hands, running callused fingers over the carving that was almost complete. Fleeta didn't have much experience feeling nervous about her work, but the way Hank was examining every detail made her hands start to sweat.

"It's not quite done," she said.

Hank finally turned to look at her, then closed his eyes and inhaled deeply through his nose. "I swear I can smell it, that magnolia's so real." Finally he blew out a breath, the gun still in his hands. "Magnolias have a sort of clean citrusy smell. Makes you wish you could just breathe in and never exhale."

Watching him made Fleeta feel dizzy. Maybe she could smell it too. "You like it then?"

A slow grin spread across his face. "That I do." He studied the intricate carving, robbing Fleeta of the warmth in his eyes. "I can't see what more there is to do, but I'd sure enjoy watching you carve whatever it is."

Fleeta wiped her damp palms on her shirt and took the gun, pulling over a stool. "I'm not quite done with the crosshatching on this—what is it? A seedpod?" She indicated the spot near the trigger. "This is a good place to give you some extra grip."

Picking up a small chisel, she began removing slivers of wood in a crosshatch pattern. She became so absorbed in the work, she almost forgot Hank was there. It wasn't until she sat back to take in the overall effect that her eyes flicked to his once again. What she saw there shook her.

She swallowed hard. "That should just about do it. I'll sand it some more, but it's pretty much done if you're satisfied."

Hank gave her that slow smile once again. "Oh, I've rarely been so satisfied as I am right at this moment. You have a remarkable gift." He leaned forward, bracing his elbows on his knees. "I hope you don't mind, Fleeta, but I went into town to see the sheriff about Bud Lyons."

Fleeta stiffened. "You spoke to the sheriff?"

"I sure did. He said there'd been a complaint or two about unpaid bills, but nothing to cause much concern. Then I asked if there'd been any problems in other places with someone making promises, then skipping town. That rang a bell." Hank settled back in his chair. "Sheriff had a notice about a fella over in Cabell County who was buying and selling guns, found himself a partner with a nice bankroll, and then skipped town. His name was Bill Lynch, yet his physical description was awful close to the one Albert gave me for Bud Lyons."

Fleeta felt dizzy again. "You asked Albert about Bud?"

"I did. Didn't want to involve you unless I thought I was on to something. And now I think maybe I am. This other fella earned the trust of the locals and found an individual who wanted to start a business and 'sold' his going concern." Hank rubbed his hands on his knees. "And here's the kicker—when I was at the sheriff's office, a fellow came in to report that just yesterday Bud had tried to sell his wife a piece of jewelry this fellow thought might have been stolen. He said it was a heart pin with a purple jewel in it."

Hank grinned. "And would you believe he said there was a crazy blue jay hounding that man. Kept flying at him until he got in his truck and drove away. You think that might be Jack?"

Fleeta stood like she might fall over if she didn't do it just right. "Here's your gun," she said, thrusting it toward him. "Should have some finishing oil brushed over the carving, but if you'll do that yourself, we can call it even."

Hank frowned. "But I still owe you money."

"No. You don't. You've paid me for my work and then some. I appreciate your business." She turned, exited the parlor, and walked upstairs to her room where Hank would surely not follow. She didn't even look out the window to watch him drive away. The nerve of that man, sticking his nose in her mess, talking to people about her mistakes. And just when she was thinking she could like him.

Hank tried to pay attention as James and Grace showed him their favorite holiday traditions. They'd all trooped out into the woods the day before and cut not one but two evergreens. The prettier of the two was stabilized in a bucket of rocks and sand. Then Abram drilled holes into the trunk, cut branches from the second tree, and inserted them to fill out the first one. The result was a remarkably full and uniform Christmas tree. Hank marveled at the ingenuity while continuing to kick himself for upsetting Fleeta.

"Stepped all over her pride," Abram said after Hank shared his tale.

"What can I do to fix it?" he asked.

Abram shrugged. "Women," he said. "I'm still trying to figure Lydia out and she's not half so contrary as Fleeta Brady."

Now Hank gave his host family about a tenth of his attention as he pondered what he could do to make things right with Fleeta. Lydia bumped his elbow and handed him a darning needle with a long length of heavy thread. She pushed bowls of popped corn and cranberries toward him.

"You're too distracted for anything trickier than this," she said. "Don't worry about a pattern, just put on some corn and then berries—it'll look nice once you're done."

Hank gave her a grateful smile. "Lydia, when's the last time you were put out with Abram?"

"Oh now, the secret of a good marriage is not telling when you're mad at your husband." She laughed. "Or your wife. Doesn't do anyone good to air dirty laundry." She gave him a sideways look. "Although once you've washed it, you've got to hang it out to dry."

Hank raised his eyebrows and strung several kernels of fluffy corn on his thread, followed by two berries.

"I'll tell you a secret."

He leaned in closer and kept to his work.

"The main thing any woman wants from a man who's upset her is . . . an apology."

Hank paused, a red berry in his fingers. "You mean just walk up to her and say 'I'm sorry'?"

Lydia nodded as she continued sifting through a box of ornaments. "That's a start, sure enough. But the best apologies have something to hold them up. Maybe a bunch of flowers you cut out in the woods, or a tin of tea from the store. The words are the main thing, but it's nice to have something to remember them by." She smiled and touched a basket of pinecones on the end table beside her. "Doesn't need to be fancy, just from the heart." She tapped Hank's chest. "The heart's where healing lives."

Hank nodded and strung some more popped corn.

The whole family went to church on Christmas Eve. Fleeta deigned to put on a dress, but that was as far as her efforts went.

She didn't have anyone to dress up for. And she was pretty sure the whole community knew how Bud Lyons had taken her for a ride—although Albert and Hank were the only ones who knew the extent of it. Unless, of course, Hank had been telling folks. She shuddered at the thought.

She was still hanging on to the slenderest thread of hope that there might be some sort of explanation for the empty shop, while fearing she'd never see Bud Lyons or her mother's brooch ever again. And somewhere deep down, she might even be afraid that the brooch had taken her only chance at true love with it.

"Sit up, sweetheart." Aunt Maisie gave her a mock stern look. Fleeta tried not to slouch, but it was hard when all she wanted to do was curl up and cry. It was bad enough she'd cried in front of Hank. She sure wasn't going to do it again in the fourth pew during the Christmas Eve service.

She saw the Markley family enter and sit on the opposite side of the church, Hank in their midst. The two children rushed to sit on either side of him, making Fleeta smile, until she remembered how Hank had meddled in her business. She wished she'd never gotten in his car that day—now he knew better than most how big a fool she'd been. He looked up and tried a shy smile. She quickly looked away before he could read her eyes. Goodness knows what he'd find there—betrayal, anger . . . longing.

Someone rang the bell three times, and the congregation settled in to listen. Pastor Lyman stood and held his worn Bible aloft. "'The true light that enlightens every man was coming into the world. He was in the world, and the world was made through him, yet the world knew him not. He came to his own home, and his own people received him not. But to all who received him, who believed in his name, he gave power to become children of God; who were born, not of blood nor of the will of the flesh nor of the will of man, but of God.'"

He lowered the Bible and rested it on the pulpit. "Most of you were probably expecting to hear the Christmas story from the book of Luke, but this year I want you to remember what John

had to say about the birth of Christ. About how He brought light into a dark world and adopted everyone who dares to believe."

Fleeta felt as though her wildly spinning world had slowed to attend to those verses. She knew the preacher had more to say, but she was stuck. Flipping Aunt Maisie's Bible open, she turned to the book of John, and there in the first chapter she found the words the preacher just quoted.

"The power to become children of God."

What in the world did it mean? She was an orphan, had been so most all her life. Uncle Oscar and Aunt Maisie took her in sure enough, but she wasn't really their child—their daughter. She thought about Jesus and how He wasn't received, was rejected even. That was how she'd felt her whole life, as though her own parents had cast her aside. She'd always called herself a Christian, but she felt like she was really paying attention to what that meant for the first time. Had she received Christ? And if so, did that mean she was . . . God's child?

The very idea left her breathless. Could it be that she was wanted like that? All because of a baby born on Christmas morning a long, long time ago? Light came into a dark world, and even now it shone into the dark places of her life. She'd been dwelling on her problems—the loss of her savings and her mother's amethyst pin, the loss of her dream of independence. But if she truly did belong to God, well, didn't she belong to Him no matter what?

Fleeta sat up straighter. Smoothed her skirt over her knees and tucked a tendril of loose hair behind her ear. She guessed maybe she was somebody after all. Just as good as anyone with two parents still living. Just as good—no, maybe better, or at least more blessed—than that bad man Bud Lyons, who had to cheat and steal to find anything of value. She suddenly had the notion that what Bud thought was most valuable really wasn't.

She slanted a look at Aunt Maisie, who smiled and patted her hand. Uncle Oscar sat a little farther down the pew, a look of supreme contentment on his face. Her cousins lined the rest of the pew, varying looks of attention and boredom on their faces. Fleeta found she wanted to burst with the thoughts tumbling through her. Bud might have stolen her earthly possessions, but she still had what she needed. More than she needed.

She dared look beyond her own family to where Hank sat with an arm around James's shoulders, with Grace fighting sleep against his side. And if she had what she needed, maybe she should take another look at what she wanted—brooch or no brooch.

15

Hank waited until late in the afternoon on Christmas Day, although it was hard for him not to hurry over and make amends to Fleeta sooner. He was determined to get her to take the rest of the money he'd promised and to tell her what he'd come to feel for her. He didn't want to rush her—to frighten her with the intensity of what he was feeling—but the fear that he'd lost her by pushing too far into her private affairs made him realize just how involved he wanted to be in her life. He was determined to persuade her to let him woo her. Giving her the final payment for her carving was the perfect excuse, and surely she couldn't be angry with him on Christmas Day.

Plus, he had a plan.

Hank drove over to Oscar and Maisie's after enjoying a fine Christmas feast. James and Grace wanted to come too, but Abram persuaded them to stay and try out Grace's new Hula-Hoop instead. James acted like he didn't want to play with a girl's toy, but as soon as Grace suggested that was because he couldn't do it, a competition was in full swing.

Hank pulled up to the Brady house and got out of his car, flipping a silver dollar over and over between his fingers. He dropped it as he stepped toward the porch and noticed his fingers shook as he retrieved the coin from the winter-sere grass.

Albert opened the door even before Hank knocked. "Fleeta, you've got company," he called into the house.

She appeared as though she'd been expecting him. Her lips tightened and thinned.

"Merry Christmas," Hank said, then jumped right in without any more preamble. "First thing I need to do is apologize to you for butting into your business the way I did. I'm real sorry about that."

Her face relaxed just a little, and she uncrossed her arms. "I appreciate that."

Hank smiled. That hadn't been so bad. "Now, I know you said you wouldn't take the rest of my payment on the gunstock carving, but I have a proposal for you."

She tapped a toe and raised her eyebrows at him. She was back in her pants and flannel shirt, and Hank thought she looked wonderful.

He held up the silver dollar. "Whichever one of us shoots a hole through this first, wins."

A gleam came to Fleeta's eyes. "Will the target be still or moving?"

"I thought Albert here could throw it for us. You shoot first."

Fleeta reached for her rifle in a rack on the wall.

Hank stretched out a hand and stopped her. "Don't you want to know what the prize is?"

"I thought it'd be that cash you keep trying to push off on me."

"If you win, you decide whether to take the money or not, and I don't say a word either way." He tightened his grip just a little where he held her arm. "If I win, you take the money and you let me call on you."

She furrowed her brow. "Call on me? Like a man calls on a woman?"

"Exactly like that. I know you don't care to marry, but I'd like a chance to persuade you otherwise." There. He couldn't be much plainer than that.

Fleeta's lips parted, and she stared at him. "I . . . are you saying . . . ?"

"I'd like a chance to win you, Fleeta Brady. And if I have to out-shoot you to do it, then I'll shoot better than I've ever shot before."

Color tinted her cheeks, and she blinked several times before drawing her shoulders back and nodding slowly. "I suppose I might let a man who can outshoot me have a chance."

Hank's heart soared. He wasn't entirely sure what he was getting himself into, but this was the happiest he'd been in ages. "All right then. Albert, will you do the honors?" He handed off the silver dollar.

Fleeta shrugged into a coat and cradled her .22 rifle in her arms. Her heart fluttered, and her stomach knotted. Did she want to beat Hank? Or did she maybe want to let him win this one? She'd never missed a shot on purpose in her life, but for the first time she was beginning to think there might be something better than being the best shot in the county. Maybe her ability to outshoot just about anyone wasn't the only thing that gave her worth. And maybe Hank had noticed. She breathed in and out slowly. If she couldn't get a handle on herself, she wouldn't have to throw the match to lose. Or would that be winning?

Albert walked out into the pasture, flipping the silver dollar in his hand. "I'm going to fling it out and up this way," he said, pointing. "Don't anybody get all shaky and shoot me instead of the coin." He laughed, but Fleeta thought if he knew how she was feeling at the moment, he might not think it was so funny.

"Ladies first," Hank said and made a sweeping bow.

Fleeta closed her eyes and whispered a prayer to the God she was beginning to think of as Father. If someone had asked her what she prayed, she didn't think she could say exactly, but it felt good all the same. Her hands steadied, and she lifted her rifle to her shoulder. "Ready."

Albert winked in the waning light and flung the silver dollar high and wide. As he did, Fleeta thought she saw a flicker of white at the edge of the trees across the pasture—like a deer's tail as it ran. She ignored the movement and forced her focus on the coin.

She tracked it and fired. The coin spun wildly and ricocheted back toward Albert, who jogged a few steps and scooped it up.

"You shot the *L* right out of Liberty," he said. "Took a piece out of the side. Hank, you'll have to shoot pretty well to do better than that."

Hank's jaw tightened, and he shook out his hands before lifting his own rifle to his shoulder. "Get ready to see some pretty shooting," he said. "Ready."

Albert threw the coin into the air again, and to Fleeta it seemed to take a long time to reach the arc of its trajectory while she waited for the sound of gunfire. As the coin began its descent she heard a shot, and the coin spun once again before landing in a tuft of weeds farther away from Albert.

"He hit it sure enough," Albert called out, starting toward the weeds.

Fleeta bit her lip, wishing Albert would hurry, when she heard the screech of a blue jay. It was Jack, following Albert again. Only this time, he swooped down, found the silver dollar, and launched himself back into the sky.

"Hey!" Albert hollered, waving his hat at Jack.

The bird flew to the peak of the barn and looked down at them, tilting his head one way and then the other. The silver dollar glinted in his claws. Albert ran into the house and came out with a piece of Aunt Maisie's fruitcake.

"He won't want that," Fleeta said, but Albert waved her off.

He walked toward the barn, holding the cake high for Jack to see. He broke off a few pieces and put them along the edge of the wooden crosspiece on the clothesline pole. Jack watched intently. Albert hurried back to where Hank and Fleeta stood.

"Give him a minute," Albert said.

Jack shifted on the barn roof, then flapped his way down to the clothesline. He landed, coin still clutched in one claw, and eyed the cake. He sampled a piece, and Albert began to ease toward him, crooning soft words. Fleeta had seen Albert feed the bird out of his hand before. She held her breath.

"C'mon, Jack, I've got a nice big piece for you right here," Albert said, holding his hand out with the hunk of cake.

Jack ate another crumb from his perch and hopped closer to Albert, who was almost to the pole now.

"That's right, Jack. I'll trade ya."

Fleeta swore she could see the bird squint his eyes as though calculating the risk and reward. Then he darted forward, snagged the hunk of cake in his beak, and flew once again. This time the bird went to a branch halfway up a hemlock tree where he settled in to enjoy his treat. He hopped along the branch, apparently having dropped the coin.

"I think that's where his nest is," Albert said. "Or was when he needed it last spring."

Fleeta started to say the whole thing was silly and they should just let it go, but before she could open her mouth, Hank stripped off his jacket and reached for the tree's lowest branch. She snapped her mouth shut. If the fool man wanted to risk his life to prove he was a better shot, then let him.

Hank made his way up the tree, over and under branches, until he was just below Jack's nest. The bird watched him from a higher branch as though enjoying the show. Hank finally heaved himself up to eye level with the nest. He reached inside.

"Got it." He held the coin up in the air where it sparkled. Jack fluffed his wings and screeched.

In spite of herself, Fleeta was itching to know who won the contest. "Did you hit it?"

Hank grinned. "You'll just have to wait until I get back down there." But he didn't start down right away. "Doggone. This nest is full of junk. Looks like Jack stole one of Maisie's teaspoons." He reached back into the nest and tossed down a spoon to Albert below. "Got some shotgun brass up here too." He continued to fish around, Jack flapping his wings and hopping from branch to branch.

"Will you stop fooling around up there and come on down," Fleeta said. She wanted to see that coin.

"All right." Hank pocketed another item from the nest and began to work his way back down the tree.

When he was about ten feet from the ground, he dropped his full weight onto a branch. With a mighty crack it gave way. Fleeta gasped as Hank cried out and fell to the ground with a terrible thud, flat on his back. She rushed to his side, all thoughts of the coin suddenly washed from her mind.

She knelt beside him, noting a long, bloody scratch up his neck to his ear. "Are you all right?"

His eyelids fluttered open and he tried to speak, but nothing came out. A look of panic crossed his face as his mouth gaped and he worked his throat. Fleeta grabbed his shoulders and gave him a shake. With a roaring gasp he inhaled air, then coughed and sputtered.

"Phew. Got the air knocked out of me, but I think you shook it back in," he said at last.

Fleeta gave a shaky laugh, still holding his arm as he sat up. She didn't care anymore who the better shot was. She wanted this man to woo her no matter what. And she didn't need any piece of jewelry to tell her when to fall in love either. As she tried to formulate the words to tell him just that, he held the silver dollar up to his eye and looked at her through the hole he'd shot in its center.

"How about that?" he said.

Fleeta flung her arms around his neck and buried her face in his shoulder. "I'm glad," she mumbled.

"What's that?" Hank asked, his arms wrapping around her in a clasp that was so delicious, Fleeta never wanted to move again.

"I'm glad you're a better shot, Hank. And I'm glad you won the bet."

Hank stroked her braid and gently eased her back so he could look into her eyes. "I found something else in that nest up there."

Fleeta had been halfway hoping he was going to kiss her, so she had a hard time following his words. What did it matter if he found some old bits of metal in Jack's nest? She didn't say anything, just waited, and hoped.

Hank reached into his jacket pocket and pulled out something shiny. Fleeta was too busy gazing into his face and eyes to pay much attention, until she saw something flash purple. She gasped and looked at what he held.

Her mother's luckenbooth shone in the palm of his hand. Fleeta took it with shaking fingers. "How . . . ?"

"Beats me," Hank said. "Maybe ole Jack liked it so much he hunted it down and carried it home to decorate his nest. But I hope even Jack won't mind if you take it back as your own."

A tear slipped down Fleeta's cheek, and Hank caught it with his lips. He pressed them there to her jawline. Fleeta leaned into him. She felt wanted . . . treasured . . . beloved. She closed her fingers around her mother's pin—returned to her twice by this gentle man.

As Hank shifted to move his lips over hers, she gave in to the sensations he stirred in her heart. Maybe there was something to this true-love nonsense after all.

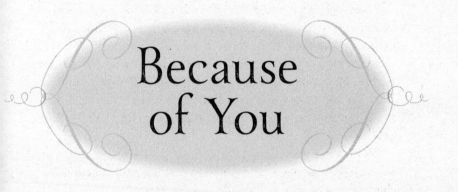

Because of You

A Bradford Sisters Romance
NOVELLA

BECKY WADE

1

Maddie Winslow met the man of her dreams the same day that her friend Olivia introduced Maddie to her new boy-friend. Which would have been splendid, except that the man of Maddie's dreams *was* Olivia's new boyfriend.

If the Venn diagram depicting Maddie's dream man and Olivia's actual man hadn't overlapped in the middle in the person of Leo Donnelly, then perhaps Maddie would be living her happily-ever-after with Leo right at this very instant.

As it was, Olivia had snagged Leo first.

Which was why Maddie felt a bit like she'd been both shaken and stirred by the words the associate pastor with the microphone had just spoken.

"Maddie Winslow and Leo Donnelly," the pastor repeated, "will form team number three." He lifted a hand to shade his eyes as he scanned the crowd, even though they were inside Bethel Church's Fellowship Hall, where there was no sun. "Maddie and Leo? Are you here?"

"Here," Maddie called, raising her hand. Belatedly, she realized that she probably looked like an overeager third grader.

287

"Here" came a masculine voice from the far back corner of the room.

Maddie twisted around and immediately spotted Leo.

He gave her a polite smile.

Her heart did what roller coasters do when they go upside down. She turned back to face the front.

"Maddie and Leo, please see Janice after the meeting so that she can hand you a Mission:Christmas folder about the family you've been assigned." Bethel's holiday ministry connected church members with families in the area facing financial difficulty or serious illness. "Now on to team number four, Hope Jackson and Walter Murray."

As the pastor continued to announce pair after pair, Maddie worked to keep her face and posture neutral. Internally, she felt anything but.

Her friend Britt's two older sisters were standing alongside her. Willow, the oldest, arched an eyebrow at Maddie in speculation. In response, Maddie projected fake calm.

Leo had signed up to volunteer for Mission:Christmas? Obviously, he had.

Ordinarily, she could spot him from a mile away and locate him through intuition, even when he popped up in unexpected places. But her Leo Sense had failed her tonight. She'd had no inkling that he'd slipped into the room on (what had been until now) an ordinary Wednesday evening.

He was wearing his black jacket with the hood, which might mean that he'd just arrived or that he'd simply forgotten to take off his jacket—either explanation was likely. The tie he'd knotted over a pale blue dress shirt looked as though it had been loosened. Black belt. Gray flat-front pants. Chukka boots.

His sandy blond hair, which was shortish on the sides and longer on top, was in a mild state of disarray. She never knew whether to call the scruff on his cheeks heavy five o'clock shadow or a short beard. Whatever it should be called, it suited him. He looked painfully appealing both in his weekday history professor attire and in his casual weekend clothing. Today, she was experiencing a slight preference for his professor garb.

Charlie, Leo and Olivia's three-year-old son, wasn't with Leo currently, which probably meant he was attending the programming the church offered on Wednesday night for peewees. The only thing more slaying than Leo in professor garb was Leo in professor garb, holding Charlie.

Maddie caught herself anxiously kneading the knuckle of her right index finger, something she did when unsure of herself. She dropped her hands.

A big part of her wanted to feel elated over the fact that she'd be working on Mission:Christmas with Leo. She put a lid on her elation, however. Platonic pleasure. That would be a more appropriate thing to feel.

She and Leo had always gotten along wonderfully. Easily. Approvingly. Maddie had with Leo the kind of relationship she had with all of her friends' boyfriends and husbands—familiar in some ways and very distant in others.

There were lines that a girl *did not* cross when dealing with a man her friend loved. Maddie had never come close to crossing those lines with Leo, despite her six-year-long crush on him.

Despite that Olivia had been killed by a drunk driver two and a half years ago.

Maddie had been a bridesmaid in Leo and Olivia's wedding, and she still thought of Leo as Olivia's husband. It seemed to her that he belonged to her good friend, who'd been outgoing and fashionable and gorgeous. Who deserved to be remembered and respected.

Maddie would need to find a way to survive her partnership with Leo without falling even deeper under his spell. She was twenty-seven years old. Already, she'd sunk the majority of her twenties into pining for him. Just last month, she'd determined that her fairy-tale, unrealistic "Leo standards" were wrecking her chance at happiness with anyone else.

She'd really like a boyfriend of her own—someone to snuggle

with and go to parties with and eat potato chips with. Someone to lift heavy stuff and empty the trash. After taking a long, hard look at her dating life, she'd firmly decided to do whatever it was women did when they moved on.

This infatuation with Leo? The opposite of moving on.

The meeting wrapped, and Leo fell in step next to her in the line before the table where Janice was handing out folders. "Good to see you," he said. His eyes appeared every bit as sad as usual, his lips every bit as beautiful as usual.

"Good to see you, too." Holy cow, what was he seeing when he looked at her? After she'd left Sweet Art, the chocolate shop she managed, she'd grabbed a to-go salad, driven to the church, eaten her salad inside her car, then dashed to the meeting. It occurred to her that she hadn't remembered to reapply lipstick after her rushed meal.

She had on jeans, Converse, and a long-sleeved gray top she'd owned for at least four years. She'd kept the shirt because it flattered what she considered to be her best feature, her fairly well-endowed chest. The rest of her was mostly average.

Her stylist had put golden-brown balayage highlights into her brunette hair recently. And she'd finally figured out how to style her current shoulder-length cut into the artless waves (which took effort to make look artless) that her stylist had intended.

Until this moment she'd been satisfied with her appearance today. Now she wished she'd made more of an effort. Olivia would have.

"So you signed up to volunteer with Mission:Christmas, too?" she asked.

"I did. When I read about it in the church bulletin, it seemed like something I could do." One of his shoulders lifted. "To help."

"Of course! I think you'll really enjoy it." Several single women were shooting her glances zinging with degrees of jealousy and wistfulness.

"Have you volunteered with Mission:Christmas before?" he asked.

"This will be my third year." She'd participated each Christmas since returning to Merryweather, Washington, after her lackluster stint in San Francisco.

"That's reassuring. You know the ropes."

"I do!" That sounded entirely too merry. She couldn't even blame spiked eggnog.

"I can be your assistant," he said.

"Fabulous. I've always wanted an assistant. My Christmas wish has already come true."

"Happy to oblige."

Once Janice handed them their folder, Maddie and Leo found a quiet spot near the side wall. She pulled free the two sheets of paper that offered pertinent details about the family that had been entrusted to them. "It looks like we've been given a single mom named Kim Huntington and her two daughters. Kim lives here in Merryweather and was let go from her job a few months back." Sympathy squeezed Maddie as she imagined trying to face Christmas as a single mom without paychecks coming in. She handed one of the sheets to Leo. They each read their sheet, switched, then read the second sheet.

"What's our plan of attack?" Leo asked.

"In the past, my partner and I have kicked things off by meeting with the recipients so they can let us know how we can help." Maddie slid the papers back into the folder.

"Sounds good."

He met her eyes and for a split second she got lost in the cloudy gray of his irises. It was a cool shade, soft like the sky over the Pacific Ocean in the morning.

By rights, God should have given the bookish and academic Leo a nerdy exterior. Instead, God had given him the sort of blatant good looks ordinarily reserved for Formula One drivers and South American soccer players. Thus, women swooned over him at every turn while Leo—when he stopped thinking about French Revolutionary history long enough to notice—wondered why they were swooning.

He looked down.

Olivia's confidence level had been at a 99. Maddie and Leo were both very competent in their professions, but socially Maddie's confidence level hovered around 85 and Leo's around 70.

"The church will lend a hand with fundraising," Maddie said. "They'll divide the proceeds from their Christmas Bazaar and their Jingle Bell Walk evenly between all the teams. Even so, my partner and I have also held a garage sale on our own in past years. That's been great because it's increased our Mission:Christmas budget, and it's also given me and the rest of my family a reason to clear out our clutter."

"I'm up for a garage sale. After that, we go shopping?"

"Yes. Then we deliver everything to the Huntingtons in time for Christmas."

"Got it."

"If it's all right with you, I'll go ahead and call Kim Huntington and find out when she can meet with us."

"Sure."

"Awesome."

He studied her, his attention both steady and kind. "Is everything going well at the chocolate shop?"

"Very well."

"And your family?"

"They're good. This is my mom's favorite time of year. She loves all the Christmas parties."

He nodded.

"How's my favorite boy?" Maddie asked.

"Your favorite boy has learned to count to twenty."

"What? I'd love to hear him count to twenty."

Leo checked his watch. "His choir practice ends in five minutes. I'm sure he'd be glad to show off his counting skills. Do you have time to say hi to him?"

"Absolutely."

They made their way down the church's hallways, talking easily about his work and hers. She was exquisitely aware of Leo beside her—his gait, his size. He wasn't extraordinarily tall. Maybe five ten? But his lean body was perfectly proportioned and also the perfect complement to her five-five height.

They came to a stop just outside the open doorway of the classroom that contained risers bearing three- and four-year-old singers. Some of the kids were staring off into space. One was opening and closing the Velcro flap on his shoe. The rest were gamely singing "Away in a Manger" and following along with the hand motions their teacher was demonstrating.

The cuteness! Amusement tugged at Maddie's lips.

Thanksgiving had come and gone just six days before, but in that time, Merryweather had switched from fall mode into full-blown Christmas mode. Wreaths hung from each light post in town. Greenery swathed the storefronts. And Christmas music danced in the air of this church classroom. Satisfaction sifted within Maddie, settling like fairy dust. She adored the Christmas season.

The teacher said a prayer and then excused each child as she recognized their matching parent. Charlie ran to Leo and threw his arms joyfully around his dad's leg.

Charlie looked very much the way Maddie imagined Leo had looked at the age of three. Both Leo and Charlie had oval faces and defined, pointy chins. Charlie's hair was white-blond, worn a little long, in a shaggy surfer-dude cut. The only visible stamp Olivia had left on her son was her eye color. Charlie's eyes were the same blueberry shade that Olivia's had been.

Whenever Maddie looked into Charlie's face, she saw Olivia's eyes staring back at her. It was heartbreaking. It was also reassuring in a sad sort of way. Olivia had died far, far too young, but she hadn't died without leaving behind a legacy. Here was her son, healthy, happy, and learning to sing "Away in a Manger."

Leo hoisted Charlie into his arms. One of Charlie's small hands curved trustingly behind his dad's neck. "Say hi to Maddie," Leo said.

"Hi."

"Hi yourself," Maddie answered. "Your dad tells me you can count to twenty, but I told him no way. That can't be possible. You're only three."

"I can!"

"What?" she asked with faux skepticism.

"One . . . Two . . . Three . . ." After ten, he paused for a moment, his miniature eyebrows inching toward each other. Ah, the confusing eleven and twelve, which really should have been called *oneteen* and *twoteen*. "Eleven . . . twelve. . ." He rattled off the rest triumphantly.

"Wow! I'm so impressed." Maddie held up her fist and he eagerly bumped it, then rested the side of his head against Leo's shoulder.

She glanced at Leo, and a pulse of delight over his remarkable boy passed between them.

Throughout their high school years, Maddie and Olivia had been part of a group of five girlfriends. In addition to the two of them, their group had included Britt, Mia, and Hannah.

Maddie let herself into her apartment, carrying the sacks of groceries she'd picked up on the way home from church. She flipped on the lights with her shoulder and made her way toward her modern kitchen.

Her apartment had begun life in 1922 as an art deco office building near Merryweather's downtown. It had narrowly escaped extinction during the seventies and eighties before its renovation, courtesy of the revitalization Merryweather Historical Village had triggered.

The bones of the building remained. Nicked and scratched hardwood floors. Enormous rectangular windows. The rest, including the drywall, had been stripped away when the structure had been converted into apartments. The exposed brick walls were weathered and varied—deep red in places, in others burnished orange, in others faded white.

Maddie had decorated with turquoise area rugs and furniture in shades of gray and white. She experienced a glow of satisfaction each time her apartment's mishmash of old and new welcomed her home.

Once she'd put away her groceries, she opened a bag of peanut, raisin, and chocolate trail mix and munched on it as she studied the photographs held to her refrigerator with magnets.

One of the pictures near the top captured the five friends during their freshman year of high school. Back then, Olivia's hair had been a light almond brown.

Maddie's attention moved to a picture taken two years later, when Olivia had decided to dye her hair black. It had sounded to Maddie like a terrible idea at the time. But it turned out that Olivia's milky skin and blue eyes looked stunning against inky hair.

Olivia had always been an assured person, but her hair color change had been like steroids for her self-image. She'd become the girl who knew everyone, who seemed to move through life effortlessly, who was at ease in every kind of gathering. Guys noticed her. Girls were impressed by her. Good things rolled toward Olivia Carroll the way golf balls rolled toward sand traps.

Olivia and Maddie had been the only two of their group of friends who'd decided to attend the University of Oregon. They'd roomed together their first year and taken turns driving to and from Washington for every school holiday.

One night, the summer before their senior year at UO, Olivia and Hannah had decided to put their newly minted status as twenty-one-year-olds to good use at Merryweather's Front Street Bar. Olivia liked to say that she'd spotted Leo one point five seconds after entering the bar that night and decided to marry him three point five seconds after that.

Leo's parents had raised their four children in Idaho. After becoming empty nesters, Leo's research-scientist father had accepted a job that brought him and his wife to Washington state.

Leo was three years older than Olivia and had been pursuing his doctorate in Idaho that fateful night at the Front Street Bar.

He'd only been in town for the weekend to visit his parents. He'd only come to the bar that night because his younger sister had dragged him out.

Maddie sometimes wondered what would've happened if *she'd* been the one to meet Leo first. She liked to think they would've hit it off. But time wasn't like that. Events happened in the order in which they happened and once they did, there could be no rearranging.

As a single, eligible man newly introduced to their region of Washington, Leo had been something of a unicorn. Once Olivia set her sights on him, Leo had, predictably, fallen for the take-no-prisoners Olivia.

The two of them—Leo and Olivia—had been a case study in Opposites Attract. He was smart, wry, and just a little bit cautious with people. She had street smarts, a quick laugh, and a personality that shone brightest in the spotlight. He was patient and steady. She could be impatient and impulsive. He had substance. She had an enviable sense of style. Her strengths and his had clicked together.

Maddie had watched Olivia butt heads with the boyfriends she'd dated previously who'd had personalities too similar to her own. A calm introvert had been just what Olivia needed to provide her with a secure foundation. An irresistible extrovert had been just what Leo needed to bring him out of his shell.

Leo and Olivia married three months after Olivia and Maddie's graduation. Affectionately, Maddie straightened the photograph taken at their wedding. It was her favorite photo from that day— not stiff and formal, but a fabulous candid shot of the bridal party, laughing at a joke one of the groomsmen had made.

The newlyweds had settled into Leo's apartment in Idaho. Leo had remained in Idaho, in fact, until this past summer, when he'd accepted a position at Abbott College.

Now that Maddie, Leo, and Charlie shared a town with a population of six thousand, Maddie saw Leo much more often.

Which was hard.

Which was exquisite.

Most people thought of "oops" babies as coming last in a family, but Charlie had been a firstborn oops. Olivia had intended to wait to have kids until at least the age of thirty, but, luckily, God had other plans.

Charlie had been less than a year old the night Olivia had kissed her baby and husband good-bye and left the house to join friends for a girls' night out. She'd had alcohol in her system when she'd been hit, but an amount under the legal limit. The same could not be said for the guy in the truck that had collided with her head on at 10:21 P.M. on June third, two and a half years ago. Both the driver of the truck and Olivia were killed instantly.

Olivia had been just twenty-five.

Maddie relocated herself and her trail mix to the sofa and clicked on the TV. She'd watch another episode of *Call the Midwife* because she could count on it to provide a dose of heartwarming emotion.

One of the midwives, peddling down a 1950's street on her bike, filled the TV screen. Maddie rested the back of her head against the sofa cushion and picked through the bag for the chocolate pieces.

Maddie was certain that Leo had never suspected how fondly she felt about him. She'd like to keep it that way, even though they'd be working side by side for the next month.

How, though? How to keep her crush under wraps?

By being friendly. By acting the way his deceased wife's friend should act.

She could look forward to spending time with him and Charlie and to giving the Huntington family a wonderful Christmas. What she could not do: allow herself to expect or hope for anything more than that.

There was only one unicorn in Merryweather.

And Olivia had found him first.

2

So nice to meet you!" Kim Huntington said as she shook hands with Maddie near midday on Saturday.

"Nice to meet you, too," Maddie said. "Leo should be here any minute."

"No problem." Kim waved a hand. "We're early."

When Maddie had called Kim to set up today's get-together and Kim had discovered that Maddie worked at Sweet Art inside Merryweather Historical Village on Saturdays, she'd suggested they meet during Maddie's lunch break.

They stood on the lip of the village's central lawn, the brick of Sweet Art at their backs, watching Kim's two daughters chase each other across the grass.

"I've been meaning to bring the girls here ever since the village put up their Christmas decorations." Kim exuded both warmth and energy. "Don't they look fabulous?"

"Fabulous," Maddie agreed.

Kim, whose voice held a distinct southern accent, launched into a story about the O Holy Night Christmas Concert she'd attended at the village and the nativity donkey who'd snuffled through her purse in search of the apple she'd stashed there.

Kim had clothed her sturdy body in relatively fancy clothing for a weekend. Heels. Wide-legged jeans, a black-and-white print blouse, purple jacket. Her dark, glossy hair hung in a layered cut. Her makeup had been expertly applied, which filled Maddie with a burst of admiration.

Though Maddie herself didn't wear a lot of makeup on a daily basis, she was somewhat in awe of those who could wield makeup brushes with the kind of skill Kim possessed.

"Do you enjoy working at Sweet Art?" Kim asked.

"I love it."

"I bet you do! Notice I'm not even looking in the direction of your chocolate shop because if I do, I'll gain five pounds." A rich chuckle. "I've only been in there a few times because those chocolates y'all make are too delicious. My willpower's not strong enough! How's it possible that you can work there and stay so thin?"

Free chocolate was a perk of Maddie's employment at Sweet Art. However, she hadn't been born with an I-can-eat-anything-I-want-and-be-thin metabolism. Like most humans, Maddie had to exercise and watch what she ate in order to stay in shape. "I only let myself have two chocolates a day. One in the morning and one in the afternoon."

"Are you the one who makes the chocolates?"

"No, Britt Bradford does. I'm convinced that she's a chocolate genius."

"Such a genius!"

"I handle everything else that keeps the shop running: I wait on customers and manage the website, the online orders, and the financial side of the business."

"That's awesome," Kim said. "I think I met Britt and her family at a function once. There are three Bradford sisters, right?"

"Right. Britt's the youngest. Then there's Nora, who works at the Library on the Green Museum here in the Village." Maddie nodded toward the museum. "Willow's the oldest. She opened her own boutique in Shore Pine this past summer."

Just then, she caught sight of Leo walking toward them, holding Charlie's hand. Both Leo and Charlie wore navy jackets over their jeans. Maddie had woken this morning to her alarm clock and a breakfast of Cinnamon Chex. Would that she'd woken up to those two. They were sweeter than Cinnamon Chex. Her heart contracted with longing.

"Did you dress Charlie like your mini-me on purpose?" she called as they neared.

"What?" Leo asked with genuine surprise. "No." He glanced at Charlie, then down at himself. He gave her and Kim a sheepish smile. "It does look like I planned this, doesn't it?"

"It looks adorable," Kim insisted, before Maddie could.

Maddie introduced Leo and Charlie to Kim, then held her arms out to Charlie. "Morning, sweetheart." He took a half unsure, half hopeful step in her direction. She gripped beneath his arms and swept him high into the air. Laughter tumbled from him.

"Again," he said.

"Please," Leo prompted.

"Please," Charlie repeated.

Maddie swept Charlie up again, then snuck in a quick hug before depositing him on his feet.

Kim's girls came to stand near their mom, panting slightly from all the running they'd been doing. Both had long espresso-colored hair, olive skin, and dark, liquid eyes. "These are my daughters." Kim ran her hand down the braid of the taller one. "Victoria's eight." She set her hand on the shoulder of the younger one. "Samantha's six."

"Nice to meet you," Leo and Maddie said.

Samantha gave Maddie a timid smile, but Victoria peered at them with worried suspicion.

"Say hello please," Kim instructed them.

"Hello," they chorused.

"Can we play some more?" Victoria asked her mom.

"Sure. I brought a Frisbee, if you want it." She extracted it from her purse, and the girls charged off.

Leo, Maddie, and Kim settled around one of The Pie Emporium's outdoor wooden tables. Even though this first day of December had dawned sunny and still, the chilly temperature had

300

inspired most of The Pie Emporium's patrons to enjoy their coffee and pie inside the shop's small confines. Only a middle-aged man reading the paper and wearing a parka also sat outside.

"We're looking forward to partnering with you on Mission:Christmas," Leo said to Kim as Charlie climbed onto his knee.

"I'm so grateful that you are! I don't mind telling y'all, though, that I feel a little guilty about submitting an application for Mission:Christmas. Until recently, I've always been fine—not wealthy or anything like that, mind you—but *fine*. I'm usually the one helping others at Christmas." Her cheerful expression faltered, revealing the stress that lived beneath. "Then I lost my job. If it was just me, I wouldn't have considered Mission:Christmas. But I adopted Victoria and Samantha nine months ago, and I couldn't bear the thought of them having to make do with next to nothing on our first Christmas together."

"I'm very glad that you applied," Maddie said. The other Mission:Christmas families she'd been paired with in the past had taught her that sometimes, in order to receive God's provision, you first had to be humble enough to ask for help. "Leo and I will make sure that your first Christmas with your daughters is a memorable one for all three of you."

"Memorable for the girls is more than enough. Please don't buy anything for me. I left that section blank on the form."

"Sorry to disappoint you, Kim," Leo said, "but we're going to have to buy you a few gifts at least."

"Leo!" Kim exclaimed, good-naturedly scandalized. "Don't get me anything."

He met her attention head on. "You're going to have to trust us, Kim."

"The girls are the ones I'm concerned with," Kim said.

Charlie climbed down and started playing with the pebbles that made up the surface of the nearby walkway.

"I'd love to know more about you and your family," Maddie said.

"Well, I was raised in Georgia, and I've worked in hospital administration ever since I got my master's degree. I've lived in Texas, Oklahoma, Missouri. Four years ago, I moved here to work at Valley View Medical Center. Right around that same time, I started to hear the Lord calling me to adopt a child. I was fifty-one years old at the time, and I've never been married. I kind of raised my eyebrows up and said, 'Lord, me? Are you sure?'" She laughed and slapped her hands together.

Leo grinned. "And was He sure?"

"He was," Kim answered. "I spent months researching adoption, both domestic and international. I decided to adopt an older child out of the foster care system here in the United States." The wind flipped a strand of her hair upside down, and she smoothed it back into place. "When the caseworker told me about two sisters who needed a home, and I saw Victoria and Samantha's picture, I just . . . I *knew* they were meant to be my babies. So I decided to take a leap of faith and become their mama."

The younger of the girls, Samantha, ran up. "Would it be okay if the little boy plays with us?" She motioned toward Charlie.

"It's okay with me," Kim said, "but you'll need to ask his father."

Samantha looked self-consciously at Leo.

"Sure." Leo turned to Charlie. "The girls have invited you to play with them on the grass."

Charlie mulled it over for a long second, his courage clearly battling against his fear, before approaching Samantha. "'Kay."

"Continue to play right here on the grass where we can see you," Kim said.

Charlie and Samantha walked side by side in Victoria's direction.

"Since you're a father," Kim said to Leo, "I'm guessing you know how hard parenting is."

"It's incredibly hard." Leo jerked open the snaps on his navy jacket, revealing a sage green sweater. Maddie might need to rethink her recent preference for his professor's wardrobe.

"I talked with all of my friends who are parents before I adopted

302

the girls," Kim said. "I knew that it wasn't going to be easy. Even so, all my life I imagined I'd make a terrific mother." Her eyes rounded with rueful honesty. "Well, motherhood's more joyful and more challenging than I expected. What I can't get used to is the fact that I'm not as terrific a mother as I thought I'd be. Please don't think badly of me for admitting that."

"We don't," Maddie said.

"I'm not the father I imagined I'd be," Leo told her. "I'm doing the best I can, but I'm fallible."

"Same here," Kim said. "I didn't realize how set in my own selfish ways I was, having had only myself to answer to for so long. It's been a journey. I've had to get over myself!" Her lips, covered in dusky rose lipstick, pulled into a smile. "Anyway, we've been finding our way forward little by little. When my boss at the medical center told me that a few other staff members were going to take over my job responsibilities because of budget cuts, I felt like I couldn't catch my breath for a week."

"I'm so sorry," Maddie said.

"The girls have been through a lot. I don't want to move them again and cause them even more upheaval unless I have to, so I've been looking for work in this area, but no one seems to be hiring at the moment, what with the holidays coming up and all."

"I work at Abbott College," Leo said. "I'll call the HR department for you."

"And I can ask my mom and dad if they know of any job openings." Maddie's father was the town's family doctor, her mom his part-time office manager. If someone dropped a gum wrapper in Merryweather, they knew about it. "Now, how about we go over the wish list you submitted?" Maddie pulled the Mission:Christmas folder from her purse. "That way, we can make sure to prioritize everything that's most necessary."

Later that night, Leo sat in the glider rocker in Charlie's room, Charlie on his lap, reading aloud the third of Charlie's three nightly board books. Kids liked routine. If Leo tried to read fewer than three or more than three books, he'd live to regret it.

He set the book aside and turned off Charlie's Thomas the Tank Engine lamp. Then he pushed the glider back and forth as he said a prayer and sang "Jesus Loves Me."

He was a terrible singer. But again, "Jesus Loves Me" was part of the routine. Routine trumped skill.

He set Charlie's sound machine to babbling brook, made sure the night-light was illuminated, then laid Charlie in his toddler bed with his stuffed dog and blanket.

"I love you," Leo whispered. He kissed Charlie's forehead.

Outside in the hallway, he drew in a deep breath and consciously forced his shoulders down. Charlie had been twice as fussy and twice as energetic this evening as Leo had had the ability to deal with.

Leo walked into a living room that had become a battlefield of toys. The kitchen was overflowing with the ingredients and utensils he'd used to make dinner.

His spirits sank.

For months after Olivia had died, when Charlie had woken up in the middle of the night crying, when it had been time for them to start cooking dinner, when the *NBC Nightly News* came on, he'd looked for Olivia.

Sometimes he'd rolled over in bed to nudge her. Sometimes he'd actually called her name. Sometimes he'd picked up his phone to dial her cell.

Then he'd remember with a fresh stab of pain that she was dead. He wasn't married anymore. He was Charlie's only parent. The only one to answer when Charlie was crying. The one to cook dinner. The one who watched the *NBC Nightly News* alone.

Thirty months had passed since Olivia's death.

Thirty months.

The panic attacks he'd battled at the start hadn't returned in a long time. He didn't call out to Olivia anymore. He didn't expect her to walk into the room. He didn't hope for her to come to his rescue.

For better or for worse, he'd grown used to his role as single parent. It wasn't what he'd wished for himself or his boy. Yet, it's what was.

Leo sighed. He'd go ahead and straighten up the kitchen and living room now because putting it off until later would only make the job worse. Except . . . maybe he'd sit for just a minute—one minute—and gather some motivation first.

Leo settled onto a dining room chair, stacked his forearms on the table, and rested his head on top. An image of a darkened theater and a stage packed with sound and color grew in his mind until it blotted out all his worries and fatigue.

His parents had taken him to see *Les Misérables* for the first time when he was ten. He was the son of two academics, and by that point in his childhood, had already been well on his way to becoming one himself. He'd been far more interested in algebra than in musicals when he'd taken his seat to watch *Les Mis* that day. Thus, his love of it had surprised everyone in his family, himself most of all.

He'd gone to see productions of *Les Mis* eleven more times since then. Of all twelve shows he'd witnessed, one particular moment from one particular performance stood out.

Several years ago, during the scene when Javert allows Valjean to escape, he'd caught sight of a woman, sitting in front of him and to the right. She was pretty. Very pretty. But it hadn't been that—at least it hadn't been *only* that—which had jolted him.

Her profile had been bathed with ambient gold light from the stage. She stared at the actors as if emotionally struck. A delicate trail of tears marked her cheek. She'd visibly reacted to that scene in the exact way he'd been reacting internally.

He hadn't said a word to her. He hadn't needed to. That moment had been absolutely perfect just as it was. That moment reminded him that there was beauty in the world and sacrifice and grace.

Whenever he needed a reminder that he wasn't truly alone, that others felt the way he did, he pulled that moment to the front of his mind.

He pressed to his feet and started unloading clean dishes from the dishwasher. After this, he'd text his mom and dad and sisters about donating to the garage sale he and Maddie would be holding for the Huntingtons.

Leo was busy this time of year. Final exams would soon be upon him. He had Christmas shopping of his own to think about. However, he didn't regret signing up for Mission:Christmas. He was glad for the chance to support Kim and her daughters. And he was very glad that he'd been paired with Maddie.

Of all Olivia's friends—and Olivia had seemed to have hundreds of friends—Maddie was his favorite. She was genuine and easy to talk to. Friendly. Intelligent. Unpretentious. He liked her independence, and he really liked how she interacted with Charlie.

He could count on Maddie Winslow. And he intended to show her through their joint project that she could count on him, too.

3

Maddie and Leo sat opposite each another at a table in the corner of a quaint little sandwich shop near Abbott College.

The fact that this lunch felt very date-like to Maddie was an aberration brought on by her own wishful thinking. *He's your deceased friend's husband. We're here to plan the garage sale! Nothing more!*

"Are you sure your parents won't mind hosting our garage sale at their house?" Maddie asked. They'd already determined that her apartment wouldn't work and that his house, which was situated ten minutes outside of town, was too remote.

"I'm sure," he said. "I talked it over with them. Their house is in town, and they have plenty of room on their driveway and in their garage. My sisters will help. It should work out well."

"Okay, perfect."

Their food arrived. Since she was celiac and couldn't eat gluten, she'd opted for a soup, salad, and chips combo. Her mouth was watering, especially due to the potato chips. Potato chips were her favorite food group. She took out her phone.

"Are you taking a picture of your lunch?" Leo asked with bemusement.

"I am. I'm a fan of Instagram. Are you?"

"No."

"Are you on any of the social media platforms?"

"I have a Facebook account that I haven't checked since 2016."

She felt her dimples crease her cheeks as she adjusted her phone, trying to achieve just the right lighting and angle. "Well, I love looking at pictures on Instagram and sharing my own. Since I don't get out that much and since this lunch is so very pretty, this photo is too good to pass up."

"I see. Do people like looking at pictures of food?"

"Indeed." She ended up having to stand and hover over her lunch like a praying mantis in order to capture the right shot. "Got it." She lowered into her chair.

He was looking at her as if entertained. "Are you going to post that now?"

"No, no." She waved a hand. "I'll post it later." She realized he hadn't made a move toward his food. "Please don't let me hold you up."

He picked up his sandwich. A man who ordered a ham and Swiss on rye with lettuce and tomato was a very reliable type of man.

Also, looking into his gray eyes was muddling her thoughts and tempting her to imagine that they *were* on a date.

You're not!

But it sure would be nice if they were. . . . if he'd never been married to Olivia and she was someone he'd just met, instead of a friend of his wife's he'd known for years.

As they ate, they talked through their plans for their garage sale.

Once they'd covered everything, Maddie decided to venture a personal question. A this-isn't-a-date type of personal question. "When you moved to Merryweather last summer, I assumed that you did so to be near your parents and Olivia's parents. Is that why you moved?"

"Yes." Leo sat back a few degrees in his chair. "Soon after Olivia died, I realized that it would be best for Charlie and me if we could live near his grandparents, but Abbot didn't have any openings in my field at the time."

Abbott College had been founded in the mid-1800s. Its campus brimmed with historic buildings, jade lawns, and the rarified air of advanced education. It was the pride of Mason County.

"A year ago, they finally posted a position that I had the qualifications for. The search committee called me in for an interview last February." He ran a hand through his sandy hair, which left sexy furrows. "I wanted the job for Charlie's sake, as well as mine, so I was nervous going in. Afterward, I worried that I might not get it."

"I'm so happy that you did, Leo."

"Me too. Abbott's enrollment is less than fifteen hundred so most of my classes have fewer than twenty students, and they have on-site day care so I can go over between classes and push Charlie on the swings."

She ate a bite of pickle. "How's it been living near Olivia's parents and yours?"

He regarded her with his straightforward, alert gaze. When talking with Leo, she never felt that his attention was anywhere else. Having all that IQ focused on her was so heady that it made her stomach tingle.

"Better than I'd hoped," he answered. "Charlie gets to hang out with Olivia's parents and her brother's kids, and my parents and sisters. They're all more involved in his life now."

"Your younger sisters are both teachers, too, aren't they?"

He nodded. "Both are pursuing their masters at the moment."

"Degrees seem to run in your family, Leo."

"Except for Audrey, who is totally unlike the rest of us."

"Is she still working in the theater world in Los Angeles?"

"Still is."

Olivia had once told Maddie that Leo had been raised in a family similar to that of Belle from *Beauty and the Beast*—brainy, creative, and just a little bit scatterbrained. "There are books everywhere," Olivia had said with fond confusion, "being read by everyone all the time." Other than Leo, Olivia had related to

Audrey best. The rest of the Donnellys, while certainly friendly, had perplexed her.

"Is Brandon still working as a bartender?" Leo asked.

Leo had only met Maddie's family members a few times, and always at highly attended occasions like weddings. Yet he remembered everyone's first name, plus details about them. "Yes, for a few hours a week. The rest of the time he's a professional slacker."

Leo gave one of his subdued smiles, and it set off fireworks within her.

Holy cow. Get a hold of thyself, Maddie.

"He graduated, didn't he?" Leo asked.

What were they talking about? Ah. Brandon. "Yes, he pursued the six-year plan and received a degree in video game design last spring before moving in with my parents. Since then, he's been playing video games, but he hasn't been designing any." Her younger brother was as content as he was shiftless. "My dad has no idea where he went wrong with Brandon and me."

"You're not in the same category as Brandon. You have a great job."

"I think so, but my dad's not as convinced." Her father had once had aspirations of etching *Dr. Maddie Winslow* and *Dr. Brandon Winslow* into the frosted glass of his office door beneath *Dr. Thomas Winslow*.

Instead, she ran a chocolate shop. Brandon slept late, ate everything in her parents' pantry, and yelled instructions to professional athletes during games as if they could hear him. "My dad was hoping that, at the very least, I'd become a high-powered executive in San Francisco."

"San Francisco?"

"I took a marketing job there right after college. I was miserable. I sat in a cubicle doing work I hated for a man who wasn't very nice. I didn't like the pressure or the anonymity or any of it. I was lonely."

"So you came home."

"I did."

Until that time in her life, she'd thought she *wanted* to be a high-powered executive. Those two years had taught her differently. What she actually wanted was to live a simpler, more slow-paced life, surrounded by people she knew and cared about.

Maddie was an achiever, but she wasn't motivated by money. What motivated her far more? The challenge of building Sweet Art into the best little chocolate shop it could be.

"You're content with what you do, aren't you?" Leo asked.

"Yes. I can post as many Instagram pictures as I want while on the job." She grinned.

"Being a doctor or a high-powered executive is overrated."

"You're a doctor, Professor."

"So I should know." He looked into her eyes, and her muscles clenched with yearning.

The Saturday following her non-date with Leo, Maddie arrived at Carmichaels Christmas Tree Farm. Carmichaels, a local institution, was everything a person could want in a Christmas tree farm. Red barn in the center. Kindly farmer and his wife manning the property. Hot apple cider.

When Maddie and Leo had asked Kim what Christmas decorations they could supply, she'd informed them that she had plenty. Her only decorative need: a tree.

Happiness tugged at Maddie when she spotted Leo and Charlie waiting for her by the hot cider stand. It didn't look like Kim and her girls had arrived yet.

Charlie ran to her on his short, robust legs. Leo had dressed him in corduroys, tiny Adidas sneakers, and his navy coat. "Hi!" he called, extending his hand as far into the sky as it would go.

Maddie knelt down to greet him. "Hi, yourself. You look extra cute today."

"You look cute today, too."

"Why, thank you. What a gentlemanly thing to say. Are you ready to go shopping for Christmas trees?"

"Yes. Daddy says I can pick out a tree for our house." Olivia's blue eyes peered at her from Charlie's mostly angelic, yet ever-so-slightly mischievous face.

Olivia's eyes. Would there ever be a time when she'd look at Charlie's face and not experience a twist of grief? Grief for Charlie, grief for Leo, and grief for herself?

"I'm sure the one you choose will be perfect," she told Charlie as they made their way to Leo. "He tells me that you've given him permission to pick out a tree for your house," Maddie called.

"I did. I like living dangerously." Leo's tan canvas jacket complemented the gold and light brown shades of his hair. His classic black Ray-Bans reflected back an image of herself standing before him, surrounded by a cool, overcast morning.

Charlie scampered off to receive a mug of cider from Mrs. Carmichael.

"You're not worried he'll pick out a twenty-foot-tall tree?" she asked, voice pitched low.

"I don't intend to show him any of the twenty-foot-tall trees." His lips curved. "Experience has taught me a few things."

Maddie smiled back. "I'm planning to pick out a tree for my apartment today, too."

"So we'll be shopping for trees for three households?"

"Correct. However, since the church hasn't given us funds for the Huntingtons yet, I want you to know that I'll pay for the Huntington's tree. I don't want you to think I expect you to open your wallet and start covering Mission:Christmas expenses right off the bat."

"I was looking forward to paying for the Huntington's tree. It sounds like the money from the church and the garage sale will pay for most of the rest. A tree is the least that Charlie and I can do."

"You're already giving of your time, though."

"So are you."

"In that case, we can split the cost of the Huntington's tree. Deal?"

"Deal."

Kim, Victoria, and Samantha hurried in their direction. "The girls are so excited about this," Kim said as she wrapped Maddie in a hug. "I just love Carmichaels. Don't you? This place is the cutest and—" Kim broke off as she spotted Mrs. Carmichael approaching, carrying a tray. "Well, here she comes now. You're about to see for yourselves how delicious this cider is," she told her daughters.

When Maddie accepted her cup, steam fragrant with cinnamon and apples filled her senses.

Their group climbed onto the waiting tractor bed and took seats on the hay bales lining its sides. Mr. Carmichael settled into the driver's seat of the tractor and towed them toward the portion of his acreage containing trees for sale this season.

"You should take a picture of this," Leo said. "For Instagram."

"Oh! Right." She spent time taking multiple shots she could comb through later in search of the best. As she did so, she could feel Leo's attention on her like heat.

Charlie kept up a steady stream of chatter with Victoria and Samantha and Kim. When they motored over smooth stretches, they all attempted sips of the cider.

After exiting the tractor bed, they'd walked barely ten yards when Charlie made his tree selection. "This one!" He pointed, jumping up and down with excitement.

Leo held the double-handled saw they'd been entrusted with. Kim looked greatly amused. Her girls appeared befuddled.

The tree Charlie had picked was perhaps the ugliest tree on the farm. Squat. Sparse. A big bare patch in front. Tilting to one side.

"Are you sure?" Leo asked, no censure in his voice.

"I'm sure!"

"This is the one?"

"Yes!"

"All right then, buddy." Leo gave Maddie a glance laced with humor while Charlie danced a circle around the tree.

"Perhaps you can turn the bald spot to the wall?" Maddie whispered.

"And trim it straight?" Leo whispered back.

"And add lots of lights so that no one will notice that it's not very . . . full."

Charlie beamed.

The little boy's delight reminded her that the heart liked what the heart liked. She and Leo bent on either side of the trunk, then worked together to cut down the homely tree.

Her own heart also liked what it liked, despite all her self-lectures and all her best efforts.

Maddie grunted as she lifted a cardboard box marked *Winslow Family China* off of a box marked *Save for Maddie*.

She was spending her Sunday afternoon foraging for items for the garage sale. To that end, she'd bravely scaled the pull-down steps that led to her parent's attic. Her father was tidy, so like the rest of the house, everything here was well organized. Nonetheless, a tinge of spookiness hung in the air.

Maddie's family and friends had supported her involvement in Mission:Christmas by purging their belongings annually in order to stock her sale. So far this December, her purging pile and her parents' purging pile were both looking thin. Her mom had mentioned that Maddie might be able to find more items in the attic, so here she was.

The *Save for Maddie* box was promising. She used the pair of scissors she'd brought with her to slit the duct tape holding the box closed. Sinking to her knees, she opened the cardboard flaps. A few well-loved, bedraggled stuffed animals rested on top. Below that, her favorite books from when she'd been small. Then artifacts from her school days.

None of this was garage-sale worthy.

After setting aside folded baby clothes and blankets, she unearthed a small, stained fabric bag, fragile with age. A bouquet of purple flowers had been stitched onto the front.

Maddie set her weight on her heels and lifted the bag. She could feel the contours of something inside, something firm. Turning the bag over, she saw that a row of letters and dates had been stitched onto the back. The topmost line read *LD 1768.* The bottommost read *FBC 1959.*

What in the world?

Gently, she opened the drawstring. A piece of jewelry slid onto her palm.

Silver had been artfully sculpted into interlocking hearts to form a base that supported a large pale purple heart-shaped stone. A single wide clasp stretched across the back. A brooch. An old brooch? She'd never seen it before. She'd have remembered if she had, surely. So why was it in her box?

She tilted the brooch to catch the light from the utilitarian bulb above. The stone seemed to draw in radiance, to glow with it . . . almost magically.

She carried the treasure down the attic steps in search of her mom and came upon Brandon watching TV in the game room. "Haven't moved a muscle since I went to the attic, I see," she said.

"Why would I?" He tilted a thumb in the direction of the flat screen. "Football's on."

"Hey, how about when I come back, you go up to the attic with me and help me hunt for garage-sale items?"

"Yeah, I would, but it might mess up my manicure."

She snorted and continued downstairs.

Her mom stood at the kitchen island, rolling out pie crust.

"I found something," Maddie said.

"Great, honey!" She had yet to look up.

"I found something *mysterious* that might be valuable."

"Hmm?" The movement of the rolling pin ceased and her mom regarded her quizzically.

Maddie displayed the brooch, cushioned on top of the bag it had come in.

Her mom's features slackened with surprise. "Oh my goodness." She extended a hand. "I'd forgotten all about that."

Maddie passed over the brooch and took a seat on one of the

island's barstools. Mom smiled at the piece of jewelry with nostalgic affection.

Her mom's face was as familiar to Maddie as her own, and still, Laura Winslow's prettiness always seemed fresh. Her mom's thick, white-gray hair ended in a crisp line near the base of her throat. Her strawberries-and-cream complexion shone with health. And her blue eyes were surrounded by wrinkles that looked wise and beautiful rather than haggard. She wore an apron that said *Kiss the Cook* over her jeans and cotton top.

"Where did the brooch come from?" Maddie asked.

"Grandma gave it to me when I graduated from high school."

They called Maddie's paternal grandmother *Nonni*. They called Fleeta Chapin, Maddie's maternal grandmother, *Grandma*. "Is the stone real?"

"Yes. It's an amethyst."

"Then it must be worth a considerable amount of money, right?"

"Possibly. Since I never planned to sell it, I never had it appraised. It's a family heirloom."

"It is?"

"Oh, yes. It's been passed down by the women in our family for generations."

Maddie raised her eyebrows.

"The women are all noted on the bag, if I remember correctly." Mom donned her reading glasses, which had been lying next to the cherry pie recipe. "Yes. See here? Each woman in our family who's owned the brooch has been added to this list."

"Those are their initials, I'm guessing. And what, their birth dates?"

"Those are their *married* initials, I think. And their wedding dates."

"Wow." It appeared that the same woman had stitched the first several lines because they were all in the same color and style. "Why does the fourth lady have four initials and two dates?" Maddie asked. "Was she married twice?"

"I don't know," Mom said.

The other lines had been sewn with different colors of thread in varying styles. The last inscription, *FBC 1959*, was overlarge and lopsided. "Wait a second. Is FBC Grandma?"

"It must be. Her married name is Fleeta Brady Chapin, and she married Dad in 1959."

"Grandma isn't the neatest seamstress."

"She's always been better at shooting than sewing."

"Why aren't your initials on here?"

"I meant to sew them on." She gave an airy shrug. "I just never got around to it."

Maddie positioned the brooch next to the bag on the island. "Why was this brooch in a box in the attic marked *Save for Maddie*?"

"Well." Mom resumed rolling out the circle of piecrust. "I packed it away in that box to save it until the time came to give it to you. For your high school graduation or college graduation or on some other special occasion. But, goodness, I must've packed that box back when you were ten. The brooch never crossed my mind when you graduated high school and college. I haven't thought about it in ages."

Mom was loving and social and cheerful but not necessarily the most detail-oriented of women. Her relaxed approach to life led to a high degree of contentment and a high number of things that fell through the cracks. Leaving a valuable piece of jewelry in the attic for years—typical.

"Sorry I forgot, honey," she continued. "This isn't as sentimental a moment as I might have hoped, but here you are." Her eyes glittered with humor as she brandished a flour-dusted hand toward the brooch. "From me to you! Mother to daughter. Enjoy!"

"Thanks, Mom," Maddie said dryly.

"Are you frustrated with me for failing to give it to you when I should have?"

"No, it's okay. It's hard to be frustrated about not receiving something you never knew existed."

"An hour from now we can celebrate the brooch over this gluten-free cherry pie I'm making especially for you. How's that?"

"That'll work." Maddie was not one to pass up her mom's homemade pie. Ever.

Mom slipped the crust into the prepared pan then began crimping its edges. "There's a legend that goes along with the brooch."

"A legend?"

She nodded. "I'll have to think on it. I believe it had to do with the bearer of the brooch discovering true love."

"Hm?"

"Yes. Isn't that sweet?"

"You mean to tell me that a brooch that might have the power to bring true love into my life has been gathering dust under baby blankets?"

Mom grinned. "That about sums it up. Not that I believe in the legend."

"Yet you said that Grandma gave it to you when you graduated from high school. Right after that, you went off to the University of South Carolina and immediately met Dad."

Maddie's dad occasionally verged onto overly intense and taciturn territory with his kids. Never with Mom, though. Mom softened him into a cream puff.

The two had become friends shortly after arriving at the university. For more than two years, Dad bided his time while planning his careful strategy to win Mom's heart. Eventually, he'd succeeded. When he returned to his home state of Washington for med school, he'd brought both an undergrad diploma and a new wife with him.

It was a match made in heaven. Of all the married couples Maddie knew, her parents' relationship was one of the best.

Come to think of it, Grandma and Grandpa had a wonderful marriage, too. They were both upwards of eighty and had been married close to sixty years.

"It was a coincidence that I met your dad shortly after Grandma gave me the brooch," Mom said.

"I certainly hope so. If this brooch has the ability to bring my true love to me then I sure could've used it a few years back."

Mom laughed.

"What do we know about the women who owned the brooch before Grandma?" Maddie asked.

"I don't know anything, I'm afraid. Call Grandma and ask. Her memory's excellent." She rolled out a second ball of dough to cut into lattice that she'd lay in a crisscrossing pattern atop the pie. "Speaking of true loves . . . are you dating anyone at the moment, Maddie?" She asked the question with casual innocence, as if she didn't know very well that Maddie loathed discussing her boyfriend prospects with her mother.

"Nope."

"Evan over at the post office is nice."

"He smells like mustard."

"What about that handsome Zander Ford?"

"Two problems there. One, he's overseas at the moment and has been for more than a year. Two, he's in love with Britt."

"How about Brenda's son, Drew? Will you let me set you up with him?"

"I've known Drew since we were four. If it was a love match between us, I think we would've recognized that by now."

"Russell Goodman?"

"He lives with his mom."

"Your brother lives with his mom!" she countered, quickly coming to the defense of her can-do-no-wrong son.

"Exactly. Men who still live at home are off my list on principle."

"The Mission:Christmas party is coming up," Mom said. "Who are you going to take?" Every year, Mrs. Pottinger, a member of Bethel Church, hosted a lavish Christmas party for the volunteers and their dates.

"I was thinking about taking you again this year." Mom had proven herself to be a convenient date. She'd never met a party she didn't like, knew everyone, and could easily spend the entire party chatting with people other than Maddie. However, should Maddie find herself awkwardly alone, she could default to her built-in wing woman.

"I'd be happy to go, of course," Mom answered. "But should you find someone special between now and then—and I really think you should give Russell a chance, Maddie—then I'll step aside. And you can go to the party with your new man." She shot a hopeful look in Maddie's direction.

Lord, have mercy.

"The brooch belonged to my mother," Grandma explained to Maddie later that night over the phone. "My father died when a log truck overturned, and my mother died not long after that—of grief, they say, because she loved my father so much. I've told you all that before."

"Yes." Maddie sat cross-legged on the floor of her apartment in front of her newly decorated Christmas tree. Its branches sparkled with brightly colored ornaments and little white lights.

"My father's brother, Uncle Oscar, and his wife, Maisie, raised me, but the brooch belonged to my mother, Marion Evans Brady."

"Which makes perfect sense because the initials above yours on the bag are MEB. Did Marion's mother give it to her?"

"I believe so."

"Mom seemed to think that the women who have their initials on the bag are all related to us."

"As far as I know, that's true."

"Has anyone studied the genealogy of that branch of our family?"

"Your aunt Susan has." Aunt Susan was Maddie's mom's younger sister. "I have the family tree she sent me around here somewhere. Once I married your grandpa, I gave up wondering about all that folderol, but you're welcome to it."

"I'd love to take a look at our family tree. If we're lucky, we'll be able to match all the brooch's initials to names."

"Give me a few days. I think those papers might be in the hall closet, but I'm not entirely sure. I'll call you when I find it."

"Perfect. Thanks, Grandma."

"Sure, sweetheart."

"One more thing before you go. Mom mentioned that the brooch has an accompanying legend."

"Yes, the legend has it that the brooch brings true love."

"Do you believe that?"

A warm chuckle. "I didn't want to. And then the brooch kept going missing and the same man kept bringing it back to me. That'd be your grandpa. I finally decided that the Lord works in mysterious ways sometimes."

4

The words *December weather* weren't exactly a match for the words *garage sale*, Leo thought as he stepped back outdoors after taking a warm-up break inside his parents' house.

Today's temperature had started out below freezing before climbing to a cloudy forty-five around the time their sale opened. He and Maddie had done what they could to mitigate the temperature. They were holding the sale between the hours of noon and four, the warmest part of the day. They had two patio heaters going. And Maddie's mom was handing out cups of hot chocolate topped with marshmallows.

Leo, Maddie, and his two younger sisters were manning the sale. They were two hours in, and so far, largely because Maddie had pitched the sale to the community as a charitable event, they were turning a big profit.

He caught sight of Maddie talking to an elderly woman. As he watched, his smile grew. He couldn't hear their exchange, but he could tell Maddie was haggling. In her very likable way, she was unashamedly trying to take the older woman for every cent she could get out of her.

So far today, whenever anyone had come up to him and proposed a price for an item less than the one they'd marked, he'd simply said, "Sure." Bargaining was not his strength. He'd never known this truth about himself until today because he'd never hosted a garage sale or attempted to bargain down the price of . . . anything.

During his elementary school years, he'd been so shy that he'd only spoken when his teacher had called on him in class. He'd barely talked to his classmates because he hadn't known how to talk to them. He'd always understood that he and his family were oddly different and completely out of step with popular culture.

When he'd reached his teenage years, being out of step with popular culture had been akin to death, so he'd decided to take action. He'd approached his coolness problem the way he approached all things—through study.

He hadn't been able to make his personality cool. But he had been able to make his clothing and hair as cool as possible. Fixing those two things had helped matters tremendously, which was a sad commentary on the shallowness of high school.

As he'd gotten older, he'd gained confidence over the years in ways that had nothing to do with clothing and hair styles. Even so, he knew that in certain social situations, he still came across as overly formal and stiff.

Maddie Winslow, on the other hand, had a way with people. It wasn't that her personality was bulletproof, the way Olivia's had been. It was more that she had a talent—despite her moments of uncertainty or awkwardness—for putting other people at ease.

The elderly woman went off to browse, and Maddie made her way to Charlie. Charlie had been bouncing off the walls inside, so his sisters had brought him outdoors a half an hour ago.

Maddie lowered to Charlie's level and straightened his winter cap before the two of them launched into a conversation. Intuitively, Maddie knew how to talk to Charlie. She'd sat on his parents' rug earlier today and played blocks with Charlie patiently, something that Leo didn't always have the time or the desire to do.

His memory stretched back to the day when Maddie and Britt had driven to Idaho to visit them in the hospital after Charlie was born. Maddie had taken Charlie into her arms and made holding a newborn—something he hadn't been very good at himself back then—look like the most natural thing in the world.

He hadn't thought about that in years.

He and Maddie had been communicating often since they'd become Mission:Christmas partners. On the way here today, Charlie had commented, "You're feeling happy, aren't you, Daddy?"

He'd realized that he was. Then he'd realized it was because he was looking forward to spending the day with Maddie.

She approached him, carrying Charlie on her hip. "Charlie's cold, so I'm going to take him back inside."

"I can take him in if you'd rather."

"It's no problem."

"In that case, just drop him off with my dad. He's probably hiding in his study." His parents often took turns with Charlie when their grandson spent time at their house. His dad would keep an eye on Charlie while his mom read. Then, like a wrestling team, his mom would tag in and watch Charlie while his dad read. He had it on good authority that it was his dad's turn.

Charlie reached for the piece of jewelry pinned to Maddie's green coat. The big gem glittering in the center of it had to be fake. Even so, he didn't want Charlie, who could destroy anything in seconds, anywhere near it. Leo peeled Charlie's fingers from it.

"That's pretty," Charlie said to Maddie.

"Thank you," Maddie answered. She turned to Leo. "I found this brooch going through a box in my parents' attic, looking for garage-sale items."

"Ah. Are you wearing it as an advertisement to sell it?"

"No. It turns out that this is a family heirloom my mom forgot to tell me about." She gazed at him with wry amusement, then swept inside with Charlie.

Leo sold a pair of side tables to a couple, then a box of records to a teenage boy.

When business hit a lull, Maddie rejoined him beneath one of the space heaters. They stood side by side, their gloved hands in their jacket pockets. She wore a white winter hat that looked like a beret, but was big enough to cover her ears. She had compassionate olive-green eyes and delicate brows. A straight, firm nose. A chin that assured him she could stick to something if she put her mind to it.

She took out her phone and snapped a few shots of the sale, then one of him.

"For Instagram?" he asked.

"Indeed."

"Are you going to put a screen on top of the picture?"

"A screen?" She wrinkled her nose. "Oh! You mean a filter? You're quaint."

"Quaint?" He pretended outrage.

"Adorably so," she said. "Look." She added a filter that turned the picture sepia-toned, typed in some accompanying words, and posted it.

"That didn't take you any time at all."

"I'm a pro." She nodded toward the elderly woman she'd been haggling with earlier. "She wants that lamp over there. It's marked at fifteen, and she offered seven. I told her I can't take less than ten."

He laughed. "What if she decides not to buy it? Then we've lost a sale."

"I know my customer. She really likes that lamp, Leo. She's trying to frighten me by playing hard to get, but she'll end up buying it for ten."

"You're ruthless."

"I'm a ruthless garage-saler, yes. You're a considerably less ruthless garage-saler, I've noticed."

"Considerably less."

She scanned the shoppers, her attention pausing on a twenty-something woman who looked like she may live on a hippie commune. "You should go tell that woman that the books she's pondering are straight out of the library of famed research scientist Oliver Donnelly."

"Are you suggesting I lie to her?"

Her face swung toward him. "No! I thought those *had* come

out of your dad's library." Her smile transformed her face and . . . he forget what he'd been about to say.

"Whose books are those?" she asked.

"Mine. That big stack of books over there is from my dad."

"I'm surprised that you had anything to donate to the sale just a few months after moving."

"I'm always buying more books." He ran through the monthly book budget he set for himself within the first two days of every month, then had to wait weeks before he'd let himself buy more.

"You don't watch a lot of TV, do you, Leo?"

"I watch soccer sometimes."

"Mm-hm. What about *Top Chef*? Or *NCIS*? Or *So You Think You Can Dance*?"

"No. The only show I watch is *NBC Nightly News*." After he put Charlie down and straightened the house, he stretched out on his sofa with a pillow behind his head and read.

"I'll have to introduce you to those shows sometime."

"I'll have to introduce you to *Robespierre, Architect of the Reign of Terror* sometime. I just finished it last night, and it was excellent."

"I love to read, but that book sounds incredibly boring. No offense."

"None taken."

"I like funny love stories or fast-paced suspense novels."

"I never disparage anyone's taste in literature."

"That's good of you, Professor."

"To each her own, so long as the cause of literacy is furthered."

The twenty-something woman was still looking through his books.

"Go over and tell her that those books were yours," Maddie encouraged. "That'll result in an instant sale."

"*Famed research scientist Oliver Donnelly* sounded a lot more impressive."

"No way. The fact that they were yours will make them far more enticing to her."

"How do you figure?"

"Because you're persuasive in your own way. You must have noticed."

"I'm an un-ruthless garage-saler, remember?"

"But you're nice, smart, and handsome. Which is persuasive in and of itself."

Maddie thought he was handsome?

"Trust me on this point," she said lightly.

When he said nothing, she peeked at him. "Fine. Let's skip the woman with the books." She extended a white mitten toward a middle-aged couple. "You can tell them you'll have to stand firm at five dollars for that electric can opener they're considering."

He surveyed the rusty nineties-looking appliance. "I'd take one penny for that can opener. In fact, I'd give *them* five dollars for it, just to keep it out of a landfill."

Looking into his eyes, she laughed.

A tide of attraction collided with him. Fast and powerful. Unmistakable.

He broke their eye contact by looking back toward the sale. His heart was beating more quickly than usual, and his balance had turned shaky.

Maddie continued talking, about the money they'd raised so far and how much they could realistically hope to raise by the sale's end. They discussed where and when they'd start shopping for the items on the Huntington's list.

The whole time, he was just treading water, keeping his end of the conversation going while his brain spun.

What had happened just now?

Maddie might not have noticed anything out of the ordinary. He could only be sure of what he'd experienced—a powerful tug of both affection and physical awareness.

What in the world?

He hadn't understood until now that he felt that way about Maddie.

They were friends. She was . . . Olivia's friend.

Maddie's mom, Laura, walked in their direction with a tall, bald guy who Leo guessed to be around his own age.

"Maddie, look who's moved back to town!" Laura said. "Do you remember Raquel Shaw's son, Kurt? He was a few years ahead of you in high school."

"I do remember," Maddie said warmly. "It's really nice to see you again, Kurt."

"Likewise."

"Kurt was just telling me that after college he went to work for the Montana Highway Patrol," Laura said. "But he recently took a job with the Merryweather Police Department. Isn't that fabulous?"

"Fabulous," Maddie agreed. She introduced Leo to Kurt and then asked Kurt questions about Montana.

Laura remained a part of the conversation, listening intently and nodding in all the right places. During the first gap in the discussion, she said, "You two should get together for dinner so that you can catch up." She looked between Kurt and Maddie. "Wouldn't that be fun?"

"It would be," Maddie answered.

Jealousy pierced Leo. Like an arrow, it shot straight into him, then stuck there after impact. He ran a hand through his hair, trying not to scowl.

How long had it been since he'd been jealous? So long that he'd forgotten how dark and miserable the feeling was. He didn't want Maddie going on a date with Kurt the Police Officer, which was ridiculous, because Kurt seemed like a decent human being.

"Are you free one night this week, Kurt?" Maddie's mom asked, as determined on her course as a shark that scented blood in the water.

Maddie's cheeks turned pink. "Mom, don't you think you should try a more subtle tactic on poor Kurt here?" She gave Kurt an apologetic smile. "Just how attractive do you think he's going to find me if you push me at him?"

"Very attractive," Kurt said immediately to Maddie. "Very attractive is the answer."

Kurt's quick-witted response both impressed and infuriated Leo. It was the kind of thing he wished he had the ability to say at the right moment. Truth was, he'd never been skilled at stringing together charming words. Sincerity he could manage, but charming was not in his repertoire.

"Kurt," Maddie scolded teasingly, "don't encourage my mom. She'll start to think her non-subtle tactics are effective."

"They are effective." He gave a sheepish shrug.

Leo really didn't like Kurt. Not at all. He wanted to sell him the old sofa they were offering today for fifty bucks in hopes that it would give Kurt a dust allergy.

The elderly woman signaled Maddie. Leo felt a sense of loss as she left his side.

"I'll give you her number," he overheard Laura saying to Kurt as the two angled toward Laura's hot chocolate table.

Leo remained alone and still.

He'd grown accustomed to aloneness, to the kind of aloneness that only another widowed single parent could understand.

For the first year after Olivia's death, he'd been buried beneath a mountain of shock and grief and responsibility toward Charlie. He'd functioned at first in numbness. Then he'd been furious at the world and the driver who'd killed Olivia and at himself. Guilt over what he should have done or could have done differently had eaten at him. Sorrow had choked him.

During that time, people had often told him they didn't know how he did it, how he managed to handle the loss of Olivia on top of the responsibility of taking care of Charlie. Before Olivia's accident, if anyone had asked him whether he could handle his wife's sudden death, he would have said no.

No.

But when he'd actually found himself in that circumstance, there'd been no choice other than to survive. He had a baby depending on him. He had to survive because he had to make sure Charlie survived.

People who experienced tragedy understood something that

everyone else didn't. They understood that God supplies exactly as much strength as is needed to get through each day. If a small amount is needed, He supplies a little. If a huge amount is needed, He supplies a lot. Leo made it through that first terrible year by hanging on to God. At the end of that long, dark time, a tiny patch of hope had finally appeared.

It wasn't that he'd ever be okay with what had happened to Olivia. He wasn't okay with it. It was more that, eventually, he'd comprehended that Olivia was gone and that he *could* live as a single father. It wasn't what he'd chosen, but he could live this way. And some days—a lot of days—could be good. At first, he'd felt shame whenever he did have a good day, as if he didn't have permission to enjoy anything after what had happened to his wife. But in time, he'd learned to accept the good days at face value, to appreciate them when they came.

When Leo and Charlie had been living in the house they shared with Olivia in Idaho, Leo had faced constant reminders of how things used to be, of the family they'd been before that tragic day in June.

But here in Merryweather, the slate was clean. He and Charlie had never lived here with Olivia so, in some strange way, it felt more bearable to go on without her here than it had in Idaho. At the same time, Merryweather connected them to Olivia in new ways. Her family was far more involved in their lives now that Leo was raising Charlie in the town Olivia had been raised in. The same streets, the same schools, the same natural beauty that had surrounded Olivia when she was young surrounded her son. Charlie's mother's town was now Charlie's town.

At no point in the last two and a half years had Leo thought that he was ready to date again. He still didn't think that. He definitely wasn't looking for more things to add to his schedule beyond his job and his little boy.

What he'd felt for Maddie just now wasn't something he'd arrived at the way he arrived at most things—through a great deal of research and forethought.

It had come out of nowhere and hit him across the head with the force of a bat.

He and Maddie had always had a great rapport, but in the months since he'd moved to Washington, Maddie had never given him a reason to think she felt anything more for him than friendship.

He reached both hands up and clasped them behind his neck. He needed to sleep on this. Maybe it had just been a random thing. Maybe he'd feel differently in the morning, and they'd continue the way they had been. Maybe he was even more lonely than he'd realized.

A picture rose in his mind from long ago. A woman's profile in a theater. The blur of bright color on stage. The music of *Les Misérables* churning the air. Tears as shiny as diamonds on her cheeks.

He was connected to others.

Life was hard, but life was good.

It would be crazy to ask out Maddie Winslow, his wife's friend. Wouldn't it? If so, then why did the idea strike him as so immediately right?

"Maddie, I finally found Susan's genealogy research," Grandma said over the phone the next night. "The papers weren't in the hall closet after all. They were inside Hank's desk."

"Thanks so much for finding them for me."

"There's a whole raft of stuff here. Might be best if I just put it all in the mail."

"Sure, that would be great."

"I'll take them to the post office tomorrow. Love you."

"Love you, Grandma."

"I hope you find whatever it is you're hunting, Maddie."

5

Anything interesting happen at the garage sale?" Britt asked
as soon as Maddie let herself into Sweet Art's kitchen for
work on Monday morning.

"We raised a thousand dollars. Then Mr. Gustafson stopped
by as we were cleaning up and handed me a check for a thousand
more."

"That's awesome . . . and also highly evasive because you know
that by 'anything interesting' I was referring to your relationship
with Leo."

Maddie hung her jacket and purse in the closet. Sweet Art occupied a building that had once been a bank before it had been
relocated to its current spot within Merryweather Historical Village. The back half of Sweet Art contained Britt's kitchen. The
shop commanded the front half.

"It really was incredibly generous of Mr. Gustafson," Maddie
said, willfully ignoring Britt's comment about Leo. "I'm going to
keep on giving him extra truffles every time he visits." Mr. Gustafson was a wealthy retiree with twinkly eyes who took his therapy
dog to the hospital for fun and was in possession of a sweet tooth.

"You give him free truffles?" Britt asked with mock outrage.
She stood at her cutting board in her white chef's coat, slicing
ganache. She'd snatched her dark hair into a top knot then added

a cloth headband for good measure. Her features were crisp and beautiful.

"Of course I give him free truffles. He pays for five times that many, and he just handed Leo and me a *one-thousand-dollar check* for the Huntingtons. I'd say the free truffles are a good investment."

"Nope." Britt smiled wolfishly. "I'm going to have to dock your pay and issue a warning."

"Can you issue my warning in the form of a Death by Chocolate truffle?" Maddie extended her hand for her morning fix.

Britt plucked up a newly made Death by Chocolate truffle and stretched across her work space to place it on Maddie's palm. "Now tell me how things went at the garage sale between you and Leo. I've been eagerly awaiting the latest installment in your tale of unrequited love."

Maddie ate half the truffle. It melted in a deep, dark, rich stream over her tongue. "My tale is going to remain unrequited, I'm afraid."

"But why?"

"Because Leo and Charlie are Olivia's guys—"

"They *were* Olivia's guys. Now they're not."

Maddie made a sound of protest.

Britt flicked a chocolate sprinkle at her.

Maddie batted it away.

"Leo is perfectly free to date anyone he wants now," Britt stated. "And so are you."

Maddie wanted to argue, but how could she? Technically, Britt was right. However, when it came to the bonds of friendship and contrasting loyalties and complicated matters of the heart, "technically right" didn't have much bearing. She had a sudden craving for potato chips.

Britt gave Maddie a forceful look. "They're not Olivia's guys anymore. You can't let that get in your head. Okay?"

"Okay, attack dog. I hear you." Maddie finished her truffle.

"What else is making you think your tale has to stay unrequited?" Britt asked.

"The fact that I don't think Leo's interested in me."

"You don't know that to be a fact. Did he do or say anything promising during the garage sale? Anything?"

"Well, two very small things did happen."

Britt cocked her head, waiting.

"He looked at me at one point as if struck by something. It was sort of an . . . arrested look? I'm not convinced, though, that it had anything to do with me. It could simply have been that he had an epiphany about eighteenth-century France."

"What's the other thing that happened?"

"My mom did what she's fond of doing and tried to set me up with an unsuspecting single man right in front of Leo. It could have been my imagination, but Leo seemed displeased."

"At the prospect of you going out with the other guy?"

Maddie nodded.

"Hmm," Britt said speculatively.

"I probably misread Leo. He probably wasn't displeased."

"Or maybe he was." Britt's almond-shaped brown eyes sparked with excitement. "Maybe he just needs some encouragement. Leo's reserved. What's that saying? Quiet waters . . . something something?"

"Still waters run deep."

Britt snapped her fingers. "Yes, exactly." She bent her head and continued slicing the ganache into perfect squares. "I think that Leo feels passionately underneath that calm demeanor. When he devotes himself to something he's *seriously* devoted. The problem for you is that men like Leo can be slow to make a move."

Britt had Leo's personality nailed. Maddie adored the fact that Leo's still waters ran deep. He wasn't glib. He wasn't the sort of guy who used flattery to manipulate and charm to seduce. Instead, he possessed the less-flashy qualities she cared about most. He was kind, intelligent, trustworthy, real, and sometimes just a little bit self-conscious. When she was with him, he made her feel like the best version of herself.

"Have you considered asking him out?" Britt asked.

The thought of that caused Maddie's heart to spiral to the ground like a wounded quail. "I couldn't." She began to knead her knuckle.

"Why not? We both know that Olivia's frankness helped her snag Leo." Britt made her way to the sink and began washing her hands. "I've asked out plenty of men in my day, and they've usually said yes."

Britt was both overtly pretty and adventurously forthright. Maddie certainly didn't consider herself to be as pretty as Britt, nor had she been born with the I-ask-men-to-go-out-with-me gene.

Rejection didn't scare Britt, but it did scare Maddie. Especially rejection from Leo. *Especially.* Maddie donned a black apron emblazoned with the shop's logo across the front in white.

"Ask him out," Britt encouraged.

"No, thank you."

"Ask him out!"

Maddie escaped by pushing through the swinging door into the shop.

Britt was determined to bolster Maddie's hopes where Leo was concerned. But it had never seemed wise to Maddie to hope that he might *actually* come to love her.

That longing seemed too unlikely, too destined to set her up for a fall.

"I'm not finished lecturing you," Britt called.

"Funny, because I am finished being lectured," Maddie called back pleasantly. "Especially about hypothetical situations concerning Leo Donnelly."

She set about the tasks she accomplished each morning before opening the shop. She brought the cash register to life, refilled the napkin containers, made sure each chocolate in the display case was aligned with all of its chocolate friends. She cleaned the glass front of the antique case, the bar that lined three of the interior walls, and the tops of the accompanying barstools.

Britt shouldered through the swinging door and came to a stop, arms crossed. "Who's the unsuspecting single man you mentioned earlier?"

"You're just now thinking to ask?"

"I was momentarily thrown off my game by my dismay over the state of your dating life," Britt answered.

"I'm dismayed over the fact that I'm slaving away while you're just standing around doing nothing."

Britt gave a sly smile. "I'm a master chocolatier, which qualifies me to stand around doing nothing."

Maddie burst out laughing. "No, it doesn't!" She tossed a freshly laundered dish towel to Britt.

The two of them worked side by side. Their long history joined them together as surely as did their town and their shared passion for Sweet Art's success.

"The unsuspecting single man is Kurt Shaw," Maddie said. "He moved back to town recently and took a job with the Merry-weather police."

"I think I remember him. Did he play baseball in high school?"

"I believe he did."

"How does he look?"

"He looks good."

Britt enjoyed dating and was extremely popular with, well, just about every available man in the county. Her relationships usually broke down after a few months, though. It was perfectly obvious to Maddie that Britt hadn't settled down long term because none of her boyfriends had been The One. Britt's friend Zander was very clearly The One for her, in everyone's opinion except Britt's.

When Zander returned to town . . . if Zander returned to town . . . Maddie had high hopes that the two of them would finally find their happy ending together.

"Keep your sights off Kurt for now," Maddie said. "I'd like to keep him in my back pocket as a maybe."

"There's no reason to keep him in your back pocket as a maybe, Maddie. Your destiny lies with Leo Donnelly."

On December seventeenth, Maddie and Leo met to shop for clothing for Kim's daughters.

Leo held up a conservative children's turtleneck and jumper. "How about this?"

Maddie's eyebrows sailed up. "Um . . . no," she said kindly.

"No?" He glanced at the jumper then back at Maddie. The gold tones in his hair shone beneath the store's lights.

"Nope. That outfit, while a very worthy suggestion, reminds me of a school uniform from the year 1978. Kim's girls struck me as liking clothes a little more sparkly and modern."

Leo hung the jumper back on its track and gave her a charmingly tilted smile. "I can pick out boy's clothing, but I'm hopeless with female fashions."

The last thing she wanted was to scare him away from today's shopping expedition. The fun of this outing would vanish like smoke if he were to leave her here alone. "Be that as it may, I require the pleasure of your company as I choose female fashions."

"You do?"

"I do. Also, you're handy. If you weren't here, who would push the shopping cart?"

She refrained from saying that she loved the way he subconsciously tapped out a rhythm on the bar of the cart with his thumbs.

She loved how, unlike many men his age, he almost never checked his phone.

She loved the way his soap smelled like leather and spice.

She loved his capable hands. His solemn profile. And the faint, grave lines sorrow had chiseled across his forehead.

On December eighteenth, Maddie and Leo met to shop for toys.

They bought board games. Books. Barbies. Barbie clothes. Art supplies. Athletic equipment. Stocking stuffers. And one big gift for each girl—a dollhouse for Victoria and a mini motorized car for Samantha.

"What do you think, Leo?" Maddie asked as they stood in the toy aisle, observing the jumbo-sized boxes containing motorized cars.

Leo started. His upper arm and elbow were propped on one of the racks, but he hadn't been looking at the toy car selection. He'd been busy watching Maddie. He was having a hard time taking his eyes off her, in fact.

Maddie was so . . . alive. Not half-alive, which is how he'd felt since Olivia's death. But fully alive. Maddie Winslow was *living* her life.

"Should we go with the pink Jeep?" she asked. "Or the pink convertible?"

"The Jeep, of course. This is the Pacific Northwest. Every girl needs a Jeep so she can go off-roading in the mountains."

"A valid point if ever there was one."

"Do you think I should buy one of these for Charlie for Christmas? This one, maybe?" He nudged a camo-sided car with his shoe.

"Is three the legal driving age for miniature cars?"

"I believe it's four and a half, but we Donnelly men are high achievers."

She met his eyes and grinned. He gazed steadily back, bracing himself against the tenderness stealing through his heart.

Over the past days, he'd come to realize that the attraction he'd experienced for her at the garage sale wasn't random at all. It had turned into a pattern. A habit. Every time he saw her, it magnified in strength. Each day, he grew more certain of his feelings.

That's not to say that this thing between them didn't surprise him, because it did. It was like finding a treasure he'd never thought to hunt for, and didn't think he deserved, lying right in his path.

Maddie chewed idly on a fingernail as she considered the cars.

She was funny, sweet, and unselfish, and he had no idea how she'd react if he were to ask her out. No idea.

Maddie might think of him as nothing more than a friend. If he put her in a position where she was forced to let him down gently, not only would he be crushed, but he'd feel like an idiot. He'd then have to live beside her here in Merryweather for years with the knowledge of her gentle rejection between them.

On December nineteenth, Maddie pulled the pages her grandmother had sent her from their envelope. She scooted a chair up to the kitchen table in her apartment and smoothed the pages flat alongside the brooch, the bag it had come in, and a napkin mounded with potato chips.

Using the family tree her aunt Susan had compiled, Maddie was finally able to locate the name of her grandmother's great-grandmother. Ruth Holister Fulbright Azlin. She was the one with the four initials. She had four initials because she had indeed been married twice. It looked as though her first husband had died six years after their marriage when Ruth was only twenty-two. *Twenty-two.* Holy cow.

Working slowly, she matched name after name to the initials. With each mystery solved, a fresh dose of satisfaction gusted through her. She studied each woman's birthplace, her age at the time of her marriage, the number of her children, the length of her life.

She had the sense that history was rushing forward into the present. These women, whose blood still flowed in her veins, whose legacy she'd inherited, had sewn their initials into the fabric of this bag with their very own hands.

Her grandmother had been right. All of them were direct ancestors of Maddie's except the very first set of initials, LD. The second set of initials belonged to Sarah Gooding Everard, who'd been born in England and died in America. However, Sarah's mother's initials weren't LD.

The stack of paper contained a photocopy of a photograph that had been taken of Sarah around the end of the Civil War, when she'd been sixty. She looked out from the photograph with a secret kind of a smile, surrounded by her large family.

A few of Sarah's letters had also been photocopied. They were hard to read, but with patience, Maddie was able to decipher them. One of the letters, written shortly after Sarah's marriage, referenced a woman who'd apparently employed her in England as a companion. Lady Densbury.

LD.

"Well, what do you know?" Maddie whispered. She sat back in her chair with a huff of surprise. It seemed that their family brooch had begun life in the possession of a British aristocrat.

Maddie slid a fingertip wonderingly over the surface of the brooch's amethyst. "You have an excellent pedigree."

She intended to take far better care of the brooch than her mom had. After Christmas, she'd have it professionally cleaned and appraised. Then she'd hire someone to hand-embroider her mom's initials and wedding year into the delicate fabric of the bag.

The silver contours of the brooch gleamed beneath the light of the chandelier.

Maddie didn't actually believe that the brooch contained magic, in large part because she didn't believe that magic existed. The only higher power she believed in was God.

Yet, it couldn't be denied that this brooch, with its overlapping hearts, was a powerful symbol of her birthright. The prior care-takers of this piece of jewelry had loved greatly and been loved greatly. They'd all enjoyed long marriages. Not because of magic. Because they'd been generous, loyal, sacrificial, and committed to their relationships.

She wanted to believe that she could experience the same thing her ancestors had. For the same reasons.

At this point, though, her marriage prospects, and thus the brooch's future, were extraordinarily uncertain.

She was a twenty-seven-year-old woman who, in four days time, would be taking her mother to the Mission:Christmas party as her significant other.

On December twenty-first, Maddie and Leo met to purchase nonperishable groceries for Kim's Christmas Eve and Christmas Day meals. As had become their habit, Leo pushed the cart. Maddie consulted her list and tried not to peer at Leo when he wasn't looking.

At this point, here's what she knew for sure about the status of her relationship with Leo: they'd grown closer because they saw each other often and communicated with each other every single day.

Here's what she didn't know: whether she could expect their newfound closeness to continue after Mission:Christmas wrapped. And whether he harbored an iota of romantic interest in her.

There were moments—fleeting moments—when he'd gaze at her with pensive softness. Those moments tempted her to think that maybe he *had* come to feel something for her. But then the moment would pass and that notion would seem farfetched.

What she'd told Britt at Sweet Art continued to weigh on her mind. *"Leo and Charlie are Olivia's guys."*

Then Britt's arguments would counter. *"Leo is perfectly free to date anyone he wants now. And so are you."*

Around and around her thoughts circled.

Around and around.

6

Mrs. Pottinger was a member of Bethel Church. A recipient of the spiritual gift of hospitality. And the owner of a mansion that reminded Maddie of a modern art museum. The home's polished stone floors seemed to stretch for acres in every direction. Towering white concrete walls supported pieces of art the width of minivans.

Every year on December twenty-third, Mrs. Pottinger graciously hosted a party for the Mission:Christmas volunteers and their dates.

Maddie set a gluten-free iced sugar cookie, then a slice of flourless chocolate cake onto her plate as Rat Pack–era holiday music burbled beneath the hum of conversations.

Notecards had been placed next to several of the platters, letting guests know which items were gluten free, dairy free, nut free, vegan, or sugar free—a gesture wholeheartedly appreciated by Maddie. If a platter had no accompanying notecard, it basically signaled, "Full of all the bad stuff and extremely delicious. Eat at your own risk."

Mrs. Pottinger had chosen a dark green and white Christmas decorating scheme. Fir trees were located in every common room of the house, each tree adorned with nothing more than glittering crystal ornaments that resembled icicles. Wreathes of glossy leaves hung in strategic places, and similar garlands coated mantels and marched down the length of the tables.

The vibe was extraordinarily sophisticated and chic, which left Maddie feeling sophisticated and chic, simply by virtue of being a guest.

She added a scoop of candied walnuts to her plate.

Fortunately for Maddie, Leo had arrived without a date this evening. If he'd shown up with another woman, she firmly suspected that she would've choked on her peppermint hot chocolate. He'd found her shortly after he'd arrived and stayed by her side. They'd mingled and chatted with the other volunteers until one of his female colleagues at the college had swept him into a discussion about Abbott.

Maddie paused at the mouth of the great room. Her attention tugged, inexorably, to Leo. He was still talking with his colleague.

Tonight he wore a gray suit, white shirt, black tie. His hair was slightly disordered. Thick scruff on his jaw. He could have belonged to the Rat Pack himself, dressed as he was. If he grabbed one of those old-fashioned microphones with the long metal heads, he could cause an audience of girls to faint dead away.

In actuality, he had a brain filled with academia instead of music. In actuality, he was too humble to call attention to himself by singing to a crowd.

How long until she could wrest him back from that woman?

Maddie was on the verge of seeking out her mom when she spotted Britt's two older sisters, Willow and Nora, and decided to turn her steps in their direction.

Britt's sisters greeted her with hugs. Because of Britt, Maddie had known them for ages. She'd always liked them, and so she tried not to be envious of the happiness they'd both found over the last year and a half with their wildly impressive men, both of whom were standing alongside the sisters this evening.

Britt's oldest sister Willow, a former model, now ran a boutique in nearby Shore Pine, which was half full of women's clothing, half full of house accessories, and entirely full of *beautiful* items. A few months back, she'd married former quarterback Corbin Stewart.

Corbin was so over-the-top famous that Maddie always felt

tongue-tied in his presence. She compensated by trying to seem casual about his celebrity, as if she hadn't noticed that he had one of the most recognizable faces in American sports.

The middle sister, Nora, owned both Merryweather Historical Village and the heart of John Lawson, a former Navy Seal who now ran an emergency-response training company.

"Congratulations on your engagement," Maddie said to Nora and John. The couple smiled at each other, their deep affection palpable. "I haven't seen you since, so this is my first chance to tell you how happy I am for you both."

"Ask to see the ring," Willow encouraged. "It's lovely."

"Yes, please!" Maddie said. "May I?"

Nora extended her hand, and Maddie made an awestruck noise. Nora's ring reflected Nora's admiration for all things retro. It harkened back to another era with its square diamond and its halo of pavé diamonds. "It's gorgeous," Maddie said honestly.

"Thank you." Nora took a sip of her drink. "Has Britt been behaving for you at Sweet Art?"

"Yes, for the most part."

"She hasn't goaded you into any hikes that go straight uphill lately?" Corbin asked.

"Not since last month," Maddie answered.

"Has she acted like an eccentric artist and stayed up all night chasing inspiration for a new chocolate recipe?" Willow asked.

"Not since last week."

"Has she made you go kayaking in cold weather?" Nora asked.

"Has she talked you into bungee jumping?" John asked.

They all laughed, then the sisters, John, and Corbin began telling affectionate "Britt stories."

Maddie's attention slid back to Leo just as he glanced across his shoulder at her—as if he'd known where she was, as if he was as aware of her as she was of him. Their eyes met, and her heart took a giddy, stuttering beat.

"Honey!" Maddie's mom entered their circle, said hello to everyone, and thrust forward the Single Man she'd discovered

344

among the partygoers. "I wanted you to meet Alistair! He's from Connecticut originally but his aunt and uncle live here, and he's staying with them while he looks for work in the area."

"Awesome," Maddie said. Not awesome. Poor Alistair looked to be fresh out of college, with a boyishly cute face, and thick, curly auburn hair, several locks of which fell diagonally across his forehead.

"Hey," Alistair said to her, obviously self-conscious about being shoved at a woman who was far too old for him in front of spectators. His attention swept the group, passing Corbin, then sweeping back to Corbin with astonishment. "Are you"—his mouth fell open—"Corbin Stewart?"

"I am."

Alistair proceeded to ignore Maddie in favor of Corbin. Maddie didn't blame him in the least, but she could feel her mom coiling, awaiting the chance to display her oldest child to Alistair again the way a pet-store owner might display an aging kitten in need of a home.

Why had she brought her mom along? At the moment, she couldn't remember.

Once again, Maddie's mother was trying to set Maddie up. Leo, who was not usually an angry person, could feel his temper rising.

Ever since he'd been separated from Maddie, at least half of his focus had remained on her. He hadn't determined to keep tabs on her in the crowd. He simply *was* keeping tabs on her, as if by instinct. Automatic. Somehow his mind and body had been reset, and the new settings were attuned to her, the way a car stereo picks up a radio station.

The woman he was speaking with was in the middle of a very long story. He sent another look in Maddie's direction.

The man her mom had brought over for her was still there.

Possessiveness pulsed through him. His and Maddie's friendship had changed—the way that sunrise slowly changes to bright morning—into something more.

He thought about her when they were apart. His spirits lifted each time he received a text from her. He left work undone at his desk so that he could arrive at their shopping outings on time. She made him laugh. Her smile stole his breath.

Maddie had become one of the things, in addition to Charlie, that gave his days joy and purpose.

All that had happened, yet he'd done and said nothing to her about it. He wanted to go on a date with her—a real date. In order to do that, he needed to ask her.

He jammed two fingers into the neck of a dress shirt that suddenly seemed tight. He loosened it and his tie slightly.

He'd never been good at asking women out. The more he cared, the harder it was for him to risk himself.

The night he'd met Olivia, she'd made it very, very clear that she liked him. She'd done everything but throw a lasso around him. Because he hadn't known her then, he hadn't been emotionally invested. Asking Olivia on a date had been easy.

After things had become serious between them, he could remember feeling relieved that he'd left the world of dating behind. All that uncertainty and insecurity were in his rearview mirror forever . . . he'd thought.

But here he was again, battling uncertainty. Wanting, for the first time in a long time, to ask someone out and feeling like a rookie. Unlike the night he'd met Olivia, this time around he cared. His emotions were already invested in Maddie.

Also, he was painfully aware of his faults. He'd been married before, to her friend. He had a child. He was introverted and sometimes too preoccupied with books.

But he knew without a doubt that he would treat Maddie the way she deserved. He couldn't trust these men Maddie's mom kept finding to do the same, which is why he couldn't allow himself to stand silently to the side any longer.

"Merry Christmas, everyone!" A well-dressed older woman stood next to the DJ, holding a microphone. "I'm Peggy Pottinger, and I'm so glad that you were able to join me tonight here in my home. You've made Mission:Christmas possible again this year with your efforts. Thank you for volunteering!" A round of applause. "Now. If you knew my late husband, Bruce, then you know that he was a sweetheart, but that he was just a little bit grumpy about dancing and music. He didn't like either one."

She lowered her voice. "I'll let you in on a secret. I love dancing and music. Love!" she exclaimed, returning to full volume. "Ever since Bruce kicked the can, we've been dancing like there's no tomorrow around here!" A dip of stunned silence, followed by a burst of rich laughter from Peggy. The crowd joined in with a smattering of nervous chortling.

"We've been eating and mingling," she continued, "but now we're going to start dancing because it's my house and I make the rules! In exactly one minute, this remarkable DJ here has agreed to play Dean Martin's 'Let it Snow.' So I'm giving you fair warning. You have sixty seconds to find a partner for this first dance. If you don't, I'm going to come around and pair you up and shoo you onto the dance floor." Another bark of laughter ended her speech.

Fear arced down Leo's spine. He wasn't a skilled dancer. But given this situation, there were things worse than having to dance. Being paired by their hostess as if he were ten years old was worse. Watching Mrs. Pottinger match Maddie with the curly-haired guy was worse.

Leo excused himself from the panicking people around him and shouldered purposely through the crowd toward Maddie.

Desperate times. Desperate measures.

He arrived just as Maddie's mom was turning to Maddie, raising a hand to gesture toward the curly-haired guy—

"Would you—" Leo said to Maddie as he arrived at her shoulder.

She turned at once, an encouraging look springing to her face.

"I was hoping . . . that you might. . . ." Leo swallowed. "That is, I was going to see if you'd like to dance with me." *Shoot!* Why couldn't he have said that better?

"Yes," she answered at once. "I'd love to."

Thank God. He offered his forearm. She wrapped her hand around the crook of his elbow, and he led her to the side of the gathering couples.

"It seems the forced dancing portion of the evening has begun," she said lightly.

"Does Mrs. Pottinger enforce dancing at this party every year?" he asked.

"This is a first. Last year she insisted we play an enormous game of Christmas charades. The year before that she created a small sledding hill and made everyone sled down it."

"I'm guessing Bruce didn't like charades or sledding."

"Exactly. She seems to be taking the Mission:Christmas volunteers on a tour of all the activities Bruce detested."

"I think I would've liked Bruce," Leo said dryly.

Maddie laughed, and he found himself laughing, truly laughing.

"You could have warned me about this," he said.

"I could have. But then you might not have come."

"I'm impressed that *you* keep coming to this party year after year."

"It's good for me to step outside my comfort zone every now and then. Besides, it gives me a chance to eat delicious food and wear a fancy dress."

"I don't know if I mentioned it earlier," he said, "but you look beautiful in your fancy dress." Her simple white dress followed the curves of her body from shoulder to knee.

"Thank you." She smoothed the dress into place. "I've been waiting for a chance to wear it."

Her long earrings sparkled. Her silver high heels showed off toes painted red. The clean grapefruit scent of her perfume scrambled his thoughts. Was he . . . should he say something else?

Music expanded through the room, and they adjusted to face each other. He offered his left hand. When she placed her fingers in his, a shock of heat surrounded the contact. Rattled, he concentrated on placing his right palm at a respectable spot on her waist.

"Oh, the weather outside is frightful," sang Dean Martin.

Leo and Maddie swayed in time to the music. He didn't feel like a terrible dancer. He felt okay at it and like the luckiest man in the room because he had Maddie in his arms. For this one night, he wasn't at home, cleaning up toys and loading the dishwasher. Maddie smiled up at him, and he smiled down at her, as if the two of them had just pulled off a jail break.

"It turns out that I don't hate forced dancing," she said.

"No. Me either."

"This is kind of nice." She settled her gaze on something over his shoulder.

"Yes."

"Really nice, actually," she said softly.

He nodded. *Really nice* was still an understatement.

"Let it snow, let it snow, let it snow," Dean sang.

Leo lifted their joined hands. She spun underneath before he drew her back into position. They moved into a slow turn.

"Maybe we should do forced dancing more often," he said.

"I think you're on to something, Professor."

"Would you like to go dancing with me after Christmas? It would give you another reason to wear a fancy dress."

She searched his face as if trying to uncover his motivation.

"And I'd want to throw in dinner, too." He worked to sound relaxed instead of what he actually felt—vulnerable. "Because dancing probably makes you hungry at some point."

"I'd definitely like to go dancing with you after Christmas."

She would?

He twirled her again, and they fell back into step. "Aren't you going to take a picture of the dancing?" he teased. "For Instagram?" She looked incredibly cute every time she framed a photo. She always scowled with concentration until she'd captured just the right shot.

"Nope. I left my phone at home. I'm going to have to remember this dance through memory alone. Which won't be a problem, let me assure you."

Had she really just said yes?

Because of You

Had he really just asked her out?

Maddie spent the remainder of Mrs. Pottinger's Christmas party suspended in a level of happiness akin to that experienced by Miss Americas directly after their crowning. She talked to people. Danced. Ate two more gluten-free Christmas cookies. And the whole time, one thought reigned supreme in her mind: *Leo asked me out.* The man whose understated personality clicked with her own. The man who'd been a fabulous husband to Olivia and was a fabulous dad to Charlie. The man who'd followed through on every one of his Mission:Christmas responsibilities. The man who was as reliable as he was good. *That man* had asked her out.

The astonishing truth of it submerged her in excitement, despite the guilt that kept trying to interrupt her delight. Each time the guilt butted in, Maddie thrust it to the side. Now wasn't the time to think through all the ramifications of Leo's invitation because thinking through the ramifications was guaranteed to tarnish the pleasure.

She wanted, for this one evening, to relish the joy.

Leo Donnelly, the man she'd had a crush on for so, so long, had asked her out.

7

The moment Maddie opened her eyes the next morning, her misgivings about Leo and Olivia jolted her fully awake—and not in a good way.

She dashed both her worries and her comforter to the side. After padding into her apartment's kitchen, she got a pot of coffee brewing.

Today was Christmas Eve. Christmas Eve! She and Leo were due at Kim Huntington's house at ten this morning to unload the Mission:Christmas haul they'd carefully stockpiled for her and her girls over the past weeks.

It was going to be a busy day. A wonderful day, full of Leo and Kim and then her extended family this evening. She didn't have time for misgivings.

When Maddie spotted Leo's car parked in Kim's driveway, anticipation rained through her like sparkling confetti.

Leo exited his car while she parked. She loved the way his clothes fit him. His jacket's collar stood up, framing his neck. Simple black sweater. Jeans.

"Good morning," he said as she approached.

"Morning." They stood, beaming at each other under a cold

white sky. Maddie wasn't exactly sure how to interact with him now that a new understanding—*we like each other*—lived between them. It was an understanding brimming with possibilities.

They popped their respective trunks. When Leo spotted her trying to lift out a heavy box, he rushed over to help. "Here. Let me." He toted the box, and she carried bags in both hands as they made their first trip up the front walkway. Kim lived in a tidy one-story Cape Cod revival style house with windows symmetrically placed on either side of her recessed front door.

Maddie rang the bell with her elbow and gave a satisfied sigh. "I love Christmas Eve."

"It's the second best day of the year, next to Christmas."

"Christmas Eve may edge out Christmas Day, in my opinion. Christmas Day is full of"—she hunted for the right word—"revelation, but Christmas Eve is full of expectation. Which might be even sweeter." *Expectation is a very sweet thing indeed, isn't it, Leo?*

Now that he'd invited her on a dinner and dancing date, the snapping attraction between them was so blatantly obvious that she couldn't believe she'd been unsure of it for so long.

Kim swung the door wide. "Hello! Merry Christmas!"

"Merry Christmas," Maddie and Leo replied.

"Heavens to Betsy!" Kim waved them in. "This is so exciting. The girls are playing at a friend's house because I wanted them to be surprised when they come home and find Christmas gifts under the tree."

"Excellent strategy," Maddie said.

"Did you bring your little boy?" Kim asked Leo.

"No, I dropped him off with his grandmother earlier this morning. Unloading and organizing aren't his specialties." A smile settled across his lips. "His grandmother has a lunch date scheduled at 11:30, so she's planning to drop him off here on her way."

"Wonderful."

They set the first round of deliveries on Kim's dining room table.

"Oh!" Kim said, taking a package from one of the bags. "You've wrapped some of the gifts. How thoughtful."

"We wrapped all of the gifts," Maddie answered. "We also attached gift tags to each. If you want to unwrap some of them and set them out instead, go right ahead, of course. We just wanted to save you time and effort if we could."

Kim's appreciative gaze moved from Maddie to Leo, then back to Maddie. "Thank you. I really love the wrapping paper you chose."

Kim was a Southern belle. Maddie had guessed that she'd like a traditional Christmas decorating scheme with just a little bit of fancy thrown in. They'd bought wrapping paper in complementing patterns of red, green, and white, plus lots of wide, shimmery ribbon.

All three of them made multiple trips to the driveway to bring everything in. Imperishable groceries they'd shopped for days ago and the perishable groceries that Maddie had picked up just this morning. Gifts upon gifts. They helped Kim put everything where she wanted it, then cleaned up after themselves.

When they were done, a wide ring of presents encircled the tree that Leo and Maddie had purchased for Kim weeks before. Maddie stood next to Leo, so close that their upper arms brushed, as they admired the final result of their efforts.

Joy, the sort of joy that Christmas is truly about—the kind that springs from hope and from putting the needs of others before your own—expanded within Maddie until it permeated every point of her body. In God's upside-down economy, He'd made sure that the person who served another would somehow become the one most richly blessed.

"Good job, Maddie."

"Good job, Leo. We did it. Together."

Kim returned from the back of the house and presented each of them with a gift that had clearly been wrapped by a child. "Victoria, Samantha, and I wanted to do a little something for you, to thank you. It's small and certainly not in any way big enough to acknowledge the magnitude of what you've done for us. But I want you to know that we really are grateful."

"This is so kind of you." Maddie tore open the wrapping paper to reveal a flat, wooden Christmas tree approximately six inches tall. She glanced over and saw that Leo had received the same.

"The girls just love Mod Podge," Kim explained. "You know that sticky craft glue? Anyway, they go crazy for it. They had a blast making these for y'all."

It appeared that the girls had cut out Christmas motifs from magazines and created a collage of them over the surface of the tree. Not a millimeter of the wood showed through the charming plaster of pictures of candles, ornaments, snow, sleds, and hot chocolate. There were also angels, Mary and Joseph, the cross, and a graphic of Jesus's manger, with golden rays shooting out from it. "I'll treasure it," Maddie said.

"Thank you," Leo told Kim.

"Thank *you*," Kim replied. "Both of you. Thank you so, so much." She hugged Leo. "I can't tell you how much this means to us."

She moved to Maddie and gave her a hug. When Kim pulled back, her eyes were wet, and she had to dash her fingers underneath her lashes. "These things that you've brought are more than material things. They're a reminder that I'm not on my own. God is still with me and God still provides. He always makes a way, amen?" She sniffed and smiled tremulously.

"He always makes a way," Maddie agreed.

"I'm looking forward to seeing you in the office at Abbott once the spring semester begins," Leo said to Kim.

"Me too! Me too." She gestured toward herself. "Come back over here for one more hug, Leo."

After Leo had spoken with Human Resources at Abbott, Kim had been called in for an interview. A week ago, she'd been offered an admissions assistant position while the current admissions assistant was on maternity leave.

If Kim ended up impressing the administrators at Abbott as

much as she'd impressed Maddie, then, who knows, her temporary job might become a stepping-stone to something more permanent at Abbott. Regardless, it addressed Kim's most urgent need: income for the near future.

"And one more hug for you, too," Kim said to Maddie.

Clasped in Kim's strong arms, a verse crystallized in Maddie's mind. *The* Lord *gave, and the* Lord *has taken away.*

He'd taken away from Kim. But He'd given, too. He'd given her two girls. An opportunity at Abbott. He'd ensured that she'd be able to make this Christmas a memorable one for her family, despite the challenges.

Leo and Maddie said their good-byes and returned Kim's wave as they walked toward their cars.

Usually the two of them were surrounded by other people, like at last night's party or at the stores they'd visited. It was rare and luxurious to be with Leo like she was now. No one within earshot. No one looking.

They chatted about his Christmas Eve plans with Charlie and her plans with her family. As they spoke, she buttoned her green coat against the chilly weather. The brooch she'd affixed to it preened with historic beauty. It almost seemed smug in its role of family heirloom. Generations had come and gone, but it had endured.

The cold was probably turning the tip of her nose pink, but she didn't want their time together to end. So long as Leo was here with her, she'd stand on this spot until frostbite set in.

The phone calls and texts and lunch appointments they'd shared had been like gold to her, each one something to look forward to, something to delight in, something to remember over and over. Now that the task that had tied them together was complete, how often would she see him?

A gust of wind blew tendrils of her hair in front of her eyes. Before she could extricate her hands from her jacket pockets, Leo reached out, delicately caught the strands, and smoothed them out of her face. For a split second, he met her gaze. Then his vision fell to his fingers as he settled her hair back into place. With a look of pure concentration on his handsome features, he traced the outer shell of her ear then let his fingers trail a few inches down the side of her neck.

Conversation had ceased. Maddie couldn't have said anything if she'd wanted to. Her heart was beating double time—

From off to the side came the loud sound of someone clearing their throat.

Leo and Maddie instantly stepped apart, turning toward the noise.

Olivia's mother, Deb, crossed the street toward them.

Maddie's stomach sank. Deb had always been a what-you-see-is-what-you-get type of person. Equal parts blunt, opinionated, generous, and self-deprecating.

Maddie and Leo had been so wrapped up in each other that they hadn't noticed that Deb had parked across the street from Kim's house. She'd left her car running, driver's side door ajar. Maddie could clearly see Charlie strapped into his car seat in the back, his attention directed at the car's built-in TV screen.

How much had Deb seen?

She must have seen all of it.

In the process of dropping Charlie off with Leo, Olivia's mother had stumbled upon the two of them.

"What's going on here?" Deb asked. She was an attractive brunette, dressed today in soft pants and a red tunic accessorized with a silk scarf imprinted with candy canes.

"Deb—" Leo began calmly.

"No need to answer," Deb interrupted. "I can see what's going on." She motioned toward her car. "Charlie's with me, Leo. I don't think he saw what I saw, but what if he did?" Disappointment carved brackets into the skin on either side of her mouth. "Olivia was your friend," she said to Maddie.

Heat flamed in Maddie's cheeks. "She was."

"Well." Deb drew herself up. "I'm not sure she would have approved of what I just saw."

"Whether or not she would have approved is a moot point," Leo said. "Olivia's been gone for more than two years." He spoke gently but without apology. He regarded Deb levelly, with just a trace of warning in his expression.

I'm not sure she would have approved. Deb's words penetrated right to the center of Maddie's own concerns. Suddenly, she could no longer evade those concerns. Suddenly, it didn't matter if she was too busy or too happy to let them in. Deb had dragged them all out.

"We can talk about this later," Leo said to Deb.

"Daddy!" Charlie's voice rang from within his grandmother's car. He waved. "Hi, Maddie!"

"Hi, sweetheart," she called back. Then to Leo and Deb, "I need to head out. I'll see you both later." She'd managed to speak pleasantly, but she didn't have it in her to look either of them in the face or to hang around long enough to hear their response.

As soon as she pulled into her apartment's parking lot, she texted Britt.

Britt, in true friend fashion, had driven straight to Maddie's apartment when she'd received Maddie's text. Maddie had just finished bringing her up to speed on all that had transpired between her and Leo last night and this morning.

"You know how Deb is," Britt said. "She often speaks without thinking."

"She might speak without thinking, but she definitely says what she means. She wasn't happy about Leo and me."

"Her reaction may have had more to do with surprise and grief than anything else. She'll come around." Britt was perched on the edge of the coffee table, directly across from Maddie's position on the sofa. Britt pulled one of Sweet Art's miniature boxes, just large enough for two truffles, from her purse and handed it over. "I was at the shop making Christmas truffles for my family when I got your text. I figured that missing your twice-daily dose of chocolate was guaranteed to make this situation worse."

"You're supposed to be taking the day off. Sweet Art's closed."

"Not to me when I want to make Christmas truffles for my family."

"I'm not family."

"Just about," Britt insisted, giving Maddie a staunch, direct look.

Hot tears constricted Maddie's throat. She'd known she could trust her friend's fierce brand of support. Flicking open the lid of the box, she revealed two dome-topped dark chocolates, crowned with perfect sprigs of green fondant holly and red fondant berries. "Thank you." She couldn't eat them at the moment because Deb's words had left her feeling physically nauseous. But these truffles were evidence of her friend's love for her. That's what mattered.

"Maddie," Britt said. "Don't go all quavery on me. This isn't the end for you and Leo. You haven't done anything wrong. Deb is the one who's in the wrong for reacting the way that she did."

"It's understandable, though. It was hard enough for us when Olivia died. But imagine what it was like for her, to lose a child."

"Brutal," Britt allowed. "But that doesn't excuse Deb's behavior this morning. She was rude."

"She was upset."

"She was rude."

Maddie's phone beeped to signal an incoming text. She glanced at it. *I'm really sorry about Deb*, Leo wrote. Maddie slanted the phone toward Britt so she could see, then typed, *It's okay.*

She and I will talk it over later today, Leo replied. *I hope you have a good Christmas.*

You too.

"See," Britt said. "Leo's on it."

Yes, and she loved the way that Leo had stood up to Deb this morning. He hadn't been cowed the way she had. And yet . . . everything felt so subdued now. It was like she and Leo were two elementary school students who'd been having a great time together right up until they'd been caught and sent to the principal's office.

"Don't let this throw you off course," Britt said. "This is an obstacle, that's all. Any long relationship will have to overcome dozens of obstacles."

"But we don't really *have* a relationship yet. We haven't gone on a single date."

"Overcome this obstacle and go on your date. Then overcome another obstacle and another. Do whatever you have to do because Leo's worth it."

Maddie said nothing.

Britt gazed at her hard, as if she were a doctor trying to diagnose an illness. "This isn't really about Deb, is it? Deb just forced you to confront the guilt you already feel for liking Leo."

Maddie squeezed her knuckle. "It's hard to explain. I just . . . I don't want to do anything that might betray Olivia."

Britt's expression turned long-suffering. "Want to know what I think?"

"I'm afraid to say yes."

"I think that you were comfortable as the third wheel back when Olivia was alive and you had a hopeless crush on Leo. Now that Olivia's gone and your crush might not be so hopeless, I think that you've cast yourself as the bad friend, and you're not so comfortable in that role. So"—she filled her lungs with air—"let me set the record straight. You weren't a bad friend to Olivia, Maddie. You were a great friend to her. And Leo was a great husband to her." She paused. "Do you think Olivia would have been against the prospect of Leo falling in love again? Of him remarrying?"

"Maybe! Maybe she would have preferred that he remain faithful to her until his death."

"You're a very loyal person, Maddie. Remember when we were in tenth grade and I threw up in history class? Everyone else shrieked and rushed to the other side of the room and then started whispering and giggling. Except you. You put your hand on my shoulder, and you scolded everyone for reacting the way they had instead of showing compassion to the sick person." She laughed.

"I remember." Maddie had been surprised at herself after that incident. She hadn't realized she'd had it in her to reprimand a roomful of her classmates.

"In this case, though," Britt said, "I think your loyalty to Olivia has turned into a runaway train. Just because Olivia died doesn't mean you have to compensate by becoming hyper-loyal to her now. Leo's only thirty-one years old. Let's say he lives to the age of ninety-one." Britt's lips tipped down with skepticism. "Do you really think our kind, outgoing, bighearted friend would want the man she loved to go through life alone for the next sixty years?"

"I'm not sure."

"I am sure. She wouldn't. There's *no way* she'd have wanted him to spend the rest of his life that way after being married to her for less than three years. And I happen to think that Olivia would have preferred for him to date one of her friends rather than a stranger."

"What? No!"

"You knew her very well, Maddie. You treasure her memory." She tossed out a hand for emphasis. "If Leo dates a woman who never met her, that woman won't give a fig about Olivia. You and me and Hannah and Mia, we *want* to remember her. A stranger won't."

It was so quiet that she could hear the couple from down the hall talking as they made their way along the corridor to their apartment. The whir of the heater. The ticking of her decorative clock.

"Pray about it," Britt said. "Listen to what God has to say in response. You'll see that He agrees with me on this."

"You always think God agrees with you."

"This time, I'm doubly sure that He does."

8

Maddie hadn't driven to the lookout in years, yet her heart still knew the way. She steered along a network of small streets before parking at her destination.

The lookout was little more than a half-circle of dirt, sweeping outward from a secluded road that graced the top of Twinflower Hill like a necklace. A short cement fence had been erected at the lip of the lookout to keep cars from tumbling over the edge, because from here, the land dipped steeply away. The view revealed the Hood Canal, the distant mountains, and the town of Merryweather nestled among the trees far below.

After killing the engine, Maddie simply sat, taking in the scene. Remembering.

It was nearing two o'clock. She'd yet to eat lunch, and soon she'd need to get herself ready for her family's Christmas Eve get-together.

Soon, but not quite yet.

She, Olivia, Britt, Hannah, and Mia had come here during their high school years on weekend nights when they didn't have anything better to do, which was often. They'd usually driven here in Olivia's Chevy Trailblazer and admired the glittering lights through the Chevy's front windshield.

Maddie could still hear the thumping soundtrack of those

years: Avril Lavigne, Rhianna, Kelly Clarkson. They'd eaten hot Cheetos and talked about the future and boys and the sports they played and clothes and makeup. The interior of the Trailblazer had smelled like PINK perfume.

The sound of Olivia's laugh bubbled up from Maddie's memory, surrounding her. Olivia had a wonderful laugh. She'd laughed easily and the timbre of it had been deep and genuine.

Maddie pulled on her white, knitted beret, then her gloves, and exited the car. She went to stand at the fence, her arms crossed tightly against her chest. Low clouds rolled overhead. She felt closer to Olivia in this place where they'd passed so many hours together with their friends than she had in months.

"I'm so sorry," Maddie whispered. She hadn't known until now that that's what she wanted to say to Olivia. Her friend's sudden, violent death had stolen Maddie's opportunity to say anything final to the black-haired, blue-eyed girl she'd known. The girl who'd been on student council with her. The girl who'd driven her into Seattle on Maddie's seventeenth birthday so they could celebrate with coffee from the very first Starbucks. The girl who'd been her college roommate.

That girl had died.

And Maddie was desperately sorry that she had.

God had a plan and He was sovereign, but it still seemed unbearably unfair to Maddie that Olivia had died so young.

The verse that had come to her earlier returned. *The Lord gave, and the Lord has taken away.*

"As much as I adore Leo and Charlie, they're both rightfully yours and I honestly wish that you could've lived out your life with them." The words emerged so quietly they barely reached Maddie's own ears. "I feel guilty for liking Leo as much as I do and wanting to be with them as much as I do. If you were here, I'd ask for your permission. But if you were here, this situation wouldn't exist."

The drifting wind made the only reply.

Maddie closed her eyes. *God, forgive me if I've ever felt wrongly toward Leo, if I've acted wrongly, if I've ever said anything that was wrong in your sight. I'm not sure how to reconcile dating Leo with honoring Olivia.*

This time, she did receive an answer.

She sensed, in the deepest part of her intuition, that Olivia was well. Whole. The God of heaven and earth had control of her care now. It occurred to Maddie, as goose bumps pebbled her skin, that He could be trusted with that.

Olivia hadn't received a long life here on earth. The Lord had taken. But then He'd given. He'd given Olivia life in a place without death, mourning, crying, or pain.

No death. No mourning. No crying. No pain.

Maddie's finite mind strained to grasp the truth of what heaven was like. She couldn't grasp it, to be honest. She was going to have to accept it on faith.

Olivia was well.

She is well. Maddie filled her mind with the phrase several times in a row. *She is well.* No one, including her or Leo, need worry about Olivia anymore.

"I love you," Maddie said to Olivia. "I will always remember you, and tell people about you, and miss you. I'll never stop looking for ways to celebrate you and the impact you had on the people you cared about."

Cold pinged against her cheekbone, and she looked up to see dainty snowflakes drifting down from the sky, silent and elegant and full of grace.

Maddie smiled at the wonder of it. Some of her friends grumbled about snow. Not her. She'd always loved it. Snow! On Christmas Eve, no less.

Minutes passed. Maddie stood, a still figure amid the dance of the snowflakes. This was no angry, sleeting storm. No, this felt much more like a blessing. A gift.

Life continued even after loss.

God had taken away the summer sun, but now He'd provided something fresh and beautiful in its own way. The snow of winter.

A new season had come.

As soon as Leo arrived at Olivia's brother's house that evening, he asked his sister-in-law if she'd keep an eye on Charlie for him. Then he went in search of Olivia's mom and dad, Deb and Randy, and asked if he could speak with them privately.

Now the three of them were closeted in Olivia's brother's home office, the sounds of voices and Christmas music leaking through the closed door.

Deb's face and posture communicated shaky defensiveness, as if she suspected she'd behaved badly, but wasn't ready to admit it yet because she believed that Leo had behaved badly, too.

Randy regarded Leo with compassion.

"Did Deb tell you what happened earlier today?" Leo asked Randy. "Between Maddie and me and Deb?"

The older man nodded.

He knew that Olivia's parents felt for him the way people were supposed to feel toward their sons-in-law. They were grateful to him for giving them a grandchild. They admired his efforts as a husband and continued to appreciate his efforts as a dad. They liked him a great deal and might even love him some. But he could never, ever function as a substitute for their beloved daughter.

No one could.

Leo had never hoped to try. It's just that in this moment, the gap between what Olivia had been to them and what he was to them seemed more enormous than usual. He wished, for their sakes, that he could be a better consolation prize.

He cleared his throat. He hadn't been looking forward to this conversation, but he was determined to get it over with so they could move on. "Did you know that every Christmas decoration and ornament I own was purchased by Olivia?" He'd given some thought to what he wanted to say to them, how he wanted to start this ball rolling. "Charlie and I opened all the doors of the Advent calendar that belonged to her when she was a girl. We listened to

'Rockin' Around the Christmas Tree' when we decorated our tree, because that was your family's tradition. We walked in the Main Street Christmas parade because that's what she did with you every year growing up. We attended your church's nativity play."

Some of the defensiveness melted from Deb.

"Olivia's influence will always mark my life and Charlie's life," Leo said. "Always. She was my wife, and she's Charlie's mother. We loved her."

"Thank you for saying that." Emotion roughened Randy's tone. "Sometimes it seems like people are going on with their lives and forgetting her."

"I understand."

"We don't want people to forget."

"Neither do I," Leo said.

Deb began to blink as if fighting tears.

"The pain of losing her was so overwhelming at times that I thought I might suffocate from it," Leo said. "I know you both know what I mean."

"We do," Deb said.

"It's only recently that I've gotten over that suffocating feeling." He sighed. "It's not that I've *gotten over it*, necessarily. It's just that I don't feel like I'm suffocating all the time anymore. I've begun to hope that the rest of my life might not be one long exercise in torture. I—I hope that you won't hold that against me."

"We won't," Randy said.

Deb, however, looked conflicted. "Did you have feelings for Maddie when Olivia was alive?" she asked.

"No," he stated definitively. "We were paired together to work on Mission:Christmas a month ago. It was then that something . . . changed between us."

Deb frowned.

"I've asked her out on a date," Leo said. "Which I know might be hard for you guys, and I'm sorry about that. Really sorry, because I'd never want to cause you any additional grief. The three of us have had plenty of that." He drew in a breath. "I'll be honest with you and tell you that I'm really looking forward to my date with Maddie. It would mean a lot to me if you could find a way to be okay with the two of us dating. To give us your blessing, even."

"You don't need our blessing," Randy said.

"I'd like it just the same." Leo looked to Deb.

"I . . ." Deb's pursed lips trembled. "I apologize for the way I responded this morning when I saw you and Maddie together. I've always liked Maddie. It was just a shock, that's all. To see you with another woman."

"I know."

"Give me a few days to adjust. I can accept it," Deb said. "I *will* accept it and even support it because you made our Olivia very, very happy, Leo."

"Olivia made me very happy."

"You're a good man," Randy said, clasping Leo's shoulder. "You deserve good things, son."

"When you talk to Maddie," Deb said, "please tell her that I'm sorry."

9

Leo's Christmas Day began at 5:51 A.M. when Charlie jumped on top of him, whispered, "It's Christmas, Daddy" in an excited voice, then attempted to pry open Leo's eyelids with his fingers.

Groggily, Leo stumbled into the living area of their house ahead of his son to switch on the Christmas tree lights and get music and coffee going. Then he let Charlie loose. His little boy tore through the gifts like a rhinoceros through a swamp.

They joined Olivia's side of the family for Christmas brunch. Food. More gifts. Then returned home so that he could get Charlie down for a nap. He'd only just now managed it. He had a brief window before he needed to regroup and drive Charlie to his parents' house for more food and more gifts.

On weekend days, he usually soaked in the quiet during Charlie's nap. Today, though, he wanted nothing more than to spend time with Maddie.

Ever since Deb had walked up to them yesterday in front of Kim's house, a stone of foreboding had been pressing down on his chest.

He'd texted Maddie last night to let her know about the conversation he'd had with Deb and Randy. He'd told her that Olivia's parents had given their blessing and that Deb wanted Maddie to know she was sorry.

Still, he worried that things weren't right between him and Maddie. Things didn't *feel* right. Maddie was susceptible to hurt, which was one of the things he appreciated about her. He knew that Deb had caused Maddie both embarrassment and guilt.

He desperately wanted to fix what had been broken.

He dialed Maddie's number.

Painful hope leapt within Maddie when she saw that the incoming caller was Leo. She dried her hands on a dish towel, scooped up her phone, and took a few steps into her parents' mudroom adjacent to their kitchen. "Hello?"

"Maddie, it's Leo."

She loved how he always announced his identity. "Hi."

"Hey, I'm sure you're probably really busy and that you don't have any time to spare, seeing as how it's Christmas Day and all, but I'm at home for the next few hours. I just put Charlie down for a nap, and I'd . . . really like to see you." He made an irritated noise in his throat. "That sounded presumptuous . . . me calling and telling you that I'm at home and that you can come over. I'd come see you if I could. If you were free. But now that Charlie's asleep, I'm stuck—"

"I have some time. I'd be happy to swing by. Definitely don't wake a sleeping child."

"You're coming by?"

"Do you want me to?"

"Yes. Very much."

"Then I'm coming by. I'll be there in ten minutes." They disconnected, and she hurried into the kitchen to gather her things.

"Where are you going?" Maddie, her mom, and her dad had been in the throes of preparing rolls and ham and mustard sauce to take to her dad's side of the family.

"I'm going to swing by Leo's."

Her mom tilted her head a fraction. "Leo? I thought you guys finished your Mission:Christmas duties."

"We did, for the most part. We just have one loose end left to tie up."

"Loose end?"

"Mm-hmm," Maddie said noncommittally. She knew better than to tell her mom anything about Leo until it was absolutely official. No sense getting Mom's hopes up unnecessarily.

"We need to leave here in forty-five minutes," her dad said.

"Who's going to whisk the mustard sauce?" her mom asked.

"Brandon will have to do it. It's high time we started making him contribute to this family." Maddie pointed her steps toward the living room.

Brandon was slouched on the sofa playing a game on his phone. In one deft motion, she nudged his feet onto the floor. "Up and at 'em, little brother. You're needed in the kitchen."

"Huh? Since when am I needed in the kitchen?"

"It's a new dawn. It's a new day!" She sailed toward the door.

"What're you so happy about?"

"It's a new day!"

She practically ran to her car. She was tempted to press the accelerator to the floor as she drove across town, but she willed herself to slow down. The streets were slightly slippery and framed on both sides by the coating of snow that had fallen since yesterday afternoon.

Maddie came to a stop in front of Leo's house and peered at it through her car window. When Leo had moved to town, the house he'd purchased had been a topic of discussion between herself, Britt, Hannah, and Mia. Motivated by extreme curiosity, Maddie had driven by once or twice, but this was the first time she'd been invited inside.

The isolated location of Leo's house read *cabin*. However, its architecture read *modern sculpture*. The materials of concrete, glass, and wood combined to form a structure that resembled a box with a diagonally slanting lid.

Maddie gathered her courage, and on wobbly legs, made her way to the door.

Leo opened it before she arrived. The fact that he'd been waiting and watching for her generated a rush of affection all out of
proportion to the simple gesture.

Holy cow. She really needed to keep her composure. It may
be, of course, that he wanted to see her so he could tell her he'd
changed his mind about going on a date.

"Merry Christmas, Maddie." He wore a white button-down
with the sleeves rolled up and jeans.

"Merry Christmas, Leo." She followed him inside. His house
had the hushed quality that only homes containing sleeping children possess.

"Thanks for coming by," he said. "I feel badly about interrupt-
ing your Christmas Day. "

"It's no problem. Really."

"I called because . . . Forgive me, may I take your coat?" He
seemed a bit nervous and even more intense than usual.

Maddie's concern that he might have invited her over to commu-
nicate bad news notched higher. Her pulse thrummed in her throat.
"Sure." She handed him her green coat, and he laid it carefully over
a chair the way he'd seen her do it, with the brooch faceup.

Maddie made her way into the living area. "Wow. Your house
is great." Floor-to-ceiling panes of glass left no room for artwork.
None was needed. The nature surrounding the house *was* the art.

He'd furnished the interior with simple, masculine pieces and
filled a wall of shelves with hardback books. Honey-hued planks
of wood covered both the floor and the ceiling. She walked to the
front of the space near Charlie's Christmas tree, which looked even
more adorably pitiful now that it had been laden with ornaments
that clearly hadn't been placed by a female. Far too many of them
were grouped on the bottom right side.

Leo came to stand beside her. "You like the house?" He gave
her an uneven smile.

"I absolutely do. It suits you." The house was literary and
straightforward and beautiful—just like he was. She trained her
attention through the windows at the snow-dappled woods.

Everything in her was reaching out for him. For years she'd been stuffing down her attraction to Leo. The barriers she'd erected to hold it back were cracking now, splintering with the force of her feelings for him.

A pocket of silence opened between them. She had no words to fill it.

"I . . ." he said.

She turned to him. A ripple of power went through her as she took in the details of the spiky lashes surrounding his storm cloud–gray eyes, so somber at the moment. So earnest.

"I just wanted to say in person," he continued, "how sorry I am about what happen yesterday with Deb."

"I'm sorry too, for your sake. That moment was awkward."

"Really awkward."

"I felt like we'd been caught doing something wrong," she said.

"Right, which is why I wanted to talk to you. I could tell that it upset you. I regret that it did."

She slid her fingers into the front pockets of the black jeans she'd paired with a silvery top. "To be completely honest, there are some things about liking you, about dating you, that concern me because of my past with Olivia and your past with Olivia. I've liked you for quite a while, Leo."

"I've liked you for quite a while, too."

An eddy of happiness swept through her even though she was very aware that his "quite a while" equaled a matter of days. "I think it's safe to say I've liked you longer. But I haven't been sure if a relationship between us would be right."

Fear shifted in the depths of his eyes.

"Deb's reaction when she saw us together," she said, "forced me to confront some things I've been avoiding."

"And?"

"And I've done some soul-searching since yesterday. There might be other moments of awkwardness like the one with Deb in our future. And more guilt, too, most likely." She didn't want to sound as if she was assuming they had a long relationship ahead of them.

They hadn't been on a single date! On the other hand, it felt incredibly liberating to talk to him about this. "It's not always easy to celebrate the good things that come your way when someone you loved no longer has the chance to do the same."

"I know."

She swallowed. "Just because it's not easy, though, doesn't mean that we shouldn't still grab hold of the good things. I think that we should."

Maddie watched relief steal over his features. Leo scrubbed the heels of his hands over his eyes then tunneled his fingers through his gold-toned hair before dropping his arms. "Thank God. You had me worried there for a second, Maddie. I was afraid you were going to say that Deb's reaction convinced you that going out with me wasn't worth it."

"No," she said.

"I think we should grab hold of the good things, too. It's—you . . . are a lot more than I thought to hope for."

Was this really happening? Could she trust something this amazingly lovely? "*Oh*." It was the most coherent response she could formulate.

"Long ago," he said, "before I met Olivia and before she introduced me to you, my parents and I went to see a performance of *Les Misérables* at the Merryweather Theater. During the scene near the end when Javert makes his sacrifice, I glanced to the side and down and saw you there. You were crying and looking happy and sad at the same time. Everything on your face matched what I was feeling."

What? With effort, she pulled up the memory of that day, that show. She'd gone with her mom. She knew the scene he was referring to, the one when Javert gives his life for the convicted Valjean. It never failed to impact her like a wrecking ball. She adored *Les Mis*. "Yes, I remember. I can't believe . . . You were there?"

"Not only was I there, but I've remembered that moment many times over the years. It's comforted me."

"So . . . did you recognize me when Olivia introduced us?"

"Not immediately. The theater was dark, and you were sitting a few yards from me during the performance. Eventually, I did put two and two together and realized that you were the woman I'd seen that night."

"That's incredible."

"Yeah."

She didn't think this was the best time to scold him for not having introduced himself that night. "You're a fan of *Les Mis*?"

"Yes. You?"

"Yes."

"It's a good sign," he said, "that we both like it. Don't you think?"

"I do."

"So things are okay between us?" he asked.

She nodded.

"We're still on for dinner and dancing?"

"We are. Although I might like to see you from time to time before our date."

"I might like to see you *every day* before our date," he admitted.

She grinned because the sentiment so exactly matched her own. It was paradise to know that Leo was coming to feel the same way about her that she felt about him. It seemed like a greater miracle than the feeding of the five thousand.

His attention sank to her lips. Then, slowly, very slowly, he dipped his head and kissed her. She felt his fingers comb into her hair until he was supporting the back of her neck.

She stepped closer and wrapped her arms around him as need and love coursed through her.

After long moments, they broke the kiss, looking into each other's eyes and smiling crazily. Breath hitching. Then they kissed again.

Leo's kisses were the best kisses that Maddie had ever experienced in her life. They swirled her thoughts and caused her tummy to flip with the force of their chemistry.

The sound of rustling crackled through the air . . . a sound like someone turning over in bed.

"What's that?" she whispered.

"Baby monitor," Leo answered. "Charlie's waking up." Leo's mouth took on a wry, humorous twist. "He never did have a great sense of timing." He kissed her again.

She might just die of exultation.

"Daddy?" came a groggy voice.

Leo and Maddie separated, laughing under their breath.

"Daddy! I'm awake."

Leo motioned for her to follow him into a room abounding with shades of white and red and navy. Charlie sat upright in his miniature bed, surrounded by a blanket patterned with trains. "Hi, Maddie." He smiled at her with Olivia's blue eyes. "What are you doing here?"

"I came by to say hi."

He moved toward her, and she lowered like she always did when he approached. He opened his arms, and she gratefully enclosed him in a hug. He smelled like honey shampoo and indefinable little boy smell.

"Have you had a good Christmas?" she asked.

"Really good! You?"

Maddie tilted to look up at Leo, Charlie still in her arms.

Tenderness marked Leo's expression.

It was a new dawn. A new day.

She'd thought her childhood Christmases were the best of her life but none of them held a candle to this one. "This, Charlie, has been my best Christmas ever."

"The LORD gave and the LORD has taken away;
may the name of the Lord be praised."

Job 1:21

Author Bios

Christy Award finalist and winner of the ACFW Carol Award, HOLT Medallion, and Inspirational Reader's Choice Award, bestselling author **Karen Witemeyer** writes historical romances because she believes the world needs more happily-ever-afters. She is an avid cross-stitcher and shower singer, and she bakes a mean apple cobbler. Karen makes her home in Abilene, Texas, with her husband and three children. To learn more about Karen and her books and to sign up for her free newsletter featuring special giveaways and behind-the-scenes information, please visit www. karenwitemeyer.com.

Kristi Ann Hunter graduated from Georgia Tech with a degree in computer science but always knew she wanted to write. Kristi is a RITA Award winner, an ACFW Genesis contest winner, and a Georgia Romance Writers Maggie Award for Excellence winner. She lives with her husband and three children in Georgia. Find her online at www.kristiannhunter.com.

Sarah Loudin Thomas is a fund-raiser for a children's ministry who has time to write because she doesn't have children of her own. She holds a bachelor's degree in English from Coastal Carolina University and is the author of the acclaimed novels *The Sound of Rain* and *Miracle in a Dry Season*—winner of the 2015 Inspy Award. Sarah has also been a finalist for the ACFW Carol Award and the Christian Book of the Year Award. She and her husband live in Asheville, North Carolina, because she can't bear to leave Appalachia. Learn more at www.sarahloudinthomas.com.

Becky Wade is a native of California who attended Baylor University, met and married a Texan, and moved to Dallas. She published historical romances for the general market, then put her career on hold for several years to care for her children. When God called her back to writing, Becky knew He meant for her to turn her attention to Christian fiction. Her humorous, heart-pounding contemporary romance novels have won the Carol Award, the INSPY Award, and the Christy Award. Becky lives in Dallas, Texas, with her husband and three children. To find out more about Becky and her books, visit www.beckywade.com.

Books by Karen Witemeyer

A Tailor-Made Bride
Head in the Clouds
To Win Her Heart
Short-Straw Bride
Stealing the Preacher
Full Steam Ahead
A Worthy Pursuit
No Other Will Do
Heart on the Line
More Than Meets the Eye

A Cowboy Unmatched from *A Match Made
in Texas: A Novella Collection*

Love on the Mend: A Full Steam Ahead *Novella*
from *With All My Heart Romance Collection*

The Husband Maneuver: A Worthy Pursuit *Novella from* With
This Ring? *A Novella Collection of Proposals Gone Awry*

Worth the Wait: A Ladies of Harper's Station *Novella*

The Love Knot: A Ladies of Harper's Station *Novella from*
Hearts Entwined: *A Historical Romance Novella Collection*

Gift of the Heart from *The Christmas
Heirloom Novella Collection*

Books by Kristi Ann Hunter

HAWTHORNE HOUSE

A Lady of Esteem: A HAWTHORNE HOUSE *Novella*
from *All for Love Novella Collection*
A Noble Masquerade
An Elegant Façade
An Uncommon Courtship
An Inconvenient Beauty

HAVEN MANOR

A Search for Refuge: A HAVEN MANOR *Novella*
A Defense of Honor
Legacy of Love: A HAVEN MANOR *Novella* from *The Christmas
Heirloom Novella Collection*

Books by Sarah Loudin Thomas

Miracle in a Dry Season

Until the Harvest

A Tapestry of Secrets

The Sound of Rain

Appalachian Serenade: A Miracle in a Dry Season Novella from *With All My Heart Romance Collection*

A Shot at Love: A Sound of Rain Novella from *The Christmas Heirloom Novella Collection*

Books by Becky Wade

My Stubborn Heart

THE PORTER FAMILY NOVELS

Undeniably Yours

Meant to Be Mine

A Love Like Ours

Her One and Only

A BRADFORD SISTERS ROMANCE

True to You

Falling for You

Because of You: A BRADFORD SISTERS ROMANCE Novella from
The Christmas Heirloom Novella Collection

Sign Up for the Authors' Newsletters!

Keep up to date with latest news on book releases and events by signing up for their email lists at:

karenwitemeyer.com

kristiannhunter.com

sarahloudinthomas.com

beckywade.com

More from the Authors

Seeking justice against the man who destroyed his family, Logan Fowler arrives in Pecan Gap, Texas. But his quest is derailed when, instead of a hardened criminal, he finds an ordinary man with a captivating sister named Evangeline. Is getting revenge worth risking his chance at love?

More Than Meets the Eye by Karen Witemeyer
karenwitemeyer.com

Forced to run for her life, Kit FitzGilbert finds herself somewhere she swore never to return to—a London ballroom. There she encounters Lord Wharton, who believes Kit holds the key to a mystery he's trying to solve. But she can't reveal the truth without endangering those she loves.

A Defense of Honor by Kristi Ann Hunter, HAVEN MANOR #1
kristiannhunter.com

After a mine accident in 1954, Judd Markley abandoned his Appalachian roots forever. Then he meets the privileged Larkin Heyward, who dreams of serving the poor of Appalachia. Drawn together amid a hurricane, are their divergent dreams too great an obstacle to overcome?

The Sound of Rain by Sarah Loudin Thomas
sarahloudinthomas.com

Willow Bradford is content taking a break from modeling to run her family's inn until she comes face to face with NFL quarterback Corbin Stewart, the man who broke her heart—and wants to win her back.

Falling for You by Becky Wade, A BRADFORD SISTERS ROMANCE #2
beckywade.com

BETHANYHOUSE

More Novella Collections

Three of Christian historical fiction's beloved authors come together in this romantic and humorous collection of novellas featuring prequels to their latest series. *All for Love* includes Mary Connealy's *The Boden Birthright*, Kristi Ann Hunter's *A Lady of Esteem*, and Jen Turano's *At Your Request*. These sweet love stories will touch your heart!

All for Love by Mary Connealy, Kristi Ann Hunter, and Jen Turano

Take a journey across America and through time in this collection from some of Christian fiction's top historical romance writers! Includes Karen Witemeyer's *Worth the Wait: A* LADIES OF HARPER'S STATION *Novella*, Jody Hedlund's *An Awakened Heart: An* ORPHAN TRAIN *Novella*, and Elizabeth Camden's *Toward the Sunrise: An* Until the Dawn *Novella*.

All My Tomorrows by Karen Witemeyer, Jody Hedlund, and Elizabeth Camden

The path to love is filled with twists and turns in these stories of entangled romance with a touch of humor from four top historical romance novelists! Includes Karen Witemeyer's *The Love Knot*, Mary Connealy's *The Tangled Ties That Bind*, Regina Jennings's *Bound and Determined*, and Melissa Jagears's *Tied and True*.

Hearts Entwined by Karen Witemeyer, Mary Connealy, Regina Jennings, and Melissa Jagears

BETHANYHOUSE